I0826825

BOOK ONE: THE ALHAMBRA DECREE

Lilian
Gafni

Second printing
Published by Lifeline Publishing Books

Book and cover design modifications by Ellie Searl, Publishista®

All characters and events in this book are a work of fiction as well as those based on true historical accounts. Any resemblance to actual events or living persons is purely coincidental.

ISBN-10: 0970273517
ISBN-13: 978-0970273512
LCCN: 2013900561

Printed in the United States of America

10 9 8 7 6 5 4 3 2 1

Lifeline Publishing Books
La Quinta, CA

Also by Lilian Gafni

HELLO EXILE

LIVING A BLISSFUL MARRIAGE: 24 STEPS TO HAPPINESS

ENDORSEMENTS

FOR

Flower from Castile Trilogy

Book One: The Alhambra Decree

"AUTHOR LILIAN GAFNI TRANSPORTS THE reader into the rich and evocative world of Spain back when Columbus readied to venture to the New World and the church fomented its Inquisition against the Jews and war against those worshipping Allah. Gafni captures the smells, tastes, and textures of this time while drawing you into the heartbreaking and complex stories of those caught on opposing sides, with the church in the middle. A master storyteller, Gafni will reveal to you a world that will open your eyes and show you a piece of important history while keeping you riveted wondering what will happen next. A must-read!"

~ C. S. Lakin, author of *SOMEONE TO BLAME AND INTENDED FOR HARM*

"GAFNI'S UNDERSTANDING OF THE TIME period seems paramount, and her plot is solid. Isabella's movement between different cultures allows readers to explore what it was like to be a Catholic, Jew, or Moor during one of history's darkest periods."

~ *Kirkus Reviews*

"*FLOWER FROM CASTILE TRILOGY: BOOK ONE: THE ALHAMBRA DECREE* is an accessible novel that inspires interest in, and relays the complexities of, a fascinating period in history."

~ *ForeWord Clarion Reviews*

"IN *FLOWER FROM CASTILE TRILOGY BOOK ONE: THE ALHAMBRA DECREE*, truth and convenience all too often pit themselves against one another. The Alhambra Decree is the first book from Lilian Gafni's Flower from Castile trilogy, discussing the late fifteenth-century wars between Islamic and Catholic Spain, as the two faiths form two nations and battle over the Iberian Peninsula. Isabella Obrigon, blessed with a noble life, finds that she has the power to turn the conflict if she faces the truth. But in doing so, she makes many enemies but few friends. A riveting tale of medieval Spain, The Alhambra Decree is an excellent choice for fans of historical fiction."

~ *Midwest Book Review*

"GAFNI USES HISTORICAL FICTION TO retrace the steps of displaced Jews during the Inquisition. She writes with passion—her experiences a springboard."

~ *The Desert Sun/My Desert*

"LILIAN GAFNI'S *FLOWER FROM CASTILE TRILOGY* is the human account describing the atrocities inflicted on the unfortunate Marranos and Sephardic Jews, and even on the Moors living in the Iberian Peninsula. So much human cruelty and so many wars caused over the centuries by different religions. The detailed dialogues provide historical information, and make the protagonists more real. This book is a monument to the Marranos that suffered and lost their lives."

~ Manuel Luciano da Silva and Silvia Jorge da Silva, authors of *CHRISTOPHER COLUMBUS WAS PORTUGUESE!*

"GAFNI TAKES THE READER ON a journey through time - placing us amid the struggles and conflict caused by religion. As a historical fiction, Gafni gives us everything we need to walk through the towns and villages and feel, taste and smell the ambiance and lifestyle of that time. And thankfully, she never bogs us down with unnecessary details that slow the story. Both my husband (who has very different literary tastes than me) and I loved this book and enjoy discussing it. Gafni is a superb author!"

~ Ann White, Rabbi and Chaplain, Radio Host, Transformational Author and Speaker, and author of *LIVING WITH SPIRIT ENERGY: BRING BALANCE AND HARMONY INTO YOUR LIFE AND WORLD*, *THE SACRED ART OF DOG WALKING: MAKING THE ORDINARY EXTRAORDINARY,* and *PEBBLES IN THE POND*

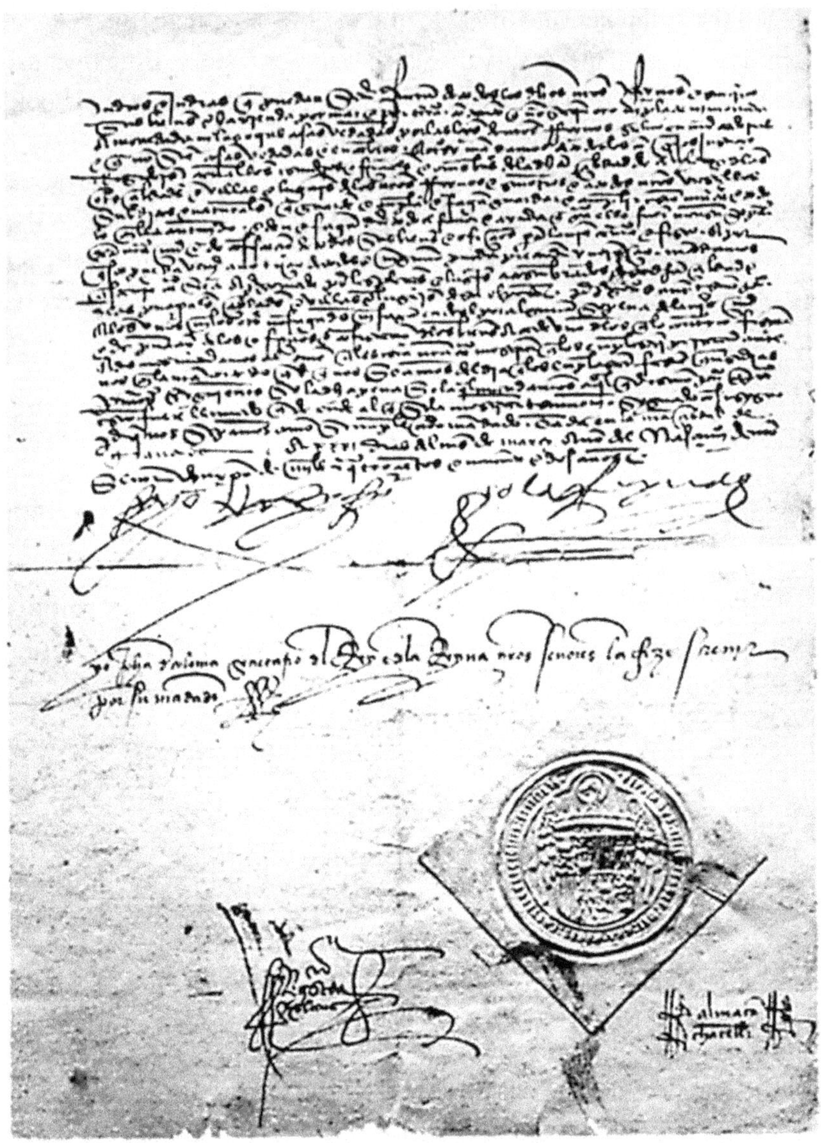

The Alhambra Decree signed in Granada, 1492 by Queen Isabella and King Ferdinand.
~ Courtesy of Wikipedia

This Book Is Dedicated to

Inquisition Victims Whose Voices Were Silenced

Acknowledgments

My gratitude goes to Susanne Lakin for her wonderful patience and impeccable editing skill and to Ellie Searl, Publishista®, for finding errors I had missed in the manuscript and for the great cover and design content.

I also want to thank my husband Joel for reading the first draft, and his unlimited patience in willing to help while I disappeared for hours on end to write this story.

View of Seville 1560–1600. Madrid Museum.
~ Photo by Alonso Sánchez Coello, 1531/32-1588.

Vista de la ciudad de Sevilla en el siglo XVI. A través del río Guadalquivir llegaba la Flota de Indias, la flota de galeones que conectaba a la ciudad con los virreinatos Americanos.

View of Seville in the sixteenth century. Through the Guadalquivir River, Indies Floats arrive, the galleons floats that connected at the city with the American Viceroyalty.

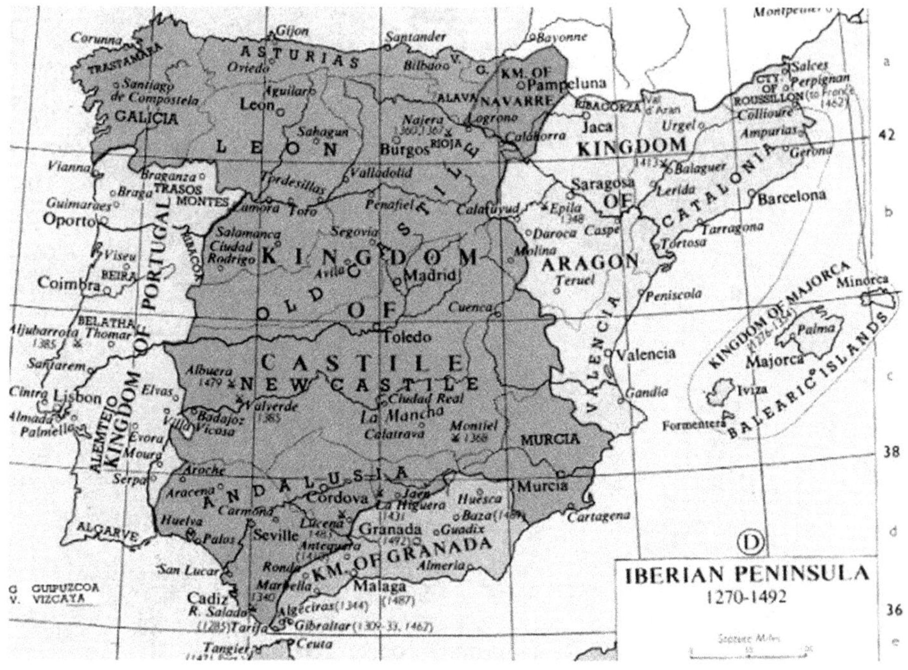

Iberia, 1492. (Col)

Adapted from Muir's Historical Atlas: (1911)

~ Internet Sourcebooks Project University of Manchester

A character list is found at the end of the book.

1

Isabel

July 1453

LOVE FILLED ISABEL'S HEART AS she gazed at her little son. She knew Salvador would grow to make her proud. If only her cursed, weak heart did not stop her from seeing her wish come true! Baltasar, the physician, had warned her that her heart would give out unless she took to her bed. She laughed in his face and told him that her parents and grandparents had lived into their seventies. Why wouldn't she follow in their footsteps? Everyone knew that only hardy people came from Sintra, the only town in Portugal that had centenarians. She was from Sintra. Nevertheless, Baltasar cautioned her to ease off. *Ease off?* She smiled at the thought. How could she slow down?

With the extra laundry she took in each day and her cleaning work for Dona Elvira, no time was left to slow down or rest. No. She had to continue working hard so that Salvador could have all the things she dreamed for him: an apprenticeship with the nearest blacksmith, then an education at the best maritime school. His father, Fernando, duke of Beja and Viseu, would approve, and so would his grandfather, the famed navigator João Gonçalves Zarco.

She looked up at the castle on the hill and sighed. Fernando hadn't visited her lately. Nor had he brought her the allowance she was waiting for. The last time he came to her with rent money was last spring. She recalled the days before Salvador had been born, and how wonderful their love had been for each other. From the start, they both had kept their relationship secret so that Fernando's father, King Dom Duarte, would not find out. Summer had long passed and her rent was overdue. She had been able to forestall her landlord by paying meagerly with vegetables from her small garden and daily fresh eggs from her hen. Sooner or later, her landlord was bound to throw her out. She shuddered. What would she do to shelter Salvador?

"*Mãe, Mãe,* look!" Salvador called from the water's edge. Standing near the water on the wet sand, he was dwarfed by the landscape of the wide and empty beach. Isabel felt fear in her heart to see how vulnerable her son was. She watched with apprehension the seagulls flying above his head, but they swooped down into the water to catch fish, and flew back up to the cliffs above the beach, where nests dwelled among the lichens in the rock. Isabel looked up at those cliffs to see her little house near the places where thistle grew in abundance, and thought it was high time to go home.

She ran to Salvador, who held a starfish struggling to free itself from his hands. She smiled at him. "It's a beautiful starfish, my son. It is like the star in the heavens you will be someday."

Salvador returned her smile, then threw the starfish onto the sandy beach.

"No, no, Salvador, *meu filho*. You must return him to the ocean, where he came from. You see,"—she picked up the starfish and kneeled down beside Salvador—"you have to love the starfish because he loves the ocean. And if you love the ocean, then the ocean will love you and be good to you." She picked up one end of her billowing long dress and tied it to her waist, and then she and the boy stepped into the gently lapping waves. She guided his hand as they both threw the starfish into the oncoming waves. She grabbed his hand, then turned away from the ocean while Salvador trotted after her on his small legs.

"Do you love the chickens and sheep, *Mãe*?"

"Of course I do!" Isabel exclaimed.

"But why do we kill them?" Salvador asked.

Isabel was surprised by her son's astuteness. "Because we have to eat," she replied. "We still have to be good to animals the way we have to be good to people. Don't you ever forget it."

Salvador nodded with his full head of reddish curly hair, and his light-blue eyes smiled at his mother. Isabel's heart warmed at the sight of her son's beautiful features. She sighed again at the thought of his father's prolonged absence. When she had inquired at the castle, one of the servants told her that Fernando had traveled to Cadiz and would be gone for a long time. Then the servant looked at her suspiciously. "Why do you ask?"

"Oh . . ." Isabel had said. "It was the farmers who were curious about the *Rendeiros* tax collectors . . . he wasn't doing his rounds to check the land and collect the rents."

"When the young master is gone, the master of collections is in charge. You shouldn't worry," the servant had told her. "He will soon be knocking at your door."

Isabel sighed again at the recollection, picked up her son, and returned to her small thatched house.

December 1453

A funerary procession made its way through the cold December rain on the path leading to the town cemetery. At the head of the procession an old man held the hand of a protesting boy. The man wore black clothing, and his sagging face bore a pained expression. He leaned heavily on a cane with his right hand while his left hand held the hand of the young boy.

"But I want her!" cried Salvador. "She promised to take me to the ocean. She promised!" He wiped his tears on his sleeve.

"I know, Salvador. I know she promised you." He nodded at the boy. "I will take you to the ocean, and when you grow up you can sail the ocean all by yourself to the end of the horizon." He made a sweeping gesture with his hand. Salvador's eyes followed the gesture. He raised his wet eyes to the old man and said, "You promise, *Tiyo* Abilio?"

"Yes, I promise. Now wipe your face."

Salvador wiped his eyes again with the palm of his hand, sniffled, and bowed his head.

The procession stopped at an open grave that had been dug in the early morning hours. A man wearing a white gown and a skullcap advanced to the grave's opening and recited a short prayer. "*Yit gadal ve yit kadash shmeh raba* . . . Exalted and sanctified be His great name. Amen. Isabel Gonçalves Zarco. A woman of valor who can find? Her value is far above jewels . . ."

"Is *Mãe* in there?" The boy pointed to the coffin.

"Yes."

Salvador started to cry again and screamed, "Come out! I want *meu Mãe!*"

"Shuu, shuu," Abilio said as he patted Salvador's shoulders.

The pinewood casket was lowered into the grave, and handfuls of soil were thrown down by each one attending the funeral. Salvador refused to grab a handful of soil. Instead, he kicked it and spread the soil with his shoes.

After the last shovelful of dirt filled the grave, Abilio slipped his hand into his overcoat pocket and brought out small pebbles. He put them at the head of the grave and gave some to Salvador. The old man wept silently as he watched the boy lay the small stones onto his mother's grave. Isabel had been like a daughter to Abilio since she moved next door to him in Sintra. She had filled his cupboard with food, brought woodchips to keep his house warm during cold winters, and entertained him with Salvador's exuberant clowning and contagious laughter. Abilio promised Isabel, while she lay on her deathbed, that he would find a good family to care for her son, and to make sure that Salvador grew up to become a Navy sailor. She confided in him before the end that Salvador's father, Dom Fernando, would honor the paternity and see to the boy's well-being and future. It was up to him now to fulfill Isabel's wish. In time he would do just that.

His thoughts were interrupted by Salvador's sobs. The boy was pounding at the wet clay with his small fists. Abilio pulled a handkerchief from his own pocket and wiped his muddy hands.

"Let's go, Salvador. We will visit *Mãe* tomorrow." He pulled Salvador away from the grave.

The gravediggers, who had finished their work, watched the reluctant small figure of the three-year-old following the bent old man with his cane slowly walk away from the cemetery ground overlooking the port.

On the following morning, when the sky was delicately lit in shades of pink and blue, and the air had a deep chill, Salvador, dwarfed by the figure of Abilio, his protector, boarded a carrack ship bound for Genoa.

2

Brewing Rebellion
April 1491

DUSK HAD JUST SET IN on a Friday, the kerosene lamps lit up the windows in homes throughout the city, and the people inside washed before their nightly meal. A lone figure cautiously approached the Juderia, the old Jewish quarter in Seville, looking furtively to see if anyone was in his path and checking that his crucifix was well hidden. He was tall, approximately forty-five years old, with white hair and piercing green eyes that searched an alley only wide enough for one man to pass through in the descending darkness. He felt a shiver when he entered the round Puerta de la Carne gate into the Juderia.

He was uncomfortably aware that there was only one other gate by which to exit because the adjacent Royal Fortress walls, the Alcazar palace wall, Ibarra Street, and the city wall hemmed in the Juderia's Jewish quarters. He shivered again, remembering his father's tale of massacres, of his great-uncles and great-grandparents being butchered. A hundred years before on July 6, 1391, the archdeacon of Écija incited mobs to rush through both gates to prevent Jews from escaping, then murdered four thousand men, women, and children in their homes, in their beds, and as they prayed in their synagogues.

Deep in thought, he moved through the dark alleys of the Juderia lit by torches attached to outer walls and arrived at a white-thatched house at the end of a forked cobblestone street. Green hanging plants decorated the windows, and a small fountain added the sound of bubbling water. He tried to look through the windows, but they were covered with black curtains. He knocked cautiously on the heavy wooden door decorated with metal scrolls. After a long silence, the window curtains were pulled apart, and a pair of blue eyes peered at him. The door swung open, and he entered a red-brick courtyard.

"*Buenas noches*, Téresa," he said to the red-haired woman who let him in.

"*Buenas noches*, João."

"Are we safe here?" he asked.

"I made sure everyone came here one by one after the streets were nearly empty. I also sent my children Miguel and José to stay with Conchita, an old woman I trust." She led João into the house through a low-ceilinged room and into a narrow hallway, then stopped at a closed door. The floor creaked as João followed her into a small bedroom to a woolen rug lying along the bedside. She lifted the rug and exposed a trapdoor. They both pulled it open and descended a narrow staircase to a small windowless, dimly lit room. Several men and women sitting around a square pine table lifted their heads as João and Téresa entered. João could only distinguish their chins and mouths; the rest of their faces were lost in darkness. Large burning candles flickered at each end of the table, filling the air with their paraffin smell.

"Do you know everyone here, João?" she asked him.

João shook his head, noticing that the assembly was made of Conversos with large crosses at their necks, and Jews wearing the red badge on their sleeves. Téresa made the introductions. "Maria Donarojo, Alfonso Sabatin, and Hernán Çavallos, whom you already know." Both men smiled as they acknowledged him, and Téresa continued. "Pedro Grasin, Ester Castelan, Salamon Moresco, Ana Saraual, and Benvenide Matigoro."

They smiled at João and nodded when Téresa mentioned their names. "João will tell you all about our plan." Téresa motioned to João to proceed.

"*Gracias* to all of you for welcoming me into your assembly," he began. He sat quietly with his head bent for a moment as if reflecting on what he was going to say next. Raising his head, he said, "The Inquisition has hounded us now for more than ten years, and there is no respite from

The Church and Torquemada." At the mention of Torquemada and his cruelty, a chill fell on the room.

João continued. "As you well know, it was in this same Jewish quarter a hundred years ago that mobs ran through the Juderia and massacred thousands of us, killing fathers and mothers, brothers and sisters. Whole families disappeared. They butchered us. It was the hate-filled sermons of the archdeacon of Écija, the Jew-hater, who incited the mobs. Now there are only a few dozen of us living here, the majority of the homes having been expropriated by the rest of the population." He stopped, took a breath, and went on. "What I would like to propose to you is a way out of this never-ending cycle of persecution."

The man called Alfonso laughed nervously. "What makes you think we can find a way out? They've been persecuting and killing us for centuries, and we haven't been able to free ourselves from their clutches."

"You are true to your words. I, too, haven't been able to escape their hate. I, too, spent years in prison . . ." He stopped hesitantly. He was glad that the darkened room hid his face distorted by hate and pain.

"What do you intend to do?" asked Pedro.

"There's a rumor that a voyage is in the making by a Genoese voyager. You also know that España and the monarchs are on the verge of completing the Reconquista by invading Granada?" Everyone in the room nodded. Their eyes hung on João's face.

Impatiently, Salamon urged, "Go on?"

"As soon as the Reconquista is over, I intend to find passage to the Indies. Anyone, be it a converted Jew or unbaptized, can join me in this venture. This could become a haven for all free men, and especially Jews," said João.

Alfonso, a Converso, asked, "How do you know if the port authorities would let us go, and if it would be safe to travel the seas with pirates or storms?"

"I don't have an answer as how you can leave the country, and have no guaranties that we would be safe. But I can tell you this much. We have no assurance that staying in España is safe either. Unlike the unbaptized Jews"—with a respectful movement of his head, João acknowledged the Jews in the assembly—"who have to wear the Jewish red badge on their shoulders that guarantees poverty because the Gentiles ostracize them, some of us as Conversos have achieved a standing in the community. As Conversos, or converted Jews, we can trade with anyone; we can hold properties and employment. Yet, we can lose that security at any time with The Church's constant suspicion of our whereabouts. To them, we're still Jews, and they can punish us any time as lapsed Christians. Tell me if this is the life you want. Who knows when they will start a new Inquisition against us?"

They all fell silent to João's argument. Salamon asked, "Do you have any assurance that we'll make it to the end of the voyage?"

Téresa interjected, "João gained years of sailing experience when he worked with my beloved husband, Nahum. May *Ha Shem* keep him in peace." She kissed the palm of her hands and looked up to heaven.

João nodded his head in sympathy with Téresa. "I can't give you any guaranties. What I know for sure is that the passage to the Indies will need manpower on the ships, boatswains as petty officers in charge of the deck crew, the rigging, etc. They will need seamen, carpenters, cooks, and tailors. Once we land in the Indies, you can then bring your families."

Alfonso looked unconvinced. "I, too, have plenty of sailing experience. What makes you so sure we'll be employed or hired by those ships?"

"Look, I can tell you that we have no guarantees that this might happen. On the other hand, the alternative isn't any better. We can only try," João said. "I will detail my exact plans the next time we meet."

"We can meet at my farm," Maria said. "It's on the outskirts of Seville, and we won't be disturbed there."

"Are we all agreed?" João asked.

They all nodded their heads.

Téresa went to a low pinewood console to retrieve two black wrought-iron candelabra; the candles were half melted and had been used sparingly. Too many candle purchases meant heretical Sabbath practices. She put them both on the table and lit them. She covered her head with a scarf, then covered her eyes with both hands. *"Baruch Ata Adonai Elohenu Melech haolam Asher kedishanou be Mitsvotav ve hitsevanou lehadlik ner shel Sahbbat, amen.* Blessed be God, King of the world, who blessed us in his wisdom to light the Sabbath candles. Amen."

"Amen," everyone repeated after her, then they shook hands and kissed each other on the cheeks as they wished for a good Sabbath. Afterward, they each drank a small glass of wine and shared a loaf of bread.

João got up and saluted everyone. "Until our next meeting." He turned to Téresa and said quietly, "I want to talk to you and Maria when everyone has left."

Téresa nodded and made a sign to Maria to stay.

After the assembly left, João turned to the two women and said, "I have a sure plan to reach our goal, and I wanted to get your agreement before I tell the group at the next meeting."

"What plan?" asked Maria.

João bent down and mumbled some words; Téresa and Maria had trouble hearing them. When they finally understood, their faces blanched.

"This is dangerous," Téresa said. "Do you realize the consequences?"

"Yes, I thought about it, and I am solely responsible for my actions. But think about the card we will have in our hand."

"Yes, we'll have more persecution, and they'll hound us like never before." Maria huffed.

"Think of the difference it will make!" João exclaimed. "They'll hound us no matter what we do."

Maria and Téresa gave each other a sidelong glance. After a long silence, they nodded their heads in agreement with João.

"You do what is right, and we'll follow you," said Téresa.

"In that case, let us part here until our next meeting," he said, turning to the staircase.

Each morning sixteen-year-old Isabella woke up and greeted the light air and shadows made by the warm sunshine moving through her room. She allowed herself to luxuriate in bed for a half hour until her nanny, dada Hannah, came in huffing like a dragon, scolding and spewing dire predictions of what would befall her if she were not up on her feet in a hurry. This morning was no exception; Isabella heard dada Hannah's heavy footsteps on the corridor's red slate tiles, accompanied by loud breathing from her enormous chest. Out of breath and red-faced, the older woman flung open the door.

"I won't say it again! I gave you instructions half an hour ago to be ready for breakfast—and you're still in bed!" She flung her fleshy arms up in the air. "You'd better be ready when I come back shortly!" With that, she turned her back and stormed out of the room.

Isabella jumped out of bed, knowing too well that dada Hannah would report her immediately to her father, who would take away her evening walking privileges in the park. Indeed, that would be severe punishment. It would separate her from Juan for that day, and that would be an eternity. Her dada looked the other way each evening when Isabella and Juan spoke a few words to each other as they greeted on Fernando Road. If, however, they dared touch hands, dada Hannah would look at both Isabella and Juan with sharp eyes that cut like a knife, and they would quickly withdraw their hands. Isabella would plunge her hands into her dress pockets and Juan would cross his arms behind his back. Juan often turned red-faced while Isabella's clear laughter echoed down the cobblestones in the plaza de la Madonna del Dio.

Isabella's anticipation and desire to see Juan each night put her in a feverish state throughout the day until the evening arrived. Both her father and mother looked favorably at the courtship between the youths. His parents, Don Pedro Escobar and Doña Maria Escobar de Santilla, a *Grandee*, also approved and gave their blessing for the match.

Juan Escobar de Santilla was seventeen, and in one year expected to be married to Isabella in the imposing cathedral in Seville. Their parents were already preparing for the wedding. Don Pedro was paying for a small house in the blue gypsy quarters of Seville, and Isabella's father, Don Arturo Obrigon, and her mother, Doña Estrella Obrigon, planned to pay for the sumptuous wedding to take place at their palatial house near the Guadalquivir River.

It seemed nothing on earth would prevent the young couple from marrying; they were in love, they were in the prime of their young lives, and Seville was, after all, the city for lovers. Many couples sanctified their weddings in the great Seville Cathedral under the gaily ringing bells on the Giralda Tower. The soothsayers and *falajas* of Seville said that to be married there was to have a good and lasting marriage. Their words were taken seriously because of their predictions about the future of married couples. Only one couple had not fulfilled the predictions of blissful coupling. They had died in a tragic accident right after the wedding when their coach overturned on a country road on the way to their honeymoon home. The falajas, or palm readers, explained that accidents could not be foreseen in the predictions of happiness. Nevertheless, both Juan and Isabella looked forward to great happiness in their future with no hitches along the way.

Isabella finished dressing and ran down the gleaming red-tiled hallway as fast as her cumbersome long skirts would allow her. She entered the imposing spacious dining room furnished in rich mahogany furniture and damask draperies. A fire crackled in a limestone fireplace even though the weather was beginning to warm up. She prepared herself to face her parents' feigned admonition for being late for breakfast. Her parents could never bring themselves to be cross with Isabella. She could usually break up the frown and furrows on her father's forehead by giggling and laughing, and both parents would end up laughing with her. Dada Hannah cautioned them many times against giving in to Isabella's whims. "Mark my words," she warned, "she will have her way each time until she brings you down to your knees, where you won't be able to refuse her anything!"

Today was different. When she entered the dining room, Isabella found her parents silent and their breakfast untouched. A veil of anxiety hung on her mother's usually serene features, and her father's face looked grim. Isabella felt her heart tightening, and with a plaintive voice asked, "What is it?" In her young mind she visualized with dread that something may have happened to Juan. "Is it Juan? Please, *Padre*, tell me!" She ran to her mother, who shielded her with both arms and consoled her by caressing her lustrous black hair.

"No, no, my flower. Juan is in good health. It isn't that. Your father will tell you."

"My dearest Isabella." Her father stopped for a moment, wiped his forehead with a linen handkerchief embroidered with the Obrigon family crest, swallowed, and cleared his voice. "I received a letter that is puzzling to your mother and me. We can't understand what it means. This letter is written in ancient Hebrew text, and we already consulted with Father Angelo early this morning."

Isabella ran to the letter on the dining room table, picked it up, and saw unrecognizable strange characters written on it. "I can't understand what it says. Please read it to me," she pleaded with her father while feeling great anxiety descend upon her.

Don Arturo took the letter from her hand and read: "'Do not allow your daughter to marry. A great calamity will befall your house if you do.' That is all it says." Her father wiped his forehead again.

"What could it mean?" Isabella asked, puzzled as well.

"I don't know nor do I want to consider it. I have no enemies, and who would want to harm one hair of your beautiful head?"

"Where did this letter originate? And who brought it to you?" Isabella insisted.

"It was found by the gate in the egg basket that Maria brings to us on Friday," her mother said.

Maria, being the old woman who prided herself in possessing the healthiest chickens in all of Castile at the outskirts of town, always delivered her best eggs to the Obrigon family at dawn. Nevertheless, Isabella could neither understand nor believe what she was hearing from her father's mouth.

"We must fetch Maria. We must! I'm not going to let this old wretch give me orders," said Isabella.

Her mother, who had been quiet until now, spoke to Don Obrigon. "My dear Arturo, can't we drive right out of town to Maria's farm and have words with her?"

"Not now. I'm due to meet with Seville's mayor in one hour. It will have to wait till I return this afternoon."

"But how can we wait?" Isabella asked her father. "Isn't my happiness more important than affairs of town?" She felt completely abandoned by her father. He had nurtured every request and desire she had while growing up, and could never say no to her. He had given her the beautiful blue-tiled fountain adjacent to her room, where twenty colorful blue jays sang all day long, and had not refused her when she wanted to invite all her friends to the country, housing them in a morada near the enchanted gardens. She knew that her father had spoiled her as a child, but this was a different matter. Her union to Juan was a matter of life or death to her. She could not live without him, not for one day. "If you don't care about my happiness, I'll have to go to Maria myself!"

"Don't be a fool! I'll be back in a few hours, and then we'll decide what to do," her father said. With that, he left the dining room, leaving his breakfast untouched.

Isabella stared with her mouth open at the dining room doors through which her father disappeared. In all of her sixteen years, he had never spoken to her with such harshness. This letter and the threatening message must have frightened her father somehow. She couldn't understand the seriousness of the threat. She thought maybe it was a merchant who had not been paid for his wares who was trying to extort money from Don Obrigon. Nevertheless, sadness fell upon her like a heavy black *mantilla.*

Doña Estrella's heart broke to see tears streaming down Isabella's beautiful face. She looked at her only daughter with the fierce pride that sometimes threatened to cripple Isabella. Isabella was a great beauty. Everyone who set eyes on her concurred that Isabella had the most striking face that the Obrigon family had ever produced. Of all the paintings displayed in the grand gallery of their home, not one ancestor possessed her features. Theirs showed rather stern, harsh faces that were bent under the weight of their heavy coiffures, lace hats, and elaborate dresses. When Isabella laughed or stomped her foot when she wasn't given what she asked for, her green eyes burned as two emeralds in a white satin skin, to which, dada Hannah claimed, even the Milky Way could not compare. With her full red-ruby lips, Isabella could outdo a *berbeliko* nightingale. When she sang accompanied by her guitar, her voice rang out crystal clear. Don Arturo and Doña Estrella guarded her health almost fanatically, protecting her from the humidity and hot sun in summers, and the cold evenings of the Castilian winter months.

A sudden chill passed over Doña Estrella. What more could she do to protect her daughter from harm? Isabella's movement was limited throughout the day. Various tutors who came to their home gave lessons in

Latin, foreign languages, music, and grooming in the social graces. The tutors had come highly recommended by the duke de la Mancha, Isabella's godfather and the minister of finance in Seville. Every moment of her day was occupied, leaving her little time to dream, except when it came to Juan. At that warm thought, Doña Estrella smiled and began to forget the projected threat upon her daughter's future wedding.

"Mother!" Isabella's voice shook Doña Estrella out of her reverie.

"What is it, *mi amor*?"

"My life hangs on a thread, and neither *Padre* nor you, Madre, are worried."

"You know how much we love you, my dove—both your father and I. We must wait for your father's return before we make any rash decisions."

Seeing no reaction forthcoming, Isabella said, "Well . . . if no one will help me, I will now return to my room."

"Go, my child. I will see you before lunch is served," her mother said with calm eyes that did not betray the turmoil inside her. She let out a sigh at the untouched food on the breakfast table.

"Make haste!" Don Arturo Obrigon ordered the carriage driver as he sat back on his seat inside the coach. His thoughts went back to Isabella and the blackmail letter. Who could have foreseen that his daughter would be in danger? What he needed right now was a soothsayer. He surprisingly smiled at the thought. As a rule, he never took old wives' tales seriously. He only believed in scientifically proven hard facts.

His wife, Estrella, though, had been told by her servant Miranda, who read teacups, that she would meet a handsome man who was a healer. During their courtship, Estrella told Arturo the future Miranda predicted. "You will be thrown off your horse Vega, and be treated by a handsome physician who will marry you." It was another estate horse, not Vega, that had kicked her, bringing Arturo to treat her sore ankle. Not quite as had been foretold by Miranda, but pretty close, no? He had to admit that Miranda had been right when she foretold the birth of a girl so beautiful that everyone would covet her.

Young men had flocked at their gate when Isabella was but twelve years old. Both Arturo and Estrella discouraged all young suitors, and also some old men who were widowers vowing to wait for Isabella to grow up to the marrying age of sixteen. But when Juan Escobar showed up at their door one day accompanied by his father, Don Pedro Escobar, all resistance vanished. Juan's handsome features, his proud gait, and intelligence seemed to pierce Isabella's heart with cupid's arrows. She fell in love the moment he addressed her, melting her with his passionate black eyes. Arturo had seen his daughter lower her green eyes in modesty at this sudden welling of passion in her young heart. He knew that from that moment on Isabella had sworn herself to Juan in the secret depth of her heart.

Isabella exploded with joy when her parents announced that Juan had asked for her hand. Don Escobar, however, hampered that joy on the condition that they wait to be married for one year until Juan turned eighteen and completed his engineering studies the following spring. Pleading and crying, she begged her parents to move the wedding day sooner, but they chose to honor Don Escobar's condition.

The abrupt stopping of the carriage at the mayoral building of Mayor José de Gerondi pulled him out of his thoughts. Don Obrigon alighted and was shown into the antechamber, where he was told that an important visitor was consulting with the mayor.

Arturo tried not to fidget as he waited and reminisced about his lifelong friendship with José. They had met while in the naval academy when they were sixteen. His parents and José's parents had insisted that the young men perform naval duty before they each married or settled in their respective careers. José chose to go into civic duties, while Arturo chose the medical profession. After Arturo finished medical school practice in León, he set up a small practice in Castile.

Arturo fidgeted on his chair and sighed at the thought of having to wait much longer. Finally the door to José's office opened up, and out strutted King Ferdinand of Aragon followed by his servant. Stunned, Arturo quickly bowed to the king.

"Don Obrigon, how good to see you. How is your charming wife and your beautiful daughter?" King Ferdinand waited for Don Obrigon to kiss his ring and then waited to hear news of his family. "Come on, man. The cat's got your tongue?" he joked when no words escaped Don Obrigon.

"Oh no. I was just waiting for Your Majesty to speak first."

The king laughed in a low baritone voice. "Very wise indeed. You must visit us with your family at the palace some day next week. After all, you named your daughter after the queen, and we're gratified by that choice."

"Thank you, Your Majesty. It is we who thank you for allowing us to use the queen's illustrious name."

"All right, Don Obrigon. Send word to the court as soon as possible."

Don Arturo bowed, and the king with his attendant disappeared through a door that led to a small courtyard. Don José looked at Don Arturo and said, "I always worry whenever the king comes to the mayoral house. I've told him it isn't safe, but he insisted on seeing me today. Come in, Arturo."

Arturo followed him to his chambers, which were decorated with tapestries and a large dark walnut desk presiding over the entire room. Sunlight fell from the high-ceilinged windows, illuminating the center of the room and capturing floating dust particles in its rays. Two chairs stood in front of the desk, and José invited Arturo to sit down. Arturo sat in his chair and wondered if he had taken the same seat that King Ferdinand had just vacated. It gave him a fleeting feeling of importance.

"What's so urgent that you sent for me this morning?" he asked José, who sat close to him in the other chair.

"It has to do with the king's visit," said José.

Arturo felt his stomach tighten. A visit from King Ferdinand was bound to signify a serious request from José, whether it was affairs of state or additional taxes. Either way, it would mean additional hardships on all the country. They were already heavily taxed.

"You know, Arturo," began José, "I would not have asked you here unless something was afoot in the palace."

"Every time you ask to see me, José, it's for more revenues for running this city. I've contributed already—very handsomely, if I may say so—to your budget, but my reserves are not limitless."

"I know, I know." José rushed to agree with him.

Arturo, nevertheless, guessed that José would use another one of his convincing arguments that every head in Castile was in jeopardy unless they forked over more *maravedís*, for more religious or public projects.

"But you see . . ." José continued, "I know how helpful you've been whenever I came to you. This time it's urgent and vital that we find three hundred thousand maravedís."

"Three hundred thousand!" Arturo cried with shock. "I could never raise this sum even if I were a close friend to all the princes of Europe and the Levant! You're asking too much, my friend."

"I'm not asking you to do that from your own monies. What I'm asking you is a different favor this time."

Arturo sighed with relief, then looked questioningly at José.

"You do have as patients some of our richest members of Castilian families here in Seville. I'm also referring to the rich Jewish merchants who come to you for their health. I'm speaking of Don Abraham Senior, and especially the financier Don Isaac Abravanel. I'm told he has the ear of Queen Isabella."

"If Don Abravanel is in the confidence of the queen, perhaps you should ask him personally."

"But you're the only one he trusts, and he has been your friend since you established your practice. There's good reason why I'm asking you personally. Something grave has come up."

Arturo sensed a veiled meaning behind the remark. Don Abravanel had loaned him funds to open his medical practice a number of years before and had referred all of the Hebrew community to him and his expert medical care for many years. "You know I owe him a tremendous gratitude for all he has done. But I've repaid him every maravedi I borrowed. I owe him nothing!" Arturo was beginning to feel uneasy with José's request and abruptly changed the conversation. "I have something more important to deal with right now. I've received a blackmail letter that has threatened my daughter's own happiness."

"What do you mean?" asked José while raising both his eyebrows.

Arturo related everything that happened that morning, including Isabella's dismay. "So you see, I have to trace where the letter came from as soon as possible."

"This is serious indeed. I'll send away for Inspector Guerida's help. You know you can depend on me. I wouldn't want anything to happen to your beautiful Isabella. Sometimes I wonder that if my son hadn't squandered his fortune, our families would have been related, adding depth to our friendship." José sighed. "You know I wouldn't have asked you unless it was urgent. I know I can confide in you."

Arturo was remembering that the reason he and his wife, Estrella, had rejected José's son was that he had tarnished many young señoritas' reputations, not due to lack of dowry for the match.

"Arturo? Are you with me?"

José's voice pulled him out of his thoughts." "I'm sorry; you were saying something about a grave reason?"

"Yes. And I know I can trust you not to breathe a word to anyone."

"Of course. You have my complete confidence."

"You know that the armed men of King Abdallah have been staging coup after coup since last year?"

"Of course. I get news every day of the wounded coming home."

"Well, news of the utmost secrecy has reached the palace that several Berber battalions from Morocco and Tangier will cross the channel to join the Moors by next spring. King Ferdinand has vowed to eradicate them from our frontiers and Granada. We used many maravedís to conquer one-half of the kingdom of Granada, and we've been fighting them since 1481. Almost ten years! The treasury is almost empty." José stopped, out of breath. He then continued. "Baza, Alméria, and Guadix surrendered to our brave soldiers two years ago. Now we need to conquer the city of Granada itself. But we need funds to enlist at least two hundred thousand foot soldiers and officers. Let me remind you that Seville is only two hundred kilometers from the frontier in Granada and from our homes. This is a battle we can't lose. If we do . . . there is no telling what might happen to our very own existence—our lands, our wives, and our daughters."

At that last word Arturo jumped. If anything harmed his daughter, he wouldn't forgive himself, nor would his wife forgive him.

Without hesitation, Arturo asked, "What exactly do you want me to do?"

"I want you to go to Don Abravanel and ask him personally for the funds without telling him the real reasons. You know that Don Abravanel has also been giving loans for a number of years to the many cities in Granada. You know what that means, don't you?"

Arturo thought for a moment, then it became clear—José was asking him to blackmail Don Abravanel, and question his allegiance to Queen Isabella and the kingdom of Aragon. How could José ask him to do that when he himself was being blackmailed?

He suddenly felt a heavy weight pressing on his chest, and he fought for air. He said, "You know, José, my allegiance to you and to the queen. But you're asking me to do something abhorrent to my honor. You're asking me to blackmail Don Abravanel!" Arturo pulled out his linen kerchief to wipe sweat beads on his forehead.

José defended himself. "No, no, Arturo. All I'm asking you is to intimate to Don Abravanel that the funds are needed to help our wounded and their families."

"But you're asking for a fortune! I don't see how he would part with that immense sum."

"I do know that Don Abravanel is the queen and king's treasurer and is amazingly rich himself. He has amassed fortunes of his own. He is the only one who can keep the dominion from ruin."

Arturo stayed silent for a few moments. Then he sighed. Nothing was going to dissuade José from giving him this mission. He would have to think of a persuading argument to have Don Abravanel part with his money.

"All right, I'll do what you ask of me. But don't forget that the queen has to know that I'm the only one taking on this enterprise."

"The queen will thank you and your family personally. I promise," said José solemnly. He then went to Don Arturo and embraced him. "Just think about it. You're saving the realm."

Arturo strode from the room without answering.

Isabella paced back and forth in her bedchamber while mumbling to herself. *What should I do?* At times of crisis in her young life, she usually turned to her parents. Don Arturo and Doña Estrella had come to her rescue, but so far, her protected and abundant life had been marred only by small disappointments. Now she was facing the ultimate fear—losing Juan. She never imagined any harm happening to her. Rather, if anyone were to be harmed, it would be Juan. Juan had a short temper and had used his sword to defend slights caused by misunderstandings among his peers at school. She also knew that Juan spent his days at school studying engineering and learning fencing—as every gentleman in his class did. The thought of his vulnerability made her fear for him. A shiver ran down Isabella's spine.

She chased the thought from her mind and concentrated on the threatening letter her father had read to her. Maria must know where the letter came from; she delivered the basket this morning. The only solution was to ask Maria. Isabella decided to find out for herself since her father was too busy to take on the task. With that thought, she rushed to the imposing carved mahogany closet and pulled out the black hooded coat hanging among her many dresses. She slipped it over her blue velvet dress and pulled the hood over her head, leaving only her eyes uncovered. She grabbed several maravedís coins from a silver chest on her dressing table and slipped them into a small string purse. Next, she took the brass key to open the locked gate in the small garden behind her room.

She slipped the key into the lock, but it resisted her attempt. She tried again and again, but the lock remained frozen. She rattled the gate with a cry of impatience. How else could she leave the house? Every servant working in the house would notice her leaving through the front door and would try to stop her. She could only leave the house escorted by dada Hannah or her parents, or one of the servants to take her to the market.

She stepped out of her room into the long hallway, trying to see if any of the servants were in sight. The hallway was silent, meaning that the servants had already cleaned that part of the house. She had to slip quickly across the rooms beyond the hallway. She swiftly walked past the reception room and prepared to slip out the front door when dada Hannah appeared before her. She gasped.

"What's this?" dada Hannah exclaimed. "Why are you dressed in this coat? It isn't winter yet! Go back to your room and take it off. You have a guitar lesson beginning in ten minutes. Have you forgotten?"

"I forgot!" Isabella hit her forehead. "I just felt a chill and wanted to keep warm." She lowered her eyes, hoping that her dada would not see the lie in them.

Dada Hannah came close to Isabella and touched her forehead with concern. "You have no fever." She looked relieved. "Go to your room quickly and get ready for your lesson." With that, dada Hannah left her.

Isabella turned around, slipped her coat off, and pretended to be heading for her room, but she stopped midway to see if dada Hannah was out of sight. After a few seconds, the entry hallway was clear. She bolted for the door and then stopped to face a small alcove in which the Madonna stood. She crossed herself, opened the door, and closed it silently after her. She ran across the courtyard and down the street away from the house. As she turned the corner, she glimpsed her music teacher's carriage stopping at the front door.

She jostled pedestrians as she bolted down the narrow alleys, and found an open carriage with the driver asleep in his seat high up on the forward bench. His whip lay on the pavement, so she picked it up and rudely tapped his thigh.

"Wake up, wake up, Driver!"

"What is it?" The driver opened his eyes and took the whip from her hand. "Where to?" he asked, as he glanced at his well-dressed passenger. "Where is your chaperone, señorita?"

"Never mind!" she quickly replied. "Take me out of town to the farming district. Do you know Maria's farm? The chicken grower in the town of Dos Hermanas?"

The driver thought for a moment, then said, "Climb aboard, señorita." After she clambered into the carriage, he whipped his horse into a trot down the cobblestone streets.

Isabella tapped the driver's shoulder and yelled, "I want to avoid the market streets in Olivera Plaza. Is that understood?"

"Very well, señorita," said the driver, and the carriage lurched into the streets that were emptying for the approaching siesta.

3

The Royal Palace

WHEN THE SPOTTED AND CREAM belly thrushes began their spring chattering in the trees around the palace in Seville, the servants began the ritual of folding and storing the winter blankets in pine chests. They rubbed the blankets with pine oil and then dried them before storage. Carmela, the head household maid, smoothed and rubbed her knotted and muscled hands over the folded blankets and began to pile them up into the chests.

"Make sure each blanket is rubbed thoroughly," she said to a young apprentice servant watching her.

The apprentice nodded her curly head and took the wooden paddle from Carmela's hand to beat the blankets one by one.

Leaving the apprentice at her task, Carmela left the servant's quarters for the seigniorial wing of the palace. She crossed the vast reception room, now empty of delegates and dignitaries, and entered the separate wing that housed the queen's chambers.

Doña Beatriz de Bobadilla, the queen's favorite lady-in-waiting, was pacing outside the queen's rooms.

"Carmela, see that the queen's chamber is cleaned last. The queen isn't feeling well this morning, and she's not to be disturbed. Is that understood?"

Carmela bowed, then turned around to leave the corridor, but Doña Beatriz called her back. "Don't come back until I tell you to do so."

Carmela bowed again and left as fast as she could. She was curious about the queen's request not to be disturbed. She had seen Queen Isabella early this morning in the rose gardens adjacent to her chambers in the east tower. It was odd for her to have gone back to bed. The queen took her morning walks seriously and preached temperance in diet for her and Ferdinand.

As a rule, Queen Isabella rose early, walked in the garden, and then had a light breakfast in her chamber. After eating, she started poring over the requests from citizens and the affairs of state that were presented to her each day. Carmela was puzzled. Could the queen be meeting a dignitary early this morning? She wondered how the queen's blankets could be removed from her chambers without disturbing her.

Carmela remembered that the queen's receiving antechamber was located next to her sleeping quarters. She received her closest advisors there when a crisis occurred. She could put on a robe, leave her bedroom, and be available to her ministers in the antechamber within minutes. If the queen was consulting someone right now, Carmela could slip into the bedroom through the back end and retrieve those blankets. Heart pounding, Carmela glided silently in her leather moccasins to the corridor reserved for the queen and slipped into a small alcove where a doorway was hidden. She searched for the ring attached to her belt and found the right key. After unlocking the door, she stepped into the queen's bedroom and was about to open the chest near the four-poster bed when she heard the low murmuring of voices in the antechamber. She froze with fear. Before she could flee, a word by a man's low, gravelly voice grabbed her attention.

"We've got to go through with it!" The voice grew louder. "Only the apostates should be investigated! My dear queen, we must make a distinction between the secret Judaizers—the *Marranos*—and the faithful New Christians. The New Christians loyal to our Catholic faith will not be prosecuted nor pursued. It is these secret heretical apostates—these Marranos, who were baptized but continue to practice the Law of Moses—that are infecting the New Christians by trying to bring them back into their fold. It is the Marranos who committed a most abominable sacrilege by merely pretending to accept the Christian faith."

Carmela crept closer to the door, when she heard the queen's voice murmuring, ". . . makes you . . . believe that they're not . . . loyal to the realm?"

Carmela put her ear to the door and heard clearly, "Because they swore allegiance to the Christian faith, while the Marranos will not budge and still practice their Sabbath's evil rituals."

The queen's voice grew stronger. "All my subjects are loyal to my policies and my faith. I can't discriminate among the Catholics and non-Catholics. I am monarch to all of my subjects, and as such they're under my wing and protection."

"My dear illustrious Queen Isabella. Your parents, King John II and Queen Isabella of Portugal, may they rest in peace, were also magnanimous. It cost them the price of quashing a revolt from the nonbelievers and infidels."

"But that was ages ago. The realm has changed since then. The only enemies we have now are the Moors in Granada."

"That's exactly my point, my queen. I have it from a credible source that Don Isaac Abravanel is meeting secretly with the Moors while financing their coffers."

"Don Abravanel has been loyal to the realm. He's been a strong supporter these last ten years in our cause against the Moors, not to mention filling our royal coffers for those battles. I need time to think about this information."

There was a pause during which Carmela plastered herself against the door to hear better. Then the queen's voice became loud, and Carmela backed slightly away from the door, ready to flee if the queen stormed her bedchamber. When nothing happened, she returned her ear to the door.

"I want you to keep an eye on anyone who conspires against me, Torquemada," the queen continued. They will be punished severely. You have my consent to carry out sentences against treachery from anyone—except you are to wait on the matter of Conversos and Abravanel."

Carmela had never heard the queen's voice raised much above a whisper. What she was hearing now was the angry voice of one who felt betrayed in her rule and in her faith. Queen Isabella changed from a lamb into a lioness whenever her authority was challenged, and she did not let go of her ire until the traitor was punished or eliminated altogether. Carmela could visualize the Dominican Torquemada's cruel smile of satisfaction at the queen's statement. Everyone feared him, including Carmela herself. Whenever she crossed paths with him in the palace corridors, she crossed herself after she passed the stoop-shouldered man dressed in his woolen frock. Whether the offense was minor or as grave as that of spying against the realm, Torquemada made even the strongest offenders wince with fear. She trembled at the thought of being so close to him behind the door.

"*Vaya con Dios,* Torquemada, and keep me informed on any rebellion from the nonbelievers."

"My queen." Carmela heard Torquemada's voice and didn't wait any longer. She furtively left the bedchamber without completing her task.

The carriage carrying Isabella Obrigon arrived in the farming town of Dos Hermanas a long and bumpy hour after leaving the city. The driver guided his carriage through the narrow streets and stopped at a low farm on the outskirts of town.

"Here it is. Maria's Donarojo's farm," said the driver.

Isabella alighted from the carriage and gave the driver four maravedís. "Thank you, señorita." He lifted his cap, lightly flicked the whip at his old horse, and left Isabella standing by the dusty road.

Isabella squinted in the bright sun and prepared to climb the few steps leading to the main house. She heard the clucking of chickens in low wooden shacks around the property. A slight breeze from the southeast blew through the larches and cypresses and brought the strong odor of manure to her nostrils. She put her handkerchief to her nose to ward off the unpleasant smell. Before she could knock at the door, a woman carrying a bucket of eggs stopped her.

"What do you want, señorita?" she asked her with a rude tone of voice.

"Are you Maria?" Isabella asked her.

"Yes. And who wants me?"

"I am Don Arturo Obrigon's daughter." As Isabella pronounced these words, she stood erect and looked down at Maria, who was a head shorter. "You deliver eggs to our home each Friday."

"Yes, yes. What about it?"

"Can we talk inside your house? It's a serious matter," said Isabella.

"All right. Follow me." Maria left the egg basket by the door and led Isabella through the front door. Isabella saw that Maria lived humbly, with few furnishings in the large low-ceilinged living quarters. A wooden staircase led to a second floor. Maria cleared the oak table laden with dirty dishes and shooed off the chickens sitting on the long benches. They ran out the door, clucking their rage in high-pitched tones.

"Sit down."

Isabella made sure the wooden bench was clean of feathers or dirt before she sat down.

"Well?" asked Maria, standing in front of Isabella with both her hands on her hips.

"This morning when you delivered the eggs by our door . . ." She hesitated for a moment. "There was a note in the basket."

Maria stared at her and waited for her to continue. "This letter was a threat to my marriage with Juan Escobar. It said that if I marry him a terrible thing would happen to my family."

Maria blanched slightly. Isabella took note of that but pressed her further. "What is the meaning of that letter, and who gave it to you?"

After a short silence Maria said, "It's for your own good. I can't explain it to you, but your welfare is at stake."

"So you admit it!" Isabella was surprised at how harsh her voice sounded.

"I admit nothing. Someone delivered this letter to me. This person is high in the ranks of the community. I cannot tell you who it is."

"You can't! You know that my father is an important person in Castile. He can have the chief of police after you! You know the penalty for blackmail!"

Maria didn't answer. She repeated the same answer she gave her before. "It's for your own good."

"If you can't tell me, perhaps they'll loosen up your tongue in prison!"

"My dear child—"

"Don't patronize me. I'm now an adult about to be married." Isabella stomped her right foot twice on the floor, raising the dust lying thickly on the hard-beaten floor.

Maria didn't respond. Her eyes were transfixed on a door leading into the house. The door flew open with a bang, and two men lunged toward Isabella.

Isabella opened her mouth to scream but nothing came out. Her throat was constricted, and her feet felt frozen to the ground. The two men grabbed her arms and dragged her into the next room. She suddenly found her voice and blasted at them.

"Let go of me! Let go, *brutas*!"

They pushed her so hard she stumbled over a wooden bed in the little room and hit her head hard on one of the wooden posts. The loud bang of the door being shut was the last thing Isabella heard before losing consciousness.

When Isabella came back to her senses, she was lying on a bed of straw on the ground. She moved with difficulty, feeling pain on the right side of her head. Instinctively she touched her head and was relieved to see no blood on her fingers. A strange smell suddenly filled her nostrils. She sat up and rubbed her eyes and found herself in a barn with animals. On one side of her, two cows munched on hay, and on the other, a couple of sheep dozed on a straw bed. In a sudden rush of memory, she remembered being dragged by two men. Throughout her life, Isabella had never feared dangers to herself because her padre and madre had protected her and so had her dada Hannah, who constantly watched over her. Tears welled in her eyes and a nascent fear began to grow in the pit of her stomach. Why was she being held prisoner? Who were these men, and why was Maria their accomplice? If they were going to hurt her, they would have done so by now. The threat in the morning note warned of harm only if she married Juan, but now they were holding her prisoner without reason. The thoughts swirled in her aching head, but she couldn't come up with an answer.

The sound of metal grinding on metal came suddenly from the barn door, and she heard the sound of a chain being dragged on the other side. The barn door opened, and a woman entered the gloom. Isabella was blinded by the sunlight flooding in through the open door, but she tried to identify who was there. The woman was of average height with red tresses tied around her head. She wore a modest blue dress with a lace mantilla covering her shoulders. She held a steaming bowl in her hands and carried a wrapped bundle under her arm.

"Who are you? Why are you holding me?" demanded Isabella. She tried to get up, but her body was too weak, and she remained sitting on the straw.

The woman put the bowl down and placed the small bundle on the straw. She unwrapped it, and in it was a chunk of black bread. Isabella turned up her nose and grimaced. "I'm not eating this food! Give it to your animals!"

"If you don't eat, you won't be strong enough to walk."

"Why, where are you taking me?" Isabella was suddenly anxious.

"We'll let you know in time, *hija*," the woman replied.

"Don't call me 'daughter.' Only my mother can call me that!" Isabella said, indignation replacing her anxiousness.

"Never mind. Everything will be explained to you in due time."

"I want it explained to me right now! Get Maria now!" cried Isabella.

The woman didn't answer. She turned her back on Isabella and walked out of the barn.

In a fit of anger, Isabella flung the bowl and its contents at the door, followed by the bread, which bounced against it. The startled animals stirred, and the frightened cows began to moo.

A raging Isabella stood up and ran to the barn door, shaking her fists and pounding on it. "Open that door! Let me out! My father will have you arrested! Do you hear me?" After a long silence with no other sounds except the lowing of the cows, Isabella went back to her corner. She sank onto the straw, panting from the exertion of her outburst.

4

A Mother's Last Request

THE NEIGHBORS CRANED THEIR NECKS to see over the wall surrounding the Obrigon property. Two armed guards stood by the entrance while two other guards kept watch as Don Arturo and Doña Estrella stood outdoors with Inspector Guerida next to his carriage.

"I wonder what this family is hiding in their home?" one neighbor murmured to another.

"I never noticed any comings or goings of infidels," said the other.

"I always suspected something fishy about this family and their beautiful daughter."

"I don't know what you're referring to. I know they possess a certificate of pure Spanish blood. A Castilian blood, mind you. The Obrigons' maid told my maid. The one who cleans their home."

"I don't know. It's still fishy to me why the inspector came to . . ."

The said inspector shook hands with Don Obrigon, and the woman fell silent. Don and Doña Obrigon said good-bye to him. Doña Obrigon was in tears.

"I'll let you know as soon as I hear anything," Inspector Guerida said, entering his carriage. He left the Obrigons' home, and the horses trotted down the narrow cobblestone road.

Doña Obrigon saw her neighbors across the street nodding in sympathy. She nodded back to them, then entered her home with her husband. She turned to him and pleaded, "Promise me, Arturo, the minute you hear anything—*anything*— you'll send word."

"I promise. Now I want you to rest, querida." He led her to her chamber. Assisted by the maid, he helped her lie down on her bed. "Here, take this glass of wine and powder. It'll help you sleep." He handed her a glass of soporific—a mixture of wine and pure alcohol diluted with herbs.

Doña Obrigon began crying again, harder than before. "*Mi hija* . . . my poor *hija*. They'll hurt her, I know." She broke down in a torrent of tears. Don Arturo gently poured the liquid into her mouth, watching as some of it dribbled down her chin and mixed with flowing tears. He covered her with the damask coverlet and saw that the powder was already beginning to take effect.

"It's all . . . your fault . . . Artur . . ." Then she was asleep. Arturo shook his head with sadness and looked up at the maid.

"Let me know as soon as she wakes up, Pilar."

"*Sí, Don Obrigon.*" Pilar curtsied as Don Arturo left the room with his brows creased and his shoulders bowed as by a heavy burden.

Several men and women sat pensively in Maria's farmhouse. They wore no jewelry or ornaments, nor swords at their waists.

"I bring bad tidings," said one of the women at the table.

Everyone fell silent.

"I overheard the queen talking with Torquemada in her antechamber. They decided to impose new measures on Conversos and continue arresting those who are suspected of proselytizing."

Maria turned pale. "I can't see how much worse it can get, Carmela. With the new bans they've already decreed upon us, we can't shop for the Sabbath or buy meat on Fridays. We can't even wear clean linen on the weekend. What else can they do—arrest us?"

"I'm just reporting what I heard. You ought to be careful where and when you meet. They could be watching us right now." Carmela lowered her head. When she lifted her face, she spoke to Maria with gravity. "You know that I have a debt to your Converso family. If it weren't for your parents, may they rest in peace"—she crossed herself—"I would not be alive today. I'll always be grateful that your parents fed and clothed me, a Christian child, while my parents starved to death during the hard times we went through."

"Yes, my parents couldn't see children go hungry no matter what their faith was. And I'm indebted to you now for alerting us to this new danger from Torquemada." Maria turned her eyes to a man in his forties, who looked prematurely aged. His hair was almost white except for black streaks at his forehead, and his face was crisscrossed by deep wrinkles. His rough hands were those of a laborer or foundry worker. "João, you know all of you cannot remain here any longer. Before long they're bound to seek you," Maria said to him.

"Yes, we know that, Maria. We didn't anticipate that the child would force our hand. We had to seize her before we were ready. Now we must hurry and keep her hidden without telling her why."

Salamon Moresco, a young man with red hair and light-blue eyes said, "That's too dangerous too. We can't keep her much longer." Both Alfonso Sabatin and Pedro Grasin nodded their heads in agreement.

"All we can do right now is remain quiet and avoid any attention," João said.

"That's easy for you to say," said Téresa Costa. She wore an apron over her long skirts tied on one hip with a knot at the waist. "We will be hounded and arrested if they find us here. I say we move her to another city. Benvenide and I will make sure she gets there safely."

Benvenide Matigoro nodded his head. "I have no one to look after, so I can drive her wherever you want me to."

"Téresa is right, João," Maria said. "I say we move her to Granada. At least there she won't be found."

After a long silence, João acquiesced. "We'll start tonight after sunset. Meanwhile, don't talk to her when you bring her food."

"All right," said Maria as she left to continue her chores in the chicken coops.

At the prearranged hour of six o'clock in the evening, Benvenide, wearing a brimmed hat low over his brow, arrived at Maria's farm. He drove an open cart drawn by two horses and piled high with straw. Téresa, draped in a dark linen cloak with the hood covering her face, was waiting by Maria's side. Isabella was sandwiched between them with her face covered by a black veil.

João came close to Isabella and lifted her veil. He raised his right hand and patted her cheek. Isabella pushed his hand aside and pulled back from him.

"Take your hand off me!" she yelled.

João's shoulders slumped.

"*Vaya con Dio*, Téresa, and take good care of her," João said. "And you too, Benvenide," he added in the direction of the driver.

Téresa turned and waived to João after loading Isabella into the cart, as Benvenide whipped the horses onto the road. Maria and João watched as the cart turned a bend and disappeared from view.

"I hope she'll be protected." Maria sighed.

"She will, with God's grace. I made a promise long ago that I would see to her safety," João said.

Téresa Costa and Benvenide Matigoro sat silently as they led the wooden cart, traveling at a snail's pace on the uneven and worn stones of the pavement. Night had fallen with the swiftness of an eagle, and they passed the kerosene lamps being lit in the thatched homes of the small farming community of Alcalá de Guadaira. Téresa thought that most of the inhabitants had washed off the sweat and grime from their day in the fields and mills and were looking forward to supper. The families were saying grace before the meal, and none of them noticed the sound of their cart with its wooden wheels rolling past their small farmhouses. She sighed as she thought of her sons, Miguel and Josè, left unprotected.

The cart passed a bend in the Guadaira River, shining silver in the moonlight, and the abandoned Moorish Alcalá fortress. A Mudéjar church with minarets and a cross at one of its highest towers shone under the moonbeams. Téresa thought that two centuries ago the Moors lived in the same hamlets and houses they had passed moments ago. She could see how the Spanish church had taken over this part of the country, little by little, through conquests and Catholic conversion. She then thought that Spain, and its Catholic fervor, would achieve the Reconquista by pushing back the Moors into the Mediterranean Sea to join their Berber allies. Then what would become of the Spaniard Jews? Would they meet the same fate? She could no more conceive of herself remaining a New Christian than joining the Moors. João was right. The Jews in Spain had to find a new land away from the Inquisition. With God's help, this much-rumored expedition could be the Jews' salvation. *What would become of her small Converso family if she remained in Spain?*

Benvenide pulled her out of her reverie. "We still have to travel for another half hour until we get to the inn. We've been lucky so far; I hope we get there without brigands blocking our way to rob us."

"Don't worry, Matigoro," she soothed. "I've traveled this road many times with my husband, Nahum, when he was alive. The seal I carry will allow us to pass any roadblock."

"I'm worried about that seal, Téresa," Matigoro said. "They're bound to ask why you posses this important seal."

"Carmela instructed us not to show it unless they ask, and to tell them we're carrying this shipment for a royal party traveling soon to this part of the country."

Matigoro didn't answer. He flicked the whip on the horse, and the cart picked up speed. He glanced at the back of the cart to make sure the cargo was secure and then turned his attention back to the narrow country road.

Isabella lay motionless under the mound of straw. It took all her strength just to breathe in the dusty air. She tried to listen to the conversation between her kidnappers, but the words were garbled to her ears. Her hands were tied with hemp rope, and the skin of her wrists was painfully sore. She managed to dislodge some straw above her with movements of her head, which allowed a whiff of fresh air to enter. She began to feel cold. Her stomach growled and distracted her mind from escape, making her sorry now she had thrown the gruel against the barn. She wanted to scream to her captors to let her out of the scratching straw, but she was tightly gagged with a bandana. Tired of her circular thoughts, she let the swaying of the carriage seduce her into sleep.

"*Halt*! You there! Come down!" The loud voice woke Isabella with a start. She heard feet scurry down from the carriage, and the driver's heavy footsteps against the cobblestones.

"What are you carrying in that carriage? *Speak*!" the voice boomed.

"Only eggs, Jandarmá," a voice replied.

Isabella tried to scream through the tight bandana, but she only succeeded in irritating her throat. If she could just alert the jandarmá, her freedom from the kidnappers would be assured. She tried to move under the straw, but only scratched her face and forehead. She froze when she felt a hard instrument shoved into the straw and graze her hips. *A sword!* She thought with horror if its sharp tip was pushed any further, it would end her life right now. When the search ended, she was not sure if she should be grateful to the guard who missed her body with his sword or be furious with him for not finding her.

"Where are you taking this shipment?" It was the jandarmá's voice.

"If you please, Officer. We have to make an important delivery. This food delivery is going to a royal party in Andalusia. I have signed documentation with the royal seal," said the woman.

Isabella could no longer hear an exchange of words. The officer must've been satisfied because the carriage started rolling again, and they were on their way. Where to? Perhaps as the night advanced, the danger of robbers might force her kidnappers to stop. Maybe then she could end her captivity. As soon as this thought fleeted away, she felt the carriage slowing and stopping. The straw was parted from the top, and a woman's face appeared to her. It was the same woman who had brought her food in the barn the previous evening.

"Now listen to me carefully," she whispered to Isabella. "My name is Téresa, and we're stopping here for the night at this inn." Isabella tried to peer through the pile of straw, but all she saw was the faded outline of a roof. "And you're going to act like a young mistress. Any movement on your part to alert the innkeeper will put this blade in your back. You understand?" Téresa's voice was low, and the knife in her hand gleamed through the moonlight. Isabella shook her sluggish head with difficulty. She said nothing. Téresa appeared to accept her silence as an indication that she understood her request.

Téresa untied the bandana and the hemp rope, and then she helped Isabella out of the straw pile. Isabella rubbed her bruised wrists and took a deep breath, clearing her nose and lungs from the wagon's dust. She brushed the straw off her hair and clothes.

"Quickly, take me to a room. I want to wash and eat," she said to Téresa.

Téresa smiled faintly. "Just walk in front of me. I'll be your maid. Matigoro, drive the carriage into the barn and eat your meal there."

Matigoro nodded.

As Téresa followed her into the inn, Isabella could distinguish through the dimly lit room a number of men seated at the main table eating and drinking. The portly bearded innkeeper approached the two women and wiped his hands on his greasy apron.

"Señorita, what would be your pleasure?" he asked.

"I want a room now, and bring us some food. We're tired and have been traveling all day." Isabella's voice was peremptory and authoritarian. *This should keep that evil woman from threatening me with her knife.*

The innkeeper bowed and made a sign to follow him upstairs. He led them up a narrow staircase to the second floor and opened a squeaky door at the end of the hallway to reveal a small room with a large bed. Two chairs and a night table stood in one corner with a washbasin and a water urn.

"Señoritas. This will be ten maravedís. Paid in advance." He stood with his hand outstretched.

"Pay him, Téresa," said Isabella.

Téresa pulled a purse from inside her bosom, paid the innkeeper, and closed the door.

Isabella turned on her with fury in her eyes but was brought up short by the woman's hand over her mouth and the flat part of a blade pressing against her back. "Don't make me remind you every time. The innkeeper is still around," Téresa breathed in Isabella's ear. Isabella nodded, gasping with fear. Téresa dragged her by one arm to the door. She flung it open with one quick movement to reveal the surprised innkeeper standing on the threshold.

"Forgive me, señorita—I was just going to ask you if you wanted wine with your meal?" he said sheepishly.

"Yes, yes," answered Téresa, sounding impatient. "The señorita wants it fast." She closed the door in the innkeeper's face.

When the innkeeper's steps faded down the stairs, Téresa released Isabella, keeping the blade in her right hand. "These greedy innkeepers always want to know who their travelers are. This way they can ask for more—"

Isabella interrupted Téresa with a motion of her hand. "Now tell me why I'm your captive and what is your ransom." She stepped backward away from Téresa.

"I can't tell you yet. But as soon as we get to our destination, everything will be revealed to you."

"What is our destination?"

"I can't tell you that either."

Isabella gave Téresa a piercing look but kept quiet, eyeing the blade still in Téresa's hand.

"I won't give you away if you hide the blade."

Téresa nodded and hid the blade in her voluminous skirts. "All right. I won't use it if you keep your bargain." Isabella acknowledged with a nod of her head.

A knock on the door interrupted them, and Téresa went to open it. A servant brought in a tray of bread, wine, goblets, and two bowls of stew mixed with some bits of meat. After the servant left the room, Isabella washed the grime from her face and hands with water from a small urn on the night table. Téresa followed her, using the leftover clean water in the urn while watching Isabella. They ate, watching each other in silence.

Isabella broke the silence first. "Can you tell me how long will I be held?"

Téresa shook her head. "All I can tell you is it's for your protection and well-being. So finish eating, and let's get some sleep."

"What well-being? All I've gotten so far is bad treatment since yesterday!" Her voice rose in anger.

Téresa didn't answer. She got up, pulled the blankets back on the bed, and indicated for Isabella to get in.

Reluctantly, Isabella slipped into the bulky bed. Téresa pulled the coarse cotton blanket over the girl and pulled the two chairs together and lay down with her eyes open. From her bed Isabella watched to see how fast Téresa would fall asleep. She reasoned that all she had to do was to get the knife, leave the room quietly, and alert the innkeeper. After all, she always got her own way! But before she could execute her plan, she fell into the deep sleep of fatigue.

Over and over, Christophero Columbus studied the unfurled map with inquisitive eyes. He tried to observe the various sea routes indicated for the voyage. One route was to sail to Africa, then navigate in a westerly direction with the winds. His preferred itinerary was to sail from Seville's port along the Portugal coast, then from Porto Santo to the Canary Islands going west to the unknown. A sudden fear took hold of him. *What if they were never to return?* He castigated himself for this thought. All would be well if he stuck to the map and his sailing knowledge. For many years he had channeled this knowledge and experience of cartographic maps to his advantage by working in the Custom House near the royal palace in Lisbon. "I can't understand," he muttered under his breath. "This route seems to be the safest, yet it is the longest, making for more dangers to confront." He knew with certainty that the currents from the island of Gomera became stronger as they sailed west and made better sailing. Yet there was great danger from the unpredictable gale-force winds.

The voice of Luis de Santángel, Christophero's long-time friend and supporter said, "You've been studying these maps all your life. You need to make a decision." He moved closer to Christophero. "You are to meet the queen soon. You must be ready to propose this voyage again to her assembly."

"Yes, yes, I know," Columbus replied with an absent look in his eyes. He became transfixed on Zarco; the Portuguese navigator's map was sprawled on the pine table. He could clearly see Zarco's route. If he followed the famous navigator's recommendations, he could reach Cathay by taking a westward route. Zarco had bequeathed his papers to him twenty years ago when he died, and Columbus had been studying them ever since. In his letter Zarco, affectionately calling him by his nickname, said, "My dear Salvador, you are named after me, and I know you'll accomplish great ventures in your life. Please study these papers carefully for they'll help you navigate the westward seas." Columbus never knew why Zarco took an interest in him, unless he'd known of his many requests to navigate the westward seas. Nevertheless, these papers were invaluable to him, and he was grateful to Zarco.

Columbus straightened up from leaning low over the maps, looked out the windows of the monastery, and fell into a reverie as he remembered those years. A sudden vision entered his mind in which he saw the lines of a woman's face, also urging him to the sea. Then another image superimposed itself upon the previous one. This time it was a beautiful apparition of thick, sweeping black hair surrounding fine features and emerald eyes in an oval chiseled face. He had not thought of that face for many years now. A pang nabbed at his heart at the recollection. *She was beautiful, my Sarita,* he thought. He had been desperately in love with her. Those years had brought him much pain and conflict. At that time, he was torn between marrying her and his ambition to navigate the seas. He had dreamed about it throughout his youth. In the end, the sea won. Many years later he had gone back to the small town of Sintra in Portugal to look up Sarita and found no trace of her. The old neighbors had moved away, and the new ones didn't know who Sarita was. Perhaps she had married a young sailor and moved away. He felt her loss for a long time and missed her terribly. *I wonder where she is now,* he thought. He then admonished himself. Better not to think of her, and he shut his mind to the painful memory.

"My dear de Santángel, you know how much I want this commission." He turned to look at his friend. "The king and queen have turned me down before—especially at the Council of Salamanca. I still can't get over the slap in the face by those ignorant mathematicians who couldn't add and who negated my calculations. This time I must make them see their errors. I'm trying to map out this voyage flawlessly." He stopped, then said, "If they can't see it, I only have one choice—that is to submit my request to King Charles of France."

De Santángel pleaded with him, "You've waited all these years. Don't give up now. This time we have to give all the reasons in favor of this voyage. You must show them the advantages of gaining souls for the

Catholic Church, the gold that you might find in these lands, and the wealth beyond imagination that will pour into Spain."

De Santángel continued, "Meanwhile, I will confer with Fray Juan Perez. You know Juan was confessor to the queen. I'm sure he'll vouch for you and speak to her on your behalf."

Christophero put his head in his hands. "In the meantime, agonizing over their decision can drive me mad."

"Patience, *amigo*," soothed de Santángel. "She's bound to listen to your plan. She admires you for all your knowledge and travels. Don't forget your experience with sea exploration. Your voyages to Iceland in the north, the Azores in the west, the Gulf of Lion, and the Tyrrhenian Sea are well known to her. And don't forget that any treasure you find will be hers, and your share will be immense."

"If the queen does not respond to my request to finance the voyage, can't you influence King Ferdinand? After all, you are his household secretary in Aragon."

"Yes, I am that, but he only listens to the queen. I'm your friend, and as such will do my utmost to convince the queen on your behalf."

"Thank you for being my friend. You always believed in me."

"Rest assured that my interest is served here," de Santángel said. "If the Jews can find a haven in Cathay, then they'll escape from Torquemada's tentacles. They'll thrive in a new land and live in peace."

Columbus stayed pensive for a moment, grasping the small crucifix hanging from a chain around his neck and stroking it absentmindedly. He suddenly let go of his crucifix. "I'll wait here at the convent of La Rábida until I hear from Fray Pérez."

De Santángel looked inquisitively at Columbus. "At least you don't have to fear for your life, Colón."

His friend always preferred to call him by his Portuguese name, Colón, instead of the Italian *Columbus*. He avoided de Santángel's probing eyes. He could never confide his secret, even to his closest friend. He was not afraid for his life but for his life's ambition—his dreams borne since childhood—and for his sons Diego and Fernandez. No, his true identity had to be concealed forever. He was a good Christian and always would be in the depth of his heart.

Fray Juan Pérez was the queen's primary confessor and had been from the time she was a small girl in the town of Arévalo until ten years ago. He progressed from friar to bishop and all the way to confessor for Queen Isabella.

He admired the queen's deep beliefs in the true faith, and she always followed his advice. Queen Isabella had been to him a paragon of faith, devotion, and moral courage. He admired her magnanimity and devotion to her subjects as she followed her minister Ximenes's advice on reforms. There was nothing that Fray Pérez could refuse her if she asked him. If the queen became amenable to Columbus's voyages, he personally would help in any capacity. Unfortunately, preparation for war with Granada had taxed the queen's patience and coffers. How was he to plead Columbus's request to sanction this voyage when such conditions existed now?

No matter—he would travel to the queen's palace in Castile and plead for an audience. He prostrated himself before the alcove of the Virgin Mary and prayed for a successful outcome with the queen

When Isabella opened her eyes, the sun was high above the horizon. She jumped down from the towering bed and touched the rough grainy pine floor with her bare feet. She saw that Téresa had left the room, and she dashed for the door. The door handle resisted her efforts. She pulled again, but the door didn't budge. Frantically, she searched for an open window and saw one with wide-open shutters and no bars to stop her exit. She approached the window and was enveloped in the scent of jasmine from the climbing vines. She saw that the second floor window was not too far from the ground. Looking again, Isabella realized that she would have to slip out of the window and make her way down the knotted vine lining the wall. She was about to proceed when a key turned in the lock and Téresa appeared on the threshold.

"Save your breath, my child. You can't jump that far without your shoes, and besides, if you break a leg, it would easier for me to keep you captive. So be a good girl and eat your breakfast." Téresa placed a tray with food on the table and sat herself comfortably on the chair.

Isabella was still seething with disappointment but saw that her flight would have to be postponed for now. She sat at the table and ravenously ate the black bread and boiled eggs in front of her. The fresh milk reminded her of dada Hannah's admonition: "You must drink this milk to the last drop if you want your complexion to remain white and creamy!"

When she was full, she asked Téresa, "Where are you dragging me today?"

"Now I will tell you, my sweet. We are inside Granada's frontier—"

"Granada!" cried Isabella. "But we will be killed! There's war raging between the queen and the king's troops and King Abdallah! You're a fool to bring me here!"

"Don't you worry yourself. We're protected here. No one will harm one hair on your head."

Tears streamed from Isabella's eyes and rolled down her cheeks. "You took me away from my home, my parents, and my fiancé, Juan. You'll pay dearly for this crime!" Isabella's face turned red and she shook her fist. Téresa sat placidly in her chair.

"Remember what we told you before we took you to this place?" asked Téresa.

Isabella spoke between sobs. "You said everything will be explained. I want to know now what you're going to do with me!"

"Well, the time is now. We'll take a short ride to the next city, where it will become clearer to you."

Isabella didn't reply. In her mind she saw another uncomfortable ride in the bottom of the straw cart in stifling air.

Téresa said, as if she had read Isabella's thoughts, "You'll travel in a closed carriage. Get ready now." She added, "Don't bother alerting the innkeeper—he's on our side."

Téresa opened the door to the room, retrieved Isabella's slippers, and handed them to her.

Isabella looked at Téresa with fury in her eyes, but she put her slippers on and followed Téresa down the stairs. The innkeeper waited at the foot of the stairs. He smiled at Isabella. "Thank you for staying with us, señoritas." He then bowed.

Isabella stormed out the door behind Téresa without a word. A carriage coach with two horses in harness waited with the driver Matigoro. The horses stamped their hooves on the dusty road and were keeping Matigoro busy trying to control them with soothing words.

Téresa waited for Isabella to climb the two metal steps and climbed into the coach after her. Inside, the padded coach was quiet and protected from the dusty road, along which she could see workers in the distance harvesting in the fields that bordered the inn. Isabella had never seen a harvesting sight before. Whenever she had traveled to their country estates in the mountains to escape the summer heat, her parent's carriage passed shanty homes lining the road, and the poor who watched them pass by had a saddened look upon their faces. Some of the peasants wore tattered clothes and seemed to have been left to fend for themselves.

When she asked her parents why these peasants looked so dirty and poor, her father replied, "Those are gypsies from Portugal. They have no other home, and our monarchs let them stay here to escape the poverty where they came from." Here in Granada, however, Isabella could see that the farm laborers looked hefty and worked energetically at their task with intermittent chatter. A chant rose from a group of them in the field as they sang in their Moorish tongue.

Isabella turned away, detached from the scene, and caught Téresa observing her.

"In Granada these Moorish farmworkers are happy to work in these fields," said Téresa, "They have homes, work, and food. Not like some of the farmworkers in Castile who have to give their land to grazing sheep. In Castile, the peasants have to let grazing sheep and cows onto their planting fields. That destroys their crops, and puts them further into poverty."

"But the king and queen wouldn't allow it!"

"But they do," said Téresa. "The monarchs have to protect the precious merino wool that brings revenues to the Mesta societies, or to the rich owners who own the sheep. It's by decree. It brings revenue to the crown and enriches wealthy foreigners making profit on our single export commodity."

Isabella was confounded by this revelation. She couldn't believe that Spanish peasants had to bow to the rich landowners "Our farmworkers are well fed! You should be ashamed of yourself taking sides against our compatriots. You speak treason!"

Téresa didn't answer her. She wore that exasperating smile and looked squarely in Isabella's eyes. Isabella sustained her penetrating gaze for a moment, then looked away and concentrated on settling down for the long ride. They crossed a large river and were making their way to the mountainous region looming on the horizon.

"We'll be ascending the Sierra Nevada Mountains soon," Téresa said. "If everything goes according to plan, we should be arriving by six o'clock tonight."

Isabella again didn't answer her. *Arrive? Arrive where?* Anxiety about a journey that would take her far away from home and her parents overcame her. She sank back into the carriage bench and remained silent for the rest of the day.

The carriage continued the long and monotonous ride over a narrow road, trying to skirt huge boulders, crossing several bridges over fast-moving rivers, and passing burned-out fields and groves. The charred trees and fields spreading for miles made her wonder if the Spanish armies were responsible for their destruction. One moment she rejoiced inside over the enemy's defeat, and the next she reprimanded herself for a lack of pity for the enemy's women and children who would go hungry this winter. She thought about her parents, her dada, and Juan. How she wished she were home now. She would gladly attend her guitar lessons without any reluctance. *Why are they holding me captive?* If it were for a ransom, she was sure her father would have paid it by now. This captivity might never end, and she might not be found. *Granada.* The thought of it gave her the shivers.

Dada Hannah told her tales of young girls and women being captured as slaves to caliphs, and about cruel Moors who hung their victims by their hands on poles until they died in the hot sun. After dada Hannah had told her those tales, and after countless nightmares, Isabella's father had forbidden the nanny to tell them again. Dada Hannah had still managed to tell her about the excursions of Moors into Castilian territories, setting fire to fields and homes in the neighboring frontier towns of Jaén, Ojos de Huescar, and the conquered cities of Guadix and Almería, which had left Spain mourning for their nobles and sons killed in battle.

The carriage came to an abrupt stop, jostling her out of her memories.

"We're stopping to eat," said Téresa. "It's our only stop until we arrive tonight."

Isabella didn't reply and ostensibly followed her reluctantly. *I might as well not antagonize Téresa. Better to make a friend out of her, win her confidence, and then make an escape at the proper time.*

The three travelers entered a small low-lying building that had a yard full of cackling chickens. A heavyset woman in peasant garb broke into a huge smile at their sight.

"Téresa. *¿Cómo estás*?" the woman said in a local idiomatic language. She hugged Téresa and kissed her cheeks, then kissed Matigoro as well.

"Estoy bien," Téresa said. She murmured some things in the woman's ear. The woman took a quick look at her and nodded her head, seeming to understand what Téresa said.

"Come. Sit here," the peasant woman said to them.

They sat on a bench near a long table, and the woman brought them cheese, black bread, and mackerel fish stew in a saffron and lemon sauce, followed by a jug of wine.

They ate in silence, After the meal, the woman glanced at Isabella, then asked Téresa, "How far are you going?"

Téresa didn't answer at first, but then she said, "Just beyond the mountains."

"We have a day's travel," added Matigoro.

The woman seemed to understand what Téresa meant. Isabella searched her mind for the meaning of "beyond the mountain and a day's travel," but came up with nothing.

"All right," said Téresa after they had finished eating, "we must leave now, *rengrasyo*. Thank you for a good meal."

Outside, the women settled into the carriage, then Matigoro whipped the horses and the carriage lurched back onto the road.

After several hours that seemed an eternity to Isabella, with monotonous fields following more fields, the carriage stopped. Téresa opened the carriage door and climbed out. Isabella followed her, but drew back at the terrifying sight of perhaps a dozen mounted men dressed in long cotton tunics with turban headdresses, and armed with scimitars and lances. The reins of two horses without riders were held by a horseman. Isabella's first reaction was to run away, but Téresa firmly grasped her trembling arm.

"These men won't hurt you, but remain still," Téresa said.

Isabella still trembled, but obeyed her for the first time.

Téresa let go of Isabella's arm and spoke quietly to one of the horsemen. He listened to her and then looked in Isabella's direction. He nodded and gave orders to his men.

"We'll ride horses from now on, and these men will accompany us. You'll ride on the same horse with me," said Téresa.

Resigned, Isabella climbed on the horse behind Téresa with Matigoro's help. He mounted the other horse, and the whole company slowly moved out, single file, onto the narrow road leading to the mountain passes. They rode in silence, paying attention to the road. The horses' hooves sounded unsure as they halted and then reluctantly resumed their climb on the gravel road. Within an hour they began the ascent into the mountains.

Narrow ledges and precipices terrified Isabella as the horses slipped now and then. She was reluctant to hold on to Téresa's waist, but a couple of slips frightened her enough to grasp Téresa's arm tightly. There was no point in endangering her life, she thought. Several hours later the temperatures dropped, making Isabella shiver in her light clothing. Téresa noticed Isabella's hands turning blue and motioned for the riders to stop. She spoke a few words to the leader, and he brought out heavy capes for all three of them. Feeling warmer under the coarse but protective garment, Isabella concentrated on her surroundings. Frost covered the ground as they climbed higher; ravines surrounding them became deeper, and loose rocks and gravel underfoot made the climb more dangerous. Isabella felt tired and sleepy from the swaying of their ride, but was too terrified to fall asleep. What if she slipped from the horse and fell into one of those deep ravines? It would be instant death! She shuddered and held on tighter to Téresa's arm.

"Qef!" The head horseman dismounted and shouted orders to his men. With haste his men laid blankets on the ground, then produced their

traveler's meals of bread, cheese, and fruit, with jugs of water to wash it all down.

"Sit down, Isabella. We might as well nourish ourselves and bring back warmth in our veins," Téresa said.

Isabella took the food and ate the rations offered to her. "How long are we going to be climbing?" she asked Téresa while munching on her bread.

"Mmmm . . . perhaps two to three hours."

"That long?" exclaimed Isabella.

"We could've taken the main highway, but that would've put us into the hands of the Spanish authorities. Or maybe that is what you want the most?"

Isabella didn't reply. She agreed wholeheartedly with part of Téresa's comment about the Spanish authorities, but was surprised to find she didn't want Téresa to get caught. She still felt resentment and anger over Téresa's role in her abduction, but she didn't want be a part of Téresa's demise over the entire affair.

"Imshee!" The leader barked the order to resume the climb. The members of the party mounted their horses and continued their trek. After two hours of skirting more ravines at dizzying heights, they came upon a plateau overlooking an immense valley. A walled city comprised of a red palace and fort with many crenellated towers came into view. Lush gardens and houses with terraces surrounded the palace. On a hill above the main palace grounds stood a smaller palace with vast gardens. The men surrounding them shouted with joy. *"Alhamdulillah! Alhamdulillah!"*

"We've arrived," said Téresa quietly. "This is the famed city of Alhambra and realm of Granada."

Isabella looked again upon at the palace and her chest felt tight. Would this be her jail now? When she looked down the valley, she clearly noticed an army encampment within close proximity to the Alhambra.

"What is this town?" she asked.

"That is where the Spaniards wait for Alhambra to give in. But she never will!"

Isabella was surprised by Téresa's strong conviction. Since Téresa was a Spaniard herself, these words made her into a traitor. She couldn't understand this treachery. What could possibly have bred this hatred in

Téresa's heart? Perhaps she stood to gain monetary rewards for kidnapping her. Téresa must've been far more evil than Isabella had imagined.

They began their descent, and within two hours they reached the bottom of the mountain. Instead of leading their horses toward the Alhambra, the lead horseman swerved away toward a gentle hill, which surprised Isabella. She waited to see where they would take her. Within a half hour, they arrived at a rock wall abutting a hill and dismounted. The lead horseman gave orders to his ten men, all of whom pushed on a flat stone that rolled on its side, revealing a dark cavern. Isabella, Téresa, and Matigoro filed into the damp, dark cavity followed by the rest of the men leading their horses. The men lit torches and rolled the stone back into place, closing the entrance. As she followed the whole procession of men and horses, Isabella could see into the dark passage, by the flickering light of the torches, a winding corridor that took them only minutes to travel through to a dead end. The leader gave new orders, and the men moved another rock, revealing the exit.

The strong sunlight hit Isabella's eyes as she stepped out of the cavern. The party climbed a small hill on a brush-covered path, and a magical world revealed itself when they reached the top. A meandering river flowed on a valley floor, dividing a palace and a smaller stately residence upon the hill. Isabella looked down on cypress trees lining a cobblestone avenue leading up to a fortress, and she marveled at the lush green surroundings interspersed with clear water fountains. Groves of citrus trees, date palms, pomegranates, and figs were separated by descending terraces and encircled by fragrant hedges of roses and myrtle. Isabella rubbed her eyes thinking this paradise was a dream, but it was real. Téresa and Isabella descended the hill and were stopped at the entrance by guards.

Téresa spoke a few words to an overseer who let them in through the arched entrance with two gigantic polished brass doors. Ushered through a series of gleaming marble corridors and vaulted ceilings with intricate filigree patterns and arabesques decorations, they found themselves in a large paved courtyard with colorful canvas awnings used to shield its occupants from the sun. The paving stones were made of red brick, and at the center of the courtyard were multicolored tile mosaics. A large central fountain dominated the middle of the courtyard surrounded by four palm trees with deer statues standing at attention between each tree. Colorful flowerbeds encircled the fountain in repeating patterns of red and yellow flowers. Servants carried large trays of lamb, rice, flat breads, and onions to an alcove at the end of the courtyard. The tangy scents of orange blossoms mixed with the aroma of grilled meat wafted through the air.

"*Assalamou Alykoum!* Come in, come in, my friends," a soft Moorish voice called from a tented alcove. When Isabella peered into the tent, she saw a diminutive man clad in a richly embroidered green satin hayk tunic over baggy *shalwar* trousers. He was seated on a rug with silk pillows scattered about him. His long face bore an expression of melancholy accentuated by hollow cheeks, a black mustache, and a goatee. Téresa turned to Isabella and whispered in her ear, "This is Boabdil, King Abdallah of Granada. In Spain we call him Boabdil *el Chico*."

Téresa approached the king and spoke a few words in the Moorish tongue while Isabella trailed behind her. Isabella immediately understood the words spoken.

"I understand everything you said, and I'm not staying here!" Isabella said.

Téresa looked at her surprised.

"My household servant was a Moor," said Isabella. "She taught me a few words in secret from the time I was a young child."

"Very well," Téresa said. "I'm sure the pasha will not object if we continue in Castilian." She turned to the pasha and he nodded in consent. Téresa lowered herself onto the yellow silk cushions piled on the carpeted floor and motioned to Isabella to do the same. Reluctantly, Isabella dropped down to the pillows on the ground and sat uncomfortably with crossed legs.

The pasha asked Téresa in flawless Castilian, "What news do you bring me from Castile?"

"Your Excellency, King Boabdil," started Téresa. "There is nothing to report at this time in your old cities of Guadix and Almería. The Spaniards are regulating both cities with an iron rule. They still have a strong garrison there in Almería."

"Ahhh . . ." Boabdil sighed. His face grew more melancholic. "My beautiful Almería. The jewel of all my territories now lost forever. For the last two years I've been here in exile, remembering its glorious times."

"One day you will recoup those territories," Téresa said.

"I'm afraid now for what is going to happen to Granada," Boabdil said. His voice grew fainter.

"Granada will never surrender. Your people are prepared to die for her." Téresa's voice became persuasive.

"Insha'Allah," Boabdil said.

Isabella looked at Téresa with contempt. Not only was Téresa a kidnapper but she was also a spy and a traitor!

"And what is this beautiful apparition?" asked Boabdil. Isabella saw admiration in his eyes, but she returned his look with one of contempt.

"She is my friend's ward. I would like to leave her here under your protection, if possible, until we return for her."

At first Isabella became perplexed at Téresa's words. What could she have meant by the word ward? She then dismissed the thought. Téresa was a liar, along with her other sins.

"A friend of yours is also a friend of mine, and she is welcomed in my house," Boabdil pronounced.

"I won't stay here!" Isabella said adamantly, finding her voice after the initial shock of learning their intentions. "I won't! You can't make me!"

"My dear child," answered Téresa, "no one will harm you. You have my word."

"Your word is the word of a traitor!"

Téresa looked at her with a smile. Isabella's accusation had no effect on her. "I've told you that everything will be explained to you when we arrived. Now is the time for revelations."

Isabella jumped up and covered her ears with her fists. "I won't listen to you! You're a criminal. Your words are worthless! Worthless! You hear!" She stamped her foot.

Téresa looked at her with a motherly expression on her face. She got up and prepared to leave Isabella in Boabdil's care. As Isabella watched Téresa walk toward the wide exit doors, she saw that the only link to everything familiar was about to disappear.

"No! Don't go!" Isabella heard her voice break in a near sob. "I'm prepared to hear what you have to say." Her voice quieted.

"All right," said Téresa. She returned to her cushions. Isabella followed and resumed her cross-legged position on the floor.

Téresa turned to Boabdil and said, "His Excellency will be a witness to my words." Then she turned to Isabella and spoke. "We brought you here for your protection."

Isabella looked at Téresa again with contempt.

Téresa continued. "You're not the daughter of your parents. You were adopted as a young baby by your present guardians and parents."

After a stunned silence Isabella yelled, "No! It isn't true! It isn't true!"

"It is true. If you could ask them now, I know they wouldn't deny it. Your true mother was a Jewish woman who lived in Portugal. It means that you're not a Catholic Spaniard but the Jewish daughter of that woman. Unfortunately, she died giving birth to you. Your uncle then took you to dada Hannah, a Jewish woman who had converted, and she was a housekeeper for your adoptive parents. Since she was already working there, she could help look out for you."

Isabella was stunned. Then she remembered dada Hannah telling her stories from the old Bible when she was a young child, stories about Moses and Abraham, the "God of Abraham," Joseph and the Maccabees, and other events from a Jewish perspective in history. Her parents reprimanded Hannah many times about filling the mind of a young girl with exaggerated tales. Now, Isabella remembered the look between her parents when the subject came up, but still couldn't believe what she was hearing.

Isabella felt her heart was breaking into pieces, and when she recovered, she said to Téresa in a choked voice, "Even if what you're saying is true, why have you brought me here? Here, where the barbarian enemy lives. Don't you care about my welfare?"

Téresa glanced at Boabdil. He only nodded his head, and his face remained placid, seemingly unfazed by Isabella's insult.

"I do care for your safety. That is why you're here. You know that converted Jews everywhere in Castile are watched and spied upon to see if they relapse. Before long, the arm of the Inquisition is bound to find you and brand you, too, as a Marrano."

"I'm not a Marrano! A secret Judaiser! I was raised as a faithful Catholic and will remain so no matter what you say!" Isabella was now in tears.

Téresa had a pained look on her face. "No matter, my child. It's too early for you to believe what I just said. Just remember that we are truly looking after your welfare. Good-bye, my child." Without another word, Téresa left the courtyard.

Isabella sat numb for a moment, not grasping fully what was happening to her. What she had just experienced and heard was worse than any nightmare. Before she could understand her action, she jumped up from the cushions and ran after Téresa. "Wait! Wait for me!" She ran back through the corridors by which they had entered, but Téresa was nowhere in sight. When Isabella reached the exit to the palace, she saw the horses galloping away on the avenue. She ran down the gray cobblestones after the horses as fast as she could, but they gained ground and disappeared from view. Exhausted, she threw herself on the ground and sobbed.

A hand gently grasped her shoulder, and she looked up to see a young veiled woman with a soft expression in her eyes. "Come, come with me," she said quietly in Moorish. She helped the sobbing girl up from the ground and led her by the hand to the main entrance leading back inside the palace. Isabella followed her as in a dream. Part of her wanted to scream and run, and another part of her followed in shock. The woman, dressed in aqua veils and emerald satin *shalwar* pantaloons, led her to a wing of the palace barred by two great metal doors. In front stood two guards with naked chests and wearing red *shalwar* trousers bound by black belts. On their sides hung unsheathed gleaming sabers. The veiled woman led her into an antechamber where many women reclined on silk sofas and satin pillows surrounding a pool. The surface of the rectangle pool was covered with lily pads and rippled by the motion of a tiered fountain spilling and splashing its crystal waters into a central pond. The women chatted with intermittent laughter. If Isabella hadn't been in shock from the crushing feeling of her predicament, she might've enjoyed the entire colorful but—to her—eerie scene. Instead she felt unmoved by the enchanting sight, and felt self-conscious with all those women's eyes turned toward her and the veiled woman.

"This girl is a guest in our midst. Treat her with respect," the woman said.

"*Aiwa*, Noor," the women replied in unison, bowing their heads in respect. Noor turned to Isabella and said, "Follow me."

Isabella followed Noor deep into the palace quarters reserved for the harem. Near the junction of two corridors, she opened a door and took Isabella inside.

"This will be your room. You'll have a maid to serve and help you. You'll find clothes in that wooden chest." She pointed at a large carved chest covered with Arabic lettering.

"I'm fine just the way I'm dressed, *agradecer*," she said, thanking her.

"If you want to remain in your dirty clothes, no one will attend you," Noor said.

Isabella nodded her head. She could no longer stand her filthy state after her barn stay and journeys in dusty straw and the hot carriage. Noor left her, but a beautiful ebony woman with chiseled features and coal-black eyes waited on her throughout her bath. Isabella's soiled clothes were taken away, and she dressed in the unfamiliar harem garb of green pantaloons gathered at the ankles, a black sequined embroidered vest over an aqua silk camisole, and a gold veiled headdress. She stood in soft heelless slippers with her toenails covered with henna. She looked at her reflection in the highly polished glass standing mirror and didn't recognize herself. Her eyes were kohl-rimmed, and a henna streak covered her chin. She might have passed for one of the concubines she saw in the harem. Isabella walked away from the mirror and was prepared to lie down on the floor-level bed when Noor came in.

"You'll have supper now with His Excellency."

"The pasha?" Isabella was surprised.

"Yes, Boabdil himself. Every guest in his palace gets to partake in his meals."

Isabella followed Noor back to the main reception room, where Boabdil sat at the end of a table heavily laden with food.

"Please sit down next to me, my child," said Boabdil.

Isabella didn't like being called his child, but stopped at the thought of insulting her host. She sat down quietly. She thought she saw a paternal expression in his eyes, similar to the look her father showed her. The thought of her father brought tears to her eyes.

Seeing her distress, Boabdil said softly to her, "You are right to feel sadness after being separated from your parents. Every child needs protection, especially a young woman like you."

She had a fleeting moment of suspicion when she thought she saw a different expression in Boabdil's eyes—a type of admiration that made her uncomfortable. *No. That cannot be. The pasha has many concubines. He doesn't need another.* Nevertheless, a slight worry lingered in her mind.

"You are to be my guest as long as possible, and no one, no one," he repeated, "will harm you."

Isabella nodded, somewhat reassured. She realized how hungry she was when she began to eat the delicacies spread before her on the table. She enjoyed the lamb and wasn't surprised to find no ham on the table among other foods, fruit, and nuts. She knew that the Moors didn't eat pork. One of the servants in her father's house was a Moor who had been forced to convert to Catholicism, but still wouldn't touch any pork. The other servants teased the servant constantly, but he remained secretly true to his previous faith. This could've earned him imprisonment and excommunication from The Church, but her father saw to it that none of his Moriscoes and baptized Muslim servants were harmed, and had warned his Christians servants to treat them with respect. She also knew that Jews didn't eat pork, and the thought brought her back to what Téresa had told her. Could Téresa be right? *No!* The idea was absurd. It simply couldn't be true. She quickly chased the thought from her mind.

After the meal, she took leave from Boabdil when Noor came to fetch her. Noor led her through a series of corridors to a different wing of the palace that was heavily guarded. They entered a palatial suite that Isabella instantly saw was the pasha's bedchamber. Before Isabella could say a word, Noor disappeared. Isabella ran for the door but it was too late—Boabdil had entered. She recoiled, thinking about her earlier suspicion. *No! No! That can't be!* Was she to be his concubine? She tried to open the door, but Boabdil motioned her to sit down on a low sofa.

"My dear child, don't be afraid. As I promised, I will not hurt one hair on your head. Sit down." He motioned again.

Isabella stood trembling by the door, afraid to advance toward him.

"I'll sit here," Boabdil said. He then sat on one of two low-lying plush sofas. "The reason," he began, "I brought you here to my quarters is a ruse to fool my other concubines. Otherwise, they'll suspect that I'm hiding you here, but if you're another concubine, or wife, they won't suspect anything. Otherwise, they'll hound you and treat you with disrespect. Every woman in the harem knows that she will be privileged to spend one night with me. That is why I brought you here."

Isabella wanted to believe him, but she still stood near the door. He pulled out a square wooden box with ivory decorations and sat it on the low carved table between the sofas. As he opened it, Isabella could see from where she stood that it was a game.

"We call this game *Shesh Besh.* Come and sit."

Isabella stood still for a moment, then slowly approached him. Each of the two halves of the chest was marked with twelve opposing pyramid-shaped bars. She recognized the game of backgammon she had played since childhood. Boabdil scooped up two ivory dice and threw them across the board.

"Come and sit down. We need to play most of the night to confound my concubines." He chuckled. His mouth broke into a wide crescent, revealing yellow teeth. His face bore a mischievous look, and Isabella thought he seemed to delight himself by fooling those around him.

Isabella's fear slowly subsided when she saw that Boabdil meant to be kind to her. She began to understand the harem's jealousies and hierarchies. She had to play her part if she were to leave the palace alive. She slowly approached Boabdil's sofa and sat cross-legged across from him on the other sofa. She told him, "We call this game Tavla."

He smiled and said, "First, I roll one die and you roll the other one." He handed her the one die, then rolled his. "I have a three," he called out. "Your turn."

Isabella grabbed the remaining die and rolled it, getting a number six.

"You go first," Boabdil said.

Isabella played her hand with both dice this time and rolled a four and a three, advancing seven spaces. Then Boabdil rolled the die and advanced to the next half of the board. As the evening progressed, Isabella's fears vanished, and she played her hands on the *Shesh Besh* with confidence. Boabdil won two games, but Isabella beat him afterward at every game. Finally, he said in frustration, "You win every time!" His complaint was half-serious, but he smiled.

Isabella replied, "I've played with my father since I was a child. He taught me the best moves." She yawned.

"In that case I give up. Besides, I see that you are tired, and it is very late now," Boabdil said. He put away the game, then approaching his bed, he unruffled it, giving it the appearance that it had been slept in. Afterward he grabbed a brass drumstick and hit a brass drum next to his bed. Immediately, a servant glided in and bowed to him. "Take her back to her quarters," he said.

Silently, the servant motioned to Isabella to follow him.

Isabella turned to Boabdil and thanked him. *"Shukran."*

"Assalamu alaikum." He bid peace upon her.

When Isabella reached her bedroom chamber, she undressed with the help of her maidservant and plunged into bed. She crossed herself, and before she closed her eyes prayed to the Virgin Mary to keep her safe.

5

Prelude to War

DON ESCOBAR WAS LOOKING AT a map of Seville's countryside while helping Inspector Guerida chart a plan of action to find Isabella. He raised his head for a moment to see that Juan sat nervously grasping the sculpted head of his sword. His knuckles were white with tension.

"We're wasting time! I say we go right now to Maria's farm and arrest her!" Juan's voice blasted.

"Calm yourself. We're going to do that, *mi hijo*," Don Pedro Escobar said.

"Your father is right," said Inspector Guerida. "If we descend on the farm just now, we're bound to arrest only Maria. We need to know who's behind this kidnapping."

"But they must've fled by now." Juan stood and started pacing the room. "If anything happens to Isabella, I'll kill them myself!"

Don Escobar felt sad to see his son's anger. Juan was his only son. If anything happened to him in a duel or while chasing these brigands, he would never forgive himself. Juan had inherited his impetuousness and his bravery along with his looks. He felt proud of his son's erect posture, especially when he wore his maritime uniform. Juan had a high forehead—a sign of distinction for a Grandee—and intense dark eyes that could look through a man. Grandees were titled nobility from a long line of crested families. Juan had the physical characteristics and required upbringing to become a truly great Grandee.

"I promise you, my son, we will retaliate tomorrow if nothing is detected at Maria's farm," Don Escobar said. He looked at Inspector Guerida, who nodded.

"I'll send twenty guards to surround the farm. This way no one will escape," said Guerida.

Guerida's comment quieted Juan's restlessness. Don Escobar knew that Guerida's word of honor could be relied upon; the inspector would put the plan in motion and follow it resolutely. It was disturbing to the don that no one had seen Isabella before she went missing, and no one had any evidence as to her whereabouts. She had now been missing for two days, and he knew that his son despaired. He hoped, for his son's sake, that she hadn't been harmed, and that she was under the protection of someone who would see to her welfare. He felt sure that if they were looking for ransom, she would be safe. He reasoned the kidnappers hadn't made their demands yet so they could increase the amount. Feeling comforted by his own thoughts, he turned to Juan.

"Promise me, Son, that you won't do anything?"

After a long silence, Juan said, "I'll wait until tomorrow."

Don Escobar let out a sigh of relief. "I'm glad you see eye to eye with Inspector Guerida. We'll wait for your word, Inspector."

"We'll let you know as soon as we encircle the farm," Guerida said. He saluted and left to rejoin his headquarters in town.

Don Escobar was about to address Juan when there was a knock at the door. "*Entra*," Escobar said.

A servant entered with a missive in her hand and handed it to Juan. Juan leaped up and tore open the seal. Don Escobar saw his son's face turning pale. He fell back into his chair.

"What is it?" asked Don Escobar. He was alarmed at his son's reaction to the message.

Without a word Juan handed him the missive.

Don Escobar saw that the letter belonged to the military high command of Captain Gonzalo de Córdova. The insignia at the top of the letter bore Queen Isabella's seal. Don Escobar's alarm increased. The captain had the power to conscript anyone of age to join his command. Don Escobar knew which post the great captain needed to cover with more recruits. Granada was the last bastion of the Moors. His chest tightened at the thought. A half hour ago he feared Juan's life would be wasted on brigands. Now his fear reached greater proportions. If Juan joined the forces sent to fight the Moors, he may as well be dead to him and his mother. Juan had been training for the eventuality of fighting for his homeland, but Don Escobar had been able to pretend it wouldn't happen. Now it was real. His son's life was to be spent over the infidels. He felt weak, and his shoulders slumped. Noticing Juan sitting prostrate in his chair, he straightened and with great effort said, "You'll join your regiment as scheduled and be proud to fight for your homeland, España!"

"I love our homeland and our queen, Padre. You know nothing can stop me from fighting the infidels! It's the timing that's wrong. I need my efforts to be for Isabella." Juan's head hung low. After a moment that felt like an eternity for Don Escobar, Juan raised his head and stood up from his chair. "Padre. I will not shame you. I will fight for you and *Madre* and for Isabella."

"That's the spirit, my son," Don Escobar said. He was deeply proud and just as deeply worried for Juan. "I only ask that you delay telling your mother until tomorrow."

"All right, Padre." Juan then stood resolutely to ready himself for his trip with the regiment.

As the door closed behind his beautiful son, Don Escobar could no longer hold back tears. They ran until he forced them to stop, and scolded himself for this momentary weakness. *My son will fight and will return home safe and sound, through God's grace.*

Téresa looked at her two sons and felt great concern for their safety. If something were to happen to her, the Inquisition's tribunal would expropriate and seal her house. Where would her two sons go? She didn't understand at first why João had selected the Obrigon family in particular. She told him this whole venture was dangerous and foolish, and she wanted no part of it. Then he revealed that the Obrigons' daughter was adopted and was in fact his niece. He convinced Téresa that as Isabella's only true relative, João was concerned only with his niece's welfare. Téresa began to trust João's reasons for this plan.

Téresa was solely responsible for her two children, Miguel and José. Her querido husband, Nahum, had been dead ten years. She was told he had died in prison of heart failure, but she knew he was killed under torture. Nahum had been a good converted New Christian, as had she. They decided that converting from Judaism was the only way for them to preserve their small family and the future of their sons. But their good intentions had failed because of the malice of neighbors, who gave them away. Téresa was seen purchasing a cut of meat in the old Jewish quarters of Seville to cook on Friday instead of the tasteless mackerel fish they had been forced to eat according to Catholic dogma. That detail alone caused Nahum's arrest and conviction. Now she and her two sons were alone. Téresa's and Nahum's parents also died ten years ago at the hand of the inquisitors.

For many years, she felt the burden of knowing that her actions had caused Nahum's death. Then this terrible guilt changed to anger at the Inquisition and the bloody hands that had killed her husband. Her rage had long been seething behind a calm façade. With Nahum gone, she'd had to support her sons by doing laundry and mending. She carried the heavy baskets of clothing to the river, dragged them back uphill to her house, and hung the laundry in her courtyard. Afterward she pressed the clean clothes with a hot iron and delivered them, using up most of her day. Keeping her small home clean and raising two sons added to her burden. Every day, she was more and more tired, and shortness of breath plagued her. She dismissed the thought that her health was worsening, and talked herself into believing it was temporary. Her soul lifted, nevertheless, as she watched her two sons grow. Each spring, at the sight of nature renewing itself, she believed that she, too, was gaining strength.

They lived in a modest whitewashed house with two rooms on one floor. The boys slept in a comfortable bedroom while she slept on a hard metal bed covered by a thin mattress in the room where they ate their meals. With the little she made as a laundress, she was able to support her family. She kept Blanko, her old white mule that the boys rode daily, in the small courtyard outside the house, Miguel and José would fetch water at the communal fountain in town and buy food from the vendors. Except for money needed for food and lodging, all her resources were saved to pay for Miguel's engineering education.

"¿Madre?" Miguel's voice jolted her out of her thoughts.

"What is it, my son?" she asked.

"You've been dreaming," Miguel said.

"I've been thinking about your future, my sons."

"You haven't touched your food either," her younger son, José, whispered as he affectionately grasped her arm.

She looked lovingly at her nine-year-old son, with his tousled red hair and light-blue eyes, his round and soft cheeks—an image of herself at that age.

"I'm not very hungry," she replied.

"You've been like that since you came back from that trip," Miguel said. His eyes were looking squarely into hers.

"I already told you where I'd been. I went to Cordoba to ask our relatives for help."

"You never told us about relatives in Cordoba!" José exclaimed.

"I didn't tell you because there was no need to. We haven't been on speaking terms since your grandparents died."

"Why is that?" asked José.

"That is because they came from a branch of the family that decided to remain in Cordoba."

"It doesn't make any sense to me," José said. "Were they too rich or did they think they were too far above us?"

Miguel looked at his younger brother and stayed silent.

"No. That wasn't the reason," Téresa said. "That's enough questions. Go to bed, you two."

Both Miguel and José got up from the table to kiss their mother good night. "Have good dreams," she told them softly.

After her sons left the room, Téresa remained for a long time at the table thinking about the risks brought on by her actions. All in the rebel group had agreed that their lives in Castile were precarious as long as they each remained suspect in the eyes of The Church and the civil servants. It was the same for Nahum and herself when they had converted; it had brought with it suspicion, persecution, and arrest. Téresa bent her head under her weighty thoughts for a moment. Then she got up and cleared the table and washed the dishes in the barrel containing water, remembering to drain it for the morning wash. She jumped when the door behind her squeaked. Miguel stepped out of the bedroom he shared with José.

"It's only me," Miguel said in a whisper.

"You gave me a fright." She lowered her voice, not wanting to wake José.

"Why should you be afraid, Mother?"

"Never mind," she said. She brushed a curly lock of black hair off his forehead and kissed him on the cheek.

"You must go to bed. You have a school exam tomorrow. I want my son to become a wealthy engineer."

Téresa looked at her older son with love and admiration. He looked just like his father: tall, with blue eyes, dark hair, and handsome features. He also had his father's good nature. All her efforts in the ten years Nahum had been gone were concentrated on Miguel. He was about to turn eighteen and ready to attend Castile's prestigious Salamanca University.

"Mother," Miguel ventured, "I didn't believe your story about the relatives. Now that José is asleep, will you please tell me the truth? Where did you really go?"

"I've already told you."

"Are you hiding something from us?" Miguel said.

"Why are you being a . . ." She stopped, hearing a sound coming from the front yard. She ran to the window and looked into the darkness enveloping her small house and the street beyond. Nothing moved except a rustle through tree branches. Neither passersby nor anyone moved in the semidarkness lit by torches that were hooked on walls lining the alley. She turned to Miguel, whose expression was one of worry.

"What is it, Mother? Is someone outside? What are you hiding? Don't you see that this could affect all of us if you don't take me into your confidence?"

"Shh . . ." Téresa put a finger on her lips, trying to tone down her son's baritone voice.

Miguel looked at her, then grasped his mother's arms and forced her to sit down. He urged her in a low voice that was barely audible, "Tell me."

Téresa bowed her shoulders, and in a whisper said, "Yes, I lied to you and your brother. But I was protecting both of you."

"How can you protect us from the authorities if we don't know what we're facing?" His voice was rising in volume. "Whatever happens to you happens to us too."

Téresa looked in his eyes and read fear and panic on her son's face. She said, "I didn't go to Cordoba, but we do have relatives there. The family name is Beneluz. Isaac Beneluz. Remember this name. Also, remember the name Isabella."

Miguel gently pressed her arm.

"The Beneluz family is Jewish. Not like us, who converted years ago. They are a wealthy and well-connected family. If you're ever in need, you and your brother are to go to them in Cordoba. They live near the Puerta de Almodóvar in the judío Quarters. You can't miss it; the house has a crenellated top and a small barred window above the door. Do you understand?"

"Yes I do. But you will be with us, won't you?"

"Now listen carefully. My dear Miguel, please understand that I had to do what I've done. That young girl I told you about is in Granada. I want you and your brother to go there and claim her. The caliph is our friend. He will help you and the girl."

Miguel was stunned. "Granada? The caliph?" he asked with indignation. "But they're our enemies. We're at war with them! How could you align yourself with them!" There was disbelief in his eyes.

"Please don't judge me harshly, my son. The same people who pretended to be good Christians killed your father. They converted us in good faith, but then they persecuted us. We followed everything to the letter to be good Christians, but they never forgave us for being Jews in the first place. I know you can't believe my words. But we are still Marranos, or Jewish swine, in their eyes." There was anger in her voice. "Your father was arrested and died in their dungeons just because I bought meat instead of fish on a Friday night. How I've hated them all these years and wanted to take revenge on them. Now I have that revenge!"

"I can't believe what you're telling me!" Miguel cried. "Why . . .? What did you do?" he asked alarmed.

"We have kidnapped a young girl, the same Isabella in Granada. She's two years younger than you."

Téresa saw her son was shocked by her confession. It pained her to reveal to him that his father had died for the slight offense she had caused. Over the years she had told Miguel and José how he became so sick while traveling that his illness took him to be with God. Miguel was almost eight when his father died. Night after night, she heard him crying in his bed, and she witnessed his changed behavior. He no longer attended Catholic school or church because he was angry with God for taking his father away from him. Throughout the years he kept asking her questions about his father's face and mannerisms, his voice, and even his displeasure when Miguel forgot to study. It was a difficult task for her to convey to him the essence that was his father. She reminded him of his soft voice and his constant vigilance for Miguel's education that began early through the church of Santa Maria.

A sudden noise in the front yard made them both jump.

Miguel said in a hushed voice, "Someone's out there."

"Quickly," Téresa said. "If something happens to me, you are to ride our mule, Blanko, and go with your brother to Cordoba. On the way I want you to collect Isabella and take her with you to safety. She is the adopted daughter of Don Obrigon."

"The noted physician?" Miguel asked with surprise.

"She's also João's niece. You've known him since childhood. He has been our protector since your father died and since he himself left prison."

After a long silence Miguel nodded, then said with solemnity, "Whatever you decide for us, Mother, we will do."

Téresa was about to kiss her son's forehead when the front door crashed open, ripping off one of its hinges. A group of soldiers with swords stomped into the room. They grabbed Téresa and tied her wrists with a rope. Miguel hung to her neck while shouting at the men, "Leave her! Leave my mother! She hasn't done anything . . ." One of the soldiers grasped both of Miguel's arms behind his back and pulled him backward and away from his mother. Another soldier clamped a rough hand over the boy's mouth to silence him.

"*¿Por favor?* If you have sons?" Téresa begged. "Leave my son alone! He's only a boy!"

The door to the other room suddenly opened with a thud, and José stood on the threshold looking surprised. "What's going on? Leave my mother alone!" he cried.

"Hush, my José," said Téresa.

"Where are you taking my mother?" José yelled.

"Ask Torquemada," one guard said with a sardonic smile.

Téresa's voice tried to conceal a sob. "Don't you worry, Miguel and José! There's nothing to worry about. It's a mistake. You'll see." She looked from Miguel to José. She wanted to imprint their features, their voices, and whole demeanor into her memory. A small voice in her head told her it might be the last time she would set eyes on her sons.

Téresa saw Miguel trying to wiggle himself free from the soldier's grasp, but to no avail. His eyes gazed upon her, and she saw his eyelids closing and opening, sending her a muted message.

"Stay safe, my sons!" Téresa screamed in agony.

As the soldiers dragged her out, the soldier holding Miguel released him. He and José ran to the threshold to see the soldiers mounting their horses. Within minutes they were all gone. Miguel dragged himself back into the house, followed by José, and fell on a chair sobbing, feeling utterly defeated but trying to decide his next step. After a few moments he knew what to do: follow his mother's instruction. He turned to his brother and said, "Pack some belongings. We're leaving too."

"But where to? And what about Mother?" José asked. Tears stood in his eyes like frozen clear beads.

Miguel hugged him. "Don't worry. We'll come back for her soon."

It only took a short time for the brothers to pack their few belongings and load them onto Blanko. With José walking behind him, Miguel steered southeast toward Granada.

The morning dew had already evaporated when Torquemada woke up. He could feel the climbing humidity as his body became sticky. His baptized Moor servant knocked at his door, awaiting permission before entering. The servant set a breakfast tray on a plain round wooden table and waited for more instruction.

Torquemada slid off his modest bed into a pair of slippers and shuffled to a pine chest of drawers. He poured water from a jug on the chest into an empty terrine and began to wash his face with a washcloth. With his index finger he rubbed his gums, then wet his salt-and-pepper ring of hair. As he dried himself with a cloth, he examined his image in the polished metal mirror attached to the chest. What he saw did not please him. His face had lately taken on a gaunt appearance, with concave cheeks and sunken eyes. He turned to his servant and said, “Pedro, bring me my audience clothes immediately. I will be meeting with the queen this morning after Matins.”

Torquemada looked with satisfaction at the youth of sixteen who wore a cross around his neck; he had been converted to Christianity in childhood. After the invasion of Alméria by the queen and king’s army and the death of the boy’s parents, he had been brought by a soldier to the Cathedral of Seville to serve as an altar boy. Torquemada told him many times how lucky he was that The Church had adopted him. That without the benevolent church his life would have been poor at best, or miserable at worst.

Pedro, meanwhile, laid out the priestly clothes and waited for Torquemada to finish his breakfast of black bread, cheese and gruel. He then helped him button up the front of his black cassock vestment and handed him a white surplice topped by a gold pectoral cross.

While dressing, Torquemada thought about hurrying after the service to meet the queen. He’d just returned from Rome with convincing arguments for finalizing his plans. Lately, he thought, The Church had relapsed and looked the other way in overseeing the signs of heretical rituals. It was up to him now to stop and convict these immoral acts immediately and extirpate heresy from the land once and for all. He also had definite orders from the Pope to reopen the full powers of the Inquisitorial Tribunal.

After the church service at the appointed hour, Torquemada was introduced into the queen’s chamber in her summer palace in Seville. He bowed before Isabella, kissed her outstretched hand, and then raised his head. She looked especially beautiful this morning. She wore a rich blue brocade dress upon which lions and castles were embroidered in gold filigree. A white silk bonnet encircled her determined oval face and highlighted her expressive blue eyes. Right now those eyes were fixed on him with what appeared to be a benevolent look.

"Come, come sit next to me, Father Tomás."

Torquemada felt extremely pleased that Queen Isabella used his first name as a sign of familiarity. He had been her confessor in childhood in Arévalo. She trusted and respected his opinions on matters of The Church. Now, however, Fray Fernando de Talavera saw to the purity of her soul, although she still confided in Torquemada when affairs of church took priority.

"What news do you bring me from Pope Innocent?" she asked.

"Beloved Queen, I have great news. The pontiff has agreed that we reestablish the holy office while placing and appointing me again as the papal grand inquisitor of Castile and Aragon."

Queen Isabella made a sign of displeasure with her hand. He had known her as a child to make this same gesture whenever she had disagreed with a reason put before her. She said, "We already spoke of this subject the last time we met. You know my displeasure with this entire affair. The last ten years have been deplorable for all of my subjects."

"But, my dear queen, Rome acquiesced in these matters. And we also did get rid of heresy in your realm."

"In matters of faith, I approved the writ myself. Now, however, I find it objectionable to resort again to those means."

"I understand and respect your noble nature, my queen. In the affairs of conversions, though, we are lagging behind. Many New Christians, who converted, have lapsed and are guilty of apostasy. We hear that after attending church, many Conversos go back to their homes and perform their evil rites. Baptismal waters are washed off of their infants as soon as they close their doors. Linens are still washed on Friday. We have caught many practicing their Sabbath by lighting candles and reciting their foul prayers, but the clergy entrusted with this holy work have just about given up."

"I am very grieved to hear it. I believed that measures to eradicate these rituals were in place to prevent a relapse."

Torquemada protested. "We have been faithful hour by hour to prevent them, but as soon as some are found and punished, other new converts revert to their old faith under the influence of unbaptized Jews."

"You know how the king and I feel about this subject. We both objected to the purity statutes when they began under the Jeronimite Order. Many of our contemporaries also objected. Alonzo de Cartagena and Alonzo de Montalvo, our own jurists, argued against the statute saying it treated all converts as ready to commit heresy before it happened. These Jeronimite friars completely ignored our displeasure with the statute."

"Indeed, my queen. The most damning evidence, though, is defilement of our own pure blood. These Conversos influence Catholics. They're infected by everyday contact with Jews. Please think about Christian souls lost forever. If Catholicism becomes infected by heresy and contact with Jews, Moors, and foreigners, who can say what would happen to the spiritual soul of España?"

Queen Isabella remained silent yet attentive to Torquemada's plea.

"Your Highness, if you agree to reinstitute the Inquisition, as agreed by the Pope, you and King Ferdinand would become the Catholic monarchs decreed by the Pope. I beg Your Highness's permission to remind you of your promise. You said, 'upon inheriting the throne I will stamp out heresy for God's glory and our Catholic faith.'"

Isabella's face remained placid when he mentioned the tempting reward by the Pope, but he noticed her furrowed brows when he mentioned the possibility of Spain becoming anything but Catholic. "This is indeed ominous news. Let me give this frightful possibility some thought. I need to think of a solution."

"I have thought of one, my queen," Torquemada said. A pleased smile briefly illuminated his pale face.

"I am listening," said the queen.

"Your Highness is aware that the clergy has tried for years to make good Catholics out of these infidels."

Isabella nodded.

Torquemada continued. "After ten years of instilling fear in them through imprisonments, auto-da-fés, publicly announcing sentences and executions for heresy, nothing seems to deter them. Even the sure knowledge they'll burn in hell doesn't stop them."

"I am well aware of all that. What are you trying to arrive at?"

"I thought . . . that the only way we can eliminate the problem is to get rid of all the infidels and foreigners in Spain."

Again Isabella appeared displeased but confused. Before she could ask Torquemada, he said, "We have to get rid of all the Jews in Spain by expulsion. We will finally rid ourselves of this old problem." He paused for a moment to gauge the effect of his words on the queen. Seeing that he had wedged a slice of doubt in her mind, he continued. "The rewards for Spain will be immense for purifying the land of all infidels—Jews and Moors alike. With the establishment of the holy Inquisition, heaven will aid Spain by shining a light upon our conquest of Granada."

Torquemada stayed silent for a moment to gauge the effect on Isabella. She stared pensively, looking at the clerestory and multifoil windows high above the arcade and the rosette pattern of light falling upon the marble floor. While she watched the intricacies of colorful glass cast its light on the floor, her fingers toyed with the blue silk flower hanging from the sash encircling her waist. She raised her head and looked straight at Torquemada.

"I can't approve of this plan yet. I'll have to confer with my husband, King Ferdinand. There is the kingdom of Aragon to consider as well as Castile. We're now making plans to amass soldiers on the outskirts of Granada. The army is ready. We only have to construct temporary shelters for our soldiers, and I will be there myself to supervise the construction. Come back in a fortnight, and we'll give you our answer."

Torquemada tried to conceal his disappointment. He bowed to Queen Isabella, and after walking backward three steps, he turned and left the queen's reception chamber.

Don Obrigon entered Don Abravanel's home and was shown directly to his study. At the sight of his old friend, Don Abravanel got up from his desk and came to greet him with a large smile. "Don Obrigon, my friend. What a pleasure to see you!"

Don Obrigon sat in the chair that Don Abravanel pointed to and wiped sweat off his dripping forehead. "It's much too hot for this early hour," he said.

"I agree," Don Abravanel said. "I've instructed my whole household to finish their chores by eleven o'clock and take an early siesta."

"Very wise indeed," Don Obrigon said. He was impatient at having to chat about details that didn't concern him, but did not show it. "Please forgive me for intruding on you this morning. I have grave news to report."

Don Abravanel's face showed concern. "What has happened?" he asked.

"You're probably not aware," said Don Obrigon, "but my daughter has been missing for several days."

Don Abravanel looked shocked. Before he could make a comment, Don Obrigon continued, "We're following a plan to find her as we speak. I haven't slept in two days, and I haven't been able to get my wife to take any sustenance. I'm very worried about her health."

"My dear Don Obrigon! I'm truly appalled that this sorrow has fallen upon your family. Please don't hesitate to ask me anything. What can I do to help?"

Don Obrigon hesitated for a moment. "We have Inspector Guerida on the trail to search for Isabella. Thank you for offering help. But I'm here for another reason."

Don Abravanel raised one of his eyebrows and waited for Don Obrigon to speak.

"I have been sent here by Seville's mayor, the Honorable José de Gerondi."

"I haven't seen the mayor for quite some time now," Don Abravanel said.

"He has expressed his good wishes for your health and for your family."

"My sincere thanks to him for those wishes. You know how I respect the mayor. We go back a long time, the mayor and I. But you know that."

Don Obrigon nodded his head. "He also sent me on a mission."

Don Abravanel raised both eyebrows in a questioning look. "Does it concern me?" he asked.

Don Obrigon hesitated at first, and then said, "Yes. You also know that the army has been fighting for over ten years? The palace is indebted with gratitude to you for all you have done to help monetarily."

Don Abravanel nodded his head. "Yes, I know. The palace has been indebted to me many times." He looked down at the floor in a modest gesture. "But I won't talk about it. It's confidential, and I respect our monarchs enough to keep their secrets."

Don Obrigon didn't acknowledge Don Abravanel's confidential information. He had to feign ignorance. "I know very little of your affairs with the king and queen, and I, too, respect your confidentiality. All I do know is that the mayor asked my help to make a special request."

"Please speak, Don Obrigon."

"As I was saying, the army has been the loser in those ten years, so to speak." At the surprised look on Don Abravanel's face, he hastened to explain. "As you know, the queen has pawned her jewels to help our brave soldiers. Those same soldiers had to forgo much of their pay so that the army could invincibly conquer territory from the Moors."

Don Obrigon saw a fleeting smile on Don Abravanel's face. Don Obrigon thought about the rumors that the queen's jewels never left her possession nor helped the army with one maravedí. He had known this bit of information for some time from his own servants and the palace's servants. It was more the Jews' money that paid the armies.

Don Abravanel made a gesture with his hand to concur with Don Obrigon. "Yes, those soldiers paid dearly with their lives and with no rewards."

Don Obrigon let out a sigh of relief, seeing that Don Abravanel was being entirely agreeable. This was going to be easier than he thought. "Therefore," he continued, "the palace is short in paying the soldiers' payroll now many months late."

"What are we talking about?" asked Don Abravanel.

"In the vicinity of three hundred thousand maravedís," he said in one breath.

"That much!" Don Abravanel exclaimed.

"The mayor knows it is a great imposition and a burden on your wealth. But he intimated that the interest rate would be higher than previous loans."

Don Abravanel pondered the request in silence.

Don Obrigon knew that Don Abravanel wouldn't ask the percentage rate. That would be impolite, showing that he didn't trust the mayor and Don

Obrigon. Business was always concluded with a bow of the body, and the documents were drawn up afterward. “Tell the mayor that I will find this sum in one week’s time. Please have the mayor send an emissary to my home by next Friday.”

Don Obrigon broke into a smile. His mission was accomplished. “I thank you from the bottom of my heart. Now I’ll be able to concentrate on the disappearance of my daughter.”

“Please let us know as soon as you hear anything. I’ll have my wife call on Doña Obrigon and see what she can do to help.”

Don Obrigon thanked him and took his leave from Don Abravanel.

Maria sat in the large dining room of her farm trying to stay calm as night descended. Turmoil rolled deep inside her in prickly waves, and terrified thoughts stormed through her head. When will they descend upon the farm? Would she be arrested? What about the others—would they escape Guerida’s armed men?

“Maria? Maria?” A voice startled her. She looked up to see João with an inquiring look on his face. “We’re ready to leave. You know you can still come with us.”

Maria shook her head. “No. My place is here. Besides, what can they do to me? And where would I run?”

“You know you’re risking your life. Come and flee with us. We beg you.” João appealed to her sense of preservation.

“You go, my friends, and I’ll stall them for a while. Go in God’s benevolent name.” She looked around at the small group of friends surrounding her and could see that they were not convinced. Alfonso looked stern with knitted brows. Hernán stared at the floor, his lips a thin line.

“If you survive prison, they’ll pry information from you about our location. All of us may be caught,” Alfonso said.

“Don’t worry,” Maria said. “They can’t make me say anything that would hurt you. You can trust me!” Her voice sounded convincing.

“Maria,” João said. “For your own safety, we can’t leave you behind.”

Maria shook her head. “My mind is made up.”

"Look, Maria. I've spent ten years in a rat hole. I've experienced prison, torture, a near miss with death, and lost years. You can't forget the smell of prison, and the smell of blood. Once they have you in their hands, there's no telling where it would stop. This is what's waiting for you!" João pleaded with Maria.

Maria didn't respond.

João pushed on. "If the frontier could be crossed within two months, traveling by night between Spain and into Portugal, our safety would be assured."

João saw that Maria wouldn't budge. Nothing would dissuade her. João knew why she was determined to stay behind. She was about to sacrifice herself to stand between her friends and Guerida's men.

He embraced Maria for a long time. Maria hugged him back and brushed her eyes as if to chase a fly. João gave her a last look. Then, flanked by Hernán and Alfonso, he left the farm through a small forest behind the chicken coops while Maria watched the darkened front yard for Guerida's men.

As João and the men accompanying him made their way into the mountains, the air became sharp and sweet with pine scents exhaled by the trees. Dry leaves crunched under their feet, and a few squirrels disturbed by their presence skittered across the narrow path. If life could be this peaceful, thought João with a half smile, who knows—he might survive to old age. He felt unusually old for his early forties, having spent one-forth of his life in prison. Now that Isabella was safe, his mission was complete. He had sworn to his dying sister, Sarita, that the infant entrusted to him would be cared for. Sarita requested that Isabella marry within the faith, and he repeated that promise, word for word. That was sixteen years ago.

João remembered telling Sarita that the man she loved was a stranger in Portugal, that he was a dreamer, and that he would amount to nothing. Sarita, deeply in love, refused to listen to him. He was proved right—the man she loved and trusted with her life left her for several voyages and never returned.

When he delivered Sarita's infant daughter, through dada Hannah, to the childless couple that was chosen in Seville, they had to promise him that they would keep her Jewish identity a secret. He had also made them swear that Isabella would not marry until seventeen years of age, and within her faith. Don Obrigon and Doña Estrella, who had been childless for many years, swore to keep the girl's origins secret and raise her as their own. Somehow, destiny had precipitated Isabella's future when João found out she was about to marry Juan de Santilla. Dada Hannah served him well by communicating that information to him.

The climb into darkness became steeper and more treacherous, rousing João from his thoughts. One false step could be deadly. The humidity in the forest surrounding them was oppressive with heat. Alfonso and Hernán were sweating profusely, and João had to stop several times to retrieve a hand cloth from his pocket to wipe his face. No breeze cooled their sweaty bodies, and birds were silent in their nests. The silence was disturbed each time one of them sent a rock rolling down the cliffs. On cue they stopped to listen. If Guerida's men were following, they would be upon them within seconds. Each slow hour that went by as they ascended the cliffs placed a wider barrier between them and Guerida. After four hours, the three men reached the summit.

"Let's rest here for a short time," João said to Alfonso and Hernán.

Both men had been his companions in prison for five years. João knew their families had succumbed to the Inquisition in the murderous riots in Seville. They swore that they would do everything in their power to fight Ferdinand and Isabella's evil realm, and they kept in touch with each other after their release.

João took a loaf of black bread from his sack and split it three ways.

Alfonso took a bite of bread and asked, "What are your plans, João?"

"We should keep traveling northwest by night, then head south. We can cover more ground at night by staying inconspicuous during the day to evade Guerida's men. We should reach Palos's shores within one week. It'll be dangerous to stay together, so we should split and go separate ways. We can reunite at the maritime port in Palos."

"What will you do then?" asked Hernán.

"I prefer not to tell you right now in case one of us falls into Guerida's hands," said João. "But I'll tell you when that time comes."

Both men remained brooding and silent. João knew they understood the wisdom of not revealing each man's whereabouts in case they were captured and tortured. João hoped that Guerida would search closer to Seville, so heading toward Palos would delay their falling into Guerida's hands.

Maria fed all her chickens extra grain and filled their water container to the brim. An extended absence on her part might cause her hens to starve. She straightened her back with difficulty and saw a black speck riding a cloud of dust in the distance. The speck grew to galloping horse riders approaching her farm. Minutes later, ten guards led by their lead horseman dismounted and climbed the steps to her small house. One of the guards left behind to watch the horses spotted Maria leaving the coops.

"Here she is!" shouted the guard as he ran to seize her by the arm.

"What are you doing? Let go of me. You're hurting me!" she yelled at the guard as she tried to free her arm.

"Be quiet, you bitch!" the soldier snapped and hit her across the face.

Maria stood stunned for a moment. Putting her hand to her face, she found blood coming from her nose. She cupped her nose and remained silent. The superior and his men ran back to his guards and asked, "Is this the woman?"

"Yes, Inspector Guerida." He saluted him.

"Put her on one of the horses," Guerida commanded.

Kicking and biting the hands of the soldiers manhandling her, Maria was thrown across the back of a packhorse. Tied to the horse, and gagged with her hands bound, she struggled to remain on the horse's back as it galloped to keep up with the rest of the company. At a faster gallop now, the small detachment of men reached the outskirts of Seville and within minutes was dismounting at the garrison's barracks.

Maria was brutally yanked off the horse and dragged into a barracks. Inside, a passive clerk sitting at a table took one look at her and pointed to a document. Maria looked down at the vellum document and saw her name at the top of the page.

"What's this?" she asked.

"It's only a statement that you arrived at this garrison on such and such day and time," The clerk said.

"No. That's not what it says here. It says I'm a convicted Marrano criminal."

"Just sign," the clerk said.

"I won't. You can't make me do it!"

"Yes, we can," the clerk said, smirking.

Maria didn't answer him. She knew what that smirk meant. Not only would they make her sign the document by force, or under torture, but they would also add more lies to it. She took a deep breath, remembering João's pleas for her to join them. She quickly put the thought out of her mind. She wouldn't succumb to weakness. She was helping them put distance between themselves and Guerida's men, she thought. She grabbed the quill and signed the document. At least it didn't brand her as a traitor, which was a more serious charge.

As soon as Maria put the quill down, the clerk grabbed the document and called a guard. "Take her now."

"Where to?" asked Maria with a slight tightening of her throat.

"You'll know soon."

Maria followed the guard, feeling doomed, and climbed into an open cart. It headed for the fort on the distant hill. She knew what the fort hid: the torture chambers of Torquemada's hell. Before she could descend into despair, the small woman straightened her back and raised a proud head. *I won't give them this satisfaction*, she thought in a flash. *I've given the men the advantage of time by remaining behind. My lips will be as silent as the grave.* This brought a sardonic smile to her lips. She looked up to find a strange look in the eyes of the watch guard.

6

Audience with the Queen

THE OPULENT ANTECHAMBER TO THE throne room was filled with men and courtiers milling about and speaking in hushed voices. Small groups gathered, then broke up and gathered again with different participants. Christophero Columbus huddled with his supporters: Luis de Santángel, Fray Antonio de Marchena, and Don Isaac Abravanel.

"I say we go gently on your proposal," said Fray de Marchena. "We don't want to push the queen too hard. Both King Ferdinand and Queen Isabella are busy with the plan to take Granada."

Columbus was impatient. "I can't postpone my voyage because Granada is to be conquered." He turned his head to the many windows filtering the sunlight from the outside. *It's been ten long years,* he thought with bitterness.

"That's quite true," agreed de Santángel. "But you don't want to drive the queen to a categorical no, either. The war with Granada is bound to delay your mission to the Indies. Once Granada is conquered, the queen will be completely receptive to your proposition."

Don Abravanel, who had been silent till now, said to Columbus, "We'll continue to support your voyage with manpower and funds from our own coffers. As soon as the conquest is achieved, a whole new world will await you."

"I'm grateful for your support. Without your help, I would've been lost," Columbus said. "From the time I worked as a cartographic clerk in the

Custom House in Lisbon to this moment, in which I can taste the salty sea air in my mouth, I've dreamed of this voyage."

"That's why you need to be patient a while longer," said Don Abravanel.

"I've fine-tuned all of the sailing and maritime requirements to the Indies until I know them by heart and can recite them in my sleep. I'm going to need at least five sailing ships and five hundred men to cross the Atlantic. Supplies, tools, food, wine, and gifts for the natives would be subsidized by loans."

"You needn't worry about funding," said Don Abravanel. "We'll all see to it." Abravanel looked to Luis de Santángel and Fray Antonio de Marchena, and they both nodded.

"I couldn't take another rejection. King João II of Portugal also rejected my plans the first time, seven years ago in 1484." The shameful rebuff at Salamanca in 1488 also came back to haunt him. The court had been filled at that time with ignorant men who believed that the ocean sea was infinite. They believed that if a ship sailed west, it would never come back, or a ship might fall off the ocean, since the world was flat. He said suddenly, "I'm getting on in years, and if Queen Isabella doesn't approve of this voyage, I'll be an old man facing death before this mission can—"

A page banging his staff on the herringbone parquet floor of the antechamber interrupted Columbus.

"The king and queen!" he announced.

Through the ornate gold-painted side doors from within the palace, Ferdinand marched in holding Isabella's hand. The monarchs smiled benevolently at the assembly, nodded their heads gracefully, and stepped confidently up the three steps to their golden thrones. After King Ferdinand brushed aside his sword and waited for Queen Isabella's retinue to help her with her train, they both sat down.

Queen Isabella ruled each Friday over disputes and conciliations, observing this long-observed tradition since 1474 with her husband, King Ferdinand. Together, they presided over disputed territories in Castile dueled over by the chaotic and long-standing feudal lords in the realm.

Ferdinand sat with her over cases involving their Castilian subjects' disputes, but he took no part in the proceedings. As king of Aragon, he couldn't pass judgment on civil cases or of a public nature. The affairs of Castile, appointments of civil and military affairs, and the nomination of ecclesiastical benefits couldn't be made without Queen Isabella's consent. King Ferdinand had been prevented from doing so when Castile and Aragon were united by a treaty specifying that Queen Isabella was the only ruler in Castile. Ferdinand was only a Castile king "in waiting." By Castilian law, he was *de jure uxoris*, king of Castile by right of his wife.

King Ferdinand addressed the court from his deeply carved throne. "We're here today to discuss the voyage to the Indies as requested by Christophero Columbus."

"I concur and reiterate what my husband the king has said," Queen Isabella said. "We'll look into the proposal by Columbus and have this distinguished assembly give us sound advice. Please approach us, Columbus."

Columbus removed his cap and bowed before the monarchs. "My dear king and queen of the ocean islands. May you always have health, wealth, and wisdom in your entire life over all your realms," Columbus began.

"Have you brought us new supporting evidence for the expense of this voyage?" asked Queen Isabella. Her blue eyes appeared patient as she looked at Columbus.

"Yes, my Queen," said Columbus. "I have all my calculations with me. May I respectfully submit them to your court?"

"You have my permission," said Isabella, turning to King Ferdinand. Ferdinand acquiesced with a sign to his attending pageboy, who descended the three steps from the throne and took the map from Columbus. He brought it back to King Ferdinand while Queen Isabella looked on intently.

"I have here," started Columbus, looking down while unfurling his duplicate map, "the best way to reach the Indies." He raised his head to the monarchs to see if King Ferdinand was following his explanations. "As I mentioned previously at the Council of Salamanca, if I go straight in a westward direction, I'm bound to reach sight of the Indies and Cathay. We already have seen Dragon trees and driftwood not of this land come across from the ocean. We have also found carved sticks and two flat-faced corpses floating in the water."

"But how are you going to navigate these waters without knowing exact measurements to reach Cathay within permissible human time?" asked King Ferdinand.

"I've spent my entire life studying the circular wind patterns and the maps of previous illustrious navigators. We know from the mapmaker Henricus Martellus that the total landmass is 270 degrees. From Cape Vincent—the furthest point in the west from the mainland of Portugal and Spain, to Cathay—lies 90 degrees of undiscovered ocean. That's only 90 degrees of ocean between the Orient and us. To cross that ocean, with your permission, noble King, by using the quadrant fixed on celestial bodies and the astrolabe for the motion of the sun, we can find our way and calculate our speed by leagues, and our location by latitude and longitude," Columbus said. He knew King Ferdinand liked the measuring complexities of naval descriptions, having been trained himself as a seaman in his youth.

Suddenly Cardinal José de la Modena interjected, "That might be fine for land, but on a ship surely you have some distortions?"

Columbus knew that the cardinal had long disliked foreigners and opportunists. He also knew that he was a diligent watchdog of money allocations designated for wasteful enterprises. The cardinal also strongly supported those monies to being used for the poor and for building new churches. Rather than antagonizing the cardinal, Columbus had to convince him that it was in his and The Church's best interests to have this voyage undertaken.

"Venerable Cardinal," Columbus addressed him, "this mission is not only for glory and fame. It's for The Church, and I'll sacrifice my life, if need be. When we find land, we'll gain Christian souls. Millions of them will convert to our faith."

"My dear Columbus," said Queen Isabella," We have no doubt that your primary objective is to win souls for The Church. We don't know, however, how many souls dwell in those lands and what religion they already practice."

"Any religion they may have practiced in the past will pale in comparison to our exalted true religion, the Catholic faith," Columbus said.

Queen Isabella, pleased with Columbus's statement of faith, acquiesced with a nod of her head. "What other benefits does this voyage have for The Church and España?" she asked. She still appeared unconvinced. Columbus looked for support to King Ferdinand, who had been listening, but the king remained silent.

Columbus turned again to the queen. "My illustrious Queen, we'll gain immeasurable treasures, trade, and the manpower. Cathay has pearls and gold in large quantities, and vast amounts of minerals to be worked from the land itself. Their cinnamon and myrrh clean the blood, and ginger cleans and pleases the palate, as do sweet sugars that España loves.

"As you know, Venetians have become rich with trade with the East since Marco Polo set foot on that land. Moors trading with each other in the Cairo bazaars bring spices to the shops and profit from the trade.

"The Moors block high-quality goods such as silk and wool from getting to us. They navigate the seas around the cape and keep our vessels from reaching these markets. The Jewel of the East, Constantinople, has been lost to the Christian faithful for the past forty years. We can't go past the Rumeli Hisar Fort without being blown off the sea. The enormous price for passage through the Bosporus set by the Ottomans prohibits us from undertaking the usual route to Cathay. The Ottomans have a stranglehold on all western navigation to and from the Black Sea."

Queen Isabella appeared impatient at being told those facts. "Please get to the point, Columbus," she said.

Columbus continued. "By navigating on a westward route, we can avoid that blockade and save millions of ducats and maravedís. Most of all, Your Excellencies"—he addressed both Ferdinand and Isabella—"think about our food that spoils fast or arrives in a putrid state. The spice that preserves meat can be used in many dishes and for many days." Columbus stopped when he saw an expression of disgust on Queen Isabella's face. He realized this last argument might've hit a sensitive spot: spoiled food caused the Spaniards many ailments.

Silence befell the hall for a long moment. Several dignitaries murmured in their neighbors' ears and nodded their heads. Columbus thought they were nearly convinced. He decided to make the final point. He faced the hall.

"Noble assembly, we want most of all to rid ourselves of the Moors, don't we? They're gaining the upper hand in trade, money, and loans to Europe. This is our opportunity to vanquish them and become the major force governing all the Christian lands. The exorbitant fees charged by the Moors have impoverished Chios Island and Genoa. Eventually we'll become impoverished as well."

Queen Isabella nodded in approval at Columbus's last words.

"I'm convinced that is the route we'll take," she said.

Columbus bowed to the queen, his heart pounding.

"How can we reward you when you find these rich lands?" Isabella asked.

Columbus cleared his throat. He thought this was the propitious moment to ask for the fulfillment of his lifelong dream.

"Dear Queen. For all these undiscovered lands, the goods to be traded for many years to come, the precious gold, jewels, and the many Christian souls to be welcomed into The Church, I ask only for what is fair. I humbly request to wear with honor the title of admiral of the Ocean Sea, viceroy of lands I discover. The material rewards can be one tenth of all precious minerals and trade to be conducted in the name of Spain." Columbus stopped to catch his breath. There it was. He had asked for the assured economic freedom from his life's debts.

A heavy silence floated above the assembly. Neither monarch uttered a word to him, but no voice rose to protest his request. For Columbus, this was a good omen.

Queen Isabella cleared her throat, and after a glance at Ferdinand turned to Columbus. "My dear Columbus. We've heard your explanations of the voyage and your request for reward. We'll deliberate on that request as soon as our campaign against the Moors is accomplished. Meanwhile, we offer you a living while you wait for our response."

Her words were a blow to his heart. Columbus lowered his head. He tried to blot the queen's last words out of his head, but they echoed in his ears. *"While you wait, while you wait, while you wait."* The same dreaded words he had heard sometime before. He was bitterly disappointed, but he concealed it.

"Thank you, Your Highnesses." He bowed to the queen and king and shuffled from the assembly hall, leaving his patrons and supporters aghast. He left the palace halls and descended the steps one after another, trying to unravel his scrambled thoughts. *This will not be. My dream will not die this way.* He was through waiting. His only recourse was to go to France and offer his services to King Charles VIII. The French monarch had turned him down before, but perhaps now he might be more receptive. He would pull his brother Bartholomew Colón from the inept court of Henry VII of England and send him to the French court to negotiate an audience with the young King Charles the VIII.

After Columbus left the assembly room, Queen Isabella turned to the protesting assembly.

"This Genoan foreigner is pretentious and arrogant," said a minister who was a long-time supporter of keeping España away from all foreign influence.

"With deep respect and devotion, my Queen," said another minister, "Columbus's proposal to replace Admiral Fadrique Enriquez would be a personal affront to the Enriquez family. He's been a loyal supported to the Crown."

"I'm well aware that he's one of my most devoted subjects. His whole family has supported the Reconquista against the Moors these last ten years. I wouldn't do anything to harm his name," Queen Isabella said. "We'll adjourn and deliberate on Columbus's request in time." She nodded for her attendant to proceed with the next item on the morning's schedule.

"My dear illustrious Queen, Captain Gonzalo de Córdova is here requesting an audience with Your Highnesses," said her court attendant.

King Ferdinand raised his right hand to proceed.

At the sight of the young captain, all the ladies in the court turned their heads. He was in his early thirties, wearing a tight-fitting shirt over his muscular chest and shoulders covered by a vermillion cape. His blue eyes contrasted with his tanned face. He strode toward Isabella and Ferdinand and bowed. Isabella extended her hand, and he kissed her ring.

"My dear Captain, you've spent many years serving me," said Ferdinand. "What news do you bring us?"

"My King. We've succeeded over the years in recapturing our territories of Cordoba, Saragosa, Seville, and Tortosa. Now our army faces its biggest challenge. It's time for the end of the Reconquista that began centuries ago to oust the Moors from Spain."

Ferdinand and Isabella nodded. "You know well, my king and queen, that the caliph's men have been infiltrating our territory and killing our soldiers. We're ready to fight back as soon as you give me the mission. Now is the time to strike at the heart of Granada."

"When King Boabdil was taken prisoner, after the battle of Lucena, he agreed in 1487 to rule Granada as a vassal kingdom. It was on this condition that we gave him his freedom," Queen Isabella said. "Granada should've yielded to us at the conclusion of the treaty of Guadix in 1489. It's high time that the Moors should, and without delay, hand in the keys to the city."

"The Moors won't surrender," Captain de Córdova said. "Boabdil, King Abdallah, excused himself from surrendering his capital, saying that he no longer controls the city. The inhabitants are entering and foraying into the Christian territories of Castile, then killing our soldiers and watch guards and retreating. They've also incited revolt in the city of Guadix, which is now in Christian hands."

"The queen is right," said King Ferdinand. They should've yielded by now. It's time for Spain to fight the Moors on their own terrain." The king looked at his queen. "My kingdom of Aragon is prepared to fight the Moors in their last bastion—Granada. I'll allocate an army of fifty thousand horse and foot soldiers to surround and besiege the city until the Moors surrender."

The queen added, "We'll oust them by camping outside the city walls. My soldiers and subjects must have comfortable shelter, especially if the siege extends into winter." She looked at the captain. "I command you, Captain, to raise a town where the encampment is to be."

"An excellent plan, my Queen. We'll call the town Isabella in your honor."

"I thank you, Captain," said the queen. "But I want the town to be called Santa Fé, for our trust in divine providence."

Captain de Córdova lowered his eyes and head in agreement.

"Then, my King and Queen, give me the order to go ahead, and we'll win Granada for the Spaniards."

"*Vaya con Dios*, my Captain," the queen said. She stood and descended the few steps separating her from the captain. She pulled his sword from its sheath and gently tapped his head and shoulders. "In the name of the people of Spain, who gave me this consecration as queen over Castile y León, I give you the sacred mission by the grace of our Savior to conquer Granada for España!"

The audience bowed down, crossed themselves, and applauded the monarchs and the captain.

Gonzalo de Córdova kissed the queen's hand again, saluted the king, and made a deep bow. He walked backward three steps and left the assembly room.

In the dungeon of St. Jorge's Castle, where Maria was held, a savage scene of torture unfolded. The dank, putrid odor of urine and feces made anyone coming from the outside nauseous. In the darkness of the rooms, it appeared that the ghostly and emaciated bodies hanging from the walls with rusting metal chains may still have a thread of life. The bodies were old beyond their years; gray beards fell from their chins, and their heads were nearly bald. A few prisoners hung their heads, apparently lifeless, until guards prodded them with sticks. The prisoners opened their empty eyes for a moment before falling back into a stupor.

She saw a prisoner in his prime lying in an alcove stretched over a rack that two men operated. The wooden screws were turned one more time, and a shrill, inhuman voice escaped the prisoner's lips. In a recessed corner sat a notary scrupulously writing with his quill every bit of information uttered by the prisoners or guards.

"No, no, nooooo . . ." The voice died down to a sob.

Maria lay in another alcove gagged and tied to a plank bed. Her head hung lower than her body, and her arms and legs were tied with ropes. Each time the wooden screws tightened and the ropes were pulled taut, her limbs jerked out of control.

"Maria Donarojo, are you recanting?" a gravelly voice asked from a dark corner.

Maria tried to lift herself, but the ropes held her down. She jerked her head and spit onto the floor beyond the planks. "I won't. I have nothing to recant!"

"Then you'll suffer the consequences," the voice in the darkness said.

She remained silent, and tried to ease the knots pressing on her wrists and ankles by lifting her body off the plank bed, but no relief came to her.

The man who had spoken to her a few moments earlier moved into the filtered light coming from a narrow strip falling from a high ceiling window. He was sheathed in dark robes and stood above Maria. In front of her stood the most hated and evil mind in the entire realm. His face was gaunt, with sunken yellow eyes. It was Torquemada. Thomás de Torquemada, who had burned thousands of victims at the stakes throughout the previous decade. Torture was his pastime, and he relished the suffering of his victims. Now she knew that she would neither remain nor leave this dungeon alive.

Torquemada asked again, "Either you recant and we spare you from the flames, or you say your prayers now to bypass hell."

"Hell is right here! Who needs to pray!" she yelled.

Torquemada made a sign with his head to the hooded man standing at the foot of the bed. The man turned a tourniquet, stretching the ropes another turn. At the tightness of the rope, cutting into her wrist, Maria let out a scream of pain. Blood began to drip where her skin had torn under the hemp rope.

"Are you going to recant and confess that you practiced Judaism on the Sabbath?" Torquemada asked her.

"I have nothing to confess. I'm a good Christian. I practice only the tenets that the good church taught me." She stopped to catch her breath. "Go and ask my neighbors."

Torquemada smiled. "You have no neighbors. You live kilometers away from your nearest neighbor."

"Then how can you accuse me? How could anyone see me light Sabbath candles, and what proof do you have?"

He came close to her face and looked straight into her tearing eyes. "I have proof, all right. You're suspected of abducting the Obrigons' child. Aren't you?"

She was stunned. How could he have known? "I don't know what you're talking about."

"You know exactly what I'm saying to you. If you won't recant, at least confess where your victim is!"

"I don't know what you're talking about," Maria said again.

Torquemada made another sign to her torturer, and he turned the tourniquet several times. Maria made rattling sounds in her throat and lost consciousness. She was awakened by water splashing on her face.

Torquemada stood above her. "We'll give you a couple of days off, then we'll start the water treatment." With a shuffling of his black robes, he quietly left the basement.

The mist lifted from the vast treeless plains revealing an inhospitable landscape seemingly devoid of life except for an occasional vulture or eagle circling above their heads. Miguel painstakingly led their mule, Blanko, on which his brother Josè slept straddling their belongings. They traveled through the night, leaving Seville and stopping only to rest for an hour at a time. They bypassed the towns of Alcala de Guadaira and Osuna to avoid arousing suspicions as to why two young lads were traveling alone. Miguel knew the danger they were facing; many travelers who braved the road on their own never made it to their destinations. Some were robbed, others terrorized, tortured, or killed. He was braving treacherous mountain passes with a young charge, and he had no sword or knife to protect them along the road. He had a new concern: the road was burnt-out on both sides. Fields were destroyed and blackened where trees stood with branches frozen as the limbs of men burned to death. An acrid smell of burnt wood and grass permeated the air. *Fierce fighting must have taken place in this valley*, he thought.

A deep weariness seeped throughout his entire body; his clothes smelled foul and dusty, and he was exhausted from staying awake at the rest stops, worrying constantly that someone would find them asleep. He watched José as he slept, struck by how young and vulnerable his brother was. Miguel had promised his mother he would take care of him until they reached Cordoba. He loved his brother more that anyone except his mother.

Miguel remembered his father's strong hand touching his shoulder. He remembered the summer he spent with his father when he was eight years old. He had accompanied him on a short trading trip along the southern coast of Castile. Nahum exchanged wool, silk, and finished garments between the

Moors in North Africa, Granada, and Castile for precious spices and dried lambskins. Miguel asked his father why they were trading with the Moors since they were the enemy.

"Christians need the Moors' goods from the east, but won't deal directly with them," his father said. He let this sink in, then continued, "Your mother could enter the women's harem to sell them clothes and jewelry, so she accompanied me on my travels before you and your brother were born."

These memories came back to him like a curtain lifting before his eyes, and other bits of life with his father came to mind. He remembered his father saying, "Whenever you find you dislike someone, always look for one good thing in him." At the time, Miguel was hard-pressed to apply those words to his classmates, who threw mud in his face and called him Marrano or swine: the sobriquets for New Christians who converted from Judaism to Catholicism. He never understood why they called him names. He'd never known his parents to deviate from their Christian faith. They went to church on Sunday, practiced the religious holidays, Christmas, and placed their faith in God, Christ, and the holy church.

He tried to blot out the terrible years after his father's arrest—the visits to the city prison, then the disappearance of his father. He had asked his mother when they would visit his father again, but she didn't answer and shed silent tears. Now he understood her silence. She had wanted to protect him from the terrible news that his father died in prison. Miguel felt tears on his face. He wiped them off surreptitiously before his brother Josè could wake and see them. The younger boy didn't remember his father at all, having been barely one year old at the time. He was given the half-truth that his father died on one of his trips to Granada.

"Miguel, Miguel, look!" José said suddenly, waking from his sleep on the mule's back.

Miguel looked in the direction José was pointing and saw a long caravan of men on horses marching in the distant horizon. Upon closer look, he could distinguish soldiers marching with swords and mounted horses following them. The sun glinted off their swords over the Sierra Mountains and into the vega, creating a shimmering burst of light.

"Get off the mule!" he yelled at José. "Hurry!"

They retreated to a clump of old pine trees extending their branches over the field in front of them. Miguel took a grain bundle from a saddle pouch and offered it to the mule, which began to munch avidly. Then Miguel pulled down a low branch on the nearest tree and held it down to create a curtain. He peered through the makeshift shelter at the column of soldiers marching toward them.

"What is it?" José began to tremble as he saw Miguel trying to conceal their presence.

"It's all right. Don't be afraid. If they stop us, we'll tell them we're lost." Miguel tried to reassure his brother. Inside, however, he, too, trembled. If they were caught, their flight would end right here and their induction into the ranks of soldiers would begin.

Studying the approaching soldiers, Miguel saw they were outfitted for battle. Their standards, armor, helmets, and lances all gleamed as the sunlight became stronger and higher on the horizon. Miguel put his arm around José's shoulders as they sat watching the men approach.

"Halt!" shouted the man on horseback at the head of the column.

Shaking slightly, Miguel pulled his brother closer to him and waited to see if they had been spotted. He saw another soldier approach the horseman on foot. He held a large linen sheet that appeared to be a map, which he showed to his superior. They conferred for a while and seemed to be consulting each other while pointing in the direction of Granada to the south. From their hideout, Miguel and José could not understand their words, but they knew that the column of men had stopped for directions.

"Onward!" shouted the mounted man, and the soldiers resumed their march. Miguel and José trembled as the column passed their shelter. They were done for if their mule began to bray at the other mules. But Blanko continued to munch on the grain. When the last man passed and retreated into the distance, Miguel and José breathed sighs of relief.

"Quickly," Miguel said. "We don't have any time to lose. We must get to Granada before these soldiers."

"How are you going to do that?" asked José incredulously.

"We're going to take a shortcut through the mountain pass. The soldiers will avoid the mountain ravines because they fear being cornered in the narrow passes if the sultan's watchmen attack. But that should take them twice as long to make it to Granada's fortified walls."

"You know best," José said.

Miguel helped his brother get back on Blanko, then mounted behind him. The mule balked at the extra weight at first, but Miguel stroked his flank and spoke soothing words in his ear until he started walking.

It had been a week since Isabella arrived in this strange world that was so different from her Catholic upbringing. Every morning and throughout the day, minarets resounded with the Muezzin calls to prayer. The faithful unfurled small carpets and bowed down. Five times a day she heard the phrase *"Allah Akbar,"* day and night repeatedly. It drove her to retreat to a small courtyard to block the sound of prayers with soothing water sounds from a fountain.

The solace she sought from the constant din of prayer isolated her further from the rest of the women in the harem. A strange lethargy had overcome her since her arrival. From the moment she woke up till the time she hit her pillow, she felt tired. She had an overwhelming desire to sleep at all hours. The women in the harem didn't bother her and seemed to have accepted her as another of Boabdil's concubines. After that one night, when she stayed up all night trying to beat him at Shesh Besh, Boabdil didn't seek her company. Perhaps he had been busy with the rest of the women. She was glad she had been forgotten and was safe for the moment.

This morning she was overcome with sadness as she sat in the tiny courtyard she could access from her chamber. She reclined on a wrought-iron bench and looked at a fountain filled with colorful birds drinking from its trough. Delicate ferns and fragrant flowers surrounded the fountain, and palm trees shaded her from the burning sun. Under different circumstances, no burden in the world would have touched her in these surroundings, but she could take no pleasure. Her thoughts were filled with sorrow for her mother and father, who must be desolate with grief at her disappearance. She longed for the way Juan would smile at her and touch her tenderly when dada Hannah would look the other way. *What are they doing now?* She wondered if they were still shedding tears for her. She held back tears that suddenly came to her eyes. She must be brave now and try to think of a way to escape and return to Seville.

"Why are you so sad?"

She was startled by a voice near her.

She looked up to see the graceful figure of a veiled young woman standing in front of her. Her black hair fell in a cascade of curls over her shoulders, and blue eyes sparkled over high cheekbones. She was more beautiful than any of the other women in the harem.

"I am not sad," Isabella replied with a shake of the head.

"Then why aren't you smiling?"

Isabella forced a weak smile. "I have nothing to smile about."

"But you do," the young woman said. "You're young and beautiful. You have all the attention of the pasha and his subjects. The women in the harem say that you might someday be his favorite concubine."

At the word *concubine*, Isabella broke into tears. She sobbed for a long time until the young woman put her arm around her shoulder.

"Shh, shh," said the woman softly. "What seems to afflict you?"

Seeing that the woman was genuinely concerned for her, Isabella stopped crying. After wiping her face with her sheer sleeve, she fell quiet. "I can't talk about it," Isabella finally said.

"You don't have to confide in me if you don't want to," the woman said.

"It isn't that I don't trust you. My life will be at risk if I'm found out."

The woman remained quiet, but she kept the same benevolent air about her.

After a few moments, Isabella said, "I'm calm now."

"That's good. My name is Sarah, and I've been here for a long time."

Isabella looked at her with confusion. The woman's name was not a usual Moorish name. The other women had names like Aisha, Noor, and Amina.

Sarah said, "I'm not a Moor like the rest of the women. I'm a Jewish woman."

Now Isabella was thoroughly confounded. "But how can you be a concubine in a Moorish palace?"

"Oh, but I'm not a concubine. I'm here only to seek refuge."

Isabella felt a bond with Sarah, who seemed to share her predicament. She suddenly felt the urge to confide in her. "I'm not a concubine either. I'm also here, supposedly, for my protection."

Sarah looked at her with inquiring eyes. "What do you mean by supposedly?"

"Because I don't believe the story I was told," Isabella said.

Sarah said, "Perhaps they know of danger awaiting you. I was brought here because my parents were arrested and sent to prison." Her face grew sad. "I don't know where they are or if I will ever see them again."

At those words Isabella began to cry freely. "I'm never going to see my parents again either. My parents are noble citizens and aren't in danger. That's why I don't understand why I was brought here far away from my family and home."

"Now, now. I've made you cry. Forgive me," Sarah said.

"It's all right." Isabella wiped her tears on her other sleeve. "The woman who brought me here kidnapped me. I'm a Catholic."

"But why were you kidnapped?"

Isabella told Sarah the whole story.

"But then, you're a member of my faith."

"I was born Catholic and I'll always be Catholic!" Isabella said with indignation.

"But didn't you say that Téresa revealed your origins?"

"She was just lying! Just lying to keep me quiet so all the kidnappers could get their share of the ransom."

"You mean others helped bring about your misfortune?"

"Yes. And when I'm found, I'll give them all away to the authorities."

Sarah remained quiet for a moment. Then she said, "The important thing right now is for us to remain friends. Please try not to view King Boabdil as an enemy; He saved my life, and I owe him a great debt."

Isabella smiled. "I'd like to be your friend."

Sarah hugged her. "Good. So it will be. Let's go to our noonday meal."

The only light Miguel could see came from the stars sparkling in the velvet sky. He was reluctant to light a fire in the sparsely wooded forest for fear that a farmer or soldier might see it. He and José, found a small cavern to shield them from the cold and the dangers of the night. Miguel tied the mule to a nearby tree and then fed him and watered him from a thin creek running down the mountain.

"But no one would see a small fire through this rocky shelter!" begged José, shivering in the cold mountain air.

"No. We can't take a chance. Anyone could see us."

"What about animals? Like a boar or a bear?"

Miguel laughed. "Boars won't attack in the night, and bears are nonexistent in this part of the country."

"But I'm afraid of the dark," José whimpered.

"Go to sleep now. I'll be watching over you. You have nothing to fear." Miguel's paternal voice reassured José, who closed his eyes and was soon asleep.

Within minutes Miguel could hear the muffled breathing of his younger brother. Then he lay down on the blanket and tried to get some sleep. Sleep eluded him and his mind raced. It was true that a small fire wouldn't have been spotted outside the cavern, especially since it was hidden behind a thick curtain of pines. Yet, he preferred not to take a chance on inviting trouble. In two days they should arrive in Granada to begin their search for Isabella. Feeling reassured, he plunged into a peaceful sleep.

The sounds of voices and braying mules woke Miguel. He crawled to the entrance of the cave and adjusted his eyes to the bright morning sun. Through the trees and brush covering the entrance to the cave, he saw a caravan making its way up a narrow trail on the opposite cliff. The trail curved around the mountain to reach their cave. Spaniards led the way, followed by a few travelers on mules loaded with provisions. He recognized a few holy pilgrims with long gray beards, leaning on their staffs and carrying their packs.

"Quickly," he called to José. "Wake up!"

José didn't stir, still in a deep slumber. Miguel ran to him and shook him.

José finally opened his sleepy eyes and looked around him. "What is it? Are we under attack?"

"No, silly. A caravan is making its way up the mountain. We can join them and travel under their protection."

José looked incredulously at Miguel, but leaped to obey him. Within minutes their belongings were loaded onto Blanko's flanks, and they waited for the caravan to reach their position.

When the head muleteer took notice of them, he signaled the caravan to halt. Miguel approached him while José waited behind.

"What are you two *ninos* doing here in this *contrabandista* region? Don't you know you're endangering your lives?"

"Yes, we do. But we have to travel northeast to my uncle's home in Cordoba." Miguel hoped his words rang true to the head muleteer.

The aged muleteer was weather-beaten and appeared experienced with mountain travel. Nevertheless, he listened without suspicion to Miguel's explanation. "It'll take you many days to reach Cordoba. You can join us, and for a few maravedís, we'll protect you."

Miguel reached into his vest pocket and brought out a few coins. "How far are you going?" he asked, dropping the coins into the muleteer's roughened hand.

"You can travel with us as far south as Osuna. We'll part there. You'll need to head north to Écija. From there it's two days travel to Cordoba. We continue south to Loxa. We'll only stop at night and travel by day."

Miguel nodded. He helped José climb onto their mule, grabbed the mule's reins, and took his place in line. The whole caravan moved slowly up the mountain with a few travelers on foot behind trying to keep up with them. Miguel looked at his fellow travelers and found them to be merchants and seasoned muleteers. The lined faces and dark sinewy hands told of many years of pulling their loads back and forth to markets. The mules' flanks were heavily laden with panniers and *alforjas* overflowing with goods. Compared to the other mules, Blanko's panniers looked almost empty. Miguel feared that their trip would leave them hungry to the point of near starvation, but he had to concern himself for the present with the safety of his brother and the mule.

The head muleteer called out to Miguel, "You can stay with me in front of the caravan, and you can call me Pedro."

Miguel rushed and pulled the mule to catch up with Pedro's mule. When he came close, he said to him, "I'm called Miguel, and this is my brother, José." He tilted his head toward his brother seated on the moving mule.

"What is your family name, Miguel?" asked Pedro, rocking side to side on his mule.

Miguel faltered at the sudden request and then said quickly, "Gonzales." José threw a surprised look at him, but kept quiet. *That's good,* thought Miguel. *José is learning fast to beware of strangers.*

Pedro looked unconvinced, and kept looking straight at Miguel.

Miguel took a deep breath and then said quickly to keep Pedro from pondering their true identity, "This mountain air feels good."

Pedro agreed with a nod of his head. The climb proceeded in silence as the caravan kept climbing. The mountain became steeper and more desolate. Dangerous cliffs rose before them, keeping all of them silent with caution, and the air became more rarefied. Only the bells adorning the mules' necks rang in the stark landscape. Afternoon passed as they ascended, vegetation grew sparsely, and birds practically disappeared. Dusk began, making the scraggly road undefined and treacherous under their mules' hooves.

"Halt!" Pedro shouted. The dusty caravan slowed down and came to a stop. Pedro withdrew a leathern bottle from his saddlebow and took a long drink.

"We're going to bed down here for the night."

The muleteers unloaded their mules and spread their blankets on the ground. Miguel and José followed suit and then took out their meager rations of black bread, cheese, and scallions and began to eat.

"How long are we going to follow these men?" asked José.

Miguel took a bite of his bread and wetted it to the mush in his mouth with water from his leathern bottle.

"Let's not be too hasty." He lowered his voice. "We can go as far as they'll take us and then we'll go our own way." His voice reduced to a whisper. "Don't let it slip that we're going to Granada. They'll kill us right now if they found out."

In the dying light, Miguel saw José's face blanching. The boy nodded his head.

The mules were tethered around a large rocky outcrop, and one of the muleteers took a guitar from his pack and began to play. The quavering string notes rose among the boulders and escarpments surrounding them in a plaintive melody of love, passion, sadness, and loss. The songs spoke of a long-ago land filled with the scent of orange blossoms, Malaga wine, and pretty dark-eyed Andalusian señoritas.

Miguel felt drowsy, and he turned to look at José, who had fallen asleep on his blanket. He covered his brother and lay back on his blanket. Above them was a velvet firmament studded with flickering stars. Perhaps their mother was now watching the same skies from her jail cell while mentioning softly her sons' names. The dozing feeling he had felt moments ago made way for anger and helplessness at their mother's plight and senseless arrest. As the distance grew between them and Seville, so was the chasm between their mother and themselves. Will they ever see their beloved mother again?

He suddenly became aware that his hands were clenched into fists. He hit his right fist at the blanket, but only succeeded in hurting himself by hitting the hard ground. He turned away on his side when he caught Pedro watching him. Miguel closed his eyes, feigning sleep, but within minutes he dozed off.

Don Abravanel came forward to greet the emissaries from the queen. "Please come in. The queen honors me with her envoys." Don Abravanel bid them to follow him into a large hall in his opulent home. Brilliant white marble floors spread to opened terrace doors, admitting a gentle breeze that stirred multicolored curtains, and urns filled with white lilies spreading a heavenly scent in the air. "Please, please, sit down," Don Abravanel urged, pointing to a low white silk-covered divan. The visitors followed his request and instructed their guards to stand by the main door.

"As you know, we are here on behalf of Her Royal Majesty to request funds from Your Excellency. The queen also sends her gratitude and documents to records those sums."

Don Abravanel nodded his head and took the document handed to him by the minister. He studied the queen's seal, took a quill pen and a blotting paper from a credenza, and affixed his signature at the bottom of the document next to the queen's handwriting. He repeated his signature on an identical second document, blotted both of them, and handed them to one of the ministers. Don Abravanel signaled his servant, who disappeared from the hall and returned with two other servants carrying a sealed chest, which they placed at their master's feet. Don Abravanel opened the chest to reveal gold pieces filling the entire chest.

"As you see, three hundred thousand gold coins, as promised to the queen."

Both ministers stood up, took stock of the golden coins, and made a sign to their guards, who came forward.

Don Abravanel raised his right hand suddenly. "Please. Let my servants carry the chest all the way to the palace. They are trustworthy and have been in my service since they were children. Your guards can give them the protection they'll need." The ministers hesitated for a moment, considering this change of protocol. They decided it was acceptable, nevertheless, and acquiesced to his request.

"I'd like you to remit to Queen Isabella this letter of commendation." He handed them a rolled parchment tied with a red ribbon. "It was due to Don Obrigon's request that I'm making this loan to the Crown. It was he who brought this need to my attention and made an appeal for these funds to help the war effort."

One of the ministers took the document from Don Abravanel. "I'll make sure it's delivered into the queen's hands."

The retinue made their way out of the house to a carriage and six horses. In a cloud of dust, the carriage took off on the road to the palace, followed by mounted guards.

Don Abravanel sighed as he watched the small fortune carried away from his home. *I hope it is put in a good and wise service,* he thought.

The neighbors at La Calle del Padre lined up as they usually did when a gossip-worthy event happened at the Obrigons' home. They knew the doctor had been called in on an emergency, because Carmelita in the Obrigon household had told Chiquita in the Perez household across the street, and she had told the other neighbors. Rumors flew that Doña Obrigon was ailing, either from being despondent, or from heart palpitations, or from having being drugged with sleeping antidotes. No one knew better than Arturo Obrigon that his wife's health was failing by the day. He tried everything he knew to cure her condition. No coaxing, supplicating, or threats had brought her out of her despondency. She seemed to have given up on living altogether. She refused to eat, drink, or to listen to Arturo's words of hope.

"¿Mi querida, mi amor, beve un poco mas?" he begged his wife, trying to force a concoction made of eggs, milk, orange pulp, and powdered wheat through her closed lips. Rivulets of the liquid dribbled down her chin, neck, and onto her silk gown. Estrella Obrigon gagged on some of the pulp being forced through her lips, spit it out onto the coverlet, and coughed repeatedly, trying to clear her throat. She sank back with exhaustion onto her pillows, her face disappearing into the white feathered cushions.

Don Arturo looked up, defeated, at the physician standing on the other side of the bed. "She won't take a drop. I don't know what to do anymore." His voice broke.

The physician came around the bed and pulled him gently by one arm. He walked Don Arturo to an alcove in the room, far from Doña Estrella's ears. "Patience, *amigo*," said the physician. "You know well that if the patient has no will to live, it will not help in the least, but you can help with encouragement and patience."

Don Arturo bowed his head and hid a sob. "I can't lose her. It's enough we may have lost Isabella. I can't lose her too."

"Shush, shush. Don't you lose hope too," said the physician. "All will be resolved in time. Try to give her hope. It's the only thing that will help right now."

Don Arturo nodded his head, wiping tears from his face. "Thank you, Don Alvarez. You've been a great help."

"Anything I can do, just ask."

Don Arturo nodded his head again as he accompanied Don Alvarez to the door. Then Don Arturo returned to his wife's bedroom and sat on the bed next to her. He gently took hold of her limp white hand and caressed it.

"*Mi amor,* I have good news to report. The inspector's men have located the farm from which Isabella was taken." He looked at his wife for any sign of interest, but she remained motionless except for the slight rise and fall of her chest. "They even spotted the men and women who were mixed up in the kidnapping. Some are already in jail." He rubbed her hand again.

At those words, Doña Estrella opened languid eyes and tried to speak, but Don Arturo made a sign for her to remain quiet. She forced a smile. Don Arturo kissed her forehead and said, "Try to rest, querida. I'll let you know as soon as I hear anything."

She closed her eyes again and fell asleep.

Don Arturo turned to dada Hannah and communicated with his eyes for her to remain with his wife. Then he left the room, closing the door silently behind him.

Left alone in the room with her patient, dada Hannah looked down at Doña Estrella. She felt anguish at all the misfortunes that had befallen the Obrigons' home. Isabella had been in dada Hannah's care since infancy. For Doña Estrella, who had never borne children, Isabella was a comfort and joy. The child was lovely—mischievous and stubborn at times—but a loving child. Dada Hannah remembered the famous little gestures Isabella had been known to make. Doña Estrella used to tell visitors about the affectionate demonstrations, to everyone's delight.

"*Mi hija querida* took her own breakfast and gave it to her dada. Just yesterday, she wanted to give her dada a bath." Doña Estrella had thrown her head back and laughed, her lustrous mane of long black hair sweeping down to her waist. The assembly followed suit, clapping with joy. Yes, those had been happy days for the household.

Isabella's upcoming marriage had also been a great occasion to celebrate. Her engagement celebration was still talked about in town. Musicians and exotic fandango dancers performed in front of the guests who had been dined as royalty. Cardinal Cisneros, who was a special guest, was sent expressly from the king and queen with generous gifts for the betrothal. It was the most celebrated evening in Castile, and all the guests were treated to lavish parting gifts. Ladies received delicate fans embroidered with Isabella and Juan's names in golden letters. Men were given canes with handles made of silver.

Tears filled dada Hannah's eyes as she remembered those happy days and contrasted them to the present gloom and darkness in the household, which was sufficient to put everyone in a melancholic mood. The cook and servants moved silently about the house, and few visitors came to the door. Dada Hannah sighed and clasped her hands tightly. *"Dio Bendicho,"* she said, shaken. "What a terrible deed!" Seeing her mistress asleep, she wiped her eyes and silently left the room.

7

Searching Heaven and Earth

BOABDIL SAT IN THE HALL of ambassadors weighed down by gloom. His downcast mood felt the same as when his father died, leaving a great void in his heart. And as soon as his father Muley Abul Hassan had died, his uncle El Zagal usurped the throne from Boabdil, the true heir.

Only a short time before, Granada's people reviled his father for the loss of Alhama's fortress and castle and incited the king's brother, El Zagal, to fight for their lost lands and cities. Yet, no sooner had his father died than Granada's people mourned for their old monarch. He was now a dead hero and a saint. *How fickle his people were,* Boabdil lamented inwardly. The line of inheritance had been a chaotic back-and-forth monarchy, split between him and his father and between him and his uncle, and between the people's factions and beliefs in one king or another. As a young king, Boabdil's soft reign tended to lean more on making peace with the Spaniards than stirring the winds of war. His uncle, however, had broken all treaties during his reign.

Now it was Boabdil's chance at destiny: to reclaim Malaga, Guadix, and the rest of his realm from the Spaniards. He was still, though, their vassal. As such, he couldn't tempt their ire by going to war against them. He'd had to abide by the Treaty of Guadix when the Spaniards released him from prison and he agreed to become their vassal. He must calm and reassure his people that the siege of Granada would end soon, especially with winter approaching the vega. No soldier could fight in the swelling torrents coming down from the Sierra Nevada mountains.

"Your Excellency?" queried Aben Comixa, his trusted counselor.

"Please continue." Boabdil urged Aben.

"As I was saying, my prince, the beauty of Granada has vanished. Commerce that crowded our streets in the *suqs* and *qaysariyya* shops and workplaces is gone. All merchants are in fear for their lives. They no longer wait at our gates to enter, and consequently our reserves are getting dangerously low. We can't pass the winter in Granada without replenishing our provisions."

"What about getting supplies by sea? The Berber tribes swore to help us in time of crisis."

"The sea is blocked by Spanish ships, and we've been surrounded by the enemy on land for the last ten months," said Aben Comixa. "We'll run out of food first before we run out of water. Thanks to Allah for raining his blessings on us with crystal waters coming down from the Sierra Mountains. But grain and fruits will be scarce if the Spaniard dogs don't stop burning our fields."

"We must—" A commotion down the marble halls prevented Boabdil from replying to his vizier. "Whoever stopped this council better have a good reason, or he'll be thrown to the dogs!" Boabdil said between his clenched teeth.

"Your Excellency, the pasha's mother, the Sultana Ayxa La Horra, is here requesting an audience," said the court announcer with a sheepish look on his face.

Boabdil's face didn't conceal his annoyance at this ill-timed intrusion. *I wonder what her demand is now?* He nodded to the announcer, who went out to fetch her.

All those present bowed when Axya La Horra, his mother, strode in with a sure gait and approached the throne.

Boabdil rose respectfully for the sultana, who didn't smile at him. Instead, she motioned him with a gentle pressure of her hand on his shoulder to sit back on the throne. Boabdil sat back down and smiled at his mother. He knew too well that his mother's influence on affairs of state was one to be reckoned with. Her energetic advice and infectious spirit moved everyone in the palace. Even now, with the factions leaning toward war, she had not lost that power. He remembered that when his father was alive, and she and the rival second wife, Zoraya, were at odds, his mother was the one who successfully influenced his father. She fought Zoraya, who cunningly connived to place one of her two sons on the throne. His mother fought valiantly against the harem jealousy and had triumphed by placing him, Boabdil, the true heir, on the throne. Everything he now possessed he owed to his mother, who was correctly nicknamed *La Horra* or "The Citadel" due to her long-standing virtue and allegiance to his father, the caliph. Boabdil was aware of his unending debt.

"To what do I owe this pleasure, my mother?" Boabdil asked.

"I came here," she said, "to warn you of a rebellion brewing among the people."

Boabdil raised an eyebrow to his mother's warning. He was proud of his mother's caring and concern and her ability to alert him in time of trouble. "What's stirring the heart of my people? Haven't I done all a monarch can do to protect them?"

"Yes, my son. You've followed your father's valiant steps in your attempts to repel the enemy at the beginning of your reign. But it's not enough. Now the enemy is at your door. I warned you about that, more than a year ago, when you refused to fight against the Christian king. By agreeing to become his vassal when they released you from prison, you sold your heart and soul to the devil! I warned you to fight him, that one day this devil would be knocking at your door asking for the land of your people." The sultana stopped, out of breath, but her eyes held a look of contempt.

Boabdil had remained silent during the long speech. Now, however, he felt unjustly singled out.

"You know well, my mother," he began slowly, "that when I became king, I organized many sorties, riding in front of my warriors, and leading them against the Spaniards. And you know," he said, looking her straight in the eyes, "you know why I signed this odious treaty and became their vassal. The alternative would've been slavery!" Looking at his clenched fists, he said, "I did it to save my people, who were besieged and starving for three years while I wallowed in prison." He lifted his head. "These same people are now complaining of my not doing enough!"

The sultana said, "You know, my son, that—"

Boabdil interrupted her. "You also seem to forget, my venerated mother, that with the help of the Spanish king we were rid of my uncle El Zagal, the traitor who usurped my father's throne."

"But why, *why* did you have to sacrifice Granada, the jewel in your crown, to the infidel?"

"It was part of the treaty! I *had* to sign it! Those were the terms of my release from prison. For three years I prayed to Allah. To save the people, I had to give up some territories. And if Almería, Baza, and Guadix were captured, I would have to give up Granada as well."

"But why Granada, why?" The sultana wailed and railed against her son, not accepting Boabdil's explanations.

"Because it was part of the treaty," Boabdil repeated again in a controlled tone of voice. "Would you rather have the dead body of your son?"

"Couldn't you have disagreed with the terms of the treaty?" she asked. "Couldn't you have held out for your most precious jewel—the crown of the Moors?"

Boabdil remained silent to her admonition and anger, knowing too well he needed her alliance to regain the trust of his people.

Meanwhile, the rest of the court had remained respectfully silent, not wanting to interfere. It was then that Muza Abel Gazan, an old general warrior who had fought under Boabdil's father, intervened between the two.

"Forgive me, my king." He then turned to the queen mother. "All's not lost, virtuous and venerable Sultana," he said in the flowery speech of an old cavalier of noble descent. "We can fight them and repel them from our grounds, where they sit in their tents. We can show them we're not women leaning on distaffs. We can show them the fire still burning in our veins!"

The sultana didn't reply to Muza's appeal. She looked fixedly into her son's eyes to see if he had been moved by Muza's words.

After a long silence Boabdil stood up, paced up and down, and turned to his vizier and general, Yusef Aben Comixa, who had supervised his campaign against the Spaniards for the past few years. "My trusted general, how much gold and silver remains in the treasury?"

"Our treasurer here, Moussa El Zayari"—Aben Comixa turned to a silent and thin man—"gave me the figure just this morning. We have enough gold and silver left to last us for another six months at the most. With our sea route blocked by the Spanish ships, and the battalions closing all routes to Granada, we will run out of coins to pay the army."

Boabdil's face turned pale. Without pay, the soldiers may not fight. He suddenly felt the desperation of lost hope. No other salvation loomed in the horizon for him and his people.

"What's the state of our defense at the present time?" Boabdil asked Aben Comixa again.

"Dear Sire. Our troops are exhausted by day-and-night forays against the Christian king. Our ordnance and arms are in short supply. Even our bulwarks, being repaired as we speak, are lacking in wood to reconstruct the breached walls. May I remind Your Excellency that because our forests were burned by the Christians, wood has now become scarce?"

"But the walls of our city mustn't be breached! You must protect the inhabitants from these murderers of women and children!" Boabdil admonished Aben Comixa.

"But, Sire, we have been!" Aben Comixa protested. "Day and night we have rained down showers of arrows and hot pitch on the soldiers who approach our walls. We've killed hundreds of their cavaliers and soldiers, but more keep coming."

King Boabdil lowered his head. He wondered if he was *El Zogoybi*, the unlucky king the court astrologers had predicted at his birth.

"What do you suggest we do now?" he asked Comixa.

"We must capitulate and remain vassals of King Ferdinand. We must pay the tribute in arrears that we owe to the Catholic monarchs."

Ayxa interjected. "That you will not do, my son! They'll have to climb over my dead body!"

Boabdil didn't reply to his mother's fury. He said to Comixa, "How can we pay tribute? Our coffers are empty. If they besiege all our towns, castles, and roads, how can we do commerce?" King Boabdil's normally pallid face became red with anger. "We can't increase our gold coins if we're not selling our goods!"

"Yes, my prince. The people have been complaining about that. And now hunger is looming ahead." Aben Comixa echoed the king, affirming a second calamity brewing in the wings.

"The people! The people!" Boabdil repeated with exasperation. "If they'd followed my lead instead of my uncle's, we wouldn't be in this predicament."

"My dear prince," began Muza ben Abel Gazan, his fiercest and oldest cavalier and fighter, "why talk of surrender, when you have all the Berbers and mountain people ready to die for you?" Muza came closer to the throne, bowed to King Boabdil, and repeated his demand.

"We'll strike the Christians during the night and set fire to their camp. We'll topple the sacrilegious faith of the infidel and throw them out of their towers and fortresses. Don't you see, my lord, we can't give in to the Spanish monarchs yet. If we don't fight for the ground we stand on, we have no country to die for. I'm ready to die for you and Granada! We are Allah's right arm. No other means is left for us but to reconquer our territories that have been taken by the infidel!" Muza stopped to catch his breath, his soldier's body still arched in mode.

Boabdil, stirred by his courageous fighter, strode to the high windows overlooking the once fertile vega plain. Below the embankments past the still-smoking burned-out fields and groves, squadrons of fresh Spanish recruits poured into the Christian encampment. Their arms and shields glimmered in the noonday sun, and the soldiers raised a fine dust with their boots as they tramped into the camp. He remembered the long line of defeats against the kingdom of Granada, against all the towns and fortresses that had existed for the last seven hundred years.

He had believed the Christian king when he said the lands of Granada would not be assaulted. Yet, one city after another had been conquered. He began to feel that he had been tricked into colluding with the Spaniards, to sell away his land. His people had changed a rugged land into one of lush vegetation over the past seven hundred years. Citrus trees bent under the weight of sweet oranges, lemons, pomegranates, and peaches. The Moors had made advances in science, math, and maritime skills. Their water engineering feats were admired, evidenced by their singing fountains and amazing irrigations canals. Where was his kingdom now? His heart was ready to break for his beloved kingdom of Granada—for Zahara, Alhama, Malaga, Loxa, Lucena, Almería, Ronda, Baza, Guadix . . . His head began to spin at all the lost battles. All that remained now was the capital city and fortress of Alhambra. Boabdil turned away from the windows with heavy heart, his spirit overwhelmed. He looked at his valiant soldier, who waited for his command.

"How many men and horses have we at our disposal?" Boabdil asked.

"Sire, there are thirty thousand foot soldiers and ten thousand horses to be joined by the Gomeres tribes waiting for your signal in the defiles and mountaintops. Ten thousand of the fiercest horsemen are ready to fight for their land," said Muza.

Boabdil remained silent for a few moments. "We'll march at dawn for Granada and for Islam, and may Allah protect and declare us the victors!"

A great cry arose from the assembly's lips. "You're not the 'El Zogoybi'! You're the leader of the Moors!" An answering clamor resounded from the people outside the palace who wanted war as word traveled that they would fight at dawn.

Boabdil turned to Muza and said, "I place you in charge of my armies. I know you'll conduct this war for Allah, and I put all my faith in you. You'll command the cavalry to defend the gates, and repel all the enemy's sallies. I want the strongest men posted on the towers. Take the best men to be your adjutants."

Muza's jubilant face displayed his pleasure at his king's decision to fight the enemy. He bowed to Boabdil. "Thank you for your trust, my prince. I'll take my leave now, and assemble the men for battle." He bowed again respectfully and left the council hall.

As soon as Muza left, the sultana rushed to her son to kiss the hem of his garment. "You're the true son of your valiant father, Abul Hassan. May his soul smile on you and us in this hour of need."

Though war was abhorrent to his peaceful nature, Boabdil nodded his head at his mother. He knew he had to fall in line with her and her followers' lead and go to war.

Aben Comixa, meanwhile, had fallen silent at this outburst of Moor patriotism. His face had turned ashen at the unexpected turn of events. He took leave of his king and shuffled out the hall.

As the Granadian dusk fell on the Sierra Nevada mountains, smoke signals rose on every mountaintop. Through the squares and narrow streets, arms were polished; steel scimitars were chiseled to fine cutting edges in fires glowing in the hot foundry ovens. In every fighter's home and in the palace grounds, warriors prepared. Steel shone from poniards and the silver saddles of neighing horses. The impatient young Arabian thoroughbred horses, the best horses bred for speed, echoed their master's vigor for the fight, pawing the dusty ground with their hooves.

Women and maidens in every home stoked the fires and encouraged their husbands, fathers, and sons. But they felt great foreboding, knowing this night may be the last time they beheld their loved ones. Nevertheless, they blessed their names, and their valor in defending their homeland and protecting their wives and children from being sold into slavery. The whole city was now at a fever pitch preparing for war. The main gates of the city were bolted with massive chains and guarded by strong men. The mounted horsemen waited impatiently for Muza's orders.

Inspector Guerida knew that his reputation was at stake in the case of the Obrigons' missing daughter, Isabella. Denying to himself that progress had not been made was easy in comparison to lying to the Obrigons about being closer to a breakthrough. For the lies to the frantic parents, he felt remorse. Sleepless nights were holding him in a deathly embrace, making him sweat at the thought of retribution from the queen's tribunal. He'd tried everything, including resorting to spies throughout Seville and having all vessels searched at ports in Andalusia and Aragon and into Portugal. The queen herself had sent an envoy to the Portuguese court to keep an eye on gypsies or foreigners hiding a young Spaniard girl in their midst. *She must be hidden in an area not under Spanish control,* thought Guerida. *But where could she be now?* No. *Isabella had to be hidden under their nose, perhaps closer than they thought.* He would intensify the search to include every hamlet and town between Seville and the frontier in the south.

As he ruminated on his bad luck at not cracking the case, one of his men barged into his barracks.

"Your Excellency, Your Excellency! We found a lead in the Obrigon case!"

Guerida felt his heart about to leap in his chest. He jumped out of his seat and greeted his second in command. "What is it, Ernesto? Tell me!"

"The Obrigons' daughter was spotted last week traveling south toward Granada!"

At the name, Guerida broke into a cold sweat. "But that can't be! No one from España would dare go near Granada. Especially with the queen's garrison camping in the vega! That's not possible!"

"But the people we questioned remember that they saw a young and beautiful girl," he emphasized. "She was accompanied by another woman and a carriage driver. The travelers dining there said that the woman and the girl disappeared into an upstairs room while the driver took his supper in the barn."

"Where was that inn?" an anxious Guerida asked.

"On the outskirt of Loxa, sir."

"The woman with the girl—what was she like?"

The sergeant looked down to the floor. After a few moments, he raised his head, his face beaming. "The men said that the woman looked like a peasant, but more like a foreigner."

"What do you mean, Sergeant?"

"You know," the sergeant hesitated. "More like a Marrano. She didn't have Spanish features. She wasn't dark, nor did she have olive skin. She had reddish hair with blue eyes. And she wasn't wearing a cross. But the young girl had an expensive cross about her neck. Oh, and now I remember one of the travelers had heard the young girl say to the woman, 'Pay him, Téresa.'"

"Good work, Sergeant!" Guerida was pleased. "If you hear anything else, I want to know right away, you hear?"

The sergeant saluted and nodded his head before turning on his heels and leaving Guerida's barracks.

"I've got them!" Guerida jubilated as he banged his fist on the table "They can't escape me now!" He ran to the barracks door and called his adjutant. "Prepare my horse and five of my mounted men. We're leaving for the holy office in Seville."

Rain hit Seville with gale force. The torrent fell over the city with the regularity of night and day, turning the muddy soil into a quagmire for pedestrians and horses. In the military camp outside the city where Juan and Antonio huddled in their barracks, the rain didn't prevent water leaks and water-clogged wood, which groaned under the extra weight caused by successive drenching. The order had come down from military command that a march to Santa Fé would begin at dawn, and Juan was busy packing his belongings for the long trip the next day. Antonio sat idle and moody.

"If this damn rain doesn't let up, we'll be in a sorry state tomorrow," Antonio said from his cot. He mumbled another phrase that Juan Escobar couldn't understand.

"Stop your grumbling and go to sleep. We have a long day beginning at dawn tomorrow," said Juan while polishing his boots.

"It's easy for you to say," said Antonio, grumbling again. "You and your father's honor. How can we fight? We're at a disadvantage from the start—the weather, the long distance, and the cold."

Juan felt anger well up in his chest at Antonio's derision. Even the darkness in the dimly lit barracks couldn't hide his anger at the insult of his honor.

"You're the one who should be ashamed—of your lack of honor!" he told Antonio.

Juan saw Antonio sit upright with clenched fists.

"Are you going to fight me too?" Juan said mocking. "Remember, I'm your friend. Not the enemy."

Antonio didn't reply. After a few moments he said, "I didn't mean to insult your family's honor, my friend. It's not that I'm afraid to fight for España tomorrow. It's that we're at a disadvantage."

"We can't invoke good weather just to suit you, my friend, nor can we only fight when the sun is shining. Remember your enthusiasm to kill as many Moors as possible?"

Antonio lowered his head. When he raised it again, he had a conciliatory smile on his lips. "Yes, I remember those exact words. Thanks for the reminder."

Juan laughed. He reached down and gave Antonio a friendly slap on the shoulder. "Now go to sleep, my friend, or you'll be exhausted on the battlefield."

Antonio didn't reply. He leaned back on his pack and closed his eyes.

Juan took this opportunity to go to the barracks' door and stare through the rain outside toward the immense vega hidden in the darkness. Antonio's reminder of the family name and honor still rang in his ears. There was more at stake here than his good and aristocratic name. There was also Isabella Obrigon to consider as part of the equation. He had no fear of dying. That, he believed, might not happen to him because he carried within him the seed of invincibility. His whole family, from his father to many generations back in the mists of his history, had fought admirably in many campaigns and survived. From the beginning of the Reconquista, winning land after land from the Moors, his ancestors had preserved the family honor on the battlefield and lived to tell tales of valiantly won battles. No, dying was not what he feared most; losing Isabella was what he feared. He couldn't imagine her betrothed to anyone else but him. His quest in this war was to win for his beloved. There was less than a year left before their nuptials. Plans had been made, a home prepared. All that was left now was their love for one another to be consecrated by The Church. As soon as she was back home.

The women in the harem were young and eager. They wagered among one another as to who would most please the king. Fights and skirmishes sometimes ensued, but usually only bloody noses occurred, leaving their beautiful faces unharmed and unscarred. Boabdil's mother, the dowager Ayxa la Horra, would enter the women's den to establish order and make sure all the women were accounted for. One false move, such as flirting with the guards or escaping into the farthermost corner of the gardens, brought harsh consequences. When Zoraya, Ayxa's rival, broke the rule by dallying with her captain from the *Abencerrages's* tribe, he was promptly put to death, and his body exposed to vultures on the nearest Sierra mountain peak.

Boabdil's wife, Morayma, was a loyal and dutiful companion to the dynasty, but she was conflicted about the upcoming battle. She had carefully tended to the upbringing of their young son, Ahmad, only to see him torn from her arms and taken captive by the Spaniards in exchange for his father. When Granada was delivered to the Spanish crown, the young prince would be freed. It had been nine years since her beloved son had been snatched away, and in her heart, Morayma secretly cursed both the Spaniards and Granada, the city that had stolen her son. In the confines of that heart seethed a mother's desire for her child, even at the cost of the surrender of her native land, her husband's kingdom. Fate was cruel. The moment her son returned to her would be the moment he would lose his inheritance and status as a prince of Granada. She counted the days until Granada surrendered. For now, she sat in a cove retreat in the harem's hall, away from all the women, and listened to a woman musician playing melancholic notes on the *al'ud* strings. Her servant brought morsels of food to her, but she refused them each time.

In an atmosphere of uncertainty about the days and months ahead, Isabella Obrigon kept quietly to herself. She sat in a corner of the harem's hall, refusing to enter the games and chatter. This morning when Sarah entered the hall, she brightened immediately at the familiar face.

"Do you want company?" asked Sarah.

"Of course," Isabella answered, and she slid sideways on the silk sofa to let Sarah sit next to her.

"It seems unusually quiet in here today," Sarah commented.

Isabella smiled. "I can't imagine how much noisier these women could be. This is the most I've heard so far."

"Have I told you of the most raucous fight they've had?"

"No. Please tell me," Isabella said eagerly, anxious to break the monotony.

"Well," began Sarah, "it happened about a year ago. The women were toying with a small puppy dog that the king had given one of them." Sarah motioned with her eyes to a cove in the hall where a slim redhead of extreme beauty exposed sparkling white teeth in laughter as she interacted with two other women. "That's Amina. She's now the king's favorite."

Isabella followed Sarah's gaze and discovered that this same woman had kept a watch on her for some time. Once, they crossed paths, and Isabella saw disdain in Amina's eyes. *I have no quarrel with you,* Isabella had tried to express in a mute message of total disinterest in vying for the king's favors. Amina, though, kept an unfriendly stance whenever Isabella entered the hall to partake of meals.

"I don't know why I feel she dislikes me," Isabella said to Sarah in a low voice.

"It's because you're younger and more beautiful than she is. She feels you're a threat to her."

"She has nothing to fear from me," Isabella said.

"Don't you think she looks a bit old for the pasha? I'd say an old carcass," Sarah joked.

Sarah's comment succeeded in making Isabella laugh, something she hadn't done in a long time. Sarah joined in Isabella's laughter, which aroused Amina's curiosity and a frown on her face. Amina got up from her couch and approached the silk sofa on which Isabella and Sarah sat.

"What're you laughing about?" Amina asked.

"We weren't laughing at anything in particular," Sarah said cautiously.

"I'd say that you were laughing at me!"

The rest of the women ceased their chatter right away, paying attention to what was being said between the three principal women. Some of them moved closer, expecting a fight, but Amina didn't give them this pleasure. Instead, she caressed her stomach as she came close to Isabella and stood in profile, making sure everyone saw that a budding paunch was there.

"See," Amina addressed both Sarah and Isabella. "I have here the next heir for the pasha."

At those words, the women of the harem let out a gasp and quickly looked to Morayma's retreat to see if she would come down hard on Amina. Morayma, though, sat silently without stirring.

Amina approached Isabella's slim stomach and rubbed it. "I don't see anything in there.".

Isabella's face turned red. "I don't know what you mean!"

Amina came close to Isabella's face and said, "Of course you don't know. That's because the king got tired of you, after one night." The women surrounding them laughed at Amina's comment.

Isabella's face turned crimson, but she didn't take Amina's bait. She turned to Sarah. "I'm not going to be insulted any longer." With that she bolted from the hall with the sound of laughter following her. Sarah ran after Isabella and stopped her partway down the white marble corridor, startling the guards standing at intervals.

"Wait, wait!" Sarah said and tried to catch her breath. "These women don't mean to make fun of you. They're just bored. Amina can't be taken seriously."

Isabella stopped short and turned to Sarah. "I'm not the pasha's concubine. As a matter of fact, he never touched me. He was extremely respectful to me."

Sarah's face became serious. "I believe you."

"I've been engaged for the last year to a wonderful soldier. We were to be married as soon as his studies were completed." Isabella suddenly burst into tears. "Now I don't know . . . if I'll ever see him again!"

Sarah hugged and held her close. "Shh, shh," Sarah urged her. "It'll happen. You'll soon be found, and your future husband will move earth and heaven to find you."

The encouraging words that Sarah said to her produced the opposite reaction. Isabella fell into a paroxysm of choking sobs and tears that ran down her face, wetting her veil. "I don't . . ." Her voice came out strangled under the emotion. "Can't understand . . ." she sobbed, ". . . why Juan hasn't found me yet?"

"He will, he will. You'll see."

Isabella regained her composure. She wiped her wet face with her sleeves and turned to Sarah. "I don't know what I would've done without your friendship."

"Nor I without yours," replied Sarah. "Let's go into the garden to refresh ourselves."

Isabella followed her, and with the ubiquitous guards following, they descended into soothing green aisles of hedges and fragrant roses.

Guerida followed the monk along the geranium-scented cloister to a room in back of the abbey. As he waited for the grand inquisitor with a touch of anxiousness, he recalled his role ten years earlier during the trials of Marranos. All he'd had to do was to report any heretic activities to the inquisitor. Usually, the charge was delivered on a small paper, denouncing the blasphemer. Any citizen could claim another, usually a new convert that had deviated from his Catholic rites and practiced Judaism or Islam. All that the informer had to do was to slip the incriminating note with the name of the accused through the open mouth of a carved stone lion jutting from a wall. Guerida shivered as he recalled those days. He had turned in a distant relative of his father's who was marked by the Inquisition due to his Morisco blood. He, himself, had been lucky. His family had been Catholic for generations.

The door opened with a grating sound, pulling him out of thoughts as Torquemada made his entrance. Guerida got up to greet him, but Torquemada motioned him back to his seat.

"I asked you here because you are working on the kidnapping of the Obrigons' child."

"Yes, Your Excellency," said Guerida.

"We're holding one of the conspirators, a woman called Téresa Costa. She hasn't confessed yet," Torquemada said. "We hope to get a confession soon." Torquemada stopped, examining Guerida through his recessed black eyes, partly hidden by drooping eyelids. "I want you to find her children, Miguel and José. They're eighteen and nine years of age. They disappeared the night of the arrest, and the trace has been cold since this—"

"Your Excellency, if I may humbly interrupt. We have a lead on Isabella Obrigon."

Torquemada opened his half-closed eyes and sat upright on his chair.

Guerida recounted the fresh lead. "I already dispatched my men to Loxa to bring back the innkeeper."

Torquemada smiled faintly. "You're a proud asset to the queen's force, Guerida. I want you to bring those children back!" Torquemada's eyes burned like smoldering coal. He made a sign of the cross. "Go with the Blessed Virgin."

Guerida crossed himself at the name of the Virgin, bowed to the inquisitor, and left on horseback with two of Torquemada's guards. Guerida smiled triumphantly at the thought of promised wealth and promotion. *This is the biggest case I've had yet. Nothing can stand in my way.* Eyes focused on the horizon, he sat erect on his horse and galloped toward Loxa.

In her cell, Téresa prayed to her one God, *Elohim*—the God of her ancestors. Her "conversion" to Catholicism had lasted for only a short time. The moment she returned home on that day, she washed the sacrament waters off her and let her Judaism emerge anew.

She remembered when Nahum announced one day that for the sake of their young son, Miguel, and for their survival, they had to convert—or they would perish. She was shocked, but Nahum persuaded her that no other choice was left to them, so she reluctantly agreed. After their conversion and the baptisms of their sons Miguel and José, they practiced their ancient faith in secret without their sons.

"Elohenu Hakadosh," she murmured silently. Was the death of Nahum, and her sons being left unprotected, a punishment for having converted? She fell to her knees on the hard floor and cried bitter tears. Why had she been abandoned? What crime had she committed in her past to merit this punishment? To worship one God or another was to live a pious life, wasn't it? The name Isabella floated to her consciousness. How could they have known she helped kidnap her? With all her precautions, she must've been seen with the girl. Téresa trembled as she thought of Miguel and José at the mercy of bandits and ruffians on the road. She couldn't bear to think of them being taken by the Inquisition within the Roman Catholic Church. She knew Miguel would follow her orders, and she trusted in his ability to evade the authorities. She was relieved that her two sons would be soon out of the reach of Torquemada.

No sooner had she reassured herself than the door to her cell creaked and Torquemada appeared before her. She recoiled at his apparition, but then she stood up from the floor keeping her gaze steady.

"*¿Como estãs esta mañana*?" asked Torquemada. His face remained unperturbed, with a seemingly benevolent smile.

The Devil himself would have been less deceitful, thought Téresa.

"I could be better if you let me go back to my home and my sons." She looked at Torquemada, not believing her own words.

Torquemada exploded in cruel laughter, his voice bouncing off the gray vaulted masonry and arches of the damp cell.

"I can grant your release immediately," he said. "But first, you must tell me—where is Isabella Obrigon?" Torquemada crossed his arms, looking patient.

The moment for confession has come, Téresa thought. I can tell him now or hold out until my two sons are in safety.

Torquemada waited.

"I know nothing of this Isabella. I have no connection with her or her family," she said.

"You know that your sons will be disinherited because of your mistake, don't you?"

She trembled at the thought. The little she had, the small house and some savings, was not much, but it would help if she didn't survive Torquemada. Even that would be taken away from her family. *The bastard!* She cursed him under her breath.

"Are you practicing 'the sins of the fathers are visited upon their sons'?" She let those words slip, but regretted it a moment later.

His reaction came instantly. "Guards!" Torquemada shouted to the outside of the cell. Two guards rushed in at his command and took hold of her arms, bending them backward until one snapped. Téresa nearly lost her balance in pain. No cry passed her lips. She would be brave as long as *Adonai* gave her strength.

"If you don't confess to your crime, you will be convicted of heresy," Torquemada hissed.

She trembled. There was no exit from that charge. They would prove it against her no matter how long she protested. But it would give her sons time to flee to safety. She gathered her courage and looked him in the eyes. "Do whatever you want with me, I will not confess to any crime!"

Torquemada hesitated for a moment at her audacity. "Take her to the Great Room!"

Téresa knew what the Great Room was. Nahum may have met his death there. Vast numbers of prisoners confessed there under the duress of inhuman torture, then died.

The guard grabbed her by her long red hair and dragged her outside the cell and into the hall. One of her moccasins was ripped off, causing her to trip over the uneven stones and cut her foot. Blood smeared the stones as they dragged her down the corridors. Two guards stood at an arched door and scurried to open it for Torquemada and his victim. Inside, arched alcoves surrounded a large hallway. Each chamber held a torture plank that was occupied by a bound victim. She was pushed into an alcove where metal pulleys hung above her head and iron instruments lay on a square wooden table. Near her an old man sat at a table with quill pen in hand ready to write on a vellum sheet.

Téresa murmured to herself, *"Adonai she bashamim Hagen al ha yelading sheli."* She repeated her plea over and over for God in heaven to protect her children.

The guard hovering over her fixed his eyes on her mouth. "What are you saying, you mad woman!" he blasted at her.

She didn't reply and repeated the same words in her head without her lips moving. From the corner of her eye, she saw that the scribe was furiously writing down every word she pronounced.

Just then she heard a squeaking sound and a rope descended from the ceiling. The guard tied her wrists together behind her back with the rope still attached to a pulley from the ceiling. Téresa waited, ready to die. The guard then drew on the other end, slowly raising her arms behind her back. Soon her whole body was lifted in the air, her whole weight pulling her stretched arms.

Torquemada came near, and with foul breath said in her ear, "Do you confess now to the crime of kidnapping?"

Téresa hung silently without acknowledging the question put to her. Torquemada nodded to the guard.

The pulleys were hoisted again and with a sharp movement dropped her a few feet from the ground. Pain shot out from her upper torso and arms, taking her breath away. Her wrists and arm sockets took the brunt of her weight and radiated pain under the strain. The guard pulled the rope again and she was lifted higher, stopping short of the ceiling. She panted in her effort to remain silent.

Torquemada addressed her, "Is this enough for you?"

Téresa closed her eyes, negating his presence. *He is nothing to me. He's a beast crawling under me. A cockroach.* She tried to repeat those words to herself over and over. Another turn of the pulley released her from the heights and plunged her down onto the floor, stopping inches from the stones. Her arms cracked out of their sockets, and she could no longer contain a cry of pain. *"¡Oy, oy, mi madre querida!"* She screamed in pain as she struggled to catch her breath.

Again Torquemada's laughter reached her ears as in a distant fog. She was still quivering with the pain and sweating profusely when weights were attached to her ankles, adding more stress to her throbbing shoulders and wrists.

"Again!" she heard. The next pull up to the ceiling wrung out of her another cry. This time she couldn't help herself. "May you burn in hell, *maldicho*, cursed man!"

"Drop her!" Torquemada said.

She was dropped again. The floor rushed to her as a sea of sawdust-covered stones that enveloped her in blackness and blissful numbness.

Torquemada waited impatiently for Téresa to return to her senses. He paced back and forth in front of the limp body lying in a heap.

"Take her back to her cell," Torquemada said.

The guard stooped to untie her arms, but she lay limp on the stones. He looked for a sign of breath, but didn't detect any.

"She is dead, Excellency," The guard said. "She probably had a weak heart."

Torquemada's face turned red with anger. From a wall full of torture instruments, he took a whip in his left hand and whipped Téresa's body over and over until beads of sweat formed on his forehead. The guard grimaced but kept silent.

"Throw her into the pit," said Torquemada, storming out of the torture chamber.

The pit contained the bodies of prisoners who died during torture.

This one was lucky, thought the guard. She escaped.

The scribe recorded the last moment of a woman's life.

~

As they reached the town of Osuna, the caravan halted. Pedro, the head muleteer, rode back to Miguel and José's position near the end of the caravan. Facing them on his horse, he lifted his arm in a parting gesture.

"This is where we part, *niños amigos*. Now you need to head straight north to Écija, then Cordoba."

"Rengrasyo, y con mucho respeto," Miguel said with a bow.

The muleteer gave him a solemn smile. *"Vaya con Dios, niños."*

Miguel and José watched Pedro the muleteer and his train of mounted mules disappear south into the morning mist. Miguel pulled Blanko's reins, leading the mule ridden by José toward a small and dusty path away from the main road and toward Cordoba.

Another obstacle surmounted on the trek for safety, thought Miguel. He and José still had many kilometers to go, bypassing towns and crossing mountain passes. The sooner they arrived at Loxa, the safer they would be, but first they had to pass Estepa, La Roda de Andalusia, and Archidona. After Loxa, it would be easy to reach Chauchina, then Granada was within reach, if the king's guards didn't catch them at Santa Fé. Any one of these towns, however, could still be a trap for them if they ran into Torquemada's men or residents who were eager for reward.

The sun blazed on the horizon and ascended over low-lying purple shaded hills in the distance. All around them on the vega, peasants had been toiling early, before sunrise. Miguel lifted his hat to the peasants, leading José's mule.

"We have at least another hundred and fifty kilometers until we get to the Sierra mountains," said Miguel.

"Hope we get there soon," José said. "My sore arse needs a respite." He stood up on the mule and rubbed his back end.

Miguel exploded in laughter, the sound reverberating through the emptiness hovering over the valley. He laughed so hard he had to wipe tears from his eyes.

"I wish mother could see you. She'd come to your rescue with padding to soothe your royal end!" Miguel laughed again. José sat mortified on Blanko. He bent his head low and kept quiet. José had never known their father, and Miguel had tried to replace that father love that his brother never had. He missed their mother now. Her absence pressed heavily on his heart. He longed for his mother, her caring touch, and her compassionate gaze when she looked at him and José.

Miguel looked up and noticed his brother's trembling lips and his eyes beginning to fill with tears. "What is it, mi hermano *querido*?" he asked José. "I was just teasing you. You know I didn't mean what I said. And because right now we only have each other in this world, we mustn't stop loving and caring for one another."

At these words, José cried in earnest. "I miss Mother," he cried. "Why are you being mean to me?"

"I'm not being mean to you. You have to trust that I'll take care of you while we're away from our mother," Miguel said. "I, too, miss her very much."

José remained silent, pouting.

Miguel felt sad with the longing for their mother's love and reassuring smile. A sudden anger rose in his chest. Why were they being persecuted? Hadn't they observed the Christian faith to the letter? He knew several Jewish families who remained faithful to Jewish law, and they weren't persecuted.

He'd befriended two Jewish boys named Essua and Zac. His mother cautioned him not to encourage these friendships and to remain far from them. But why was his family persecuted and not these boys? His mother explained that because his father and mother had converted, and he and José had been baptized, they were monitored for slipups or relapsing into Judaizing. The rewards for their conversion were numerous; he had been able to join a university, his father permitted to travel to non-Christian lands to pursue his commerce, and his mother allowed to service the old Christian neighborhoods with laundering, and using her skills in needlepoint and knitting that brought a few more maravedís into the household. The Jewish boys and their family were not allowed to join learning institutions or climb into the higher gentry class. They would remain living in poverty from generation to generation.

"Miguel? Miguel?" José's small voice pulled him out of deep thoughts. He looked up at his brother and saw a remorseful face. José knew from early age how to have anyone forgive him by showing a contrite expression, and a will to meet halfway.

"I knew you were teasing me before. I'll be good. You'll see."

"All right, José. Promise?" asked Miguel.

"Promise," José repeated.

As Miguel led Blanko near cultivated fields in the flat plain, he observed the peasants bent and toiling under the rising heat, their heads covered by flat caps, their shirts open at the neck, and curved knives in their hands gleaming and reflecting the sunlight as they cut the ripe melons from their trailing vines. The women followed the men, collecting the fruit in a large basket. Their long skirts tied at the sides of their waists revealed sturdy young legs. Miguel surveyed the scene as they ascended the mountainous path getting further away from the workers below. He was glad the peasants concentrated on their labor and not on two young lads traveling on their own. As they left the abundant fields behind them, the terrain began to change from the flat plain to a gentle climb into the mountain. If they could cross the summit by night and descend on the other side toward Granada by morning, the rest of the trek should go smoothly. The surefooted mule climbed the rocky path into the looming and snowy Sierra mountains. As they climbed, Miguel saw that vegetation became scant on the trail lined by rocks and boulders teetering at the edge of the abyss.

After long hours of climbing, Blanko began to slow down. The ground below his hooves became a sheet of miniscule pebbles that moved as he stepped. A small avalanche of tiny stones frightened and caused him to jump sideways, his eyes rolling and mouth dripping with white foam. José clung, looking panicked. They had been lucky this time. They could have tumbled down the deep ravines dropping away from the path.

"Hold on!" said Miguel. "Come on, Blanko, come on," he whispered in his ear and gently caressed his upper jaw. With a jerking movement Blanko came to a stop, his long ears raised at attention. Miguel heard a slow rumbling sound below the mountain. He looked down, but couldn't see below the path, the vega having disappeared many hours ago while they were the only travelers on the mountain. He coaxed Blanko again when José called out, "I see men riding on their horses!"

Miguel spotted Moors mounted on horses with scimitars at their belts. He spun around and said, "Quickly, let's hide near these rocks!" He led Blanko behind a boulder jutting near the path. José climbed down and was about to crouch behind the boulder, when Miguel pointed to the cliff wall.

"In here!" Miguel pulled Blanko, followed by José, to a hollow in the cliff that had been hidden by the large boulder. The older boy drew a cloth from a bag on Blanko's flank and covered his eyes while speaking softly into his ear again. José crouched on his haunches, his whole body trembling. He looked up to Miguel for protection. Miguel put a hand on his brother's head and tried to reassure him. They heard horses' hooves scraping the gravel and men's voices.

"I'm afraid," José whispered, his face turning white.

"Hush," Miguel breathed.

After what seemed an interminable number of minutes, they couldn't hear the caravan or horses any longer. Miguel slipped out of the cave to check for stragglers. Seeing an empty path, he told José to come out. José, still pale, led Blanko to Miguel, who helped him mount. They looked cautiously around and then continued on the path up the mountain. The route got steeper and steeper, making progress slow. When sunset began, Miguel stopped Blanko with the words "Ho, ho."

"Why are we stopping?" José asked.

"Because we're both tired," Miguel replied.

"Look, Miguel," José cried, attracting his attention.

Miguel looked where José's finger pointed and saw the mouth of a cavern. He and José entered a dry space large enough to provide refuge for them and Blanko. Gray ashes in a fire pit indicated travelers, possibly traveling monks, had used it. Miguel found a flat space for them to lie down, pulled the two blankets from the satchels on Blanko's flank, and spread them on the ground. He fed Blanko first, then split more of their bread, dry cheese, and scallions between his brother and him.

"Come on," he urged José, "we need to rest now."

They ate silently. Miguel noticed that José had fallen asleep holding his bread, so he covered him with the blanket. He could hear José's quiet breathing as he slept soundly. Miguel then rested his head on his blanket, his mind numb and empty, before he fell into an exhausted sleep.

A sharp poke to Miguel's arm awoke him abruptly from a sound sleep. Several men surrounded him and José with glaring torchlight that blinded him. Miguel jumped to his feet with his arms extended over José, who had just awakened.

"Miguel! Miguel!" José cried from his blanket. A look of terror spread over his face at the sight of several men standing in the small cavern.

"What is it you want?" Miguel asked in a firm voice, showing no fear. These men were neither Spaniards nor soldiers. Perhaps they were farmers from a nearby town, he thought.

"What are you boys doing here?" asked one of the men in a broken Castilian dialect. He wore a cotton turban with a caftan over his striped tunic, and a scimitar hung from his girdle on one hip.

Miguel hesitated, trying to come up with a plausible explanation, when one man pulled his scimitar with a quick movement of his wrist and placed it across Miguel's throat.

"Speak, Infidel!" he bellowed in Miguel's face.

José jumped up from the blanket and began to cry and shake violently. "Don't kill us! Please don't kill us!" Two of the men grabbed a frightened José by his arms.

Miguel raised his hands in front of him and said to his brother in a calm voice, "It's all right, José. These men are friends of ours."

The man holding the scimitar applied more pressure, and Miguel felt it cutting slightly into his skin. He put his hand on the scimitar and quietly said, "You don't want King Boabdil to be mad or kill you if you harm me or my brother."

The man eased up on the scimitar slightly, but kept it on Miguel's throat. "You better give me a better reason than that, otherwise you're both dead!"

At those words, José's legs buckled underneath him and he slumped downward, unconscious. The two men holding his arms lifted him back up and slapped his face several times. José regained consciousness and began to scream and cry.

"I'll tell you exactly who we are if you let go of my brother," Miguel said. He felt a slight tremolo in his voice even though he tried to sound calm.

The man who still held the scimitar made a sign to his men and they let go of José's arms. Rubbing his bruised arms, José ran close to Miguel.

Miguel said, "We we're headed for King Boabdil's palace and found this cavern to rest for the night."

"How do you know King Boabdil?" he blasted at Miguel.

"My mother sent us on a mission to him. I can't divulge the reason right now."

"If you can't tell us, then King Boabdil will have to force it out of you." He made a sign with the sword that sent a shiver down Miguel's spine. "Put those two swines on the mules!" he commanded his men.

Miguel and José were pushed and dragged outside, where horses waited. Blanko was tied to another horse, but they didn't get to ride him. They were thrown and tied onto mules. The caravan jostled its way to descend the other side of the mountain. The night was still cold and opaque except for the constant stars in the black sky. Darkness made the trip on slippery pebbles even more treacherous for the mules, who brayed their fear and reluctance. Sometimes it felt to Miguel that the entire mountain might slide on top of them, burying men, horses, and mules. He was relieved when they began their descent to the other side.

Miguel practiced in his mind the approach he would use with King Boabdil. His mother warned him not to reveal the true purpose of his quest to anyone except the pasha. She revealed to him that his father had been on good terms with King Boabdil when he brought merino wools, precious silks, heavy brocades, and damasks for the entire harem. King Boabdil especially liked the translucent pearls Nahum brought back from Ceuta and Tangier. The pasha gave those only to his favorite concubine.

The trips his father made were dangerous, with brigands on land and pirates in the Strait of Gibraltar. Time after time, his father had evaded death on his voyages—only to find it at home at the hands of his own countrymen, the men of España. To Miguel, this seemed an unbearably cruel destiny. Miguel closed his right hand into a fist, silently vowing a curse upon the head of the Inquisition. One day he would return to find his father's murderer. It seemed an impossible task, since he knew nothing of where his father had been held, tortured, and killed. However, he wouldn't rest until this oath he made to himself was fulfilled.

They reached the bottom of the mountain, and the sound of raging waters indicated to Miguel that the men were attempting to cross a river. The small light of day was gradually seeping through the forest revealing the outline of trees, rocks, and the entire region itself beginning to rise from the mist. The mounted men had traveled in a southeasterly direction, and from the position of the sun Miguel gathered that they were very close to Granada. He looked fondly at José sill sleeping and felt reassured that his brother was safe for the moment, at least.

"Halt!" a voice shouted. Several men in Moorish attire stopped them on their path. The man who had first threatened Miguel dismounted to talk to one of the guards in Moorish—a language unfamiliar to Miguel.

"Al Hakim gedida. Salam alaikum." The guard saluted their captors and made a sign for them to continue their trip. The sun was beginning to pierce the scantily wooded forest, spreading diffused light on delicate ferns and vegetation. A few red squirrels with cream-colored chests darted between the horses' legs, making them balk. Miguel clutched at his mule's neck. He was glad José was still asleep. It reassured him that his brother wouldn't panic or antagonize their captors with his youthful fears. Miguel felt some trepidation himself, not knowing what to expect at the end of their journey. King Boabdil may not be inclined to protect the children of his former friend, Nahum. According to Miguel's mother, the two men had been very close. Nahum and King Boabdil were the remnants of a past life in Moorish Spain when the Convivencia—or convivial times between Christians, Jews, and Moors from the seventh century on—created a rich life for all of its inhabitants.

His father told him that it was a time of rich trade between the three religions. They lived side by side as neighbors while the Moors governed Spain. Arts and sciences flourished in universities, and great works of antiquity were translated from ancient Greek into Hebrew, then into Arabic and Latin. Miguel had heard many times that the Convivencia was a great time of peace and prosperity. Now, however, the Spaniards had conquered most of the lands from the Moors and considered trading with the Moors an act of treason. Granada was the last bastion remaining to be conquered by Spain in the name of Christendom.

José awoke with a whimper and jolted Miguel out of his thoughts. The boy began to cry immediately.

"Hush, José. We're near our destination, and everything will be all right. You'll see."

José stopped crying but looked worried. Miguel smiled at him, and José smiled slightly back at him.

The small caravan of horses, mules, and men arrived at King Boabdil's palace. Miguel saw the red fortress of the Alhambra for the first time. Turbaned soldiers manned the crenellated towers; a flurry of activity took place around them, and wooden carts were piled high with arms. Miguel's throat became constricted with emotion at being trapped in the enemy's camp. The men dismounted, and the leader made a sign to four of his men who approached Miguel and José and grabbed them roughly by the arms.

"Tell your men we're guests of King Boabdil!" Miguel reminded the leader.

"Of course you are," the leader said. He motioned to the men to take them to the king, but instead of leading them up the marble steps to the front doors they were pushed to the side of the palace, where they entered a side door. They were led down steps and through a subterranean labyrinth and thrown into a dark cell. Metal doors slammed shut behind them.

As soon as he recovered from the shock, Miguel ran to the cell door and shook it back and forth with all his strength, but the door resisted his attempts.

"Let us out! We're guests of the pasha! Let us out!" The echo of men laughing, then fading down the corridor, was all he heard. Miguel turned around to José, who lay prostrate on the floor, unable to utter a word. Miguel went to him and grabbed both his shoulders.

"Listen to me, José. These men don't know we're here for a reason. You'll see—they'll be back and will free us." José sat motionless, his eyes vacantly staring at the opposite wall. Miguel tried shaking his brother's shoulders, but José remained frozen and silent.

Miguel could usually face adversity and find something good in it. His parents had taught him to bounce back in times of trouble, but his brother's withdrawn state of mind disturbed him. He felt responsible for José's well-being. Maybe it was best for José to withdraw from his present reality. They didn't seem to be in danger at the moment. Although, a worse fate could be waiting for them: torture or death.

Miguel felt a shiver pass over him. He chased away this last thought, and gathered his strength to go to his brother and cradle him in his arms.

8

Imminent War

In Seville, one of Andalusia's biggest military headquarters, soldiers polished their swords and lances and brushed their horses. Platoon commanders lectured their new recruits while young page boys helped dress their masters. In one tent, a young soldier finished dressing and carefully packed his belongings, making sure not to forget his sword and flat blade. A fellow soldier sat unoccupied on his cot cracking his whip back and forth with a swooshing sound.

"We start on the long march within the hour, Antonio. You'd better get ready."

"I tell you, Juan, I'll kill twenty . . . no, thirty . . . of the infidels with my sword."

Juan looked at Antonio and laughed in a clear voice that rang over the din and the tumult in the camp.

"First, make sure your sword is as sharp as your tongue."

Juan bantered with Antonio, but he admired his friend for his brave comment. Antonio had fought his way into the mounted troops, earning the rank of corporal through hard work and study. Juan had used his father's connections to get his commission into the cavalry—though he had achieved his rank by distinguishing himself during painful and grueling training.

Antonio looked disconcerted at Juan's harsh statement. "If you don't believe me, then watch me as we engage the enemy."

"I'll do that. Meanwhile, get your belongings together. We're leaving as soon as the sun sets over Seville."

"Tell me one thing, Juan."

"Yes?"

"Why didn't your father stop you from joining the war?"

"Because it's my duty to fight. My father wouldn't think of stopping me. On the contrary, he urged me to fight for España."

"But you're his only son! How can he send you on a journey that you may not come back from?" Antonio looked incredulous.

"We're not to think of death. It is life's glory we seek."

"Just the same, I can't see it your way. I'm one of many sons to my father and mother. They could certainly spare me. My other brothers will look after my parents if I don't come back. But you . . ." Antonio didn't finish his sentence.

"Come on, my friend. It's time to get ready." Juan terminated the conversation by folding his blanket and loading his pack onto his horse. He tied his heavy pack onto the saddle and ran a leather strap below the horse's flank several times. Any item lost could not be retrieved. Each soldier purchased his own tin goblet and plate, clothing, and shaving items. They carried some food—mostly dried vegetables, fruit, and staples.

His mother, Doña Maria Escobar, had filled his woolen sack to capacity. Her tears had mingled with the food as she cautioned him to look out for himself. She had waited many years to give birth to a son, and when she found herself pregnant at the age of thirty, she considered it a miracle. She told him many times that he was begotten with the spirit of the Lord, and as such he would always serve God. His mother couldn't help feeling sad that he was now on a mission for España.

When Isabella accepted his proposal of marriage, he delighted the household by dancing with joy through the entire palatial home and kissing every woman servant in the place. Juan remembered that his mother seemed less than enthusiastic. He kissed her over and over in his euphoria and laughed at his mother's long face.

"By St. George, Madre, I swear you're jealous," Juan teased.

She had lowered her eyes and said with a red face, "You know I want the best for you, *mi hijo*. I know she'll make you a good wife."

"Then what's this long face about?"

"It's just that I'll miss you terribly every day."

"You'll see me every afternoon and on Sunday at Mass. I could never part with my madre."

Juan smiled at the recollection.

"Platoon, march!" The voice of Gonzalo Fernández de Córdova, the commander in chief, boomed over their heads. The long column of two thousand mounted men and three thousand foot soldiers moved as one while their boots, swords, lances, and spurs created a deafening clanking.

Juan was proud to take part in this campaign to liberate España, once and for all, from the Moors. Once the attack began against Granada in the shadow of the Sierra Nevada Mountains, there was no retreat nor turning back. He prayed that if the Moorish citadel could be compared to the biblical, ill-fated Masada defeated by the Romans, then as Spaniards their victory over the Moors would be assured. If this similar strategy and strength of attack could be executed, the Moors will be vanquished.

Juan's anxiety about Isabella's safety abruptly rose to his consciousness. No word of her whereabouts had reached them in Castile, except for the little that was learned from Torquemada's dungeon. How and why could this chicken farmer plan and successfully kidnap the love of his life, aided by thugs and brigands? With all the able men under Guerida, none had prevented nor stopped the terrible thing that had happened to Isabella. He knew Isabella had been impulsive—he loved that about her. She loved life; the small things that came her way—such as a pigeon landing on her head—made her laugh and endeared her to him. He suddenly felt a sharp pain welling in his chest, and tears sprang to his eyes. He quickly wiped them off and looked around to see if anyone had noticed. If word got around that Juan Escobar had tears in his eyes, it would spread that his courage had failed him. His honor would be compromised—and what would Isabella think? He forced his thoughts back to the battle at hand. Between him and Antonio, they could very well kill at least ten to twenty Moors, he decided.

The sun was now shining, but strong winds raised the dusty soil before them. Juan raised his hand above his metal helmet to protect his eyes. He saw that Antonio had done the same. Their eyes met and they both broke up in laughter. The other mounted soldiers looked sharply at them. Juan could see reproach in their eyes at their irreverent laughter in the face of possible death.

As the soldiers marched forward in the dry vega, rising clouds of dust raised by horses' hooves masked the length of the marching column and true number of men advancing forward. The only men that could be seen at the head of the column were a few foot soldiers. The rest of the column was partly concealed.

Two lone figures, crouched behind a granite outcrop high above in the Sierras, watched the column marching down the plain before them.

"I only see about seven hundred to one thousand men and horses," one of the two men said. Both his hands were raised to protect his eyes from the sunlight. He continued. "I'm quite sure of my estimate."

"You're wrong, Ahmad Kalil. I see more, perhaps two thousand."

"What difference does it make if it's seven hundred or even a thousand? We can't disturb the pasha with news like that. Our orders were to sound an alarm if we saw several thousand men."

"I still think we should light fires to alert the mountain passes and warn our peasants in the fields to round up their herds and flee to safety," the other man said as he removed his turban and scratched his scalp.

"I'll make the decision here," Ahmad said.

His subordinate let out a sigh and bowed his head in submission. "Allah is great! He'll give us the answer."

"Yes, he will," Ahmad echoed. "Let's go back to the ravines, where we came from. We'll reach town before nightfall and tell the pasha what we saw."

The subordinate said in a subdued voice, "It might be too late by then." He knew he was pushing his luck, but he also knew that he was right.

Ahmad frowned and bellowed, "You're an idiot, Mansur Abbas! How many times must I tell you I make the decisions!"

Mansur lowered his head in silence and followed Ahmad to the cavern, where their mounts were tied up. They mounted their Arabian horses and galloped toward Granada through the mountain passes.

Maria had languished for several weeks in the dungeon of St. Jorge's Castle. They had stopped the torturous plank three days ago, and she lay on the dusty floor, where the stench that permeated the small cubicle reminded her of how foolish she had been not to heed João's warning. Did she gain precious moments for the men by not following them into the mountains? Would Guerida have followed their trail into the night if she hadn't been caught? She'd never know the answer. All she knew now was that the men had distanced themselves from Guerida.

She had also hoped that the inquisitors would be less savage on a woman. From her seated position on the straw bed, she let out a bitter laugh that echoed off the cavernous and dark ceiling. Man or woman—it made no difference for the extraction of the truth they wanted. As long as they obtained a confession, whether that confession was stained in blood or spoken with a death rattle, then their duty was fulfilled. She wondered what the next hours would bring her: death or freedom? She tried to move her body, but the pain from her pulled joints began to awake. For a brief moment, she hoped against hope that her jailers had tired of her. She admonished herself for this unrealistic thought. What was sure to occur next was the long descent into oblivion. Fear crept slowly into her mind that this reprieve was about to end soon. The sound of a key rattling in the cell door startled her.

Torquemada entered her cell accompanied by two attendants. Following him were the notary with his writing instruments and guards carrying a plank bed resembling a ladder.

"Maria Donarojo, do you have anything to tell me?" Torquemada breathed his foul breath in her face.

She shrank back as far as the chains pinning her to the walls would allow. "I have nothing to say to you!" she spat.

A dry sinister laugh filled the small cell, echoing off the walls. "You've nothing to tell me? You've used up my patience! Your luck is about to end—you hear me?" Torquemada's voice was shrill.

"You call that luck?" Maria replied to him despite an insidious fear numbing her limbs. "You have tortured me and starved me! How lucky can I be?" She let out forced laughter as pain began to mount in her inflamed and bruised joints.

Torquemada turned to one of his attendants and nodded. His attendant left the cell and returned with a large bearded bare-chested man wearing a black vest over black leather pants. Torquemada turned to Maria and said, "May God have mercy on you, Maria." He made the sign of the cross.

Maria's jailer and an attendant approached her, yanked the chains off her wrists, and dragged her to the *escalera*, the flat wooden ladder, to which they tied her wrists and ankles. Next they lowered the head of the escalera, supported on a fulcrum. After a few moments she began to feel blood constricting the vessels in her head. Leather bands bound her head, arms, and legs to the ladder. Any movement on her part would cut wounds in her flesh from the tight whipcord. Her mouth was forced open with an iron prong. Her nostrils were plugged with linen, and a pad of linen was placed across her jaws. The jailer poured water into her mouth. The weight of water forced the linen into her throat, and when she tried to expel it from her mouth, its bulk forced her tongue back into her throat. She began to gag under the weight of the water that seeped into her closed throat. Some of the water backed off her mouth and flooded her face, hair, and upper body, but they kept pouring more water through the linen. She choked and coughed, trying to dislodge the linen, but she only succeeded in swallowing it deeper in her throat. Next, she tried to swallow the water to allow some air to reach her lungs, but the wet cloth being soaked by more water poured into her mouth prevented it. Maria began to suffocate under its weight. She swallowed and swallowed until she could no longer breathe and felt her life ebbing out of her. Her eyes began to bulge, and darkness enveloped her.

"You can stop now," Torquemada said to the jailer. "We can only use eight measures of water, then we'll continue when she comes to." He walked away to another of his victims.

The Spaniards' camp below Granada was a flurry of activity. Mallets and hammers pounded as workers erected the temporary city of Santa Fé to shelter thousands of soldiers and prepared a makeshift headquarters for the queen and king.

Queen Isabella made a grand entrance into the settlement field on her white horse, Esperanza, to supervise the preparations for war. Seeing their queen join King Ferdinand, the adoring soldiers filled the air with thundering *hurrahs*. Isabella supervised the feeding and comfort of her soldiers, visiting them often in their tents to see to their needs. They never missed a chance to cheer and applaud her. She was their revered queen, for whom they were willing to sacrifice their lives in the cause of España. Isabella stroked Esperanza and turned to Ferdinand, who was behind her, giving him the nod to address the field assembly.

"My dear soldiers and compatriots," Ferdinand declared to the soldiers, "we are preparing our way to victory and the conquest of Granada!"

A deafening shout rose from the soldiers. They raised their powerful voices and waved their lances above their heads, clanking them against those of their neighbors.

"As you know," continued King Ferdinand, "we started the Reconquista centuries ago. You well know how we laid down our lives for this noble and blessed call to save our country, and how we vanquished the Moors in town after town." Another rumble of shouting rose from the foot soldiers and the mounted lancers. "Now is the end of our struggle for España, May she live on and prosper in this holy endeavor!"

"¡Para mi España, España!" the soldiers shouted again.

"Hurrah! Hurrah! Hurrah!" A great wave of excited voices rose up from the field.

When the voices died down, Ferdinand turned to Isabella and made a motion for her to address the soldiers.

"My dear soldiers," she began while the soldiers bowed and crossed themselves before her.

I've earned the trust of my people and the Santos label of "The Catolica Queen."

She gathered her strength and addressed the soldiers. "We have waited a long time to regain our country from the Moors. We waited seven hundred years!"

Again a formidable shout came from all assembled. Isabella's retinue of ladies from the court waved their colorful scarves, and her foot soldiers and maids held small colorful flags above their heads. The flags ruffled as a sea undulating under the mild sun of a cool morning.

"So, my brave soldiers," continued Queen Isabella, "go to victory and glory and for our Savior!"

The rumble of joy coming from the soldiers became thunderous, lasting a full fifteen minutes. Afterward, Cardinal Mendoza, who had accompanied the monarchs, raised his cross and blessed all before him. The soldiers fell to their knees, some in tears, overpowered by their love for their country and queen.

Isabella gently pressured Esperanza's flanks and caressed her shining white coat. The horse gracefully turned around, and Ferdinand's black stallion followed. They made their way back to their tents while their retinue followed at a respectful distance.

Isabella and Ferdinand dismounted and entered the large tent that served as a makeshift assembly hall for their subjects. Captain Gonzalo De Córdoba prepared to take orders from his queen and king.

Isabella addressed the captain as she sat on an imposing red velvet chair decorated with gold inlay in an intricate rose pattern. "We must make sure the provisions last us as long as the war with the Moors does. Hopefully, we'll soon conquer them and triumphantly enter Granada. It's my wish that they will abide by the treaty, capitulate, and relinquish the keys to the city."

"Yes, my queen," Córdoba said while bowing before her. "They'll have to agree to the treaty signed at Loxa with the king of Granada to surrender his capital. He agreed that with the capitulation of Almería, Baza, and Guadix, their inhabitants would be protected, free to worship their God in their mosque. He signed the treaty of Guadix saying that Granada will surrender without an arrow being fired."

"Yes, according to the terms in the treaty," said Isabella with a nod of her head. "I know that King Abdallah—Muhammad XII, known as Boabdil—went back on his promise to surrender his city according to the treaty, using the excuses that the inhabitants of his city prevented him from making good on that promise. He declared he's no longer their master. If what he says is true, and the city's inhabitants prefer to build their own defenses, then it is war."

She looked directly at him. "How ready are you to wage war?"

"We've been preparing for this blessed event since last winter. Preparations are almost complete," Córdoba said. "We'll wait till the early morning hour, when they're not fully prepared. It'll be best to do a frontal attack the moment the muezzin begins his chant. All will be prostrating and praying. That's the best time to attack."

"That is clever of you, my captain," Isabella commented. Ferdinand also nodded.

She continued. "You've been a loyal subject and as capable a captain as your elder brother, Alonso de Aguilar. I've seen your military planning and activities since I took command of the army in April of this year."

Córdova bowed at the compliment, and his face turned crimson.

The queen knew her husband King Ferdinand's estimation of the captain was nearly as high as hers. He showed the king courtesy and took great interest in his warring tactics. The king was keen in all aspects of war. His interest in mechanical innovations, commerce, and the latest advances in medicine made him one of the most inquisitive monarchs in all of the near kingdoms. She felt proud of Ferdinand.

"Go now, Captain, and get my armies ready to defend España."

9

Assault

SPANISH TROOPS MOVED STEALTHILY IN the first diffused light of dawn, stepping silently in the vineyards that had not been burned below the citadel of the Alhambra. Whole battalions held their noise in check and avoided giving away their positions by not shuffling their frozen feet on the cold, damp earth. The horses moved restlessly, stomping their hooves in the soft ground of the vega.

Two soldiers held their swords unsheathed to avoid metallic sounds while trying to balance on their restless horses.

"Whoa, whoa, mi querido," Juan whispered in his horse's ear. He patted his steed's lustrous flank, then applied pressure with his hand to keep him steady. He turned to Antonio, who rode behind him, and said with a hushed voice, "Stay right behind my horse, and don't try anything heroic unless I tell you to."

Antonio nodded his head in silence. Just then the call to prayer for which they waited began in the distance.

"Allaaaaaaah Whakbaaaaaar!" The voice rose above the crenellated walls, and then it started again, *"Allaaaaaaaaaah Whakbaaaaaaaar Sheellallaaaaaaa!"*

The repetitive chant continued for a few more minutes and then was drowned out by a great cry from the plains.

"For the glory of Spain!" The pennon of St. James held within the tight grasp of the flag bearer flew straight on the wind amid galloping horses surrounded by shouts from thousands of young warriors. *"¡Santiago! ¡Santiago!"*

Several thousand horses galloped in rank through the dusty plain, raising clouds of orange dust that blended with an orange sun rising at the horizon. *"¡Por la vida de España y Santiago!"* The voices rose in unison. Behind the cavalry, foot soldiers waving their swords and rows of lancers ran at a trot, then increased their pace to a steady run. Foot soldiers carrying tall ladders ran protected behind the lancers.

In the Alhambra towers, Moorish soldiers positioned themselves within the walls. The archers manning the towers climbed to the platform by the crenellated windows and waited for the order to start shooting. When the captain dropped his scimitar downward, a volley of arrows rained down on the cavalry and foot soldiers arriving at the wall. Several rows of foot soldiers fell when arrows pierced the flesh on their necks where their helmets ended and their chain-mail suits began. Horses, hit by arrows, fell and filled the air with their pitiful cries.

In the mêlée, Juan succeeded arriving at the wall. He turned to Antonio but couldn't see him and began a quick search. He spotted Antonio's horse lying on his right side on the ground while his friend tried in vain to coax the horse to get up. Juan applied pressure to his horse's flank to turn him around and rushed in Antonio's direction. Just then a second volley of arrows moved through the skies in sheets, raining on the foot soldiers still arriving at the walls.

As Juan's horse neared the spot where Antonio's horse had collapsed, a sharp pain suddenly pierced his back, making him reel in his saddle. He felt for his back and found that an arrow had pierced him through a hole in his chain-mail suit, but he couldn't budge it. In great pain, he dismounted and collapsed by Antonio's prostrate horse. Antonio rushed to Juan and dragged him into the shade of Juan's own horse, which still stood upright.

In a dream, Juan heard Antonio's voice calling out to him.

"Talk to me! Talk to me!" Antonio called to his friend while gently shaking his right shoulder. Juan noticed that Antonio's hands were bloody. Antonio quickly tore a strip off a cloth stuffed in his padded jacket, slipped it under Juan's mail, and applied pressure to stem the blood dripping from the wound.

"Don't you worry," Antonio tried to reassure him. "I'll take care of you."

In the harem wing of the palace, Isabella whiled away the hours and began to droop as the petal of a wilted rose. Her cheeks had lost the pink blush color highlighting her fine cheekbones, and her posture began to sag. Tears often dulled the emerald sparkle in her eyes and sapped her vitality. She now believed the prison that held her may never let her go. The boundaries of her life were the outer perimeters of the harem with its enchanting gardens and clear water pools, and the guards who never let her out of their sight.

This morning as she sat on the edge of a small round fountain, an unrecognizable reflection stared back at her from the pool: a crouched forlorn figure of a young woman contradicted the image she'd had of herself before she was snatched from her safe home. During childhood and into young girlhood, her dada Hannah, or her maid Pilar, accompanied her everywhere. There was never any indication that her safety would be compromised, excluding a pickpocket youth or two. Seville and nearby neighborhoods had been open to her as long as she had companions or the *dueña* with her. She realized with painful frankness that this state of affairs was of her own making. If it hadn't been for her youthful impetuousness, as her father patiently reminded her in the past, she wouldn't be in this predicament.

She sighed with great sadness. She would give all her cherished possessions, including the singing berbeliko nightingale in her room and all her dresses and jewelry, just to see her mother and father again. How unhappy they must be right now. She felt wretched for causing them pain. She began to cry again; this time sobs of true regret racked her chest. She, the daughter of a physician and an aristocratic mother, was doing penitence in the enemy's den. What if Téresa was right? What if she truly was the daughter of a Jewish mother and father? It suddenly occurred to her that perhaps Téresa had opened for her a more dangerous destiny, and it shook her to the core. As a Jewish girl, she would become poor and shunned as were the few families living in the Juderia.Worst of all, Juan couldn't, or wouldn't, marry her. She shuddered at the thought.

"Why are you sitting sadly by yourself?"

Isabella heard Sarah's melodious voice. She turned around to catch Sarah's shocked expression at finding her crying.

"This is a beautiful day, querida," said Sarah. "The whole earth and sky are singing for us with beautiful flowers and birds to gladden our heart." Sarah took her hand and pressed it affectionately. "Come, let us walk into the garden."

Isabella followed her, and thought how she had come to befriend and trust Sarah during her captivity. The two women had developed great affinity for each other in their mutual circumstances. Sarah told her of her parents' love for Granada and their friendship with the old caliph, dating back several decades. Sarah's father had been the private treasurer to the caliph, who had been a great protector of her family.

"Like you," said Sarah, "I was an only child to my parents with privileges accorded to the wealthy Jewish families who lived for centuries alongside Moors and Christians in Granada. We lived and worked side by side in Granada until the Spanish Reconquista began in earnest."

"What happened then?" Isabella asked curiously.

"My parents were caught during the Reconquista, which is still going on, and I was brought here at a young age. I don't remember ever living anywhere other than Granada, nor do I ever want to leave it."

Isabella caught a worried look on Sarah's face. She grabbed her arm and pressed it gently. Sarah smiled at her. The young women continued their walk down the garden path in deep silence. Isabella, though, reminisced about her upbringing in Seville.

Sarah was the first to break the silence. "I heard some rumors today among the servants."

Isabella raised her head. "What did you hear?"

"The mule caravan bringing supplies spread rumors about a Spanish *ejército* in the vega."

"An army?" Isabella repeated, her heart skipping a beat.

"There's nothing to worry about. The caliph has his own army. We're safe here behind the Alhambra walls."

Isabella didn't comment. She wondered if the Alhambra walls could be breached. Could she be freed? Tears of hope sprang to her eyes.

Sarah tried to comfort her. "You're upset right now about your family and feel uprooted and unprotected. That's understandable."

"You don't understand," Isabella said. "I'll be glad to cheer for the Spanish army when they attack and breach the walls!" Isabella unleashed a sudden string of curses. *"¡Maldicho son esto payiz y my Estrella maldicha que me traer aqui!"* She was startled by the pained look on Sarah's face and then by the intensity of her anger and hatred of the people holding her. But hadn't they been friendly to her? They saw to her every need—except freedom. It was, nevertheless, a golden cage—a cage that entranced and cajoled her senses, keeping her in a bewitched world. She was about to despair again, when her whole soul rebelled. No. She was going to be strong and reemerge again to see her mother and father—and above all to see Juan at her side forever.

Even though Sarah was mortified by Isabella's anger and curses upon their hosts, she said nothing about the outburst. She said gently to Isabella, "We're allowed to go into the king's garden if we get permission."

Isabella nodded her head with a slight smile. She let out a sigh of relief. She inhaled deeply of the pure air descending from the mountain heights mingling with the scent of citrons that permeated the garden.

Sarah clapped her hands, and a male Nubian servant appeared. Isabella marveled at the sudden appearance of the servant. He must've been in the shadows awaiting her call. Sarah spoke some words into his ear, and he left to return promptly with two guards sporting scimitars at their sides, who escorted them out of the harem's quarters.

"We're going to the pasha's summer palace," Sarah said with a mysterious look on her face.

The Nubian servant unlocked a metal door built into the gardens' wall, and the guards led them fifty meters across a bridge overlooking a river that divided the palace of the Alhambra from the summer palace on higher ground. They crossed a covered pathway shaded by cypresses on both sides and arrived at a small two-story palace with a roofed gallery overlooking the Alhambra and an open arcade with pillars near a series of gardens divided by endless hedges. An enchanting world of green foliage opened up before Isabella.

A long courtyard enclosed on both sides by low-lying buildings was bisected by a central rectangular water channel with bird-filled trees and flowerbeds on each side. The court was graced with orange, lemon, and myrtle trees, some still carrying a late summer bloom. A profusion of plants and flowers scented the air. The scent of perfumed roses dominated the other scents. They walked leisurely over a path of finely laid gravel that crunched under their feet. The air, still filled with morning dew, was delicately warmed by a low sun on the horizon that began to spread its warmth to every branch and twig. Cascading water in the fountains bathed droves of frolicking birds in their clear waters, and added a soothing sound to their footsteps. They moved from court to court under an abundant green canopy of foliage. At the end of a court, they stopped by a staircase with water channels along each marble side that fed the gardens below in the main court.

Isabella looked to Sarah, but she stopped short of the stairs. "Aren't we going to climb these stairs?"

"No," Sarah said. "There are more gardens on the premises, but the guards will not allow us to enter here."

"Why not?"

"Because one can become lost in those gardens or disappear."

"How far can we go into the king's garden?" Isabella asked.

"The gardens cover much of the grounds on the outside. All the way down the hills."

Isabella tried to conceal her excitement. She yearned for freedom with all her body and soul. "Can we go there? I'd love to see it."

Sarah turned to the two guards following them and whispered in one man's ear. The guard shook his head.

Sarah turned to Isabella. "We're not allowed to go down any further; we can only walk the grounds surrounding the summer palace."

Isabella remained silent but followed Sarah obediently. Her eyes searched the grounds, looking intently for a break in the tall wall surrounding the palace. No such breech in the massive wall appeared to exist. The mute stones seemed to mock her. Was she to remain a prisoner for the rest of her life?

Sarah and Isabella continued on their walk in silence. They strolled down a steep incline with deep ravines on both sides that followed the palace walls. On her right, Isabella noticed a single wide dirt path that ended abruptly by one of the palace walls. She also noticed a brook crossing at a right angle under their path, spilling its waters to the other side and down the hill to disappear through a hole in the wall. Suddenly, she broke away from Sarah in a skipping step down the descending path along the brook and toward the structure. The two guards became alarmed and snapped to attention in a flight stance, their hands resting on their swords.

Sarah called out to Isabella, "Come back, Isabella! Come back!" she shouted.

Isabella ignored Sarah's warning, and kept laughing as she gamboled toward the small building at the base. The guards, meanwhile, ran after her, descending the ravine with giant leaps. Then it was all over. A solid wall with no door or opening stopped her.

"That's strange—there's no door here!" she shouted back at Sarah.

She then heard an ethereal and muffled voice rising from deep down behind the thick wall.

"Who's in there!" she shouted as she stared at the wall. It was then that the word *prisoners* repeated over and over came to her ears. She was about to shout when the guards caught up with her. One of them grabbed one of her wrists while the other guard pushed her forward with his sword.

"Imshee! Imshee!" He pushed her back up the path.

Sarah came running and admonished her. "That was a foolish thing to do!"

Isabella suddenly found her voice from the shock of being manhandled by the guards. "Tell them to release me!" she screamed.

Sarah made a motion of her hand to the guards, who immediately released Isabella from their grip. Isabella rubbed her wrist and marveled at Sarah's authoritarian manner.

"I'm sorry, Sarah. I didn't mean to disobey you or anyone else. I was just curious where this path led."

"You must never do that again. They could've chopped your head off!"

Isabella put her hand over her throat at those words. She lowered her head momentarily, then suddenly changed her demeanor. Laughing, she playfully grabbed Sarah's arm.

Sarah smiled back at her. "Let's go back to our quarters. It's near the noonday meal." The two young women quickened their pace and reached the palace quarters in the harem.

When the guards were out of reach, Isabella turned to Sarah. "I heard someone calling behind the wall. It was a cry for help."

Sarah looked at her sideways. "We don't ask nor seek whose voice it was. It's dangerous and forbidden for women to inquire or ask questions."

"What if the voice belonged to someone who needed help? Wouldn't you find out who it was?" Isabella's voice became insistent. "Please!"

Sarah remained silent. She looked at Isabella and said, "If I hear anything, I'll certainly let you know."

"You're a true friend," Isabella said

Sarah smiled at her and pressed her hand in friendship.

In their cell, Miguel and José grew more desperate each day. When they were captured, they thought a sure death was their fate. Slowly they realized their captors would neither kill them nor release them. One meal was brought to them each day, in the afternoon. It consisted of flat, round breads, a paste of ground, hulled sesame seeds with chickpeas and scallions, a sweet cake made of wheat, and several gourds of water. At least they weren't starved.

In the first few minutes of their incarceration, they had made the welcome discovery of a bubbling brook. The water flowed in through the base of the first wall and found its outlet through the opposite wall. They were able to wash the grime off their bodies from their journey and discharge their own waste. The sound of running water cheered them throughout the day and lulled them to sleep each night.

Miguel lost time shortly after they were thrown into the cell. He had been able to mark the days with small pebbles carried by the brook, but when he ran out of those little stones, he lost count. The small pile he gathered showed that three weeks had elapsed. In those twenty-one days,

José became morose, not wanting to talk or chat, as was his usual habit. Miguel kept talking and reassuring his brother, urging him to eat and move around. He also encouraged José to chase him through the roomy high-ceilinged cell. Small round windows on one wall and at the base of the ceiling filled the cell with diffused sunlight during the day. At night it was pitch black, illuminated now and then by moonlight. Each night, their two guards checked on them by raising their lanterns that burned with a strange smell Miguel couldn't identify. He encouraged the guards to talk to him, but each time he spoke they threatened him with motions of their swords, slicing through the air. Miguel retreated each time.

After a number of days, Miguel noticed that José began to show signs of lethargy—sleeping longer spans of time throughout the day, eating less and less, and refusing to respond to Miguel's urgings. Miguel felt himself losing hope at the sight of his brother's decline. Nevertheless, he persevered in encouraging José.

One day as he sat on his straw bed with José sleeping near him, he heard faint laughter. He listened intently in the direction of the voice. It sounded again, clearly calling the name Isabella. Miguel sprang from his bed and ran to the wall where the sound seemed to originate. His heart began to race as he realized this was the name of the girl they were seeking! The girl his mother had urged him to yank out of the Alhambra. This had to be the same Isabella that brought them here!

He shouted out her name: "Isabella! Isabella! We're here to rescue you! We're prisoners! Prisoners!"

José woke up at the sound of shouting and became alarmed. "What is it?" he asked.

"Shh," Miguel said. "Listen."

The next thing they heard were strong male voices shouting orders. Then all was silent again. Miguel stood straight, arms at his sides and his mouth open as if in the next moment Isabella was going to materialize in front of him. But the voices were gone, like a dream that flees the moment one wakes up. He wailed over and over. When he stopped, there was only the silence. No one had been alerted to his shouts. No footsteps sounded in the corridor to their cell, and none approached their cell door. He and his brother were alone in that tomb of a prison.

Defeated, Miguel turned around and threw himself down on the straw. Now he felt discouraged to the depth of his heart. He pulled himself up and leaned against the wall. He then lowered his head to his chest and began to sob for the first time since they had left Seville.

José came close to him and said, “Don’t you worry, big brother. I know we’re going to be rescued soon.” He sat on the straw and hugged Miguel with his small arms, then rocked him to and fro.

10

An Honorable Death

THE WINDS OF AUTUMN SWAYED the myriads of tents dotting the vega, flapping canvas corners and blowing out the campfires that soldiers tried unsuccessfully to light. When the fires were finally lit, black billowing plumes of smoke escaped through the cold air. Rain showers had turned the dry soil to mud the day before, and spread a chill that permeated through soldiers' clothing down to their bones. The building of wooden barracks in Santa Fé continued, replacing many canvas tents. More barracks were to be built before winter began in earnest.

Juan lay bandaged on his cot while Antonio watched over him and held his hand. *If Juan dies, his parents will be devastated.* Antonio shuddered at the thought. He recalled that Juan had a fiancée whom he adored. Juan had told him of their wedding plans—how the parents had arranged it, and how Isabella, his fiancée, loved him back with all the impetuousness and reciprocity of deep love. Juan was distracted these past few weeks with the burden of not knowing where Isabella was held, which made him distant instead of concentrating on the impending war with the Moors. Antonio often found him staring and daydreaming when all his attention should've been focused on Granada. Juan had taken a big risk that day when he came to Antonio's rescue. The arrow that hit him had pierced a lung.

As if on cue, Juan stirred and began to cough. Antonio touched Juan's forehead and found it burning hot. Another strong fit of coughing racked Juan's body, and frothy blood dripped from the corner of his mouth. Antonio wiped it with a cloth just as Juan opened his eyes and tried to smile. The effort made him grimace with pain.

"Antonio . . . Anto . . ." Juan coughed again.

"Shh, shh," Antonio said. "Don't exert yourself."

"No, no!" Juan's voice gained strength. "Listen to me." Juan pulled Antonio by the collar of his shirt, bringing him close to his mouth.

"What is it?" Antonio asked.

"If something happens to . . . me." He stopped, turned his head away, and coughed again. This time it was a deep cough. "I want you to do me a favor."

"Go ahead," Antonio said.

"You know that my querida Isabella is a prisoner somewhere in this land." He stopped to rest. Antonio nodded. "Swear to me that you'll find her and protect her from harm." Juan had lifted his body up slightly as he gazed intently into his friend's eyes.

Antonio looked at him, momentarily surprised by the request, then said, "Of course I will. It'll be my honor and duty for you and her family." Antonio grasped the head of his sheathed sword as he spoke. "But you will be well in no time and do that yourself."

"Swear it!" Juan said.

"I swear with my life that I'll protect and return her to you and your family."

Juan rested back on his cot, his face peaceful. "Thank you, my friend."

"Now rest." Antonio covered him with the blanket lying at Juan's feet.

Juan closed his eyes. When Antonio heard him breathing quietly, he left him.

In the gardens of the Franciscan monastery Santa Maria de la Rábida, Fray Marchena walked this morning in peaceful contemplation. He strolled among the rosebushes and went around the gently flowing Madonna's fountain, filling his lungs with the clear morning air while gazing at the blue sky interspersed with a few small clouds. This was what he loved most—the balmy weather of Palos. He thought that in this province of Huelva, where the rivers of the Tinto and Odiel intersected, fate and providence would also unite to bring jewels to crown España.

"Ahhh!" Fray Marchena exhaled. *If life could be so blissful all over España, we would be close to Christ returning to earth.* On many occasions he had advised the townspeople in the village near the monastery that life, in addition to praying and confessing, was to be lived with joy and blissfulness. He counseled them to daily put aside childish wants and desires, end quarrels with neighbors and spouses, and to contemplate the blessings that this existence had to offer. The villagers bent their heads in submission, but he didn't see satisfied or carefree smiles. Yes, their existence was difficult and sometimes grueling, with crop failures and lack of maravedís to pay to their landlords, but ultimately, their luck would change—he believed it deeply in his soul. He kept exhorting the people and urging them to have patience for their deliverance.

He led a pious existence of repentance and confession. He admired the cartographer and mariner, Christobal Colón, who now resided at the monastery. Colón was also a pious man, practicing self-abnegation in the worship of God and never neglecting his daily Mass. He energized the entire monastery with his plans to sail to the east by a westerly direction. He thought of Colón as a saint and a savior. The one who'll save España's commerce and monetary future with the riches he'll bring home to Isabella and Ferdinand. Fray Marchena knew of the opposition to Colón by court's officials who shied away from him, calling him a foreigner with ambitions for himself. Fray Marchena dismissed them as jealous contemporaries vying for the queen's attention. He thought Colón was a visionary prophet who would accomplish much for España.

"My dear fray, up so early?"

Fray Marchena lifted his eyes to see the very man he was thinking about. Christobal Colón was standing before him, a smile in his eyes, toying with the astrolabe in his hands.

"You've appeared as if I'd conjured you," said Fray Marchena. "I was lost in my daydreaming, thinking about the treasures you'll bring back to us."

"That I'll do, for the sovereigns I love and the country that adopted me."

"I'm of the conviction that you'll deliver these promises to España. That's why we took care of your son, Diego, who'll grow up to make you proud."

"That he will. My dear departed Felipa Moniz e Perestrello made me promise before she died to educate him and see to his future as a mariner. I know that you've taken care of him during my absences, and for that I'm much indebted to you and to the monastery."

"It's our pleasure and duty to fulfill your desire for the child. He needs to study hard and not while away his time. Of course, he's only eleven and soon will be graduating to the reading of the Holy Bible, with the friars' help."

"He has my full support and has promised obedience to his teachers," Colón said.

"Now let's talk of your voyage. I'm certain the queen will relent this time. The monarchs are nearly finished with the new city of Santa Fé. You know how good the queen is to her army. Each of her soldiers is dear to her."

Colón nodded his head.

"What you need now is patience. I know it's bound to happen soon. Now the Reconquista is near its end. Granada will fall, and the Moors will leave this land forever."

Colón crossed himself.

"Santa Maria de Dios." Fray Marchena also crossed himself, invoking the Virgin's name for protection. "I sincerely believe that your mission will prevail."

Colón bowed to Fray Marchena, honoring the priest's predictions for a most fortunate outcome for his navigation and discovery. "España will prevail and conquer."

"Si, mi hijo benito," Fray Marchena intoned in approval.

Torquemada sat in his chamber, his head heavy with thought, looking over documents from Rome. He read over the writ proclaiming that the Inquisition was now open for apostates and showing how to successfully extirpate those who had lapsed after their conversion. He was familiar by now on how to root out heresy, and had perfected procedures for punishment. His thoughts turned to a question that had tormented him for some time. What should be done about the Jewish population? They were the culpable ones because they infected and swayed the New Christians. Vigilance was needed now more than ever. If only the queen would rid herself of all Jews; then España would have the chance of becoming a Catholic land. The queen must be convinced that *sangre limpia* cannot remain in España if these Jews kept intermarrying and tainting the pure Spaniard blood. A knock on the door interrupted his thoughts.

"Come in," Torquemada said.

His attendant came into the room leading in two sumptuously dressed delegates from Rome. They wore velvet vests over their long-sleeved satin shirts, red capes tied at their necks, brocade breeches topping their silk stockings, elegantly turned shoes, and hats carrying emblems and feathers of their family crest. The attendant politely left the room, and Torquemada turned to the two men, who had removed their plumed hats and were bowing to him.

Torquemada glanced at their rich garb and grimaced at the vanity and expensiveness of the clergy's way of life. His modest robes paled in comparison to their attire. Two hundred years ago, Pope Innocent III had cried, "Gold and silver I give to thee, and not for me!" as the poor and underprivileged scurried to catch showers of coins flung at them from the Lateran steps. *I cannot contradict The Church's way of life,* thought Torquemada, *but I can lead an exemplary monastic life devoid of luxuries and richness.* He took self-righteous pride in believing his riches were the abode pointing to heaven. His mission was to help the mendicant and the poor, and the orphan and the widow treading in his path.

"Your Excellency, High Inquisitor, we're here to convey the holy writ by the Pope," said one envoy.

"How can I be of service to you?" Torquemada's face had loosened up with a rare half smile that befitted his post and dignity. "I'm honored by your visit. I was just thinking about this holy mission," he said, his face now drawn in concentration.

"Your Excellency, we're here to answer any questions you might have about this Act of Faith. We have also documents from The Church to that effect." One of the envoys handed the documents to Torquemada.

"These documents have all rules governing New Christians and tell how to look for signs of relapse," said the other envoy.

Torquemada unfurled one document. The instructions clearly defined the steps for detecting heresy. In one portion of the document Torquemada read, "If you see New Christian neighbors cleaning their houses on Friday and lighting candles earlier, they are relapsing into Judaism. If they wash their hands before meals while saying prayers, they are relapsing. If they wear clean or fancy clothes on Saturday, they are relapsing into heresy. If you see them associating and fraternizing with Jews, they are relapsing into heresy." He raised his head from the document.

"I'm already familiar with those instructions," Torquemada said. "But I don't see how to proceed with regulation of punishment."

"With all due respect, Your Excellency, you'll find those instructions in the second document."

Torquemada unfurled the other parchment and saw that those instructions now included punishment for final executions: Death was to follow torture. The finality left no recourse even in the cases of recanting and rejoining the fold of Christianity. Those who kissed the cross would be spared the pyre and be garroted at the last moment. Breaking the neck would induce instant death. Those who refused to admit their errors would suffer the thousand deaths of being burned alive.

Torquemada nodded his head as he read the second document, stopping now and then to reread a sentence or two, indicating his approval by nodding again and again.

"I'll carry the instructions myself to Inspector Guerida in the secular branch of the city."

"Do you know if he's to be trusted? Or if he'll carry them out to the letter?" asked one envoy.

"He'll do more than that. You see, Inspector Guerida serves with our armed holy brotherhood set up by our Catholic king and queen: the *Hermandad*. He has found and arrested many of the accused. We're still prosecuting the case of the 'Blood Libel,' and that of the Christian child kidnapped from his parents and murdered. The accused tore out the child's heart for a blood ritual. I've transferred the case from Segovia to the new monastery at Avila, which has all the necessary equipment. The accused and his accomplices have confessed and been found guilty of the kidnapping and torturing of the young boy and tearing out his heart to concoct a poisonous blood potion to give to Christians. Only the stake will suffice to expiate the crimes of the accused and Conversos, Benito Garcia, and his seven accomplices. I've personally attended the trials and confessions."

Torquemada took a deep breath and sat upright in his chair. He projected pride in his thin body. No doubt fasting and praying had been his life's mission: fasting to purify his body and praying to purify and elevate his soul.

"Are the child's parents mourning for him? Have you found the child's body?" one of the envoys asked.

"We don't know where the parents are. I believe they've gone into hiding to mourn for their son."

"But what of the body of the child?" the same envoy asked again.

"The body has been hidden by the accused, and they'll confess when we bring them to the stake," Torquemada said.

At this statement, both envoys looked at each other and lifted their eyebrows. Doubt showed in their eyes. Torquemada saw the questioning look but remained silent. They had to trust that he employed all his skills and mastery for stamping out heresy.

"We now know why Rome depends on you and your obedience to The Church. Christ has in you the savior and guardian of the faith," the envoy said, conferring complete trust in Torquemada's methods.

Torquemada bowed to them and then quickly regained his effacing posture lest he be accused of self-vanity. "Thank you for your trust in my faith and obedience to The Church." Torquemada lowered his head in modesty and then got up to see the envoys to the door.

After they left him, he sat down again to further study the instruction in the documents. Satisfied, he reclined in the hard wooden chair with his eyes set to the ceiling and his hands in prayer.

In the dungeons of St. Jorge's Castle, Maria lay in her cell praying that her end would come sooner than later. Her wounds were infected and oozed with pus, and all her bones ached, begging for respite from the pulling and shoving of chains, straps, and whips administered daily. If she had to do it over again, she thought, she would have left with João. But no, she had done the right thing. The men could've been found if she hadn't delayed the search. They might be free now.

"And how are you this morning, Maria?" Maria couldn't see whose sardonic voice addressed her, but she knew Torquemada stood before her. She squinted at him and tried to clear her eyes by blinking, but to no avail—Torquemada remained blurry. She thought for a moment that this was a dream. She was going to wake up at any moment. Then she understood the weakness in her body, her brain, and her vision. She couldn't remember the last time she ate.

"What is it you want?" Her voice came out gravely, interrupted by a deep, cavernous cough.

"All we want is for you to tell us where you're holding the Obrigons' daughter, and you'll be free from the stake."

"I know nothing of that man's daughter. How many times . . . do I have to repeat it . . ." Her voice broke in a renewed cough.

"If you don't remember, we have a way to bring it back to your memory."

She searched her memory as to what other torture method they hadn't used, but none came to her sluggish brain. She'd been subjected to the whip, to the "water cure"—the choking and drowning sensation as eight liters of water were splashed down her throat. And the *Strapado* — the lifting and dropping of her until her arms became dislocated in their sockets, and endless hours of questioning until she fell asleep and was reawakened by hot irons applied to her bleeding feet.

With morbid anticipation, she waited for the final torture to give her death and peace. When torture didn't materialize, she lifted her sore upper body from the bed as far as she could, and saw that the torturer wasn't at her bedside to renew the agony. She then saw through her cloudy eyes an old woman being brought into her cell by a jailer. This woman looked unfamiliar to her; she had torn clothes, blood dripped down her legs and arms, and her head rested low on her chest.

"Who is it?" Maria asked.

Torquemada answered, "It's one of your coconspirators—Téresa Costa—who helped you plan your kidnapping of Isabella Obrigon." Torquemada had one of his rare smiles that looked benevolent until his victim saw the evil that lay deep below his serene façade. Maria turned away from Torquemada to stare at Téresa. That couldn't be Téresa, she thought after examination. This woman was much older and shorter than Téresa. Her body was emaciated, her chest ribs protruded through the thin linen robe she wore, her hair was white with scanty black hairs at the temples, and her bloody arms hung away from her body, puppetlike. This woman had fared no better than she did. Maria grimaced at the thought.

"I don't know this woman," Maria said.

"Yes, you do!" Torquemada's voice rose with anger. He turned to the guard standing next to the poor woman and nodded. The guard raised his whip and whipped her several times. The woman stumbled with cries and painful wails.

"Mercy, mercy, I don't know anything, I don't know anything . . ." She broke crying.

"What's your name?" Torquemada's gravelly voice rose.

When the woman didn't answer, the whip unleashed her tongue right away. "My name is Téresa Costa. I have two sons, Miguel and José, and may the God of Moses protect them. I live in the Jewish quarter in Seville." The words came out orderly as in a well-rehearsed lesson. Maria turned her head away with detachment from the scene.

Torquemada's voice rose again. "Where's the Obrigons' child?"

The woman raised her head in a questioning look. "What? I don't know what you're talking about! I don't know anything." The whip fell on her again, and she wailed loudly, her cries echoing off the concave ceiling. The whip came down again and again over her convulsed body until she raised her hands in an arresting motion. "I'll tell you if you stop." She sobbed.

"Where is she?" Torquemada asked while looking back at Maria's face.

"I took her to another city . . ." Her voice died down.

The whip fell on her again and she supplicated Torquemada, "I don't know. I don't know. I'm just inventing a place to satisfy you."

Torquemada's face took on a reddish tint. Rage seemed to flow from every pore.

Maria felt pity for the poor woman. Obviously, the old hag knew nothing of the kidnapping. She'd been rehearsed, by the whip, to falsify her name, but apparently didn't know where Isabella was. Only Maria, Téresa, Matigoro, and João Treves knew where Isabella remained hidden, and Maria was ready to sacrifice her life rather than reveal the hideout.

"Where are your children?" Torquemada asked, and before the woman could answer, the whip fell upon her over and over again. She responded with wails that sent shivers through Maria's body.

The old woman quieted down when the whip lay still at the guard's hand. She raised her head and directed her intense eyes to Torquemada.

"*Por la Madre de Dios,* don't torture me any longer. I know nothing of a child or a kidnapping. Give me release," she begged Torquemada.

Torquemada came close to the woman's face and breathed ominous words in her face. "We're going to find your boys and torture them too."

The woman's face revealed incomprehension, and she kept still for a moment trying to understand Torquemada's threat. At that moment, Maria knew that this poor woman had no children and had been set up to make her reveal Isabella's hideout. Her own bones hurt every time the whip fell on the woman. Maria felt torn between keeping her secret and letting the woman stop suffering for her. But she had to be inexorable and without pity. She could, though, give the woman a way out of her torture. It might be her death sentence.

"I know something," Maria said calmly.

Torquemada turned to her with eyebrows raised, and an air of victory swept over his death-pale face.

"I'll tell you if you let that woman go," Maria said.

Torquemada motioned the guard to take the woman away. As she was led out, the woman turned to Maria and said, "Bless you."

Torquemada turned to Maria and waited for her to speak.

"All I know," said Maria, "is that a young girl was taken from Seville and transported to Aragon."

"How do you know this information?" Torquemada asked.

"I heard it through town when I went to make my egg delivery to the Obrigons' home."

"You're lying! We watched your home day and night for anyone entering and leaving. You didn't make deliveries after she disappeared!"

Maria wanted to shout at him that Guerida's men were inefficient, bumbling idiots. That they came upon her house after everyone had fled the house: Téresa, João, and the men and women who met the night before. She'd been targeted because of her connection to the note left at the Obrigons' door. Why then the charade of Téresa's double, and what about her children? It was a disturbing thought. Téresa must be in danger. What's more, her children were in mortal peril of falling into the clutches of the secular arm of the justice administered by Torquemada. She shivered at the thought. She glanced at Torquemada and saw his quizzing eyes and imagined his slavering thoughts.

"I did deliver my eggs," she said quietly.

Seeing that Maria had cunningly lied to free the old woman, Torquemada flew into a rage, but no whip fell upon her. She sensed that he was through with her, but the Inquisition's tribunal was not.

"I'm finished with you!" he shouted. "You're now going to sign papers that you were a heretic, following in the Judaizing rituals in your home. If you kiss the cross and return to Christianity, you will be garroted and absolved from the pyre."

At that last word, a cold shiver went through Maria's body. She knew quite well that confessing to practicing Jewish rituals was a death sentence. Would Torquemada relent his torture without her confession? Or would there be more punishment if she didn't sign those papers? For now she would linger in this dungeon until her accusers, jailers, and the society that put her there decided her fate

.

11

The March of Time

ON A SOMBER MORNING, A gathering took place in Calle de los Madres: black coaches lined up along the entire length of the street, filling its width and making it impossible for pedestrians to walk through. The coaches were draped with black crepe, and black silk flowers garnished both sides of the horses' bridles. The animals huffed impatiently and pawed the pavement with their hooves while the coach drivers tried to contain them, hoping their coach riders would finally emerge from the Obrigons' mansion.

As if on cue, the double metal gates opened with a grinding sound. Coffin bearers walked in slow motion to the crest-decorated Obrigon family hearse drawn by six horses. In the first row behind the coffin marched Don Arturo Obrigon, supported by the duke de la Mancha on his right and Mayor José de Gerondi on his left. Don Obrigon wore a black hat matching his somber attire. He walked with difficulty, swaying and tripping as he neared his coach and climbed into it with his friends' help. In the second row of mourners leaving the Obrigon home, Don Pedro Escobar held the arm of his wife, Doña Maria Escobar. She was sobbing, and he was murmuring in her ear. Seville's city functionaries, including Inspector Guerida and his men; close friends and neighbours; and the Obrigons' household formed the end of the procession.

The coffin was loaded onto the hearse. The drivers gave the signal, and the hearse moved slowly forward, followed by the long row of carriages in a queue to the outskirts of Seville.

In the first carriage, Don Obrigon lamented, "Why did the Savior allowed this to happen? Why?" Don Obrigon wiped his eyes. "I tried everything . . . medications . . . coaxing and talking sense into her. Patience, patience, I told her. Isabella would be found. Nothing would help. Nothing!"

He wailed, tore at his garments, gasping as if he were suffocating. Mayor de Gerondi and the duke de la Mancha attended to him by untying the shirt bow around his neck.

"Breathe slowly, breathe slowly, slowly," said the mayor.

Still breathing with difficulty, Don Obrigon nodded to reassure his friend. He turned his head to the duke de la Mancha and gave him a pitiful look. He was silent the rest of the way, limp with grief.

The carriages reached the cemetery and the grave awaiting Doña Estrella Obrigon's body, where Father Angelo stood preparing his sacerdotal garment until the mourners gathered around him. He began the service with a prayer, then gave Don Obrigon the sign to read a eulogy for his wife, Estrella. The grief-stricken husband declined. Father Angelo nodded and took over the duty of extolling the deceased woman.

"In the name of God, the merciful Father, we commit the body of Doña Estrella Obrigon, who was a loving wife and mother, to the peace of the grave." Following a lengthy sermon, Father Angelo grabbed three handsful of earth, one at a time, from the mound of dirt lying next to the grave. As each fell on the coffin, he said, "From dust you came, to dust you shall return. Jesus Christ, our saviour, shall raise you up on the last day."

Supported by Mayor Gerondi, Don Obrigon moved close to the gaping hole and let a handful of soil fall on Doña Estrella's coffin. Each mourner took turns saying his or her farewell to the woman who had been the mother of Isabella.

This morning the palace was in commotion, and Friday's court was taken off the schedule. Tomás de Torquemada had sent a strange written request to the queen, whose childhood confessor he had been. The missive said that the queen must affix her signature for sentencing prisoner Maria Donarojo, but it didn't mention the crime committed by this wretched woman. Torquemada would reveal the reason upon addressing the court. Queen Isabella looked down with annoyance at the unsealed missive and nodded to her minister to let Torquemada enter.

Torquemada approached the throne with a slouched but steady gait, and Queen Isabella couldn't help but notice his emaciated body and pallid face.

"You don't appear in good health, my dear Torquemada," she said. Isabella used frankness with the inquisitor in all her dealings with him. She knew of his piety and devotion to the true faith, but his duty and love for faith went beyond the boundaries set by The Church in Rome. She knew for a fact that Torquemada fasted periodically, more than usually demanded by his Dominican order, and rejected all gluttony.

"My dear queen, your concern elevates and honors me. I assure your Illustrious Highness, I'm in the best of health," said Torquemada.

Queen Isabella nodded, then abruptly said, "My Fridays are devoted to my subjects in their daily concerns."

"Dear revered queen, it's for one of your subjects that I require an audience."

Queen Isabella raised an interrogative eyebrow.

"It's about an innocent young girl, named with your benevolent name. I'm speaking about Isabella Obrigon, my queen."

The queen raised a surprised look. "I'm familiar with the child. I promised as godmother to protect her. Her mother, Doña Estrella Obrigon, is a distant cousin of mine. We were overjoyed when we heard that she had a daughter, after a wait of many years."

"That's exactly my point, my Queen. I regret to inflict pain on Your Highness, but you see . . . Isabella's mother, may she be blessed, joined the angels about a month ago. She died of grief."

The anticipated response of shock and grief crossed the queen's serene but serious face. "I had no knowledge of Doña Estrella's death. Please convey my condolences to her husband."

"My queen," Torquemada started. He lowered his head to the large ochre crucifix hanging about his neck and, lifting it, kissed it with eyes shut in reverence. "The child has disappeared, kidnapped by a band of heretics."

Queen Isabella tried to contain her indignation. "Have they been arrested?" she asked.

"Yes, my queen, they have been. We're still searching for several men and women who have escaped. But we"—he quickly hastened to add—"we're close to an arrest."

"I'm grieved that this happened to the Obrigon family. Please keep me informed of new developments." She made a motion of her hand to dismiss Torquemada.

"Please, please," Torquemada interjected. "I'm here, dear Queen, to request a longer audience." He disregarded her silence and pressed on. "It's for that reason that we must rid ourselves of the Jews infecting our midst. We must expel them! They'll continue in their heresy to infect New Christians, and the kidnapping of our youth, as in the La Guardia Niño Santo. We must rid ourselves of these infidel Jews and Moors, once and for all. Spain will then be united under the Catholic monarchs and become the Catholic nation," Torquemada pleaded.

Queen Isabella followed Torquemada's passionate plea with great interest. She felt conflicting emotions between her duty to her loyal New Christian subjects, but losing patience with delays to her lifelong mission of ruling Catholic Spain. She had battled these feelings since her brother, Henry IV, had brought her to court. Henry had been castigated by his treasurer as a vulgar spender on frivolities to the point of emptying the royal coffers. His debauchery; his repudiation of his pious wife, Blanche of Aragon; and the alleged affair of his second wife, Joanna the Portuguese, were enough to disgust her. Isabella then swore to her confessor that if she were queen, she would rid Spain of the depraved, unbelievers, heretics, and adulterers. But to rid Spain of loyal subjects who abided by her rule was unconscionable.

She also knew that ridding Spain of its Jewish craftsmen—silversmiths and goldsmiths, weavers, winemakers, financiers, tax collectors, and moneylenders—would take away so much tax revenue it would administer a great blow to her realm. At the same time, the continuous war with the

Moors had depleted their war coffers. Isabella dismissed the whole prospect as an outrageous and dangerous idea to the realm, akin to what her brother Henry had done to Spain earlier.

Queen Isabella fixed her blue-green eyes on Torquemada with a resolute air. "I've heard and weighed your request, dear Fray Torquemada. We'll definitely wait until after the conquest of Granada to deal with this problem. Wait for my word on this subject. But we—my husband, the king, and I—will give this weighty decision much consideration after the war is settled." With a movement of her chin, she signaled to Torquemada that her audience was over.

Torquemada lowered his head with closed eyes, kissed the queen's ring, and silently left the audience chamber.

In a recessed alley in the Juderia, Ana Sarauel's two-room house reflected her pride. She kept her house with care, attending to any repairs while keeping the small garden off the courtyard filled with flowers and fragrant herbs. Her house lay within two narrow alleys from Téresa Costa's house. After the last meeting, when João Treves had made his plea for all New Christians and Jews to band together, Ana came home to her empty house made of stone and sat for a long time near the cold hearth. She used wood sparingly and would not light a fire until it was absolutely necessary; Seville didn't succumb to cold evenings, nor did it suffer cold weather as did other cities in the north. Now, however, she sat shivering near the gaping black hearth. Was it something that João had said at the last meeting that chilled her to the bone? Or was it a portent of things to come in España?

She had remained Jewish and couldn't accept baptism. Understandably, not having children made it easier for her to remain in the Mosaic faith of her forefathers. She was a midwife, a woman of humble background and modest means. She had nothing to lose except her home and a few hundred maravedís she had saved over the years.

Ana was sixty. It was time for her to enjoy her twilight years in modest comfort. But she was concerned about her friend in the Juderia. They were neighbors and close friends, and Ana had midwifed the birth of Téresa's sons. And that's what concerned her tonight. During the last two weeks, she'd noticed the door and blue shutters of Téresa's whitewashed home remained shut, and no sounds or lights came from within. Téresa's two sons often visited, but now they seemed to have vanished. Her chest tightened at the thought: *What could it mean?*

Ana knew that as a New Christian and Converso, Téresa could've moved outside the Juderia to live with the Christian population in Seville. She also knew that Téresa couldn't bring herself to leave the home she had made with Nahum. After his death, she told Ana she would remain in the same house, living with Nahum's memory. Téresa then embarked on the perilous path of holding clandestine meetings with Conversos, and she mingled with the Juderia Jewry despite the danger.

Ana feared for her life; she knew that fraternizing with New Christians might've spiked the danger for being found out. If events forced her out of the Juderia, the only recourse left to her was to go to her wealthy cousin, Don Isaac Abravanel, a financial advisor to the royal family. Ana knew that her cousin, Don Abravanel, who'd remained a Jew himself, would protect her from hate reprisals. Unlike her cousin, who was immune from wearing the badge, she had to wear the Jewish red badge on the shoulder of her gabardine sleeve. To alleviate her growing worries, she thought it best to visit her cousin's home.

It was dusk, and she had a few hours until curfew to return home before the gates were locked, sealing the Juderia from the rest of Seville. She dressed quickly and covered her head with a black lace mantilla that extended over her long robed skirts but left the accursed badge visible on her sleeve. By decree, she wasn't allowed to wear a warm cloak over her robes lest it may hide her Jewish badge. She felt cold when she exited from the Puerta de la Juderia leading outside. The day had advanced with dark clouds presaging another scarce rain of the season for Seville. The air felt almost wet.

Moving quickly through narrow alleys, she passed tiled patios and small garden homes lit by candlelight. The faint murmur of voices and laughter escaping through drawn shutters made her feel lonely. She sensed that she was standing outside of life. As a Jewess, there were constant reminders from the ruling localities to make her aware of how different she was from the rest of the population. She had to live in the Juderia, wear the badge signifying her Jewishness, pay additional taxes from which the

Christian populations were exempt, and was shut in for the night in the Juderia.

Following a series of wider streets, she crossed the Guadalquivir River and found herself in the lush garden neighborhood of the elite society of Seville. She was about to turn a corner on La Madre Street when a stern voice shouted for her to stop. Frightened, she turned around and stared into a jandarmá with a sword at his side.

"And where do you think you're going?" the jandarmá asked.

"I was just going to see my cousin," said Ana.

A corner smile appeared on the policeman's lips. "You have rich cousins living here?"

The sardonic tone was not lost on Ana. Wearing the ubiquitous Jewish badge made her a target.

She raised her head with pride but toned down her voice. "Yes. As a matter of fact, my cousin is very rich. He's a close friend of King Ferdinand."

The jandarmá looked piqued by her arrogance when she quickly said, "My cousin is Don Isaac Abravanel. Ask your superior at the police station. He'll confirm my story. I don't have much time left. I have to be back to the Juderia before nightfall."

The jandarmá said, "Go to your cousin. I'll follow you to see if you're lying."

Within minutes, Ana—with the jandarmá on her heels—came to a small white palace surrounded by walls capped with wrought-iron spikes. She pulled the leather strap to the cast-iron bell that sounded in musical tone. A servant opened the door with an inquiring look on his face.

"Tell your master that a cousin of his wants to see him," the jandarmá said.

"What's your name?" the servant addressed her.

"Ana Sarauel."

The servant closed the door and returned quickly. "He'll see you now."

The jandarmá, looking discomfited, scratched his head, then turned and left them.

Ana kissed the *mezuza* on the doorpost, containing the sacred Deuteronomy parchment of verses, and was shown into a marble vestibule, where her cousin Isaac Abravanel came forward to greet her.

"My dear Ana! It's good to see you. Come in, come in."

She followed him into his study, where he pulled out a leather chair for her. As she sat, she glanced at the richly carved beamed ceiling, the divan's cerulean-blue damask fabric, and the brocade draperies. How blessed was her cousin to own such a home. His entire family, including his three sons, was a pride to the Jewish community. Her cousin had donated many a maravedís to help the poor of the Juderia and many less fortunate than she. In contrast, her family had always been of moderate means with the craftsman skills of weaving, jewelry making, and engraving. Don Abravanel's skills were those of mathematics and money lending. Since both Ana and Isaac could trace their lineage to the house of King David, she wondered why her mother, who'd also come from the same illustrious line, hadn't been as prosperous?

"What can I do for you, dear cousin?" Don Abravanel said.

Ana kept silent for a moment, and then said, "I don't know if you're aware, but there are many rumors going on in the Juderia."

A veiled look of worry came upon Abravanel's face. "What do you mean?"

"Some Conversos I know have disappeared from their home, and the rest of the Juderia is feeling a low and rising current coming from the community at large."

"Have you heard anything that might give cause to be worried?"

Ana kept silent for a moment, then spoke in a low voice. "Well, according to a source I can't reveal, Torquemada has been frequently meeting with the queen."

"And?" He urged her on.

"He wants to rid Spain of all Jews."

Ana noticed right away the incredulous look in Don Abravanel's eyes.

"You can't believe that," he said. "I'm closely and amicably associated with King Ferdinand, and he returns my friendship. I never heard a word from him nor the queen about a mass exodus from Spain."

Ana raised her voice. "Mark my words, my dear cousin—the fire is at the gates and at your door!"

Abravanel's face turned pale at Ana's fiery warning. He shook his head. "I believe we've nothing to fear. I'm a close confidant to King Ferdinand. If there are rumors, they're being spread by alarmists."

Ana tried to remain calm. "You don't understand, my cousin. Every day there are arrests and jail sentences for the Conversos. Nothing has changed since the Inquisition was established in Castile in 1478!"

Abravanel looked indignant. "But you're a Jewess, not a Converso. You shouldn't fear the arm of the Inquisition."

"It's precisely because of the Conversos that we're in danger. They're still assembling with the Jews, and they still practice Judaism rituals. They can't give up their forefathers' faith. It would be like cutting off their own right arms." Ana kept silent about Téresa's and her sons' disappearance. "If not for the Jewish community's sake, believe it for your son's sake. It's your duty!"

At those words she thought she saw Abravanel shiver. She knew that it wasn't long ago, in 1483, that he had fled Portugal with a price on his head put there by the new king. How could he be so fearless? Seeing her cousin deep in thought, Ana asked him, "What will you do?"

"Look, go home now," he said. "I'll keep my eyes and ears open. I'll send word to you if there's danger." Abravanel searched her face to see if he had convinced her.

With a feeling of impending doom, Ana stood up, unsteady on her feet. The danger was pressing and palpable. Her cousin's stubbornness and blindness to events happening all around them may be their undoing. *We're all doomed.*

"Adonai, ayudarmos." She invoked God's help as she shuffled out of his house feeling defeated and hurried back to the Juderia.

In an alley just outside the Juderia, she thought of her friends, the Medina family. Francisco and Adela de Medina were a Morisco family of five, who were converts to Christianity from Islam. Over a century ago, their grandparents chose to remain in Castile after its conquest by the Trastámara line. Ana knew that Francisco, Adela, and their three sons still secretly practiced their *Mahomet* prayers and rituals. As their midwife, she had been privy to those rituals and knew he'd had his three boys circumcised, keeping it secret from the authorities.

She arrived at their doorstep at the end of the alley and rang the doorbell three times. Francisco de Medina opened the door. "Come in. *Ahlan wa sahlan*!" Francisco welcomed Ana.

"As-Salamu Alaykum," replied Ana. "I'm here to see you on an urgent matter."

Francisco frowned and let her in, making sure no one lurked in the alley.

Ana entered their humble whitewashed living quarters and sat where Francisco indicated—a chair in front of the warm fire crackling in the hearth. A savory aroma wafted from a three-legged bronze pot hanging over the fire pit.

"My boys and my wife are in the back room," he said. "What brings you here? I hope it's good news with Allah."

Ana looked him straight in the eyes and breathed her fears in a low voice. "They're many rumors that . . ." She hesitated before administering the blow. ". . . well, maybe not just rumors, but sayings that a great calamity will befall on the Jews in Castile and Aragon."

Francisco's face remained unmoved at first. He was a secret Morisco, practicing his Muslim rites away from prying eyes. "How did you hear of this terrible omen?" His voice seemed to tremble.

"I have my sources that I can't reveal right now. You know that the Conversos have been persecuted on and off for many years. You and your family also converted in order to survive." It pained Ana to alarm her friend with no proof or evidence.

"How do you know if you'll be safe tomorrow? You know that I consider your family like my own, your sons as my own sons. I couldn't imagine something happening to you, Adela, or your sons."

Francisco raised his hand to reassure her. "Don't worry about our safety. We're faithfully observing the Christian religion and no one can say otherwise. But pork . . ." He stopped with a grimacing face to show his contempt. "We tried to wash our mouths every time we had to taste it in public. No one has complained so far, and I don't foresee any problems in the future."

Ana forced a smile, but could only show tight lips. She got up to leave, then stopped at the threshold. “If anything happens or you need me for any reason, please let me know right away.”

Francisco de Medina smiled with effort as she left his house.

The days and nights had become one and the same for Miguel and his brother. The only break in the monotony was when the guards brought their meals. Miguel begged them over and over to see Boabdil, but to no avail. One day Miguel hatched a plan to get them out.

“José?” He called out to his brother, who was sitting in a fetal position on his straw bed.

José lifted his head slightly, and his questioning eyes peered above his crossed arms.

“I’m going to get us out of here one way or another,” Miguel said.

“What do you mean?” José’s voice sounded apprehensive. Miguel could see that he had alarmed his brother.

“Don’t you worry,” he quickly said. “I want you to do exactly as I tell you. You understand?”

José nodded his head.

At the appointed hour for their meals, the guard slipped their food through the trap door, but when he heard sobbing he opened the cell window. Miguel was standing over a straw-stuffed replica of his brother’s form, completely covered with a blanket. José, meanwhile, stood plastered against the wall near the door, ready to flee as soon as the door opened.

“What’s going on here?” The guard peered through the window.

“It’s my brother. I think he’s dead.” Miguel broke out in stronger sobs and started wailing.

The guard hesitated at first, having no backup. “You make a wrong move and I’ll kill you,” he threatened as he closed the window.

Miguel glanced across the cell at José and nodded at him. He heard the guard’s exasperated sigh as the keys jingled in the keyhole. The bolt scraped against wood, and the door creaked on its hinges. The guard came in with his saber unsheathed and cautiously approached the form in the bed. Miguel dashed to the entrance, pulled José from behind the door, and slipped outside the cell with him. He slammed the door shut as the guard ran to it, locking it quickly with the keys that were still attached to it. They scurried down the dark twisting corridors while the guard yelled for them to return. When they emerged from the labyrinth of corridors with closed cells where no other prisoner could be seen or heard, Miguel and José breathed a sigh of relief. The brightness and warmth of the sun caressed their cheeks and blinded them at the same time.

"Ahhh." Both Miguel and José sighed with pleasure.

"Come on!" Miguel urged José. "We must make haste!" He looked around him for a way out, but they were surrounded by heavy walls and were stumped to find themselves in a densely wooded area.

They climbed the nearest hill, then saw two young women walking leisurely on a hilly path above them. One of the women spotted them and cried out. "Look!"

It was too late to run. One of the guards accompanying the women ran down the hill with his raised sword gleaming in the sunlight while the other remained behind.

José began to cry with fright, and Miguel shielded him behind his back.

"Don't harm them!" One woman screamed the order. The charging guard stopped in his tracks, then retreated back a few steps. Miguel grabbed his brother's hand and ran toward the two young women. He bowed to them as he reached them.

"Please, please, Your Highnesses—save us from death!"

The two women first looked surprised, then both laughed at him. Their protective guards raised their swords simultaneously and left them hanging inches from Miguel's and José's faces. One of the women, still with a lingering smile upon her face, addressed him. "We're not princesses!" She motioned to the guards to pull back their swords. She then turned to Miguel. "Who are you?"

"I'm Miguel. This is my brother José. We've been wallowing in a cell for days!" He turned around and pointed to the low-domed building where they had been holed up. "We want to see His Excellency, King Boabdil. Our mother is a friend to the king."

"And who's your mother?"

"Téresa Costa."

One of the young women cried out, screaming over and over. "Your mother is a traitor! A traitor, you hear me? She kidnapped me and brought me here!"

The other young woman stood speechless and pale. She eyed her companion with pity.

Miguel felt a blow under the accusation he did not deny. Astonished he said, "You must be Isabella! Don Obrigon's daughter. You're the very girl I'm seeking. I came to escort you to Cordoba, where you'll be safe."

"I'd rather die than follow you. You're a traitor, too, like your mother!"

Miguel didn't reply to the stinging branding. He felt powerless to disprove her fiery words. Now he was sure to lose his head and would lead his brother to the same fate.

"I am Sarah," the other young woman said. "I'll see the king and relay your request. You must go back to your cell. I can't release you nor interfere in the king's affairs." She then motioned to one of their guards, who bowed down before her. Sarah took Isabella's arm, and they both headed toward the palace followed by one of their private guards.

With his sword drawn, the remaining guard pushed them back toward their prison. Upon reaching their cell, the guard inside the cell fell upon Miguel. He hit him hard on the back with his sword's hilt. The blow took away Miguel's breath as he crumpled to his feet, then the sword's hilt hit again on his crouched legs. "Get up, dog!" the guard yelled.

"Stop! Stop!" José yelled at the guard.

Miguel got up on shaky legs and moved haltingly toward the back of the cell. The guard hit him hard again, this time on the head. Miguel fell to the floor unconscious.

"¿Hermano querido avla, avla, por El Dio?" José prodded his brother to speak to him.

Miguel opened his eyes with a pitiful smile. "Don't worry, my little brother. I was faking it," he said while rubbing his throbbing head.

José became angry with him. "You let me believe that he killed you! You rat!"

"I know," said Miguel. "I'm sorry. But now I'm sure we'll be saved." He grabbed his brother, and it was his turn to hug him in an embrace and rock him in his arms.

Columbus looked lovingly at the rag map with the ocean as his focus. Mist filled his eyes. His most cherished venture seemed to have receded further and further away from his grasp. He clenched his hands into fists, turning his knuckles white, and painfully tried to control the anger seething inside him. At the age of forty he was considered to be an old man, with graying temples, slouched gait, and a morose attitude. It seemed he would grow very old without accomplishing his most desired dream. Why didn't the Spanish court see his worth—his knowledge and his ambition that would allow him to fulfill his destiny? Surely, he had to be patient, as his dear friend and mentor, Fray Antonio de Marchena, had urged him, but how could he be patient when his life was passing him by? The hourglass perched on his worktable reminded him of the years elapsing, day after day and hour after hour. Impatiently, he turned away from the worktable and looked out the barred window of the monastery.

The Franciscan monastery was built on a rocky mountain overlooking the place where the Tinto and Odiel Rivers merged their waters in white foaming spray. The monastery had once been a Moorish fortress and watchtower in the twelfth century, before the Knights Templar seized it to defend the inhabitants from the pirates who were sacking the coast.

Columbus turned away from the clerestory window feeling cold. On this blessed day of the Lord, the twelfth day of October, he was dressed in a fur-bordered robe because the days and nights were now getting cooler. He left his cell and moved with haste along the columned cloister and brick-paved corridors to Fray Antonio Marchena's cell at the other end of the monastery. He hesitated in front of the wooden door, then raised his hand and knocked resolutely.

"Come in," called Marchena's soft voice.

The door squeaked on its hinges, and Columbus found himself in a still smaller cell than his own, looking down at Marchena genuflecting in front of the alabaster statue of the Virgin Mary. Marchena made the sign of the cross, kissed the small silver cross he wore at his neck, then raised his eyes to Columbus as he lifted his rheumatism-stricken body off the floor with difficulty.

"This fall season is reminding me of my older knees and bones," he lamented to Columbus.

"My dear Fray Marchena, please don't remind me of old age. It's the very subject that has me coming to you in supplication."

Fray Marchena raised his eyes again, this time with a quizzical expression.

"My dear Colón," he said, using Columbus's Spanish name, "what could be more pressing on this cold night than warming oneself by the fire of the hearth and drinking a cup of warm and blessed wine?" His face broke into a reassuring smile as he headed for his credenza, where his wine carafe sat. He took two silver goblets and filled them with the red liquid.

"Let's drink to the approaching deliverance of the Catholic land from all heretics," he said as he handed Columbus a goblet.

Columbus half-smiled as he took the goblet from Marchena's hand and raised it into the air. "Yes, let's drink to the Father, Son, and the Holy Ghost. May they bring us good tidings from the sovereigns for a swift victory in Granada," he said, crossing himself.

Fray Marchena crossed himself again, then raised his goblet, and they both drained their cups. Marchena filled the cups again and asked, "What seems to be troubling you, my friend?"

Columbus was quiet for a moment, then his suppressed feelings tumbled out. "I have a foreboding that the monarchs will forget the whole venture." His shoulders caved in.

"My dear Colón, you know that I believe wholeheartedly in this voyage, and so does Fray Juan Pérez," he reassured him. "This is why he's pleading for you right now at the court in Córdoba." He went to Columbus, put his right hand on the navigator's shoulder, and forced him to sit down on a bench near the fire in the hearth. "I also believe," he continued, "that the Catholic monarchs want this quest even more that you do."

Columbus raised questioning eyes.

"What I mean is, the royal coffers are emptying at a faster rate now that preparations are almost ready for the last bastion to fall."

Columbus nodded his head. This last bastion, Granada, was delaying his own conquest: the conquest of the oceans.

"As I was saying," Marchena continued. "By the end of this year of our Lord, 1491, we'll see miracles! I'm speaking now of a unified Christian España. The glory of Christendom!"

Columbus raised his eyebrows, not fully understanding what Fray Marchena insinuated. Marchena hastened to explain. "You see, my dear friend, España will be free not only of the Moors but also of all infidels."

"You mean . . ." Columbus could not finish his sentence.

"Yes, my friend. All infidels—and that include the Moors, the Jews, and Gypsies. All who cannot see the true faith, huh?"

Columbus felt a chill reaching down to his bones despite the fire's warmth in the small cell.

"You can't mean all the Jews?"

The proof was Fray Marchena's heavy silence. Columbus felt a crushing weight on his chest. He gasped for air and rushed out the cell for breath. When he recovered, he reentered the cell and faced Marchena squarely. "You know that the voyage is to be funded by the Jewish financiers in España! The Jews will leave the land and take all their wealth with them!"

"That won't be possible. They can't take any gold or silver with them. They'll leave everything behind. They can take with them only their belongings."

"How did you hear of this?" Columbus asked, hoping it was only a rumor, not wanting to believe Marchena's words.

"Through the palace. Every time I went to see the queen, the rumors were thick. I wouldn't ask Queen Isabella; it would be arrogant on my part to quiz her."

"Now I know why I felt this foreboding," said Columbus. "I knew bad luck was plaguing me."

"No, no, my friend. It's good luck. Because once the land is free of infidels, the king and queen can devote their entire efforts to the voyage! Go, my friend, with my blessings. It's written that you'll undertake this voyage soon."

Columbus remained skeptical. Nevertheless, he concentrated on Marchena's words of encouragement. "Thank you, Fray Marchena. Thank you for supporting me and for your friendship." Columbus gave Fray Marchena a warm embrace and left the cell feeling much lighter.

In the seaport of Palos, life flowed peacefully. Each day followed the next, month by month and year by year since the Moors had been chased out of Huelva's province. The docks were piled high with export bundles and crates that arrived daily on ships from Italy, France, and the Netherlands. The ships' holds were bulging with imported grain from Italy, damasks and linen from the silk route out of China, precious metals from northern Europe, and whimsical millinery from Paris. Spain's Merchant Marine had a banner year bringing raw material to be fashioned into arms and artillery, costly fabrics for the knights fighting daily on the Moorish frontier, and grain to feed the masses of soldiers on foot. The seamen, meanwhile, worked hard for a mediocre pay of thirty sueldos per month, giving them only enough for sustenance and congested shelter in hay barns, musty home attics, and rat-infested warehouses.

On one of the docks, a robust man worked without a shirt. His linen pants were rolled up at his calves and held by a leather black belt, and a red bandana on his head was knotted at its four corners to protect him from the radiating sun. His square jaw and aquiline nose were capped by a shock of white hair, and green eyes burned from a tanned face.

Above the din of the men lifting and unloading the merchandise, a supervisor yelled orders to the workers.

"Move your lazy bones, João! At this rate your day will end at midnight! You have much more to unload!"

João lifted his head and wiped the sweat dripping from his forehead down to his neck with the bandana. He remained silent but quickened his pace. When all the bales were unloaded from the carrack ship and deposited on the docks, he straightened his sore back, then rubbed it for a moment. He looked at the blue sea beyond the breakers and fancied himself on a ship sailing west past Golfo de Cádiz and around Cape St. Vincent by the coast of Portugal. He tousled his white hair with his right hand while thinking about the escape that seemed unreachably distant. Then he hit his forehead with self-reproach.

"¡Qué bovo estoy!" he admonished himself. *I'm not going to give up my hopes to reach this Promised Land. If anything untoward happens, it will be a long wait for the voyage to materialize,* he thought. He waited daily to hear of a grand voyage in the offing, but each day passed with no such news. *Have I been overly hopeful? Has it been a chimera from my imagination?* Again he hit his forehead, seeing how quickly his good intentions dissolved.

A whistle marked the end of his day. He picked up his ragged jacket lying on a bale nearby and made his way out of the docks toward the town. He found lodgings at the Jupiter Inn, where a rented space was located near the stables. In exchange for additional chores—cleaning stables and caring for the sheltered horses—he could get by on the few *sueldos* he earned. As he entered the stables tonight, he noticed a new black horse had been brought in while he'd labored on the docks. He wondered what wealthy cavalier might have traveled on this silver horse saddle. The horse looked sturdy, somewhat soiled with dust by his travels. João lit a lantern and approached the animal. Upon hearing a gentle neighing, he extended his hand to caress his mane.

"I'll call you Black Knight," João said in his ear. The horse quieted, bent his head, and continued munching on straw while his tail swayed back and forth. João took a hand brush and began to remove the dust caked on his flank and tail, revealing the black luster of the horse's coat. João opened a fresh bale of hay and began spreading it among the horses stabled there for the night when he noticed a man standing by the stable door in the waning light. João squinted his eyes to see the visitor, but the man approached him in the poorly lit stable and stood in silence in front of him.

"What's your pleasure, noble cavalier?" João asked him, lifting his lamp above his head.

"I want to make sure you're taking good care of my horse."

"Please see for yourself," João ventured.

After a brief exam the cavalier said, "He's well taken care of. *Gracias*."

João bowed his head.

"If you're ever in want of a job, Pinzón, the docks' manager, will send you to my estate."

João bowed again, and noticed the *fleurie* Cross of Santiago de Compostela on his vest. No doubt, this cavalier was of noble birth.

"I'm Don Alonso de Aguilar. I'll need my horse early tomorrow morning. Please see that he's ready for the road."

A stunned João bowed and said, "I will."

Don Alonso de Aguilar quickly left the stable.

The illustrious cavalier was the same great general who had distinguished himself in many battles against the Moors and in the conquest of fortresses a few leagues away from Granada. Why was the general in Palos instead of preparing for war? He should've been readying for the final assault on Granada, unless the general had been sent from the queen to enquire on a voyage in the making. As these thoughts ran through his mind, he walked to a corner in the stable where a washbasin sat on a wooden crate. He cleaned himself as best he could, took the lantern to a cubicle in back of the stable, and lay down on a blanket drawn over a pile of straw. He blew out the candle and lay awake in darkness for a long time before he fell asleep.

The guard prostrated himself in front of King Boabdil, trembling. His face showed the fear of an anticipated deathblow.

"My you live long and prosper, my king, with health for many years to come in peace and in battle." The guard's body trembled with dread. "I was only carrying out orders! Ahmed Kalil and Mansur Abbas of the second brigade brought the prisoners for me to watch over. I had no idea, no idea whatsoever, they were under your protection!"

"Silence, dog!" King Boabdil shouted. He got up from his golden throne, walked around the poor trembling creature, and kicked him several times. The guard fell and rolled down the steps in front of King Boabdil's throne.

"These same two scouts were to spot King Ferdinand's armies marching toward Granada. They failed to report to me," Boabdil roared. "Kalil and Mansur were executed! They cost us an opportunity to thin the enemy's ranks!" He turned to his Nubian guards standing at attention along the walls and motioned to them. "Throw him in a dungeon." King Boabdil's face was red with anger as he returned to his throne. The reluctant guard was dragged away kicking and begging.

Miguel, watching the whole scene, decided to interject. "Illustrious King." Miguel's voice was timid. He stood near the throne's platform, holding José's hand. "Dear King, it's not his fault. I'm to blame."

"It's precisely for that reason that he'll be thrashed. What if a spy had come here with nefarious intent to take my throne or my life? He has to be punished!"

Miguel lowered his head, ashamed for questioning the king's actions. He bowed to the king and nudged his brother José to do the same.

"Now, tell me again the reason your mother sent you to us?" said Boabdil.

Miguel struggled for a moment to reply, then said in one breath, "To bring Isabella to Cordoba."

"You mean that was your mother's wish?" Boabdil's face looked puzzled. "Isabella has all the comforts here in Granada. All that her heart could desire."

"With all due respect, King Boabdil, life here in Granada, and under your benevolent eye, has been most generous for Isabella. Anyone would be blessed to spend time in God's paradise." Miguel stopped, trying not to overdo his praise for Granada's life lest the king himself would detect a hint of irony in his words. They were in a precarious situation—being inside the enemy's den but having a refuge from the clutches of Torquemada.

"No need to thank me." Boabdil raised his arresting hand. "Now we're going to supper, and I'll decide when you will take the young lady under escort on your journey."

Miguel bowed before Boabdil and proceeded to follow the king into an open courtyard where a sumptuous meal awaited them. Miguel looked in vain for Isabella. Only the king's men, closest advisors, and trusted friends surrounded Boabdil. Miguel ate in silence and eyed his brother to do the same. The food dazzled the palate, but José also ate in silence without much appetite, watching his brother carefully. When the repast ended with fruits and sweets, the two brothers thanked Boabdil and were escorted out of the open courtyard. Through white marble corridors they followed their guide until they came to a room at the end of a hall. The guide let them into a large room overlooking a small garden and decorated with damask draperies. Miguel turned around to acknowledge their guide, but he had disappeared. He ran to the door but found it locked. José's face was already turning white when Miguel turned back to him.

"Hush, my little brother. We're treated with respect by the king. I'm sure it means that we're locked in for our protection."

José stood speechless.

Miguel glanced through the open arched windows at the attached courtyard below, and discovered three-meter walls surrounding it capped by broken colorful glass. He went back inside the room and looked out the opposite windows from the courtyard. They were eight to nine meters off the ground. Jumping out on the court below would kill them. He sighed at the discovery. *We're locked in a golden cage.*

"Let us rest here for the night, little brother. Tomorrow will bring us closer to our aim."

José sat silently with tears flowing down his youthful round cheeks.

"Come on," Miguel exhorted his brother. "Let's clean ourselves and get a good night's rest.

12

A Secret Revealed

ACCORDING TO THE PILE OF pebbles she hid in a wooden coffer under the window seat, Isabella calculated she'd been wallowing for three months in the Alhambra. She whiled the hours away in her gilded room furnished with rich damask draperies, silk bedding, and an ebony chest full of Moorish dress attire. She avoided the harem, and spent most of her time in the courtyard next to her room.

The latticed windows to her room overlooked part of the immense vega that was mostly hidden from her sight. Her heart jumped one day when she saw files of soldiery making their way across her narrow field of view. She recognized Spanish standard bearers and tall horses magnificently caparisoned with colorful saddles. Is this war? If so, her captivity would end as soon as the first Spanish troops took over the palace. Then her captors would be punished for keeping her prisoner. Perhaps her querido Juan might be among her rescuers! Her heart leapt with joy at the thought of seeing her fiancé. *Could it be possible? Could Spain be this close?*

She had noticed during the last two weeks that the size of her meals dwindled, and instead of two guards she had only one. When she asked to see King Boabdil, the answer came swiftly with a warning of the guard's scimitar slicing through the air. Sarah no longer visited her chamber or met her in the courtyard. It was most curious. Where could she be?

"May I come in?" Sarah's melodious voice rang in her ear, making her jump.

"Come in, dear Sarah," said Isabella. She got up from the satin cushions below the latticed window and hugged Sarah. "I haven't seen you in days!"

"I was busy attending to the king's young children."

"How many children does he have? And what are their ages?"

"They're very young, and too numerous to count," Sarah said, laughing.

"Do you think they'll let me see them? Or hold them?" asked Isabella.

"That I can't answer. But I'll inquire and let you know."

"Sarah, did you notice strange rumors going on in the palace?" asked Isabella.

Sarah flinched, but she recovered instantly. "Why do you ask?"

"The maid who brings food used to speak to me but is silent now. And down in the vega, I saw Spanish soldiers in the distance. What do you think is going on? Is it war?"

Sarah didn't answer right away. She raised her hand and caressed Isabella's lustrous hair in a reassuring gesture. "There's nothing to worry about. If anything happens we'll be well cared for."

"What do you mean, 'If anything happens'?"

"Just that. The women in the harem will be well protected, especially you and me."

Isabella was mystified by Sarah's reply. How could they be safe if the palace was breached and taken over? Would the invaders recognize her as a Spanish subject who had been abducted and kept prisoner? Would she be harmed before she could shout that she wasn't a Moorish girl? All those questions whirled in her head in a moment that held hope and fear at the same time.

"I see that you're worried, and rightly so. I assure you that we'll be safe," said Sarah.

"How can you say that? Unless you know something you don't want me to know?"

"It's nothing you should concern yourself with. I promise you'll be safe. You'll have to trust me," Sarah said.

Isabella didn't reply to Sarah's reassurances of safety. Perhaps Sarah knew of a way to escape the palace grounds without being seen. She must trust her and rely on her knowledge. "I do trust you," she said to Sarah.

Sarah sighed with relief. She grabbed Isabella's hands and pulled her to the courtyard. "Come. Let's get fresh air in the garden."

Isabella followed her, eager to leave her cloistered room. She and Sarah stepped into the sunlight-filled palace grounds. The guard followed two steps behind, his eyes fixed on the two women.

They walked in silence until they reached the Albaicín's gardens. The citrus fragrance and scented jasmine surrounded them as they leisurely walked between two rows of oranges trees that filled the air with delicate aromatic scents. Colorful birds frolicked and chattered in the branches. In the center of the groves, they arrived at a circular platform paved with variegated stones. In its center arose a tall fountain spilling its clear waters in bursts that splashed into the several rows of troughs below.

"Let's pause here for a moment," said Sarah. They retired to a white marble bench gracing the platform and sat in silence.

Isabella was the first to break the silence. "What's to become of us?" she said, trying hard to conceal her trembling voice.

Sarah sighed at first, then said, "As guests of King Boabdil, we're safe under his protection. Therefore, no need to trouble yourself about our future." Sarah kept looking straight at the fountain, but Isabella noticed that Sarah's hands were grasped tightly together in her lap.

"That's what you're saying, but I hear something else in your voice."

Sara turned her head toward Isabella with questioning eyes. "What do you mean? Don't you believe or trust my words?"

"I trust you more than anyone in this palace or beyond."

Sarah smiled. "I'm glad we're friends. It means more to me than a world of gold or silver."

Isabella smiled back at her, and they resumed their walk. The guard kept pace with them. They walked to the end of the tended gardens to a thicket of woods spreading downward below the gardens. Sarah grasped Isabella's hand and pulled her toward the dark interlacing trees. The guard immediately made a menacing gesture by grabbing the hilt of the scimitar and pulling the blade out of its sheath.

"Qef! Qef!" The guard yelled for them to stop. Sarah turned around with deadly calm and spoke words to him that Isabella couldn't understand. The guard returned the blade back to its sheath.

Amazed, Isabella asked her, "What did you tell him?"

Sarah smiled mischievously. She bent down to Isabella's ears and whispered slowly, "I told him that nature called on both of us, and to respect our privacy."

Isabella covered her mouth to control her laughter and followed Sarah into the thick wood. When they were out of earshot from the guard, Sarah turned to her with a stern face. "I want you to remember one thing."

"What is it?" asked Isabella.

"If you need to hide or flee for your life, you'll retrace your steps to this wood and go down the hill to a stone tower. There you'll find a pair of lions carved on both sides of a stone door."

Isabella trembled at the words *flee for your life.*

"You're not to be concerned until you need to escape," Sarah added.

Isabella didn't utter a word, but she nodded.

"When you get to that door," continued Sarah, "Pull on the right lion's left ear toward you. You understand?"

Isabella nodded.

"The door will open, and you'll find a very long tunnel. At the end of the tunnel, you'll see a round stone blocking an exit. All you have to do is step in front of the stone. It'll move on its own. This exit will lead you to the vega and to safety."

"But where will you be?" asked Isabella.

"You're not to be concerned about my safety. However, I can tell you that I'll pass as a Moorish woman and receive all the safety and precautions reserved for the king's women."

Isabella couldn't understand why Sarah would want to remain behind. Nevertheless, she didn't question her friend's motives or her wish to remain behind. As a Spaniard woman, Isabella had nothing to fear—unless the danger occurred from within the palace. "I'll do as you told me," she told Sarah.

"Let's go back now or the guard will get suspicious."

They turned back to where the guard was pacing back and forth. They saw relief on his face when they reappeared among the trees.

"Imshee, Imshee." He calmly exhorted the two young women. Sarah looked at Isabella, and they both started to laugh as they walked toward the harem.

13

War Council

AS THE MORNING SUN ROSE on the vega, ghostly forms emerged from the rising mist. The soil had been drenched the night before by heavy rain that drained down from the mountains. Muddy cracks oozing with rainwater on the plain made it miserable for the Spanish soldiers struggling with their tasks. Camp sounds and chatter rose in the huge makeshift camp of Santa Fé. The clamor and din filling the camp almost drowned out the shouts of sergeants and corporals trying with great difficulty to keep their men and horses from disappearing into the white haze.

Numerous magnificent tents were reserved for the king in the center of the camp. Tapestries and silk hangings adorned the insides of the king's tents, and the floors were laced with intricate geometric patterns made of pine and oak wood parquetry. The queen's tents were similar, except her accompanying retinue and maidens had damask and silk inside their chambers. White linen tents encircled the entire perimeter of the royal quarters with colorful flags where the nobles made their headquarters. The soldiers' lodgings on the outskirts of the camp paled in comparison: they were huts with walls made of boughs and branches whose leaves now drooped with rain. In a small corner further down the camp, the friars and peddlers of goods for the soldiers were housed. Their tents were the poorest of all. They were fabricated with cheap cloth and canvas, and the floors were made of mud.

Captain Gonzalo Fernández de Córdova relayed instructions from his tent about a skirmish into the Moor's territory to weaken their defense lines. His soldiers admired and obeyed him, fully aware of his distinguished military career and that of his elder brother, Alonso de Córdova, count of Aguilar. The soldiers under his command welcomed the orders. They were tired of inaction and eager to ride forth on their stallions and slay as many Moors as their swords could withstand. The duke of Medina Sidonia and his friends Rodrigo Ponce de León, the marques of Cadiz; Don Diego, count of Cabra; and the distinguished general Hernando Perez del Pulgar were also rearing to fight. They followed Captain Gonzalo de Córdova's instructions with rapt attention.

"We have to continue the assaults into enemy land until they're weakened. Their scouts are waiting in the mountain passes, ready to pounce on our troops marching in the vega. We have to roust them from their dens. We must launch a surprise attack at dawn."

General Hernando del Pulgar shook his head slightly, seeming to disagree.

"My dear captain." He interrupted Captain de Córdova. "Sending our scouts into the passes above Granada may not be to our advantage. With due respect, the Moors have the Gomeres tribes, their best mountain warriors in those passes. We could fall into a trap."

"Yes, I'm well aware of that possibility. Remember that by cutting the supply of men in the mountains, we cut the Moors' source and means to rescue Granada," said Captain de Córdova.

"My captain," said the marques of Cadiz, an old nobleman. His entire features were red with excitement at the prospect of war. "I agree with you entirely. While we skirmish into enemy lands, we're still saving the lifeblood of our armies."

"Well spoken and true to your words, my noble marques," said de Córdova. "We must not yet use the bulk of our armies. We still have a formidable foe. Their walls are thick and strong, and many Moorish soldiers would die for their general, Muza Ben Gazan. They're getting weaker by the day, and they'll starve because of our devastation of their crops and groves. Our spies report that intrigue and dissension within the palace is splitting allegiances. We must be patient and not jeopardize the flower of our army into an early battle that'll bring no fruit. I say let's continue to weaken them by harrying them."

The men voiced their approval in loud and appreciative voices. Hernando del Pulgar, however, remained silent to the accolades for Captain de Córdova.

The captain turned to a map drawn on a linen sheet and pointed to places where his men would confront mountain fighters.

"We'll surprise these mountain men and cut them out here in Cerro de Çavallos at dawn." He turned to the marques of Cadiz and said, "I want you, Marques, and you, Duke Medina, to lead your men through this valley into the east fork of the mountain. Count Cabra, you'll lead your men through the west side across the ravine skirting the mountain with del Pulgar's men. Understood, Count?"

The count of Cabra didn't reply. Instead, he stroked his red beard and appeared detached.

"Count?" de Córdova asked again.

"I was just thinking . . . that perhaps . . ."

Every eye in the tent was on Count Cabra. Captain de Córdova remained silent and waited respectfully. The count was a venerated old soldier who had distinguished himself many times in the last ten years. His opinion was important.

"If we split into three groups at a lower elevation, we can all cross the ravine right there"—the count pointed to a dry riverbed between two cliffs—"and with the marques and the duke on the east, my men coming through the west fork, and del Pulgar descending from the top, we can surround the mountain. The enemy will have no escape route."

"By *¡Santiago!*" said de Córdova. "That's an excellent plan."

Hernando del Pulgar broke his silence and resistance to the raid. "With your permission, dear Captain, I'll take the third position on top of the mountain and descend upon them. I have no doubt that whether we win through palace intrigue or through offensive, we'll see our Spanish standard fly over the towers of the Alhambra!"

Captain de Córdova turned to del Pulgar. “Brave prophetic words are yours, Hernando. Let us now pray for a moonless night.” He turned to the assembly and said, “Tomorrow we strike!”

Several detachments of mounted and foot soldiers crept through the chill of the night on escarpments where their horses could find only narrow ledges on which to walk. They could barely see a few feet, but were aware of ravines dissolving into the darkness around them. Lights flickered in the distance on the mountain cliffs. The word went out that those were the Moors’ watch posts. Del Pulgar rejoiced to see that the Moors’ encampments were fewer than anticipated.

The Spanish soldiers reached the rocky heights of the Sierras and waited on a plateau below the snow line for further instructions.

“General del Pulgar, we’re ready for further orders,” the soldier at the head of the column said in a muted voice.

“We’ll stay concealed behind these boulders till we hear from the other detachments.” Del Pulgar pointed to a dark mass of rocks jutting from the cliffs near the edge of a precipice.

The soldiers silently led their horses behind boulders and waited. Finally, they heard the mournful cry of a Griffon Vulture. Each soldier grasped his sword or lance tightly, expecting the enemy to surge before them. The vulture squawk was repeated several times, answered by the same call from within their ranks. After a few minutes, a dark figure moved stealthily toward their position.

“General del Pulgar?” a quiet voice called out.

Hernando del Pulgar answered just as quietly, “We’re all here.”

The dark figure came nearer and saluted. “I’m sent by the count of Cabra. His detachment is waiting for the sign to attack.”

“We’re also waiting for word from the marques on the east side of the mountain,” said Hernando del Pulgar.

The word came quickly when a second soldier reached them with the order: “Go with the dawn!”

By now the barely emerging dawn light began to color the sky in pale shades of orange, revealing jagged rocks and frightening ravines where men and horses could disappear. Some of the soldiers crossed themselves and uttered silent prayers to the Madonna to spare their lives.

A few Griffon Vultures, calling repeatedly, flew low on the flanks of the mountain. Other birds murmured in their nests, and the air slightly lifted its chilliness.

Hernando del Pulgar descended the mountain with his men and horses to a plateau where the Gomeres tribe of the Moors was still sleeping.

On cue, the Spaniards loosed a great cry. *"¡Santiago!"*

A horde of foot soldiers, mounted noblemen, and archers fell upon the sleeping Moors. Their Moorish horses neighed vigorously as if to alert their masters of the danger descending on them. The more-alert Moors grabbed their scimitars and sprang to their feet. The Spanish soldiers rained blows on the surprised Moorish soldiers, who tried to fend them off as best they could.

Hernando del Pulgar's men slashed left and right while raising their metal shields to protect themselves from the skilful Moorish cavaliers. Moorish soldiers lay dying in pools of blood. The Spaniards lost a few of their men but kept pushing the Moors down the mountain, where some of them slipped and fell from the cliffs to their deaths. The duke of Cadiz's men joined from the east, and then a great number of Spanish soldiers arrived from the west.

"Mind your rears!" shouted General Hernando del Pulgar. He was now battling two Moors. He fought bravely—fending and ducking each time a fast-moving steel scimitar came close to slashing him. When he found himself surrounded by two additional Moorish swordsmen, he was sure this was his last moment on earth. He prepared to cross himself for a short prayer before death, when the marques of Cadiz appeared, followed by two of his swordsmen. They fell upon the Moors, the marques crossing swords with two of them. Hernando del Pulgar now went to the marques's aid until both Moors lay on the ground mortally wounded.

The marques and del Pulgar embraced and were rejoicing their blessed luck when a great cry sounded from above on the mountain. Their eyes instantly turned upward, and they were horrified to see hundreds of Moors descending the mountain shouting, *"Allah Akbar!"*

They fell upon the Spaniards, leaving many of them in growing pools of blood.

The marques of Cadiz, the count of Cabra, and del Pulgar retreated as they crossed swords with the freshly arrived Moors. As the Spaniards retreated and descended the mountain, they were driven into a glen with no exit. They were trapped between the abyss and the Gomeres Moors advancing on them.

A silver trumpet sound broke the air from below. Spanish soldiers led by Captain Gonzalo Fernández de Córdova, appeared behind the Moors. Now the Moors were trapped. The Moors fought valiantly, hemmed in between two rows of enemies. Dozens of Moorish soldiers fell to their death; the rest of them slid between the two rows of Spaniards and disappeared up the mountain.

The Spanish soldiers cheered mightily, and all battalion leaders embraced amid shouts of thanks and prayers. Captain de Córdova congratulated the three principal leaders for their bravery and steadfastness in battle.

The jubilation was short-lived, though. When the living Spanish participants of the offensive turned back and saw their dead fellows—the bravest soldiers of their ranks—they were filled with sorrow. They somberly transported the dead down the mountain and prepared to hear the king's pleasure at the victorious outcome, and his silent reproach for the loss of so many soldiers.

14

Fresh Tracks

INSPECTOR GUERIDA AND HIS AIDE were shown to the vestibule adjacent to the king's tent, where other envoys waited to be summoned. Guerida and his man were disheveled, covered with road dust, and frazzled from lack of sleep. Guerida looked around him and to the ceiling. The graceful folds of the tent's apex were made of pure white linen with a candle chandelier descending from its center. No luxury had been spared in duplicating the court in Madrid or the alternate palace in Seville for the sovereigns. The chairs for emissaries and nobles were of gilded wood with velvet padding, and low enamel-encrusted mahogany tables held refreshing drinks that were offered to the courtiers by servants.

Guerida thought that if one-tenth of these expenditures had been allocated to find criminals instead of this ostentatious display of wealth, he might've had better luck in finding Isabella Obrigon. He now waited his turn like others, depending on the good will of his king. Two hours later, as the audience diminished, Guerida prayed for his turn to come. Just then, the announcer's voice called out to him, "The honorable Inspector Guerida."

He stood, bowed, and entered the king's chamber followed by his aide. This room was even more elaborate that the waiting room. The walls were covered with rich tapestries, depicting victory scenes from previous battles for the Catholic king and queen. King Ferdinand wore an embroidered vest over his white silk shirt and velvet breeches. Rodrigo Ponce de Leon, the marques of Cadiz, sat on one side of him, with Captain Gonzalo de Córdova and the duke of Medina flanking his other side.

"The honorable Inspector Guerida is here to plead with Your Royal Highness," announced an attendant to the king. Guerida took two steps in the direction of King Ferdinand and made a deep bow.

"Come closer, my dear inspector. How can we help you?" asked Ferdinand.

Guerida approached King Ferdinand and bowed again. "My venerable monarch, may you reign and live a long life. I'm here on an important mission to save the life of a young girl."

"And who might this unlucky young lady be?" asked King Ferdinand.

"She's the daughter of Don Obrigon, who's under your patronage. She's Isabella Obrigon de Estrella, Sire."

"I'm acquainted with Don Obrigon. Why is her life in danger?" asked King Ferdinand.

"She was kidnapped several months ago from Seville. Now we have a strong suspicion, and proof," Guerida hastened to add, "that she's being held captive in Granada under the auspices of King Boabdil."

The assembly let out a cry of indignation at the news. A young Spanish noblewoman at the mercy of the Moors? She could be subjected to the indignities of a concubine! King Ferdinand frowned at the news that one of his subjects—one of his Trastámara's relations—was in the hands of his enemy.

"What's your proof that she has fallen into their hands?" asked King Ferdinand.

"My king, we traced Isabella and her kidnappers to an inn in Chauchina. The innkeepers have already confessed. A Morisco spy in the palace under our intelligence has confirmed having seen a beautiful young woman in Spanish clothing brought before King Boabdil."

"That is indeed ominous news," King Ferdinand said. His expression was solemn. "I still mourn for the many men who died in the battle of Cerro de Çavallos, and now more bad news."

Guerida lowered his head.

"We can send more spies into the palace, my king," Gonzalo de Córdoba said. "I have under my command one of the best men who'll follow my orders to the death. They'll find her and retrieve her under the cover of darkness."

"That will delay tomorrow's assault," King Ferdinand said.

"Sire," said Gonzalo, "we can't hold back the skirmishes of the nobles, who won't wait to bring in prisoners and collect booty. They've waited long enough to fight for the banner. They've restrained from galloping to the very gates of the Alhambra. Sire, please give us your word. When do we attack in earnest?"

King Ferdinand was quiet for a long moment. He turned to Guerida, who waited patiently. "Go, my courageous inspector. You'll take several of my men to accompany you. Hide in the nearest grove with Captain Gonzalo's spies, and wait till you hear word from the Morisco in the palace. Go now!"

Guerida and his man bowed deeply to the king and walked backward to the antechamber. As Guerida turned around to exit the tent, he glimpsed an envoy waiting to be called in. The envoy's face looked familiar, and Guerida realized it belonged to Don Abravanel the Jew, a wealthy and close confidant of King Ferdinand. How could King Ferdinand befriend a heretic? *But maybe the king was in need of his services*, thought Guerida. Never mind, he admonished himself. *I have a mission to accomplish.* His mission was to do as Torquemada had instructed him: find Isabella.

15

Crumbling of an Empire

BLASTING THUMPS OF CATAPULTS SHOOK the palace throughout the day. In a corner of a lavish room in the palace, José curled up on the marble floor, grasping his knees in a fetal position while trying to hide his ears between his shoulders. Miguel cast a pitying look at his brother, unable to comfort him.

"We'll get out of this, I promise you!" said Miguel.

José raised his head to reply but was interrupted by a whistling sound. Miguel lunged for José's corner and threw himself over his brother with arms outstretched. A loud metallic sound burst within the castle, followed by the crash of stones and mortar. Their room withstood the blow.

José freed himself from Miguel's protective arms and ran to the locked door screaming, "I can't take this anymore! I can't stand it anymore!"

Miguel ran to him and shook him by the shoulders. "Get a hold of yourself! We're going to get out of here!"

José calmed slightly at those words but returned to his downcast mood. Miguel dragged him to the divans in the center of the room where they slept. "Here, sit down and let's discuss this calmly. We have to concentrate and see how we can get out of here."

Miguel's words somehow shook his brother out of his torpor. José lifted his head and said with surprising alertness for his age, "I know! We can tie sheets together and climb down from the rear balcony."

"All right," Miguel said. "Let's do that. Then we have to find Isabella and convince her to come with us."

"Why?' José asked, looking confounded.

"Because that's what Mother told me to do. To take her to our relatives in Cordoba."

"We'll waste time and may never escape!" José said.

"Just trust me!" Miguel said. "Now, let's gather all the linens, and we'll use your plan."

They sprang into action and tore some of the silky sheets from the divans into strips. They tied them end to end into coiled ropes. Next, they pushed the heavy divans against the front door to keep out the guards. Miguel rushed to retrieve the empty sack from an alcove. He filled the sack with bread, scallions, olives, cheese, fruit left over from their meal, and additional bedding. Miguel looked over the rear balcony and the grounds behind their room, and saw no guards watching. *They must've used every one of them on the battlement.*

He and José unfurled the makeshift rope, tied one corner to the scrolled wrought-iron parapet, and threw it over the balcony. The courtyard was bathed in soft sunlight; it was a peaceful corner of the palace grounds. Polished hedges and cedars of Lebanon formed a natural curtain, which would conceal their flight. Miguel helped José climb down the rope, keeping an eye on the front door. When José reached the ground, Miguel lowered the sack filled with food, then climbed down.

"Now let's find out where they're keeping Isabella," Miguel said.

José didn't answer him.

Miguel tried to recall the scene when they had been dragged out of their cell. They had crossed a series of courtyards filled with fountains, then passed many buildings that led them right to the king. He and José slipped by the various gardens undetected and penetrated a secluded area beyond the main palace. Four large two-story buildings with screen-covered balconies stood before them. Miguel noticed at one end a tall tower dominating a building where several guards watched the grounds. Farther down the grounds many lion statues spewed jets of water in a central fountain, which was surrounded by a gallery with marble columns. This seemed an area protected from the roving eyes of the men in the palace. *We must be near the harem*, thought Miguel.

They ran from hedge to hedge through the adjacent gardens past rosebushes and lemon trees. Miguel spotted a guard at one end of the grounds watching two veiled women on a marble bench near a fountain. He grabbed José and forced him to hide behind a hedge. He thought it was curious that the two women were enjoying the garden when the palace was being attacked.

Moving almost at a crawl, Miguel and José approached near the bench where the women sat. Miguel let out a muffled cry as he recognized Isabella as one of the two young women. She had long black lustrous hair, emerald eyes, and white skin. The other woman was Sarah, who'd promised to help them. The curious thing was that Isabella seemed to be dressed with layers of silk robes and many facial veils. Why so many robes, he thought, and why the disguise? As they watched the women from their hideout, Sarah went to a guard and spoke a few words to him. The guard looked in Isabella's direction and nodded his head. The young woman made a sign to Isabella, who left the bench and walked toward an area of the garden descending beyond the women's harem. Miguel was mystified as to why Isabella had been left unaccompanied. Taking advantage of the guard's inattention while watching Isabella, he signaled José and they crawled unseen in Isabella's direction.

The garden where she walked began to recede and descended downward on a gentle slope. Tall pine trees and wild vegetation surrounded them. With a jolt, Miguel recognized the area where they had first seen Isabella. They followed her to a round stone tower, where she stopped. Miguel and José saw her pull on the head of one of the carved lions outside the tower. A low rumble sounded, and Miguel and José watched with astonishment as part of the wall slowly receded, revealing an opening into the tower. Isabella quickly disappeared through the opening, and the wall closed after her. Miguel ran with José in tow to the tower and rubbed one lion's head. The wall didn't budge.

"Pull the left ear toward you. The lion on the right!" José urged him. Miguel looked surprised but did as his brother suggested. The left ear yielded under his touch, and the wall opened again.

Miguel turned to José and said, "What would I do without you, Brother?" José smiled with unabashed pleasure. In front of them lay a dark gaping hole. As soon as they stepped in, the opening closed, leaving them in total darkness.

José's voice trembled. "Miguel . . . Miguel . . . I can't see you."

"I'm next to you, José," Miguel responded, searching the darkness with his hands. When he felt José's head, he breathed a sigh of relief. "Give me your hand and follow me quietly." Holding hands, they walked slowly into the darkness.

"Where . . . are we going?" José asked.

"Shh." Miguel tried to keep him quiet. He breathed words to José, "I hear running steps ahead of us. It must be Isabella, or . . ." He didn't finish his words, not wanting José to worry. They stopped momentarily and heard the steps distinctly. Someone was running away from where they were standing, the steps becoming fainter.

"We're going to run too. Let's catch up with her." He pulled a reluctant José by the arm, and they ran toward the diminishing sounds of the steps. They bumped into the dark cavern walls as they ran, then stopped periodically to listen for Isabella's steps. When he heard no steps, Miguel knew Isabella had also stopped to listen. After some time, her footsteps sounded closer, and they knew that they were catching up with her.

When a weak light grew in intensity, they ran faster in her direction. At an abrupt turn in the subterranean corridor, the light suddenly grew strong, and they could see Isabella holding a lit torch with her silk robes flowing behind.

"Stop, stop, Isabella!" Miguel called out to her. Isabella turned around frightened, but resumed her flight forward.

"Isabella! It's me, Miguel, and my brother, José. Please stop! We won't hurt you!" he called.

The words must've made an impression on Isabella, for she stopped in her tracks and turned around to face them in the labyrinth. The light of the flaming torch illuminated her frightened face.

Out of breath, Miguel came close to her, and she retreated accordingly.

"What do you want?" Isabella asked brusquely. "Why are you following me?"

"We only want to escape, like you!" Miguel raised his voice, and it bounced off the cavern walls. "We don't want to harm you. We were prisoners, like you, in the palace."

"You're the son of a traitor!" she yelled back at him, putting the torch between him and her in an attempt to stop him from coming closer.

"Look," said Miguel. "Let's not discuss this right now. We must band together to find a way out of here."

"Why should I help you?" She still faced him, holding her torch in front of her.

"Because, my dear lady"—Miguel put emphasis on the word lady to leave her with the sense of superiority—"we're both Castilian and Spaniards. We must help each other."

Those words may have found a resonance within Isabella, thought Miguel. She lowered her torch and asked in a quiet tone of voice, "How can you get us out of here?"

"We'll first look for an exit from this tunnel, then we'll follow the glens to the orchards and the mountains. There are many troops and scouts searching the fields and rivers for Moors. We mustn't reveal who we are or they'll kill us on sight," Miguel warned.

At those words, José began to tremble and cry. Isabella suddenly came close to José and embraced him.

"Don't worry," she said, consoling him. She turned to Miguel and faced him with a mocking smile. "I've nothing to fear. I'm a Spaniard woman, and as such, the Spanish soldiers will protect me."

"They'll kill you first, then ask questions later," Miguel replied.

"I tell you they'll save me!" Her voice rose in volume and pitch.

"With those Moorish clothes you're wearing?"

She looked down at her clothes and lifted her head with a horrified expression.

"Follow me," Miguel said, grabbing the torch from her hand.

With Miguel lighting the way, they went through the corridors in the labyrinth that twisted and turned frequently, descending deep into the mountain. After a long interval, when it seemed the labyrinth would never end, they arrived at a large cavern. Miguel used the torch to look at the walls for an exit to the outside. No such opening appeared. He said, "We'll wait here for the night." Both José and Isabella looked worried.

"How are we going to get out of here?" she asked, her voice shaking.

"We'll have to wait here until morning, when the light is brighter," he said.

"But how will you know?" she asked again.

Miguel pointed up to the opening in the roof of the cavern, from which light fell upon them. "This is where we'll escape."

Isabella and José inhaled audibly in the gloom.

Isabella sat on the floor and leaned against the cold granite wall. Miguel remembered the bedsheets in his sack and quickly gave them to Isabella and José. Isabella hesitated at first. As she reached for the sheet, her hand brushed against Miguel's. She shrank back and turned away from him.

All three of them waited for nightfall. Isabella and José fell asleep; the sound of their peaceful syncopated breathing lulled Miguel. He kept a vigil, fighting sleepiness and anxiety.

How were they going to escape? It had been an easy thing to enter the labyrinth, but not to exit. He had lied to Isabella and his little brother; he doubted they could climb the sheer walls. He sighed and put away the problem till dawn. Within minutes, he too fell asleep.

16

Auto de Fé

CLANGING BELLS AWOKE THE PEASANTRY who slept under the stars in the great plaza of Seville. They were there for the *Auto de Fé*, the Act of Faith, and had been promised spiritual salvation and rewards in the hereafter for attending. The church said the Act of Faith would give redemption to penitent prisoners through their deaths. If the prisoner admitted his or her guilt and kissed the cross, they would then be garroted instead of suffering a thousand deaths by fire.

The grotesque spectacle allowed all who were present to enjoy festive entertainment seldom seen by city dwellers or country folks, who were arriving by cartloads; food vendors hawked their wares, clowns and circus gymnasts performed, and fortune-tellers read palms. Even the gentry looked forward to the holiday atmosphere spectacle. Every one of the attendees felt secretly relieved that they weren't one of the unfortunate creatures that would die that day. Scaffolds were constructed the day before; piles of twigs and wood branches were heaped and ready to ignite at the first touch of a flaming torch. Wooden edifices had been erected near the plaza center to seat the nobles and gentry as they watched the spectacle. These were the esteemed and noble representatives of Seville's country elite, delegates from the Pontiff in Rome, and high officials from the city. Clerics were present to give witness to the expiation of the heretics' sins. The entire event purported to have but one goal: the strong perpetuation of the Catholic faith for all people.

The sound of a commotion turned all heads toward music and voices spilling from a narrow alley. Clarions, drums, and trumpets preceded a long procession of chanting friars and men in long white robes with their heads covered by black cones. The standard of the Inquisition, made of crimson damask with a cross in the middle and surrounded by the sword on one side, the olive branch on the other, and a crown at the top was elevated for full view. Following the religious train were haggard and emaciated men, with long beards and dirty, matted hair. Ropes bound their hands, and shackles restricted their feet, leaving the men no choice but to slouch forward and shuffle in their worn-out sandals. They wore the yellow *sambenito* gown with a diagonal black cross of Saint Andrews drawn on top. Some men wore black gowns painted with downward-pointed flames. These men had confessed—escaping the stake, but not death. Behind the shackled men stumbled the women, in no better condition. Their long yellow gowns had red painted flames representing heretics being burned in the fires of hell. Every one of the condemned wore tall mitres also painted with flames. Behind them came a choir of chanting youths, holding lit taper candles and large crucifixes. The procession wound around the farthest reaches of the plaza, parading through a turn for everyone to see, then made its way to the center while the spectators booed and shouted insults at the victims.

"You'll burn in hell, heretics!" one man shouted from his seat high on a bench. Peasant youths hurled stones but missed their victims.

"Repent and live forever!" another spectator shouted. Amid the crowds in the front rows, an older woman dressed in a nun's habit clasped her hands in prayer, her lips moving silently. She succeeded in approaching a woman in shackles.

"Kiss the crucifix and save yourself from torture!" the woman begged.

Maria looked back at the old nun, grimaced at her, then turned her head away, continuing her slow and painful shuffle toward the center of the plaza.

When all the victims had been paraded around the plaza as examples for everyone to see, the condemned sufferers were led in front of a black altar set up in the open. A holy official raised a tall cross in front of all spectators.

"Do you swear to uphold the faith and defend it from heresy?" the official shouted.

"We swear to uphold the faith and defend it from heretics!" The bystanders and nobles shouted back.

One by one, the victims were brought in front of judges, who were dressed in black robes. Torquemada, the highest judge, sat away from the city judges and clerics. His chair was hand-carved solid mahogany, padded with red velvet studded with gold nails and bearing the coat of arms of the Roman Catholic Church. He stood up and addressed the judges sitting in their humble chairs.

"I bring to you, honorable servants of this great city and country of España, these heretics. They have confessed and been charged with a lapse in their duty to The Church and the Savior. Do now as you will with them." He sat down and began twirling his rosary beads one by one.

A church official got up and began to read the names of the convicted men and women along with their charges. The victims were variously accused of several months and years of relapsing into Judaizing, sorcery, charlatanism; making heretical comments in a drunken state; and fraternization with Jews and non–Christians, robbers, rapists, and criminals. Those who would escape the flames would be garroted to death. The penitents with light sentences would be made to forever uphold the Catholic faith and wear the yellow garb of shame for years. Afterward the garment of shame would hang in each person's church for all to see, and for as long as the person lived. As the names and charges were read, minutes stretched into hours until noontime, when the city official stopped for a hasty meal before resuming the charges. The victims stood in their shackles, sweating under the hot sun and silently praying for their death and hour of deliverance.

Maria endured the charade and mockery and insults with the diminishing strength left in her. Her feet bled from cuts and bruises, all of her bones seethed painfully from fractures, and her swollen tongue almost touched the palate of her mouth. She was in a dazed state of torpor. It seemed a long time now since her incarceration. Days had merged into nights, minutes into hours, and events had blurred in her memory as an unbroken chain. She also had a vague notion of someone's hand forcing a quill pen into her own hand. The hand pushed hers through the letters of her name at the bottom of a document. She knew she had signed her own death decree. Now she yearned for the long sleep of death. Nothing made any sense now—not the names of the convicted, including her own; the long time spent standing in the hot plaza; her farm; her friends in adversity; and her deep beliefs in practicing the faith of her father. She only knew that everything she had done in life had been for a purpose. Therefore, her death would cap her life's achievement.

Just then her name was called. She slowly approached the black altar and stood there silently.

"Maria Donarojo, do you accept your sentence and admit to heresy, kidnapping, and black magic?'

She raised a faint voice. "I don't accept any lies or false witnesses against me."

"Then you'll burn in hell," the official replied.

Maria shuffled back to her spot among the condemned and closed her eyes wearily. She saw a vision in her mind of long ago. A voice called out to her, laughing for her to stop. She saw, vividly, a young woman in peasant clothing chasing her. How she had loved her mother. She remembered times spent in the fields, with her father cutting wheat and her mother laying a cloth on the grass with food she had cooked.

Her parents had been of strong peasant stock from a long line of country folks who dwelled for centuries in the vega of Castile near Seville. They flourished, owned their farms and lands, and made a prosperous living with crops. Then came the persecutions of Jews. Those who owned lands were taxed heavily, their land was curtailed, and they were forced to convert. Maria remembered watching her mother prepare for the holiday of Passover when she was a child. She remembered helping her cleanse the house of all leavened bread and preparing the festive meal and helping her father set the table with religious articles. After their conversion to Christianity, her parents adhered to the Jewish holidays in secret, warning her never to reveal them to anyone.

The arrest of her parents remained vividly in her mind. She never saw them again.

A hand grabbing her tore out the images. Maria was led, along with other condemned prisoners, to where the pyres were set up. Each of the condemned was tied with their hands around the post and a rope around their neck. A large screw embedded in the post was connected to the neck rope.

An inquisitional priest made the sign of the cross and gave a parchment to a city official.

"I release to you all condemned for the city justice to carry out their sentences," he said, handing them to civil and police guards.

The city official unrolled the parchment and read to the condemned. "All those condemned to be burned, we deliver you to your Maker. May he have pity on all your souls. If you confess and kiss the cross, a merciful death will be granted to you." The official finished his pronouncement, then nodded to the masked guards standing next to each of his victims.

Maria waited for her turn to be asked to kiss the cross. Below her feet a pile of dry wood awaited ignition. Her executioner stood behind her waiting for instructions.

"Adonai, Eloheinou, Adonai Eloheinou," she mumbled over and over.

The guard carrying the cross down the row of convicts asked each of them the final question: "Do you repent and kiss the cross to save yourself?"

When the victims agreed to kiss the cross, they were garroted immediately with a turn of the screw. Their necks broke and instant death followed. If they refused to repent, the pile was ignited. As the smell of burnt flesh and the piercing cries of victims rose in the air, the guard approached Maria.

"Repent, woman!"

Maria took one look at the crucifix and spit into the official's face. "You're the one who'll burn in hell!" she shouted in his face. "You're the criminals of this earth! When will you stop persecuting us!" She looked into the eyes of the official and repeated over and over, "Thou shall not kill . . . thou shall not kill . . . thou shall not kill."

The official recoiled, then turned his back on her and motioned the attendant to begin. The darkened hand of the executioner lit the pyre under her feet, and then he moved on to the next victim. Maria looked up to the heavens now obscured by heavy smoke.

"Adonai Eloheinou, she bashamaim Hagen aleinou ve al doroteinou." May our God who's in heaven protect us and guard our descendents, she implored silently.

The flames slowly began to creep, scorching the soles of her feet, up to her ankles and her legs, then engulfing her in unimaginable, throbbing pain that seared and split back her flesh into ribbons. Her heart stopped, and her last breath hung in the air until it dissipated into the blue sky.

17

The Flight

MIGUEL WATCHED THROUGH THE ROUND opening in the ceiling as the stars faded and the faint light of dawn began to increase. He dozed fitfully during the night fearing that someone might come through the labyrinth. When the early morning arrived, he breathed a sigh of relief. The sooner they left this cave, the safer he would feel. He went to wake his brother and Isabella from a deep sleep. He gently shook José. Isabella opened her eyes slightly, then went back to sleep.

José stirred with slow movements, then rubbed his eyes. "What is it?" he asked.

"It's time to move," Miguel said to him. "And our duchess here"—he pointed at Isabella—"We need to wake her sleepy head." He reached for her and shook her brusquely.

Isabella woke with a jolt this time. "Why are you so rough?" she complained.

"If we don't move soon, we could be spotted and caught by either Spaniards or Moors."

"All right, Captain," Isabella mocked, standing and saluting. "Show us the way."

Miguel stood for a moment, confused, but decided to disregard her jab.

He thought that since a secret passageway had brought them to this cavern, there must be an exit. He ran his hands along the walls but couldn't find an opening. He looked up toward the round opening at the top for rock formations they could use as handholds. The cavern was still in semidarkness and didn't reveal an obvious route.

"Wait!" Isabella shouted at Miguel, who was about to begin his climb.

He turned to her. "What is it?"

"I just remembered something."

Miguel and José looked at her.

"I remember that Sarah, the girl who told me how to flee from the palace, said that I'll find a round stone that opens to the outside."

"But we checked the walls last night. There wasn't one." Miguel said.

"But she did, she did," Isabella said, holding the sides of her head and trying to concentrate.

Miguel and José waited silently.

She ran to the end wall and stood facing it. Nothing happened. She tried another wall with no result.

"Wait!" Miguel said. He retraced his steps back into the tunnel and checked the walls again. As he walked by a niche near one wall, they heard a grinding sound. All three were amazed to see the wall rolling back and exposing an opening to the outside.

"You found it!" Isabella cried with joy.

"That's my brother," José said.

They all stepped outside, and the stone closed after them, sealing the entrance.

"Be careful as you climb down. Shuffle with small steps," Miguel alerted them.

Walking single file, they descended a gentle incline where little grass grew under their feet and few trees surrounded them. In the rising dawn, they shuffled down a few hundred meters and arrived at a flat plain with the charred remains of burnt trees. With Miguel leading, José following him, and Isabella at the end, they trekked through the countryside while Miguel tried to orient his small party. By now they were anxious, hungry, and fearful of running into marauding bands of soldiers—or worse, renegade Moors.

Miguel raised his hand and stopped suddenly.

"It seems we were headed in the wrong direction when we first descended inside the mountain."

"Where are we headed now?" José asked.

"When the sun rises over the horizon, I'll be able to tell," Miguel replied.

"Use your maritime directions, Brother," José reminded him.

Miguel replied, "We'll use the morning star if the clouds disappear."

José sounds like our mother with his urgings and admonitions, Miguel thought affectionately. His task now was to prevent Isabella and José from falling into enemy hands—whether King Ferdinand's men or Boabdil's guards. He then became aware how childish and puerile his good intentions were. They were surrounded by men at war, fighting each other to the death; by robbers looking for gold or silver; and by unethical traveling men, who preyed on inexperienced young travelers. He looked at his brother and Isabella trudging through the scanty underbrush and burnt trees and felt heavily responsible for their safety.

"Let's stop for a moment," he called out to Isabella and José. Miguel unfastened the sack and distributed bread chunks and cheese. He then gave them each a sip of water from the leather skin bottle. "If we're careful, this food and water can last us for a week."

"Why a week?" José asked.

"We'll hide in the mountains for as long as possible," said Miguel. "When it's safe, we'll head for Cordoba."

"What will you live on then?" Isabella asked.

"I still have a few maravedís left. That can hold us until we reach Cordoba."

"But what then?" Isabella asked again.

"Then we go to my relatives, and they'll take care of us."

"What if I don't want to go to your relatives—or to Cordoba, for that matter?"

"You must come with us. You're the reason we left our home—to fetch you."

"You mean the reason for the ransom!" Isabella yelled.

"You're wrong! My mother specifically instructed me to protect you if war broke out in Granada."

"So it was your mother's scheme to kidnap me." Her voice was angry. She stood in front of Miguel with her arms crossed in front of her chest.

"Look," said Miguel calmly. "It wasn't my mother's design. It was . . ." He hesitated. "It was your uncle who asked my mother and Maria—the chicken farmer—to take you to Granada, where you would be safe."

"Safe! Safe! That's all I've heard until now. I was safe in my home with my parents protecting me. What do I have now? I'm in danger no matter where I turn . . ." She choked. A sob escaped her.

José, who hadn't said a word till now, came close to Isabella. "Don't worry, Isabella. I'll take care of you,"

Isabella lifted her head and smiled at José while wiping her eyes. "Perhaps I should take care of you!"

She turned to Miguel and asked him abruptly, "Who's that uncle you're talking about?"

Miguel hesitated before he replied. "His name is João Treves. He's Portuguese and was related to your mother."

"I'm not familiar with this name." Isabella fell silent. Then she said, "It seems everyone knows about me, except myself."

"Perhaps that's something you can ask when you get back to Seville," said Miguel.

"Look," she said to Miguel. "I'll go with you to Cordoba. But you better not betray me," she warned him.

"Why would I do that?" Miguel protested. "Perhaps I should expect that from you."

Isabella's face looked piqued in the rising daylight. "I promise you. I won't do anything to give you and your brother away." She smiled at José, and he returned her smile.

Miguel nodded, pleased with this mutual truce. "Let's continue our trek with caution. If we're stopped, I'll say that I'm accompanying you to your future Morisco husband in Malaga."

At those words, Isabella looked as if she'd forgotten her good intentions to cooperate. She opened her mouth, but no words came out.

"What about José?" she asked.

"José is your brother, and your future husband is to take care of him too."

José smiled, content with the arrangement. “Then what are we waiting for?” he asked.

Miguel smiled back. *“¡Vámonos!”*

18

A Father's Search

IN DON OBRIGON'S HOUSEHOLD IN Seville, servants hurried in the early morning hours following orders by the overseer, Emilio Gomez. He supervised Don Obrigon's personal servant, who laid the clothes in a wooden chest that his master would need for his voyage. Then Emilio looked around the room to see if he'd forgotten anything. He signaled to the servant to tie the leather straps and lock it with a key that he put back in Emilio's hand.

"Go back to the kitchens and make yourself useful," Emilio told the servant, who nodded and left the room quickly.

Emilio sighed with relief that everything was in order. When Don Obrigon gave him instructions about his trip to the farthest reaches of Andalusia, Emilio had raised his eyebrows.

"I see you're dying to know where I'm going," Don Obrigon said.

Emilio nodded his head but remained silent.

"You know," said Don Obrigon, "all these months I refrained from riding my horse to search for Isabella?"

"Dear Don Obrigon, only a father would know how painful it is to lose one's cherished daughter. Your intentions were noble and pure."

"I'm touched by your affection for this household, Emilio. You've been a valuable help to the family." Don Obrigon stopped for a moment, then said, "You'll supervise the estate while I'm gone. I have complete trust in you."

Emilio bowed his head to his master. "I'll take charge with your approval, Don Obrigon."

Don Obrigon smiled at him.

Don Obrigon left his chambers to say good-bye to his servants, who waited in the front courtyard. The women servants were in tears, wondering when their master would return and what their future held. As Don Obrigon passed each servant, he personally asked after their welfare as they bowed and curtsied to him.

"Take good care of *Casa Joya* for me," he told them, causing the women to cry in earnest. He also pressed dada Hannah's hands. She was in tears and tried to speak to Don Obrigon, but she was overwhelmed by emotions.

"I know, I know, my dear Hannah. I'll tell Isabella how much you missed her." He climbed into his carriage, and the servants saw their master leave them unprotected for now.

Winter descended with fury, making all trails, roads, and bridges impassable to Ferdinand's troops. Water dripped off the canvas tents, forming rivulets that flowed down the encampment into large pools of water. The relief column that started from Barcelona weeks ago had not arrived yet. Provisions, horses, and fresh troops had become scarce. The Spanish foot soldiers' lack of sleep began to show, slowing down their successful sorties against the Moors. Whenever two battalions advanced toward the ten-foot-thick walls of the Alhambra, only half the men returned. The vega was strewn with dead bodies and the bloodied wounded. Ensigns hurried under fireballs catapulting from the battlement, leaving them vulnerable.

The Moors were ensconced behind their protective walls, but they had also suffered from the stalemate. They were weak with hunger and fought with less energy and stamina. With food becoming scarce, they began to kill and feed upon their tired horses.

Meanwhile, the Spanish soldiers shivered as they sat on wet cots in their tents, their feet resting on muddy ground. The construction of Santa Fé's new wooden barracks had progressed over the summer, but it was now at a standstill, leaving entire platoons to wallow in the muddy tents. The king's four white canvas tents were battered in the wind that had now increased exponentially. But his parquetry floors were dry in comparison to those of his poor soldiers.

In King Ferdinand's tent, a concerted effort was being made to alleviate the urgent standoff.

"We must get more supplies," Adjutant Don de Torres begged King Ferdinand.

In dismay at the stagnation of his campaign, King Ferdinand's brows were creased while he studied the maps in front of him. He raised his eyes from the map and looked at de Torres with distracted eyes.

"We sent word to the queen in Seville two weeks ago. She'll see that new provisions arrive within days," said King Ferdinand.

"Sire, with all due respect," de Torres said, "that was more than a month ago. We're still waiting. We can't keep going unless fresh troops can relieve those tired soldiers."

"My king," interrupted Captain Gonzalo Fernández de Córdova, who stood near the king. "Adjutant de Torres is right. We must send new word to the queen to scour the countryside for new supplies."

King Ferdinand's lips formed a tight line as he struggled to make a quick decision. After a few minutes, during which his men stood silent around him not wanting to break his concentration, he turned to Captain de Córdova.

"Send two squads of twenty men to scout for the supply army that is overdue."

Captain de Córdova bowed to King Ferdinand and left the tent to see to the orders. On his way to the adjutant's tent, a company foot soldier bumped into him.

"What is it?" asked de Córdova with impatience.

The soldier saluted and said, "Many pardons for stopping you, Captain. We have a very ill soldier who has asked for a favor from King Ferdinand."

"And who's this important soldier requesting an audience?"

"It's Juan Escobar de Santilla. I understand that his family has the king's benefaction and attention."

Captain de Córdova scrutinized the soldier for a moment. "What's your name?"

"I'm Corporal Antonio Peres with the school of engineering, my commander."

"All right, Antonio. Go to the king's tent and see if he'll see you."

Antonio saluted Captain de Córdova, then ran to Ferdinand's headquarters.

Sloshing in the mud, Antonio arrived at the first tent, arranged as an antechamber. Upon entering, he was stopped and barred by two guards at the entrance.

"No one enters without proper authority," the guard said.

"I have Captain de Córdova's word that I can see the king," said Antonio, trembling more from the cold than the fear of being arrested.

"What business do you have with the king?"

"I come as envoy from Juan Escobar de Santilla."

"All right. You wait here." The guard said a few words in the ear of a colonel who disappeared into the king's tent. He reappeared shortly and made a motion for Antonio to advance.

"Make sure to bow deeply to the king, and don't address him unless he speaks to you first. Understand?"

Antonio nodded his head. He scraped the mud off his feet on the threshold, then followed the colonel into the king's main tent. Ferdinand was still at his table studying his maps. He lifted his head at Antonio's appearance and motioned him to come close. "What brings you here, Corporal?"

Antonio first bowed, then saluted the king. "My king, it is with great pain and regret that I bring ill tidings."

Ferdinand nodded, encouraging him to continue.

"Captain Juan Escobar de Santilla is dying, Sire. He has a last request, my king."

"What is that request?" asked Ferdinand, who considered every soldier as his own son.

"He asks that word be sent to his parents, Don Pedro and Doña Maria Escobar, to give them his son's love and to find his fiancée Isabella Obrigon, Sire."

At the recognition of Isabella's name, King Ferdinand flinched with surprise and shock. "I know of Don Obrigon's daughter. We have underway . . ." He stopped suddenly, not wanting to reveal the search for Isabella. "I will personally follow you to Corporal Santilla's tent."

Antonio's mouth fell open with this unexpected honor to Juan. "Please, Sire, follow me."

King Ferdinand and a dozen men followed Antonio to Juan's tent located at the other end of the camp. Large parasols held above Ferdinand prevented him from getting wet in the heavy rain. When the soldiers in Juan's tent saw the king enter, they jumped off their cots and bowed deeply until they were motioned to leave the tent. The priest by the bedside bowed to the king and ceded his place to him. Ferdinand approached Juan's cot and saw a thin, bedraggled young man whose pallid face blended into the white pillow. He took Juan's hands between his own.

"I'm here at your fellow soldier's request. What can we do for you?" King Ferdinand said in a low voice.

Juan opened his eyes, and for a moment life came into them. He opened his mouth to acknowledge the king.

"My king . . . you do me . . . great honor." Juan spoke with effort.

King Ferdinand forced a smile and held back tears.

"Please, my king. Find my love, Isabella Obrigon. And . . . tell my parents—" Juan stopped to take a hollow breath. "Tell them . . . not to suffer. I go to heaven with great honor for . . . my country and king." Juan stopped and remained still.

"My dear son. I'm touched by your faith and honor for España. I'll see myself to finding Isabella."

Juan's face regained slight color, but then the pallor took over again. He closed his eyes and his lips formed the word *Gracias*.

The priest behind King Ferdinand moved to the other side of the bed and took Juan's wrist. His eyes met King Ferdinand's. They both acquiesced to the sorrow of losing one of Spain's finest youth. The priest covered Juan's face, and Antonio sobbed behind them.

"Cry my son, and give way to your sorrow," said King Ferdinand gently.

Once outside the tent, the king let go of tears that clouded his eyes. Then he straightened and turned to the men accompanying him.

"Tomorrow we march against the enemy!" he declared.

In Santa Maria de La Rábida's monastery, Columbus sat gloomily and waited for Fray Juan Pérez to join him in his room. While he waited, a lighted taper in a brass candlestick on the table projected his silhouette in black on the whitewashed walls. *It's just the same in Spain's mind—black or white,* he thought. No other thought could be conceived between two opposing beliefs—black or white, Christian or Moor, poor or rich—and that extended to every phase in the life of a man in España.

He knew the monarchs couldn't subsidize his voyage unless more funds—gold and silver—could be found. He felt certain that his voyage would fill the Spaniards' coffers for decades to follow. Right now those purses were hollow and flat, but once the Indies were reached, gold would be found aplenty. The funds for the voyage would have to be raised through appeals to men who creatively accepted his challenge. For now he'd have to wait till the winter passed and pray that the war succeeded.

The heavy wooden door squeaked, and Fray Perez stood on the threshold. "My dear Columbus, I hope I didn't disturb your prayers," said Fray Perez. He sat at on the long bench by the table opposite Columbus.

Columbus cleared the maps from the table to make room. "No, dear Fray, I was just reminiscing about the old days."

"Were those good remembrances?" asked Fray Perez.

"Most certainly. It was twenty years ago that I came to your monastery, and again recently, when you offered to care for my son, Diego."

"Yes. He's a most eager child, anxious to learn all there is to know about the faith," said Fray Perez, smiling. He turned his palms toward the small flame burning in the candlestick and rubbed them together. Then he buried his palms in his billowing sleeves to keep them warm.

"You know that I returned from the court in Madrid about a week ago? Of course I had to attend to the monastery's functions first before I could see you."

Columbus nodded his head, but felt neglected. "My dear fray, your duties are of the most important urgencies. I remain your humble and grateful guest."

Fray Perez smiled again. "I'm glad we understand each other, but . . ." He made a motion to stop Columbus, who clearly couldn't contain himself from asking about the pending voyage.

"I spoke to the queen. She's most eager to start the preparations and requirements needed for this monumental task." He emphasized the word *monumental*.

Fray Perez continued. "The queen intends to commission several ships, perhaps as many as three, for the voyage. The other necessary details she leaves to you."

Columbus's heart did a somersault. "I'm most grateful to the queen, but what of the date for this voyage? Is it soon?"

"Yes, my dear Columbus. As soon as the first day that Granada's keys to the city are in the sovereigns' hands."

Columbus opened his mouth, but no sound came. He swallowed hard, then said, "But that may take months!"

Fray Perez's face dimmed enough that Columbus could detect it by the small flickering light of the wax candle.

"You must have faith in the queen," urged fray Perez. "At least she's thinking about preparations that may take months to accomplish. That's why she wants you to go to Palos and begin the search for seamen and mariners for the voyage."

Columbus thought for a moment, trying to digest the ephemeral directive to plan a voyage by thinking about it. He was reluctant to start on a phantom promise. No matter—he'd do as she bid him. The queen, after all, held the purse strings.

"May I request from the queen, at least, some funds to contract these sailors on my promise to hire them when the time comes?"

"I can do this much. I have discussed your petition to the queen with the powerful head of Martin Alonzo Pinzón's family. This is where you'll go and confer with him. Being a family of navigators, they'll advise on what course to take."

Columbus raised his head in hope. Here was a lead he could follow. Now, though, there was another matter to discuss.

"My dear Fray Perez. You've been a godsend emissary, not to mention your piety and charitable sheltering for my son, Diego. Now, however, I must collect my son and send him to Cordoba, where my other son, Fernando, resides with his mother, Beatrix Arana. It's temporary; I'll bring him back on my return trip to Palos."

Fray Perez looked disappointed. "We'll miss the boy. He brightened our days with his tender and frank joy. Please bring him back soon." He got up and took leave from Columbus by crossing himself.

"Go with God's help." he told Columbus.

A pale sun peeked through the cloud cover, which opened momentarily to reveal the blue sky reflected in the Atlantic Ocean. This was unusually mild weather in this region of Huelva, where the inhabitants were used to soaring seas and heavy gales. A gentle breeze coming from a northwest corridor between the low hills caressed the dockworkers and passengers waiting for a signal from merchant ships to board. The marine port bustled with the loading of wool products, cork for casks destined for the European markets, wine flasks from Madeira, conserves in jars, and citrus fruit from Andalusia.

João sat eating a hurried morning breakfast of black bread and dry fish in a corner of the docks. He wetted his meal with ale and quickly swallowed the last bite, when his name was called.

"Hey, João, do I have to keep calling you to get back to work?" yelled a supervisor.

"My apologies, Overseer. I lost track of time," João said humbly. He couldn't afford to antagonize his source of subsistence. Already, paying ten maravedís per week for his lodging on the hay in the barn ate half his wages. Without wages, he would be on the streets of Palos, a target for pickpockets, or worse—an assassin. "I'll work an extra hour to make it up to you," João said to the overseer.

"Just don't let it happen again. There are ten men looking for your job."

João didn't answer the threat and marched toward the carrack ship being unloaded.

"Where were you?" a workmate asked him in a low voice.

"Hey," said João. "No questions asked."

Getting the message, his workmate continued working in silence. A few moments later, as they were coming down the wood ladder with their backs bent under bales of cotton, his workmate breathed, "We have two new recruits."

At first João didn't respond. He then said, "Gomes, keep your tongue in your mouth or we'll be dismissed."

Gomes kept quiet until the bales were deposited on the docks. Then he turned to João and said, tongue in cheek, "His Excellency is telling me to shut up!"

João restrained his anger. "Look," he said, "it isn't that I'm not interested in the new recruits. You know what the overseer said: 'No talking.'" He mimicked the overseer's demeanor.

Gomes laughed.

"Let's meet afterward for some ale," João said.

"That's fine for me, mate." Gomes's face lit up.

Just then the two new workers unloaded their bales on top of those already on the docks. João was startled to see Hernán Çavallos and Alfonso Sabatin standing on the docks.

The three men hugged in a tight embrace, laughing out loud and jumping together in joy while slapping each other's backs over and over.

"I thought I'd never see you again," a happy João said.

"Nor I, finding you here, and now," said Alfonso.

"Any word on Benvenide?" João asked.

"Nothing," said Hernán with a touch of sadness in his eyes. "Even though he had delayed in meeting us, he should've been here by now."

João felt his chest tighten. *What if Maria and Benvenide didn't reach their destination? What if they fell into Guerida's hands? What of Isabella?* These thoughts came at him with the force of a hammer pounding on a nail. *My God! What have I done?* His dead sister would turn in her grave by now if she knew. And what of his solemn word to take care of Isabella?

"What's wrong, João? Looks like you've seen a ghost," said Alfonso, his laughter ceasing.

Hernán's jovial mood also disappeared. "Yes, what's wrong?"

João quickly regained his composure. "There's nothing to worry about, my friends," he said. "I hope we hear from Benvenide someday. We better go back to work or we'll all lose our jobs."

The two men nodded, then turned to climb the ladder into the ship.

Gomes had stood aside the whole time without saying a word. When they resumed their work, he said to João, "What's the matter—I'm not good enough to introduce me to your friends?"

João turned to him. "Our meeting at the tavern tonight is still on, isn't it?"

"Of course," said Gomes.

"I'll introduce you to my friends then," João said. "Now let's get back to work."

Isabella sat shivering in her scanty silk clothes and veils. Her feet were wet and cold in her slippers, and she held Josè, who was trembling all over.

"Miguel, do something! Your brother is going to catch . . . his death here in this cold cavern." Her words came out trembling too. She removed her wet slippers and rubbed her cold feet with her right hand.

Miguel felt dejected and overwhelmed. He had completely failed to protect Isabella and Josè. The rain hadn't let up for two days, and they were stuck in a damp cave they'd found on the side of a mountain. They had no heat and no dry clothes. He thought of gathering the scanty twigs and branches lying outside their hideout, but he reasoned that they, too, were probably soaked. If he could find a way to light the soaked branches, he may be able to make a fire to keep them dry. He got up under the cavern's low ceiling and walked bent over down to its end, where he discovered another cavity branching from the first one. Feeling the granite wall with his hands, he found that it led into a rugged corridor. The darkness was thick, but he advanced slowly toward a dim light developing farther ahead. When the darkness suddenly dissipated, he found himself in another cave, this one larger than the first. A pool of water from the rain filled a depression into the center, and the light that had guided him came from the top of a natural opening in the roof. A thrill ran through him when he discovered a pile of dry branches in a corner as if someone had left them there intentionally. *This must've been a poor beggar's dwelling,* he thought. He ran back to Isabella and Josè, shouting to them.

"Quickly, I found another room where we can dry ourselves."

"Josè looked up to him and said, shivering, "But what about a fire?"

"We'll worry about that later. Come!"

They followed Miguel to the back cavern.

"I see firewood," said Isabella. "But we have nothing with which to light one." She looked at Miguel.

"You and Josè just rest here, and I'll find some stones to start the fire."

Miguel left them and ran to the outside to look for sharp stones. After finding several quartz and pyrite stones, he looked for a birch tree in the scattered tree area. When he found one, he rejoiced—then spotted fungus on the tree and cut a large chunk off it with his knife. Reentering the cavern, he went to work right away striking the quartz stone against the pyrite. After many trials he saw a spark, but it died down quickly. Furiously, he repeated the same maneuver several times, but each time the spark died down. Sweat beads appeared on his forehead, but he was determined to keep trying. The pyrite stone had now a dented groove where sparks lasted longer. Miguel put the sliver of fungus next to the pyrite hand stone. A spark rising in the channel rolled to the fungus and lit it with a glow. He waved his hand gently to fan the fire until it grew into an orange flame.

"Josè, bring me those twigs by the wall!" Miguel shouted.

Isabella and Josè ran to bring him the twigs to place above the small flame igniting the wood. A warm red-orange flame rose high above it, projecting its warmth to all three of them.

"Quickly, remove your wet clothes!" he ordered Josè and Isabella.

Isabella looked shocked. "I won't do that!" she said indignantly.

Miguel suddenly realized that he had insulted a young woman with his clumsiness. "I beg your pardon, Isabella. I was only talking to Josè. If you like go into the next room and throw your clothes back to us, we'll keep our eyes closed when you say so. As soon as they dry out, we'll do the same and throw them back to you." He then said quickly, "With our eyes shut, of course."

Isabella left the cavern, and when ready she yelled for them to catch her clothes, then disappeared back in the first room. Miguel ran to her wet clothes, surprised at the voluminous amount of dresses she had worn, and tried to dry them as fast as he could. Meanwhile, Josè had stripped naked and tried to dry his pantaloons, long-sleeved shirt, vest, and cape. Miguel followed suit and succeeded in half-drying his clothes as well.

"Isabella," Miguel called out to her.

Isabella's muffled voice came back to them. "Yes?"

"I'll put your clothes in the corridor where you can't see us."

He came back by the fire and warmed his hands and the rest of his clothes by sitting close to the flames. Isabella made her entrance, a glow over her face. She went to sit by them and smiled gently at Miguel.

"Thank you," she said to him.

"I was cold too," he said. "Now we need to plan on what to do next."

"I'm listening," Isabella said.

"So far we've evaded both the Moors and the Spaniards." As Miguel said those words, he eyed Isabella for any reaction to the word *Spaniards*, but she sat calm and composed. *Thank God, she won't give us away*, he thought.

"First we have to find food in the nearest town or farm," Miguel said.

"But what if they hand us to the authorities?" asked Josè with a tinge of worry on his face.

"We'll tell them that our father had been killed and we were taken by the Moors."

"This will be a half-truth and easy to lie about," said Isabella with irony.

Miguel disregarded her comment and went on. "What we have to do is coax the inhabitants to help us by telling them that our father was a noble and very rich. They'll be rewarded accordingly."

"Now that will be a full lie," Isabella came back.

"We must lie or cheat if we have to. Our lives depend on it," Miguel said to her.

Isabella looked about to protest, but she refrained from speaking.

Seeing that Isabella would cooperate, and at least not reveal who they really were, Miguel turned to her and said, "We'll be grateful to you for your understanding." He turned to Josè and said, "Now that the rain's stopped, we should go and find food and shelter for the night."

19

A Palace Feud

CHAOS BROKE OUT IN THE Alhambra Palace when the decree to vacate was made. The word had circulated in the morning for all civilians to prepare to vacate their homes when the order was given. The result was a sea of cries, hair-pulling, and moaning as to their fate. Emissaries shouted and ran from antechambers to the king's reception hall, and servants squealed and were confused as to where to begin first in their duties. The harem women fought among each other over possessions and which dresses to take with them, and their poor women servants trembled with fear, terrified their mistresses wouldn't take them along. Where to? No one knew yet.

With a cross look on her face, Ayxa La Horra, Boabdil's mother, burst into the harem. "I expected better behavior from you!" She yelled at the disheveled women, "You've already sold your country and home to the infidel by believing us beaten! We're still the powerful descendents of the Nasrids—your proud ancestors!" Ayxa stopped, out of breath.

"Now," she said in a calm voice, "put away your dresses and silks, and behave like sultanas."

The women, who had cowered during Ayxa's diatribe, returned to their divans muttering inaudibly. Ayxa, meanwhile, went to see Boabdil's wife, the sultana Morayma, who was in her usual alcove being fanned by her two servants.

"I'm glad that you, at least, don't give way to rumors. What a nuisance these women can be."

Morayma smiled weakly. "They're also the pasha's wives, and even though they may be young and foolish, they're my sisters." Morayma moved her full body on the divan with difficulty, letting a slight moan of discomfort that didn't escape Ayxa.

"You don't look in good health, my daughter. What's the matter?" she asked.

"It's nothing, my venerated mother. I just wish that . . ." Her voice broke, and her full red lips remained shut, her large eyes now dim and without sparkle.

"I know what ails you, my daughter. It's your son, Ahmad. Believe me, my daughter, I cry, too, about my grandson being a prisoner of the infidel. What can we do? The king was released on the condition of handing over his own son until Granada is in Spaniard hands." Ayxa stopped, choking with the emotion. She quickly got hold of herself. "I know that you suffer, but he's cared for by the benevolent Queen Isabella."

This comment did not seem to reassure Sultana Morayma. She bent her head.

"I wonder what he looks like now?" she said gloomily.

"Yes, he was only a two-year-old babe when he was handed over to the Spaniards as a tool for helping advance their wars!" Ayxa raged.

"My husband was exchanged for my son. As soon as I rejoiced that the king was released, they tore my son from my heart. How cruel and intransigent is fate! More cruel than death."

Ayxa raised her hand. "But I have good news for you."

Morayma stirred at those words, her large gold ring earrings moving with her head. "What is it?" she asked with hope.

"The envoy from the Spanish queen is here with news of your son."

"My son? My son? Where is he? Ahmad, my poor child!"

"The king is waiting for you in the ambassador's hall," said Ayxa with rare tenderness.

Morayma covered her face with the sheer veil attached to her tall headdress and lifted herself from the divan with difficulty. Followed by her mother-in-law, Ayxa, she shuffled down the corridor out of the harem to the ambassador's hall where her husband, King Boabdil, waited for her.

When King Boabdil saw his wife and his mother entering the hall, he called for the envoy. "Send him in!"

A few moments later, the Spaniards' envoy entered the hall. He was a Morisco, a Moor who had converted to Christianity, but was now dressed in Spanish garb with a sword at his hip, feathered hat in hand as a sign of respect for the Moorish king and queen, and a small bundle wrapped in linen in his other hand. He bowed deeply to both monarchs and waited for them to speak.

"What news do you bring from my son?" said King Boabdil to the envoy. Neither his voice nor his black eyes reflected any emotion.

Dear King," said the envoy, "your son is well and robust."

At those words Morayma let out a sigh. If it was a sigh of joy, it was understated. It was more a breath of pain that the queen exhaled. It was the pain of longing.

"Tell me how he looks now. Is he taller, stronger?" Morayma asked.

"That he is, Queen Morayma. I have here a drawing he made for you." The envoy came close to the divan and offered the small bundle to Morayma.

She untied the hemp rope and unwound the linen wrapping. Inside was a crude childish drawing of a woman in veils holding the hand of a boy and standing next to a crenellated palace. A cry escaped her lips. Tears welled in her wide and expressive eyes, dropping onto the linen drawing. She quickly wiped it dry with her sleeve.

"Can you tell me if he speaks of me and his father?"

"That he does, dear Queen. He speaks all the time about his land, and very proudly too. He tells everyone how he will succeed to be king one day."

"Yes, he will," echoed King Boabdil as he nodded his turbaned head.

Renewed tears came to Morayma's eyes. When she regained her composure, she turned to the envoy. "You have my gratitude," she said to him.

"How can we reward you?" Boabdil said, stroking his black goatee beard.

"Dear King, I seek no reward." He fell silent. "There is, however, one favor Queen Isabella is requesting."

"What is it? I shall grant it," said Boabdil.

"There is a young woman in your palace. A Spaniard girl residing in the harem."

Morayma's curiosity was piqued. "I don't know whom you are speaking of. What is her name?"

"She's also named Isabella, after the queen."

Morayma's eyes showed a hint of recognition. She remained silent for a moment, then said, "I didn't know she was known to the queen."

"All that Queen Isabella asks is for her release, to be reunited with her family."

King Boabdil didn't answer right away. He bent down to his minister and spoke a few words. After shaking his head, he turned to the envoy. "We'll see to it that she's released. We'll forward word to the Spanish Queen."

"But I was hoping to bring the girl back with me," said the envoy. "Queen Isabella has taken great care of your boy, dear King and Queen, and she expects the same of this young girl, who is captive in your harem."

"Until you hear from us, I'll personally see to her safety and well-being," Said Boabdil.

"May I remind you, King Boabdil, that your boy will be returned to you upon the promise of the treaty."

Boabdil lowered his head, and Morayma knew the dreaded reminder wounded him. The envoy's words ground into her heart, and the pain of missing her son surged again.

"Go, tell your queen that I'll do all in my power to release the girl," she said, speaking out of turn. Her eyes looked with supplication to her husband. King Boabdil remained silent.

The king turned to the envoy. "Go and tell Queen Isabella that the girl will be returned upon the return of my son." His face betrayed no emotion.

The envoy bowed deeply to the king and queen and left the hall. Two Nubian guards holding sharp lances followed him down the hallway, and he quickly made his way to the exit.

Back in the ambassador hall, Morayma prostrated herself on the marble floor at the feet of her husband, the king.

"Please, please, Sire, release the girl now. I couldn't bear not ever seeing my son again!" She broke down in cries and sobs.

The court, composed of Boabdil's closest minister, Yusef Aben Comixa; his finance minister, Moussa El Zayari; Muza Abul Gazan, the king's right-hand man; and his mother, Ayxa la Horra, all lowered their eyes at the sight of the queen begging.

Boabdil looked at his crying wife and descended the steps from the throne to her.

"It's not fitting for the queen to beg, even if it's to her husband the king," he said. He helped her off the floor and motioned to his mother to help her back to the harem.

Both women, one supporting the other, made their way out of the hall.

In the ambassador hall, Boabdil turned to Muza Abul Gazan and said, "Where is that wretched girl! I gave her shelter in the palace, and now my son's freedom is at stake."

A silence followed, then Aben Comixa said timidly, "We lost track of her. She slipped unseen from the gardens of the Albaicín. The two brothers staying in the palace are also gone."

Boabdil exploded at the bad news. "Gone? Gone where? Go and fetch the watch guard! He'll be executed right here!" Boabdil's flaccid face had turned dark red, and he was perspiring.

Aben Comixa turned to Boabdil and said, "Sire. We'll need every man that can fight for the Alhambra. Better he should die in battle than in shame."

"My king," said Muza Abul Gazan, "Aben Comixa is right. I can search for all three of them and bring them back to the palace."

Boabdil thought for a moment, then said, "No, I need you here. I have an omen that Ferdinand is about to attack the Alhambra soon with everything he's got. We must stay together and prepare ourselves."

"But what about the fugitives?" asked Aben Comixa.

"We'll deal with them later," Boabdil said, wiping his face. "Send a missive to Queen Isabella that the child fled and can't be found." He got up from his throne and made his way to his own chambers. The assembly bowed before him as he passed.

20

An Audience with Ferdinand

Don Obrigon was sweating under his heavy winter clothes, but stayed in his seat, afraid to pace the royal antechamber. The two guards at the entrance to King Ferdinand's council tent kept watching him, as if wondering what a noble citizen of Don Obrigon's rank was doing in a war battlefield. Don Obrigon's brocade breeches, fine embroidered vest, silk cape, and silver studded boots revealed his rank. At the rustle of damask draperies opening, Don Obrigon sat upright on the wooden bench, anticipating being called in. When Inspector Guerida appeared, Don Obrigon gasped in surprise.

"Looks like you've seen a ghost," Guerida said, laughing.

"I . . . didn't think to find you here . . . I thought—"

Guerida interrupted him. "I know what you thought. You thought I was in Seville napping on the job, didn't you?"

Don Obrigon swallowed hard, trying to explain his confusion. "What I meant was that you were working in Seville from your end to find Isabella."

"Come in," Guerida said, showing him the way into King Ferdinand's chamber.

Don Obrigon followed Guerida with some apprehension. *Did something happen to Isabella?* His chest felt suddenly tight, and his heart skipped a beat. But it couldn't be—Guerida's face was smiling and at ease. He calmed himself, ready to hear news of his daughter. When he entered Ferdinand's war sanctum, he was amazed at the fine linen drapery covering the walls and the solid, carved oak table in the middle of the tent supporting various maps and instruments.

"We're waiting for King Ferdinand to return from breakfast with the queen," Guerida said.

"I had no idea that the queen was present in this war region," Don Obrigon said.

"She always follows her husband, the king, and sometimes assists him in war decisions."

Don Obrigon was silent, his respect for the queen growing. This queen was not only magnanimous in governing her subjects, she also made decisions of the greatest outcome for Spain.

A curtain was pulled back, and King Ferdinand appeared, followed by the duke of Medina Sidonia; Captain Gonzalo de Córdova; and the marques of Cadiz, Rodrigo Ponce de Leon.

Stunned by this chivalresque and famed entourage following the king, Don Obrigon stood up and bowed deeply. He considered himself fortunate to be in the presence of these famous men.

"My dear Don Arturo Obrigon!" King Ferdinand exclaimed with surprise. His face then suddenly became serious. "I know why you're here."

Obrigon knew his face showed pain, and he struggled to control the lost feeling inside him. He smiled faintly at the king. "Sire." He bowed again. "I'm touched by your concern about my daughter's disappearance."

"Of course I am. I remember the last time I saw you in the mayor's palace. Remember how I was gratified by your naming your daughter after the queen?"

"Of course. I remember," Obrigon said. "Both my wife—" He stopped, pierced by another indelible pain in his heart.

Ferdinand quickly said, "I'm so sorry about the loss of your wife. She was a fine woman."

Don Obrigon nodded. "Even as a physician I couldn't save her." He bent his head in sorrow.

"My dear Don Obrigon. You did everything possible, I'm sure. Sometimes we can't fight the will of God. She's with the angels now. But we have good news for you," King Ferdinand added with a smile.

Again Don Obrigon's heart skipped a beat, this time with hope.

"But I'll let Inspector Guerida here tell you about it," said Ferdinand.

Inspector Guerida bowed to King Ferdinand and turned to Don Obrigon. "We found your daughter in the palace of King Boabdil in the Alhambra."

This news hit Don Obrigon like a fist in his chest. "That's most distressing news," he said, then quickly corrected his comment. "What I mean is . . . I'm grateful to hear that she has been found. But is she prisoner in this palace?"

"We traced her back to the harem of Sultana Morayma," said Guerida. He quickly added, "She's unharmed and her honor respected, we're told."

Don Obrigon sighed with relief. "When can we rescue her?"

Inspector Guerida stayed silent, and he looked to King Ferdinand for a reply, but Gonzalo de Córdova took the lead.

"My dear noble Don Obrigon. We're in the middle of a war with the Moors. We expect a swift victory, then we'll save your daughter."

"But she could be killed in the meantime!" Don Obrigon cried in despair.

King Ferdinand raised his hand to allay Don Obrigon's fears. "We have firm assurance that King Boabdil's consort will see to her safety. We also have her own son in our safekeeping under the tutelage of Queen Isabella," he said.

Don Obrigon felt unconvinced by the king's words. "I'd like to help in any way I can. I'm a physician and can administer aid to the soldiers. By the vigilance of the Virgin Mary"—he crossed himself—"very few wounded, I hope."

"This is most welcome, Don Obrigon. I'll deliver you into the capable hands of the marques of Cadiz, Rodrigo Ponce de Leon. You'll assist him in his duties." With these words, Ferdinand got up from his chair and left the tent for his chamber, accompanied by his council.

21

Two Friends Reunited

Don Isaac Abravanel sat in his study toying with a small poniard—a fine double-edged blade with a bejeweled handle. It was an heirloom passed down from his grandfather Don Samuel to his father, Don Judah, then to him. He remembered his grandfather Don Samuel, a venerable old man with creased brows and a long white beard. He cherished the time spent with him looking at the stars and learning about money. Don Samuel was a powerhouse at the Castilian court, serving Fernando IV and Castile's *almoxarif* mayor. Then Don Samuel converted to Christianity in deference to Fernando IV for the favor shown his family, and Don Judah severed relations with his own father. The rumors in Don Abravanel's family were that the threat of prison and the stake motivated Don Samuel to conversion. His father and his grandfather never spoke again. Don Judah packed up the family and left for Portugal.

"Don Abravanel?" a voice startled him.

"Yes, what is it?"

"The envoy from the queen, Don Abraham Senior, is here," his servant said.

"Let him in." Don Isaac placed the poniard in a drawer of his walnut desk and prepared to face his guest Don Senior, who was the chief rabbi in Seville and his mentor.

"My dear Don Isaac," said Abraham Senior to his compatriot in the Jewish community. He clasped both of Don Isaac's hands. "I haven't seen you in months! *¿Cómo estãs?*"

"I'm well, my friend. What brings you here? How did King Ferdinand spare you from your tasks?"

"Slowly, slowly, Don Isaac. I'll tell you everything in good time." He sat down.

"Very well. What brings you here?" Don Isaac repeated as he sat near him.

Don Senior composed himself and remained silent a few moments, while Don Isaac shuffled on his seat, impatient to hear him out.

"Well, you've heard that the war against the Moors is moving along with success," he then said.

He's finally coming to the point, thought Don Isaac. *Hopefully, he won't ask for more funds.* He encouraged him to continue. "Yes, I've heard the same. Go on?"

"The queen, and King Ferdinand," he hastened to add, "are conveying their warm regards to you and your family."

Don Isaac nodded. "I'm very much in the monarchs' debt."

Don Senior continued. "You also know that the treasury is nearly empty."

Don Abravanel tried to keep his chagrin from showing.

"I know how much you've helped with the war funds," continued Don Senior. "The queen is grateful to you for everything you've contributed." He stopped, then continued. "Now Spain is ready for the last and final push for the Reconquista. By conquering Granada, we are near the crowning of España into one unified country."

Don Isaac nodded.

"This is the last time we come to you for a loan. This time we need six hundred thousand *reales*."

Don Isaac's jaw dropped. "There's no way I can raise this amount! I've just given alms to the poor, bought the freedom for two hundred and fifty Jewish slaves caught in Fez, the rebuilding of the synagogue in the Juderia, and now this?"

Don Senior nodded sympathetically.

"We're all under obligations to the poor and the city, and I fully understand your feelings. You've been magnificent so far with sharing of your fortune," said Don Senior.

Don Isaac didn't respond to Don Senior's appreciation. Now he had to outdo those obligations to the land that had given him birth and sustenance.

"I've done the same and more for the progress of España," Don Senior said, "If I hadn't brought Isabella and Ferdinand together, their realms—Castile and Aragon—wouldn't be united. That certainly would've changed our destiny under the Moors."

"True," agreed Don Abravanel. "Yet, we Jews haven't fared any better as a race under the Spaniards. May I remind you of the massacres in 1391, in which four thousand of our brethren were murdered in the Juderia in Seville? What about the riots of Alcala de Guadeira and Écija? How about the two thousand dead souls in Cordoba? And what about since then? How many more Jews will have to meet the sword and fire? How many?" Don Abravanel's voice had risen as he ticked off his grievances.

Don Senior bowed his head, his shoulders dropped, and Don Abravanel could see his brows furrowed in painful memory. Don Senior then raised his head and said, "We've made peace with those terrible times. Now we need to move forward. The conquest of Granada will release us once and for all of all the hate begun by the Dominican brothers and the jealousy that brought this calamity upon our brothers. You'll see."

Don Abravanel suddenly felt as if he'd awakened from a long sleep. No matter how many funds were advanced to the Castilian monarchs, the Jews would always be outsiders in their own homeland of España, How true were his cousin Ana's words: "Next time the fire may be at our door."

"I'll make allowances for the funds. I'll let you know soon," Don Abravanel said.

Disappointment spread over Don Senior's face. Nevertheless, he accepted Don Abravanel's reply.

"I'm heartened to have seen you, Don Abravanel, after this long time. I'll part from you and anxiously await your word," he hastened to add.

Don Senior had been a pillar of the Jewish community in Seville. The older man's sagacity in financial affairs was weighty and considerable. As the favorite financial counselor to Queen Isabella for a number of years, he had received many fortunes and honors from the monarchs. At the age of eighty, Don Senior was at least twenty-five years older than Abravanel, whom he respected and loved as a son. Don Abravanel clasped Don Senior's outreached hand, then put his arm around him and led him toward the exit to his house.

"We'll see each other soon," Don Abravanel said.

Don Senior walked with him silently. Before crossing the threshold, he turned around and said, "We're brothers in fate and destiny, no matter what decision you come to."

Don Abravanel smiled warmly at his former mentor, then saw him climb into his carriage. The wheels creaked forward on the stone pavement, and Don Abravanel watched until the vehicle disappeared into the next street.

Don Abravanel returned to his study and sat for a long time mulling the possible outcome of the approaching war and the feeling of impending doom he couldn't lift from his chest. His beliefs and loyalties lay with his people and his family's Jewish faith, which had grown stronger after his grandfather Samuel's shocking conversion to Catholicism. Now, more than ever, he must stand strong with his people.

We'll wait and see what happens to us.

22

Cordoba

DISHEVELED, HUNGRY, AND TIRED, THE young trio trudged with difficulty over the last hill and was overjoyed to see Cordoba. The red-brown walls of Cordoba, hugging its brood of nestled houses, were laid out before them. In front of the city walls, the Guadalquivir River flowed and snaked under the roman bridge where the Almodóvar gate permitted entry. Two guards with upright lances paced in front of the gate. In the background they could clearly see the Alcázar royal palace, where the monarchs' court presently resided. Miguel remembered his mother saying that the Beneluz family lived in the Juderia, very near the palace.

José and Isabella began to descend the hill, but Miguel stopped them.

"Wait! We must wait for night time."

"Why?" José asked.

"We're still in our Moorish clothes; the guards at the gate will stop us! More importantly, we can't jeopardize the safety of my uncle's family."

"Can't they vouch for us that you're their relative?" Isabella asked.

"First we have to alert them of your presence," said Miguel.

"That's fine." Isabella crossed her arms and mocked Miguel. "First we have to alert your uncle, then we cross. But we can't cross to alert him, so we stay here for eternity."

"Not so quick," Miguel said with a mysterious look on his face. "We'll wait for dark when the guards are asleep."

"What if they wake up while we're crossing the gate?" José asked.

"We'll be very quiet and practically glide before them," Miguel said.

Isabella was not reassured, but she resigned herself to following Miguel's instructions. "All right," she said, "let us find a place to rest while we wait."

All three returned to the top of the hill, where they had hoped to enter the city quickly. Isabella peeled off one of the multiple skirts she wore and spread the garment over the damp ground. She looked up and saw Miguel and José watching her. After some hesitation, she quickly removed another two silk skirts and offered them to the young men. She now remained in her silk pantaloons and her sleeveless vest covering a long-sleeved camisole.

Miguel took the garments from her. He helped José lie down on one of them and covered him with the second. His brother slipped into a restful sleep almost immediately.

Isabella watched Miguel's protectiveness in taking care of his brother, and she began to feel close to him. His actions reminded her of her father's same gestures when they sat outdoors on cool nights. Her father had this same natural tenderness. His medical profession also equipped him with the ability to comfort human beings whether they were suffering or not. Isabella lowered her head with a slight moan. She felt her chest tightening at the recollection of her father. *Will I ever see my parents again?*

"Isabella? What's wrong?" Miguel's voice shook her out of her thoughts.

She didn't answer right away, but raised her head and looked straight at him.

"Why did your mother feel I had to be rescued? Why couldn't she have left me where I was, protected by loving parents in my home? Why?"

Miguel was at a loss to give her a reason. "All I know is my mother wanted to protect you. She never meant to harm you in any way."

Isabella remained silent to what she believed was a genuine answer, and felt relieved not to feel rancor toward Téresa.

Miguel continued. "You do have an uncle, I believe, who asked my mother to take you away from harm," Miguel said. "Apparently, you were in danger, and this uncle of yours thought it was time to remove you."

"Who's this supposed uncle of mine?"

"As I've said before his name is João Treves. And you look like him," he added.

"How do you mean?"

"I . . . only saw him for a brief moment last year. I was leaving for Conchita's house." He stopped, then continued, "Both José and I went to a close neighbor's house in the Juderia whenever João and my mother's other friends came to the house." He hesitated but added, "Your uncle was there, and you do resemble him."

In the absence of moonlight, Isabella couldn't see Miguel's face clearly, but she could see a faint profile whenever he turned his head away from her. "How do you know that we look alike?"

"He had many of your features: your face, your pale coloring, and especially your eyes."

"What do you mean by my eyes?" she asked, her heart skipping a beat.

"Your eyes . . . I mean the . . . the . . . the same color, emerald green . . ." Miguel stuttered. He coughed, cleared his throat, then remained quiet.

"You can't see the color of my eyes!"

At first, Miguel didn't answer, then said, "I can't see them now, but I remember them accurately—the shape, the color . . ."

Isabella felt her face flush despite the cold that was beginning to penetrate every layer of her clothing. She was glad that the darkness had concealed her confusion. She scolded herself for this momentary lack of control, recalling her Spanish tutor's strict advice: "You will control your girlish emotions, but give freedom to your brain. It's the only way to learn!"

An inexplicable feeling occurred to her. It had to do with the green eyes Miguel had just mentioned. She recalled earlier crossing paths with a man with startling green eyes, but where, she couldn't remember.

Isabella and Miguel fell into a deep silence. Yet, she felt connected in the silence by an invisible thread—their thoughts meshing on the same inexplicable level. Miguel was the first to interrupt the shared silence.

"If you want to close your eyes and sleep for a while, I'll keep watch."

Isabella didn't reply. She slid down on her garment covering the ground and in no time was sound asleep.

The only thing that Miguel heard now was Isabella's soft breathing. He tried to cover her with the skirt's corner, but there wasn't enough fabric. He cursed himself for leaving the sheets in the cavern. A menacing doubt began to creep in his head. Would he succeed in protecting both Isabella and José? What if they were found out or their relatives not found? Worse yet, they may not be able to prove their identity.

He suddenly felt weary from the responsibility. He winced as he thought of seeing his mother's reproachful eyes if he failed, then he lowered his heavy head and closed his eyes to rest them. Night had fully descended. No travelers were waylaid at the Cordoba gate. Commerce and merchants had come and gone, and the city was in a deep quiet, except for loud voices from a nearby tavern. The two guards at the gate's entrance were still pacing back and forth. Miguel looked at Isabella and José's still forms resting peacefully despite the cold and, hearing their low muffled breathing, wondered how to wake them when the time came. Meanwhile, the guards stopped their back and forth pacing and sat down on the ground to chat. *When will they doze off?*

As he thought, the night cold became overbearing, and he slapped his arms and shoulders to keep warm. He bolted from his sitting position, and he, too, began pacing back and forth to warm his numb feet. Just then, he saw one of the guards with his head low to his chest. The other guard yawned then closed his eyes too. He quickly went to José and shook him.

"What is it?" José asked, startled.

"Shh." Miguel's finger covered José's mouth. "It's time," he whispered. He did the same for Isabella, shaking her gently. She started and quickly stood on her feet.

"Follow me," Miguel whispered. Holding hands and following each other in single file, all three descended the hill and approached the gate on their toes. Just then, as they came close to the gate, one guard stirred, stretched his limbs, yawned, then fell back asleep with his head hanging low on his chest. Miguel, who had startled and frozen quickly, regained his composure and motioned to José and Isabella to follow him. They crossed the gate and found themselves inside the city near cascading pools by the walls. Moving slowly with frequent checks to see if they were being followed, they found themselves in a large plaza. No lights burned in homes, reassuring them that no one would see them sneaking through the narrow streets. Lit torches attached to walls were few and far between. The rest of the alleys were still and dark. They slowly crossed the vast dark plaza, and found themselves at its opposite end facing four narrow alleys branching as a fan. Miguel looked at the four dark alleys. Which one should they take?

"Isabella whispered to Miguel, "Take the first one near us."

Miguel nodded and motioned them to follow him. The alley was dark, with few torches. They followed it close to the stone houses and walls lining the street. Trees overshot the walls, their branches sweeping their faces as they proceeded with caution, and they occasionally heard water fountains in courtyards behind the walls. Miguel remembered his mother's instruction to go beyond the city center, all the way to the confines of the city where a high wall would encircle a spreading abode and an entrance flanked by two lion statues. At the rate they were walking and in the semidarkness, the odds of finding that rich enclave were low. As they came to the end of one alley, another opened up at a right angle, and they continued their search.

"What are we looking for?" asked José, who had been silent till now.

"A large estate with lions up front," Miguel whispered.

"Real lions?" José's voice trembled.

Miguel laughed low under his breath. "No, *bovo*. They're statues."

José said, "Why didn't you say that in the first place?"

Miguel was about to reply when Isabella said, "You treat your brother shamefully."

"But I meant—"

"No 'buts'," replied Isabella as she hugged José.

"All right," said Miguel, "We've arrived."

Isabella and José looked surprised, and then stopped abruptly in front of two lion statues guarding a large wooden gate. Two burning torches lit the entrance. They could see that past the tall gate many trees lined a courtyard. Miguel looked for a bell to ring but could find none. He picked up some small pebbles at the base of the walls and aimed them at the imposing bronze double doors, hitting them several times. He waited to hear any commotion in the house, but none came. He tried again and again, until a small window at eye level in the door opened up.

"Who's there?" called a bearded old man holding a candle in front of his face.

Miguel spoke to him. “We are your relatives. Nahum and Téresa Costa’s children.”

At the sound of those names, the man came out of the house and approached the gate. He brought the candle close to their faces, and then let them in the front yard. He observed them silently one by one and motioned them to follow him into the house through a narrow entrance hall, through another door, and into an open courtyard. A fountain gently trickling water into its trough with green plants and flowers surrounding it offered an inviting environment. A balcony encircled the second floor with rooms overlooking the courtyard. He led them into a room on the first floor, adjacent to the kitchen, that appeared to be a dining room. He pulled the chairs around the table and motioned them to sit down.

“I don’t remember that your mother had three children?” he asked as he stared at Isabella.

“It’s only my brother and me,” said Miguel, “This is Isabella; my mother instructed us to bring her here.”

The bearded man looked from Miguel to José to Isabella. “I’m your uncle, Isaac Beneluz. My household is asleep now, but in the morning you’ll meet your aunt and cousins.”

Isaac Beneluz left the room without a word and returned with bedding and pillows.

“Follow me,” he said.

All three followed him upstairs to a room where low divans were spread around the room, and without any other word, left them to fend for themselves.

“I presume no food will be offered to us?” José sighed.

“I’m sorry, José,” Miguel said. “We should just be grateful that we made it here safely.”

José didn’t answer, carelessly arranging his bedding and plunging into it. He slumbered immediately. Isabella spread sheets over a divan and reclined wearily into it. She turned toward the wall and fell asleep without a word. Miguel remained awake in the darkness, marveling that they had reached their destination.

What would happen to them tomorrow, he couldn’t guess, nor could he forecast his aunt’s reception of additional guests under their roof. He did know, however, that his mother had spoken kindly of her brother-in-law and his entire family. There had been a split between his uncle and his parents, and he didn't know the reason. At the age of eighteen, he could only guess that the rift between the family members may have been caused by his father's lack of nobility or money. His uncle owned a merchant fleet and had a considerable fortune—making him a *hidalgo*, or gentry, in the eyes of Spanish nobility. Now, only the future would tell if Beneluz's kindness to his brother Nahum's family would bridge the gap of past family feuds.

23

The Last War

UNDER A CLOUDLESS DAWN SKY on a chilly morning, Ferdinand's armies were lined up in the burned-out vega. Not one blade of grass, not one bush or tree to give shade or fruit, or any water canal—the Moors' lifeblood—remained. A massive wall of men and beasts faced the palace city of the Alhambra, the Moors' last vestige on the Iberian soil.

Neighing horses pawed the dusty soil with their hooves, looking for grass and showing their impatience to be released. Foot soldiers adjusted and readjusted their helmets and visors. And nobles kept their favorite horses in check while balancing round bucklers and swords, pikes, axes, and lances. Cuirasses shone in the orange light from a fully awakening sun. Every soldier, legion commander, and war tactician, including the head commander of the Spanish armies, knew this would be the last battle. They would bring glory to Spain, from nobles to foot soldiers, fighting for the blessed cause—the expulsion of the Moors from their Catholic land.

The Moors, who saw from their castle the army and noble Spanish pageantry with their rich array of silks, plumes, colorful battalion banners, and the fanfare of Spanish drums and trumpets, were taunted to cross lances with the Christians. A call to arms was made immediately by the vizier Aben Comixa to prepare the army for combat.

Ferdinand was reviewing his plans for attack and studying the terrain on a large map laid across a camp table. His vassals, nobles, and captains—

Captain Gonzalo de Córdova and his brother, Don Alonso de Aguilar; the duke of Cadiz; the marques of Villena; the count of Tendilla; and the counts of Cabra and Ureña—surrounded him.

"My king," said Don Alonso de Aguilar, a large muscular man in his midforties with graying hair, "I recommend that we attack when the sun is high on the horizon. Our shining metallic arms and mail suits, and metal swords and bucklers will blind the Moors. They won't be able to estimate our numbers."

Ferdinand reflected for a moment on de Aguilar's statement. He then looked to the rest of the assembly that waited respectfully and said, "Is there any objection to delaying an early attack?" The men in assembly were silent. "Then it's decided. We attack at noon," Ferdinand said.

The king's long-time friend, General Hernando del Pulgar, said, "My dear monarch and protector. May I point out a place to put an additional company of men?" He directed Ferdinand's attention to the map.

Ferdinand came closer to the spot where del Pulgar's finger pointed to a glen high in the mountains that overlooked the Alhambra.

"With your permission, let me show you where we can get a strategic advantage to maim the Moors. If we send a company of archers into this mountain pass, we can attack the Moors from the rear."

Ferdinand looked at the map and listened to del Pulgar's explanation. He stroked his small stubble beard and shook his head. "I prefer we keep this able company lower at the foot of the mountain. If we have need for them, they can replace any of our wounded soldiers."

Del Pulgar nodded to his sovereign. "Very well, my king." He turned to his attendant to carry out the order.

As the aide left the tent, another aide arrived. He bowed to the king and waited for Ferdinand to address him.

"Come on, speak!" Ferdinand commanded.

The aide lifted his head and said, "Sire, the queen's entourage is ready to leave."

Ferdinand turned to his assembly. "We'll resume momentarily." He left the tent and joined Queen Isabella dressed in rich damask and velvet skirts and mounted on a colorfully attired horse surrounded by her four children. The Princesses Catalina, Maria, and Juana, and Prince Juan, the heir, were also mounted on gaily dressed horses. The queen bowed her head with a smile in Ferdinand's direction. Ferdinand kissed his queen's hand.

"Go in safety, my dear wife. Everything is in ready for you in the town of Zubia. May the Blessed Mother keep you and my children safe."

Ferdinand kissed his wife's hand again, but only nodded to his children. The children nodded back at their father, knowing to keep their public enthusiasm for him in check. Young Prince Juan, perched on his horse, turned to his father.

"Take me with you, Father. I will fight for España!" He pulled a child-sized sword out of its sheath.

Ferdinand smiled at his son. "Keep your sword for other enemies for when you grow up, my son."

Juan replaced the sword in its sheath along his small thigh and pressed the flanks of his horse, urging him on.

The long train of cavalry, armed men dressed in steel mail, ladies of the court, the queen, and children turned their mounts around and proceeded down the vega on their way toward the mountain heights and past the magnificent Alhambra in Granada.

Down in the scorched vega in front of Santa Fé, fifty thousand foot soldiers and twenty thousand mounted horses presented a united front between the Spanish camp and the Moors. After the queen and her retinue had left the vega and were climbing safely into the Sierra heights, all soldiers unsheathed their swords and presented arms. Ferdinand stood on a promontory with his war council taking a grand view of the war theatre.

As predicted by Don Alonso de Aguilar, deflected sunlight hitting steel arms, bucklers, and helmets, reflected back at the enemy. The gleam of fine steel swords shone as a long wave of blinding light, making the Moors squint on the red crenellated roofs of the Alhambra Towers. The Spanish archers aimed their crossbows in the direction of the Alhambra. In Ferdinand's camp, two hundred iron cannons formed a menacing wall from one end of the vega to the other. Gunners awaited the signal to fire.

On the Alhambra side, ten thousand Moors led by cavalry commander Muza Abul Gazan welcomed the opportunity to cross lances with the Christians. They sallied from their gate, trumpeting their willingness to wage war and galloping deftly on their vigorous Arabian horses. It took them ten minutes to cover the eleven kilometers between Granada and the enemy in Santa Fé.

"Allah Akbar!" Thousands of mounted horsemen and foot soldiers thronged. Deafening war cries escaped their lips at the sight of Spaniards' shining armor and the soldiers lined up in a steel wall. Thousands of voices in the Spaniard camp echoed the war cry and filled the air with their voices. *"¡Santiago!"*

The two armies clashed. Lances broke with the initial blow, and a bloody hand-to-hand combat ensued with mounted horsemen on both sides clashing with their counterparts, sending pieces of metal flying all around them in the fury of the encounter.

Second and third detachments of Moors sallied forth from the gates to encircle the Spanish army from the right flank, but the count de Ureña and the commander of Calatrava met the challengers with their battalions. Blood poured from the Moors' side, and the Spaniards tried hard to protect themselves with their bucklers. Moors were swifter on their agile horses than were the Spanish nobles. Spaniards rode lightweight horses, but were encumbered by heavy metal mail cuirasses and their metal breeches with helmets obscured by feathers and ribbons. Moorish horsemen were vulnerable to wounding and to the slicing of unprotected flesh, while heavily clad Spaniards were better protected from blood-shedding.

Both camps advanced and retreated, under the volleys of firing cannons, with the Spaniards gaining ground and pushing the Moors back to the Alhambra. In the Spanish camp, a horseman gave the signal by slicing his saber through the air for crossbowmen to begin their volley of arrows. Wave after wave of arrows flew to hit their Moorish targets. Four hundred Moor riders and their horses fell to the dust, hit by arrows. Some riders' horses landed on them as they went down screaming in pain, adding to the din. Thousands of soldiers shouted their war cries to give themselves courage. The Moor riders who had luckily escaped the slings of arrows jumped onto their feet and fought in close combat with the Spanish foot soldiers. Men on both sides were lanced through their bodies, which penetrated and sliced their organs—the lucky ones through their hearts. Wounded horses, especially the ones trying to stand upright, added to all cries rising in the dusty and parched vega.

Moors began to fall back in disarray and panic at the sight of charging Spaniards who were gaining ground with their horses. Muza, holding the Mahomet crescent standard, tried in vain to call them back to arms. He stood on his stirrups and cried to his kinsmen, "Fight for your land! Fight for Islam and Allah!" but they fled with panic toward the city's gate with the Christians following them.

In the mêlée, charging horses trampled Moorish soldiers who fell to their knees and stumbled on their bucklers and lances. Hundreds of bodies and pieces of hardware littered the blood-soaked ground. The Moors' pointed helmets and long unraveled turbans slowed their flight toward the city. As the last Moorish horse crossed the city's threshold, the gates banged shut, trapping ten to twenty Spaniards who were still charging at them. Moments later the gates opened and the bodies of dead Spanish soldiers tied to their horses were sent out. King Ferdinand and his party watched the Moors' revenge in horror. All present crossed themselves as they prayed for the souls of Spanish soldiers.

"¡España Vive!" A great cry roared from thousands of Spanish lips. Soldiers turned to their comrades and embraced each other with great joy while jumping and hugging in their happiness. They had beaten the Moors, and now all they had to do was to collect the prize—Granada. As they were celebrating, the Alhambra gates opened and turbaned soldiers began to collect their dead and wounded. The ground was soaked in blood and horses were expiring—the carnage was total.

General Muza Abul Gazan stood on a promontory taking stock of the battle. Realizing all was lost, he cried in agony and fury. "To the next battle!" he proclaimed, and then urged his horse to a gallop, not toward the Alhambra but toward the mountains on the other side of the Alhambra to the heights of the Sierras. His soldiers followed him and disappeared in a cloud of dust as they entered the base of the mountains to the east heading toward a no-man's-land of boulders, snow, and brigands' nests high in the snowy Sierras.

Several Spanish squadrons readied in pursuit of Abul Gazan and his men, but a signal from Ferdinand's camp prevented them from the chase. "We'll deal with those renegades later," Ferdinand said. He descended from his promontory and summoned his council and the royal scribe. Within minutes the scribe entered the royal tent where Ferdinand and all his faithful advisors were assembled.

"We'll send an ultimatum to King Boabdil to surrender his city as stipulated in the treaty he signed. We won't be patient any longer!" Ferdinand's voice boomed with the anger and frustration of being close to his goal and yet not able to attain it because of the stubbornness of this king.

"Send for an envoy to Granada to begin capitulation of the city." He turned to his scribe to dictate the conditions of the surrender of Granada.

"Our demands for the fulfillment of the treaty between Spain and the king and Sultan Abu Abdallah Mohammad XII, also known as Boabdil El Chico: That on the year 1487, upon his release from the castle of Lucena, where he had been imprisoned, he consented to rule Granada as a vassal and a tributary kingdom of Castile and Aragon with our support against his uncle El Zagal and to regain his throne from him. Now, he must relinquish the kingdom of Granada as proscribed in the treaty signed by him in 1487 in the castle of Porcuna."

Ferdinand paused for a moment, then continued. "In the Treaty of Granada, the Catholic King Ferdinand II of Aragon of the House of Barcelona, and the Catholic Queen Isabella of Castile of the House of Trastámara, with our combined kingdoms and power, we promise these rights to all Moors:

"That all persons should be free to exercise their Muslim religion. That they should all take an oath of fealty to the kingdom of Castile, and that they should all be free subjects of the crowns of Castile and Aragon. That they be exempted to pay tribute to Castile for three years.

"That all residents shall be protected from harm and reside in their dwellings as before, and that they should keep all their possessions, arms, and horses. That they should all be allowed to practice their laws, religion, and functions as before. That no Christian nor Jew in public office should rule over them. That all Christian prisoners be returned and all Muslim captives returned to their families. That those who should choose not to be ruled by Christians may leave for Africa without taxes imposed upon them. That all Muslims be exempted for a number of years from our taxes.

"That they should not wear any badges, as with the Mudéjares, conquered Moslems, and the Jews. That their prayers should not be interrupted. That any Muslim wishing to become a Christian should do so after a number of days reflecting upon his actions and with the approvals of Mohammedan and Christian judges. That all the Christians who have become Muslims should not be forced or coerced to return to Christianity. That the city of Granada should be delivered, including its fortress, the palace of the Alhambra, the Alcazar, the Albaicín, and the Vivarambla, where all commerce took place, and all adjacent fields and lands, and their artillery, to be delivered in sixty days.

"These instructions should be considered as the Treaty of Granada, to be signed no later than the twenty-fifth of November 1491.

"In additional articles, King Boabdil, including his wife, Morayma; Ayxa, his mother; his children; and Zoraya, his late father King Muley Abul Hassan's wife, is to receive the power to sell his royal patrimony of lands and houses. To him and his descendents in perpetuity, he is to receive the sovereignty towns and valleys of the Alpuxarras region and the eastern vicinity of Almeria. On the day of surrender, King Boabdil is to receive thirty thousand gold pieces." Ferdinand finished his instructions to the scribe.

The scribe put down his quill, blotted the excess ink, and presented the document to King Ferdinand for his signature and seal. Just then, an envoy entered the tent and bowed to Ferdinand.

"Take those documents and have them signed by the queen upon her return, then deliver them to be signed by King Boabdil El Chico with great haste."

"I'll dispatch them with the utmost speed, my King." The envoy stepped backwards to leave the tent. His hand cradled the official deathblow to 700 years of Moorish existence in Spain.

Don Obrigon waited impatiently in the antechamber for an audience with Ferdinand. Springing from his seat, he bumped into an envoy leaving the tent.

"I beg your pardon," Obrigon said to the harried envoy disappearing out the door's opening. He then turned to a royal official sitting at his desk. "I'm here to request an audience with the king," he said to the clerk.

The clerk asked, “What’s the urgent matter for which you seek the king?”

“His majesty is aware that I’m here in the capacity of physician.”

“That won’t get you an audience. You need to submit papers to His Highness for him to decide whether he will see you or not.”

Don Obrigon, patient until now, began to feel irritated by the thoroughness of this official.

“Where do I get those papers, and where should I submit them?”

“Go to the next tent, and the official there will grant you those papers.”

Resigned, Obrigon turned to leave, when the curtains to Ferdinand’s quarters were pulled aside to reveal a host of army men and nobles assembled around the king. His general, Don Alonso de Aguilar, leaving the royal tent accompanied by his brother, Captain de Córdova, came forward.

“This must be Don Obrigon,” said Don Alonso with a smile upon his tanned, muscular face. He rubbed his peppered mustache and waited for Don Obrigon to speak.

Don Obrigon, stunned at being acknowledged by this famous warrior whose triumphs in successive wars were the stuff of legend, stuttered, “I . . . am most . . . gratified to be acknowledged by your person, General.”

“I know who you are by the king’s warm regards concerning your family—especially your daughter, Isabella.”

At the mention of his beloved daughter, Obrigon’s shoulders slumped.

“Now, now, my dear Don Obrigon. You mustn’t lose courage. We’re now very close to taking possession of the Alhambra. We’re bound to find persons who saw your daughter, who talked to her, or who know right now where she is.”

Obrigon straightened his posture and apologized profusely. “I’m confident that she’ll be found under your vigilant watch.”

“We’ll be in touch with you very soon if we hear anything. You’ll be the first one summoned,” said De Aguilar with empathy.

“Thank you from the bottom of my heart,” said Don Obrigon, bowing before de Aguilar.

De Aguilar didn’t reply, but took his leave accompanied by his brother.

Don Obrigon was left alone with the clerk, who looked upon him now with deference. How many more days or months would he have to wait to see his querida daughter, Obrigon wondered?

24

Capitulation

HIGH IN HIS TOWER, BOABDIL watched the war scene with great pain. He was now finished as a king. His remaining soldiers were weak with exhaustion and hunger; his obligation now was to capitulate to Ferdinand and expect clemency from his camp. Boabdil turned away from the barred window to the council.

"Allah Akbar! Wa la ghaliba illa Allah!" There is no conqueror but Allah! Boabdil thought.

"We're now going to surrender to Spain." His words died in his throat as he lowered his head in agony. He then raised his head toward the window that had confirmed his defeat and said apologetically, "What more can we do? They're more powerful. They have more men and horses, and they haven't been starving these past months. We're defeated."

The council remained silent until one of his viziers said, "Sire, can't we at least wait to hear word from Muza, your valiant defender? We can still fight."

Yusef Aben Comixa, Boabdil's minister, interjected, "Muza has fled with his men. He's no longer valiant, nor is he part of the people!"

Just then angry voices hit his ears and filled him with shock and pain.

"Curse upon your house, *El Zogoybi*! You were indeed unlucky the day you were born!" The raging voices rose like noxious fumes from fires in the heart of his people. "We are tired of fighting, of hunger, and living in fear of our lives and our sons' lives. Give up this land. Give up this unlucky throne!"

Boabdil couldn't bear to hear any more advice. The thoughts whirled in his head; his chest heaved up and down with the strain of the decision that was tearing him apart. He got up from his throne and went to open a window. He could hear louder cries rising from below in the town from many women wailing for their fathers, brothers, and husbands who had perished at the hand of the Spaniards.

"I can't hear the women's funerary cries any longer," he declared. "I'm indeed an unlucky child born under an unlucky star."

His wife, Morayma, awakened by the lamentations and screams of the population, hurried into the council chamber to console him.

"My husband, lover, and friend. You are the king. The people owe you allegiance. They are in grief at the moment, but in the morning their grief will be quieter; they'll be prostrated." She looked at him to see if he had heard her. But the king remained lost in his own grief for failing his people utterly, sealing his fate, and creating the certainty of losing his crown to the infidel.

"Tomorrow will bring news of our defeat. It's the end of our lives in this land. The land cherished by our ancestors and won by the blood and swords of our fathers is lost to us forever," Boabdil uttered.

Morayma remained silent when Boabdil's mother, Ayxa, entered the reception hall in a flurry of black robes.

"What have you done, my son?" she demanded.

"Nothing that I haven't done before. You've exhorted me many times to stand and fight for my throne. So I did. And in doing so, I lost."

"Nothing's lost yet!" she snapped. "The morning will bring more news, better news."

"Yes, my king and husband," Morayma interjected on a different note. "Tomorrow we may finally see our son. Our son"—her eyes sparkled—"who has grown away from us for many years and without our guidance."

Ayxa la Horra lowered her head.

"Let's go to our rest now," Boabdil said. He left the hall followed by his wife, Morayma.

Ayxa la Horra was left alone to contemplate her son's demise and the demise of the kingdom. It had happened to her late husband, Muley Abul Hassan, Boabdil's father. He'd had to fight El Zagal, his own brother, from usurping the throne, to save the earthly paradise of El Andaluz lands—its fortresses, fields, and waterways—which were now on the verge of being taken away by the enemy. She had protected her son and succeeded in placing him on the throne, at the expense of her husband. All the intrigue and backstabbing she inflicted to keep her rival, Zoraya, the infidel Christian who her husband favored over her, from placing her own son on the throne had been done in vain. Ayxa had failed as well.

25

A Family Reunited

FAR FROM THE RUMBLE OF retaliatory battle, on a cul-de-sac street in the city of Cordoba, the Beneluz family was waking up to find three new additions to their household. The patriarch, Rabbi Isaac Beneluz, had just finished his morning prayer when his confused wife entered the room.

"Why didn't you tell me we had guests? Shame on you!" she said, pointing her index finger at him.

"I didn't tell you because I didn't want to alarm you last night. Besides, what good would it have done? You wouldn't have slept a minute worrying about their well-being and what you'll cook for them. Right, Rivka?" He came close to her and looked at her with smiling eyes.

She smiled back sheepishly. Her blue eyes looked at him. "But they're your brother's children. How can we not let them feel welcome in our house?"

His face suddenly lost its smile. "We have to do more than that. I believe their mother is lost to them." He raised his eyes to the ceiling and pronounced a small prayer silently.

Rivka blanched and seized his hands. "What are you telling me, Husband?"

"Just that. I haven't asked them any questions yet. But why would those two innocent children leave the safety of their home to come to us?"

Rivka nodded her head. "I'll go into the kitchen and prepare them a large meal."

Beneluz smiled at his wife's ability to return to household affairs immediately. He turned to the matters at hand. He left his small study and climbed the stairs to the second floor, where the bedrooms were lined up one after the other. He reached the last room at the corner of the building and knocked at the door. Miguel's head popped into the door's opening. Seeing that the younger boy was still asleep, Beneluz quietly motioned to Miguel to follow him to the lower level apartments.

Intrigued, Miguel followed his uncle. They passed the center courtyard with the splashing fountain to the last room at the end of a hallway.

"Come into my study," Beneluz said to Miguel.

With curiosity, Miguel entered a retreat that revealed his host as a book-learned man. The walls were covered with old parchments rolled up and stacked along the shelves; the desk was strewn with papers, quills, and ink blotters; and papers were piled on one corner of his desk.

"I see that you're observing my everyday life in this study," Beneluz said. "However, this is not where I spend my entire day. As the community rabbi of Cordoba, I have my obligatory duties to the Jews living here."

"My mother told me of your rabbinical studies and leadership of the Jewish community. She praised you highly whenever she mentioned your name," Miguel said. He felt his heart aching and emotions overwhelming him at the thought of his mother. Tears welled up in his eyes.

Beneluz remained silent.

Miguel wiped away the tears that had come to his eyes. "I'll tell you everything that's happened," he said, then related to Beneluz his mother's confessions to him, the instructions pertaining to Isabella, and the shocking arrest of their mother.

Beneluz said with a reassuring voice, "Right now you have nothing to fear. All three of you are welcome in my home, and you can be sure that we'll protect you."

"I thank you, Uncle Beneluz," Miguel said. "There's one thing I don't understand." Miguel looked into his uncle's eyes. "What did really happen between my father and you?"

Beneluz remained silent for a long time. He then said, "Your father, my dear little brother, decided to break away from the family. He converted and moved all of you to Seville. I had warned him of the authorities' suspicions of Conversos, that in the nature of The Church there was a danger to him and your mother. Your brother hadn't been born then. I recall you as a small boy, inquisitive and playful . . ." Beneluz had somehow digressed from his story, but then his brows became creased as he continued. "I tried to bring him back to Cordoba, but to no avail. Your father's commerce with the Moors in Granada was thriving. You must remember that at the time, relations between the Moorish and Spanish monarchs were not as critical. There were even jousts and events practiced between the nobilities of Spain and the Moorish kingdom. These encounters became less prevalent, and the Moors became more confrontational. All travel to Granada became dangerous and was forbidden. Your father wouldn't hear of it and continued his trade to King Abdallah. That's why The Church used the 'Judaizing' pretext to arrest your father." Beneluz stopped.

Miguel had this horrible thought that perhaps his father had been too callous in choosing his trade over the safety of his own family. "Are you saying that my father was a traitor?"

"That's not what I'm saying!" Beneluz protested. "Your father wanted to make his mark in the world. He didn't want my help, nor did he listen to your mother's pleas to abandon his travels to Granada. All I'm saying is that your father was too proud. By then he had converted and brought your mother and yourself into this alien religion. I warned him that conversion wasn't a sure way to escape the Inquisition, and he would be under close scrutiny."

Miguel lowered his head at the painful realization that his father—the man he adored—had hardened to his brother's concerns out of pride and chose to alienate himself from his religion and family.

"I understand now," Miguel whispered. After a long silence he said, "I accept your hospitality and thank you for it."

"Tsk, tsk, don't mention it. We're family. Let's head to the dining room now, or your aunt will be cross with us for delaying breakfast."

Miguel followed his uncle to the dining room, enticed by the appetizing aroma of cooked onions. He now felt safe and was sure his dangerous trek had come to an end.

26

An Empire Fades

THE MORNING MIST HAD DISSIPATED, and a clear second day of January in the year of 1492 revealed itself throughout the vega, the snowcapped Sierras, and at the Alhambra emerging from the fog in a red splendor of towers and minarets. Granada's weather had cooperated in this day of surrender. In the Alhambra palace of his ancestors—the Nasrid Dynasty—King Boabdil stood before his people, nobles, generals, and families assembled down in the square to hear their monarch's last words.

"My dear subjects, my venerable mother, my wife, my loyal nobles, and citizens of Moorish Granada. In my haste to secure the throne from my father, I've sinned against Allah, and you, my people. For the survival of your families and your children, and for the honor of your wives and daughters, and for all our people, I've agreed to surrender our beloved and eternal capital and land of Granada. I've also agreed to surrender for your safety, your worship of Allah, and the continuation of your properties through the generations, so you may have a happier life than what my ill-omened birth of El Zogoybi brought you!"

Tears formed in the eyes of all those who had heard King Boabdil's words of submission to the Spanish kingdom. A quiet murmur followed in which one could hear muffled voices saying, "A long life to the unfortunate Boabdil." But the people had no strength to rejoice for their safety in the agreed-upon future. All they could envisage was the long sorrow of leaving their centuries-old homes and land that their ancestors had provided for them. They would never live under Spanish rule. They bowed their heads in grief but felt relief for the safety of their lives, and for no longer having to see their children hunger. They filed past their king, bowed and left silently for their homes to begin their exodus.

Abul Cazim Abdel Melic, Granada's old governor, left on his horse accompanied by his aide to deliver the signed surrender papers to Ferdinand and Isabella. Upon arrival, the monarchs' assembly greeted him. The Spanish nobility, the generals, and the armies who had fought for the crown were assembled in the immense vega in front of the army town of Santa Fé.

Abul Cazim dismounted and bowed to Ferdinand and Isabella mounted on their richly decked-out horses. The pennants of various army contingents flew gently in the breeze, and the banner of Spain with its intermingled castle-and-lion motif swayed in the caressing air from right to left as if to signify that the vega valley, the snowcapped mountains of the Sierra Nevada, the red towers of the Alhambra on the hill in front of them, and the hamlets dotting the hills in the distance were now the length and breadth of new dominions and territories acquired under the crown of Spain. A weighty silence took place while Ferdinand unfurled the Declaration of Surrender and read its contents. He turned to Queen Isabella, who nodded her head in agreement. The queen gently urged her horse to turn and face the Spaniards assembled before her.

"My dear husband and king, my dear subjects and people of this land. We've fought a noble battle throughout the years, and we've acquired all the lands in Iberia under one flag, the flag of España. The wars are over! Long live peace and prosperity!"

"Hurrah! Hurrah! Long live España!" The great shouts escaped from the lips of every soldier, and every noble and their attendants assembled in the vega. Their horses punctuated the shouts by neighing and pawing the ground. Abul Cazim was the only man who remained silent. He felt a pain in all his bones at this precise moment that Granada was no more. He mounted his horse silently and took off for Granada with his silent aide.

When Abul Cazim arrived at the Alhambra by the Gate of the Seven Floors, he found the royal procession of King Boabdil followed by his viziers, his secretary, and his Moorish nobles waiting to proceed. They made their way with a slow and precise gait of their Arabian horses and moved forward down the vega to meet with their Spanish counterparts. The Moorish royal party advanced and began to see the assemblies and the richly caparisoned royal horses of the Spanish monarchs. The Moorish cavalry led by King Boabdil came to a halt, and only Boabdil—Abu Abdullah Muhammad XII—came forward on his richly dressed horse with leather and brocade saddle and silk stirrups with gold buckles. Now that he was a vassal and subject of the Spanish king, Boabdil prepared to dismount his horse to kiss Ferdinand's ring, but the Spanish monarch stopped him with a motion of his hand. Ferdinand came to meet him on his horse with the respect due to another king. They bowed to each other, then Boabdil bowed in the direction of Queen Isabella. She nodded her head with graciousness for the vanquished monarch. Boabdil, his gentle face framed by his thick black beard and mustache, showed a sad smile as he bowed again to Isabella.

As if on cue, a great commotion burst through the gates of the Alhambra. Thousands of Moor subjects, on horses and mules packed with the personal belongings of the populace of Granada, poured through the gates.

A separate and mournful party of the royal family left through an isolated postern-gate of the Alhambra to maintain their privacy and dignity. Boabdil's mother, Ayxa la Horra; Morayma; his stepmother, Zoraya; and her son, with all their domestics and guards, were all mounted on horses and mules and followed by carts laden with the royal treasures and personal belongings. Only Morayma had reason for hope: her son should now be returned to her as promised.

They were leaving behind them centuries of tradition—not just the marble palaces of the Alhambra. The golden halls had seen countless emissaries and visiting ministers in the hall of ambassadors. The vega valley with its woods and olive groves and watered by the Genil River had given them sustenance. The lush environment of pomegranate trees and courtyards cooled by hundreds of fountains and fruit trees represented the good, rich life in Moorish Granada. Tears and lamentations that had been held in until now to keep up courage began to fill their eyes and wet their lips.

At that precise moment, Queen Isabella advanced on her horse to deliver Boabdil's son, who had been held captive for six years. The lad, riding a young mule, had grown a full head taller, with a soft face and tousled black hair. Boabdil took his son off the mule and hugged him close to his heart with strong emotion. He presented the keys to Granada to the queen, then turned his horse around. Still holding tightly on to his son, he took leave of Queen Isabella, leaving with a sad heart to join his family and head east to the Valley of Purchena over the heights of the Alpuxarras.

When Boabdil arrived at the secluded meeting place, Morayma ran to his horse and tore her son from his father's lap. She put him on the ground and crouched to look at him.

"How you've grown, my beloved son Ahmed!" Morayma cried with tears of joy.

The boy, dressed in a silk Spanish suit, looked at her curiously, then bowed in Spanish custom with his right arm folded against his midriff and his left folded against his back.

Morayma stood up and grabbed her son with both arms. She burst into tears.

Boabdil's mother, Ayxa, sat haughtily on her horse watching the scene with dry eyes.

Boabdil descended from his horse and went to Morayma. "My dear wife, we must leave now."

Morayma nodded between her tears and was helped to her horse while her son, Ahmed, was lifted by Boabdil to his.

The royal party rejoined by their family made their way up the Alpuxarras Mountains to a promontory that gave full views of the vega and Granada. The rays of the sun shone over the minarets and red towers of the

Alhambra. A necklace of green foliage wound around the red stone towers and trimmed the silver-blue waters of the Xenil River. Below the Alhambra, the Xenil River met the Darro River in a syncopated dance of clear water mixing and spilling onto the vega for life-giving blessings.

From his vantage point, Boabdil could see a giant silver cross installed on the Torre de la Vela to bring the Christian faith to the land of the Moors. A colorful Spanish banner hoisted from the highest tower of the Alhambra unfurled in a gently swaying motion that brought a wave of sobs and lamentations from the Moors assembled on the hill overlooking Granada. A sudden faint sound of artillery accompanied by smoke signaled that the city and land of Granada was now in possession of the Spaniards, and lost forever to the Moors and their descendants.

Boabdil let go of his tears. "Allah's will be done." The words came out softly among the tears.

Boabdil's mother, Ayxa, who silently contained her seething resentment at the Spanish monarchs, now vented her grief upon her son. "Weep as a woman, my son, for what you could not defend as a man!"

"Allah Akbar," cried Boabdil with freely flowing tears. "What misfortunes have I brought upon my people."

27

Destiny Rings

QUEEN ISABELLA SAT IN COURT in the marble ambassador hall in the Alhambra. Four loyal subjects had solicited an audience. Fray Juan Perez; Luis de Santángel; Alonso Quintanilla, her first counselor; and Senior, her financial advisor, needed her attention. She made it a point to listen to requests and arguments and to deliver clemency with an open mind. Her conclusions were based on her quick thinking and sense of fairness.

The morning began badly with her daily counselors complaining about the audience requested by Columbus. Columbus requested too much, they said, and took it upon himself to grant his own rewards. Columbus couldn't merit honors and monetary rewards for his pains and travails. She was weary. With the end of the Granadian wars, her mind and body screamed for a well-deserved rest. Ferdinand returned to Aragon to confer with his advisors on the state of Naples—a vassal state of the kingdom of Aragon—and its allies. Her trusted nobles had quitted her side to spend time with their families at their estates. She alone remained to give advice to her court and her people and issue the daily judgments concerning criminal sentences.

"My queen." A voice ringing in her ears pulled her from deep thoughts.

She looked up to see her court minister demanding her attention. She raised a tired hand. "What is it, Master Juan?"

"The men requesting an audience are here."

"Let them in," she said. She saw that the four men were none other than Columbus's supporters.

"I've made my decision," Queen Isabella announced. The men's mouths were still open.

"My queen," began Quintanilla, "we come to plead to you to give Columbus another chance. He's a loyal supporter to your cause. He has patiently waited for the end of the war. His only desire is to reward Spain and only Spain!"

"Yes, illustrious and benevolent Queen," said Fray Perez, his hands clasped in prayer mode. "He's the only man who could voyage on the Atlantic without fear. Columbus brings years of travel with unlimited map experience."

Isabella looked at her past confessor with warmth and friendship. She remembered her years of attendance in his church in Arévalo, and the years of his paternal guidance at Sunday church, or whenever she sought his advice. He had been her favorite confessor and friend.

"I trust your words and friendship about Columbus. It's on that trust that I gave you an audience. I would like to help him, but our treasury has been completely depleted by the wars."

Luis de Santángel, who had stood quietly the whole time, approached the throne and bowed deeply to Isabella.

"Beloved Queen. You have been more than magnanimous to Columbus, and have given him audience upon audience, and have listened to him with patience and benefaction."

Isabella nodded with every one of his words.

Luis de Santángel continued. "Now it's time for our land to reap the rewards of expansion and commerce. With great land comes the duty to populate and sow fields to feed, clothe, and educate the people."

This last word by de Santángel hit a chord. Isabella had begun reforms for learning institutions to expand and to educate the masses. She advocated expansions and new buildings to house future learned generations. That leaning on education was Isabella's legacy, along with fairness within the judicial system and peace between factions of the nobility.

"Continue," Queen Isabella said to de Santángel.

"I'll personally loan the crown seventeen thousand *florins* to undertake this voyage."

Her financial advisor Abraham Senior nodded his head.

Fray Perez jumped in immediately, and before the queen could speak her gratitude to Santángel for past loans to the realm, he said, "My dear queen. This voyage will put us on the map of Europe. Besides the riches it might bring from Cathay and Cipangu, where the streets are paved with gold, we will gain souls for Christendom. That would place you and His Majesty, King Ferdinand, as the Catholic queen and king above all kingdoms in Europe. Those were your dreams as a young girl for all the sins committed at your half-brother's court. You alone, with your consort, will regulate that Spain is Christian in its heart."

"Please, my queen. I beg you to recall Columbus before he sails for France and before all is lost for Spain," Quintanilla added.

Isabella was moved by the supplication of these men who demanded nothing for themselves, but had only the welfare of Spain in mind.

"Go and call him back! Make haste! Tell him that I agree to his demands!" She joined with the others in the feverishness of excitement and enterprise.

All four men bowed with reverence. Fray Perez went to Isabella and kissed her ring while mumbling, "Thanks to the Lord . . . thanks to our most noble queen."

Far from the masses of people surrendering and victorious men receiving compensation, Columbus observed from a distant hill the saga of an empire changing hands. For him nothing had changed. He was still poor; his dream of sailing west was still a dream and nothing more. He was still the same poor navigator having dreamed for seventeen years the same unfulfilled dream, and the penniless father of two young boys—one cared for in a monastery, and the other by his late wife's parents.

At the age of forty, he was now considered an old man with few years left. He felt bitter and angry for seventeen lost years of hope and rejection. The queen of Spain had now rejected him for the last time. His next step would be King Charles the VIII and the kingdom of France.

"Then go to him!" Queen Isabella had replied in concert with her advisers when he told her that. The rebuff and humiliation still tormented him. He only asked for a just reward for making possible the riches Spain would gain. The gold, precious jewels, and new Christian souls would make Spain a world power.

He was now through with Spain. His brother Bartholomew waited in France for his word to engage the French monarch about the merits of this enterprise. He'd join his brother and convince the French king without delay. Columbus turned his mule around toward wooded areas—toward Palos.

Columbus traveled more than nine kilometers after leaving the Alhambra. He crossed the small, stoned-arched bridge of Pinos over the gentle Genil River. He stopped his mule to take in a bucolic scene of barley fields, vineyards, and gentle hills and forget his pain at having failed yet again. Now he had to begin anew, request an audience at the French court, wait to hear about his request, and be subjected to ridicule from the court's audience. Worst of all, what was he to live on? The little living money allocated to him by Queen Isabella had now run out, and all he possessed in his pouch were a few maravedís.

Oh woe, woe is me, he thought in despair. He watched a small bird land on the stone parapet where he'd been leaning for some time. It shook its red plumage, and its constant chattering distracted him. The feathered bird had no fear of the immobile man standing next to him. Columbus stared fixedly at his plumage for a long moment. He felt a strange sensation of being at one with the bird. He wondered how many colorful birds he would find in Cathay or Cipangu. How many heathens would he bring back with him to be converted to the true Christian faith? Thinking of the gold, silver, and precious jewels he would bring back to his future benefactors made his head spin with renewed excitement and new vigor. No matter—a new royal patron was bound to be convinced of this voyage. He would never rest until this enterprise became a reality.

He left the parapet and rejoined the patient mule. Columbus fed the mule a handful of grain from the saddlebag. Then he took a chunk of black bread from his pack, wetted it with the water gourd he carried, and chewed on it.

"¡Arre!" Columbus mounted and directed the animal off the bridge with a slight pressure of his legs on the animal's flank.

He heard shouts behind him. "Stop! Stop!"

Columbus turned around to look in the direction of the calls and saw two riders galloping on the bridge toward him with a riderless horse. The first thought that came into his head was that he would be arrested for his impertinence at the court in Granada. He stiffened, his pulse racing, and waited for the horse riders to catch up to him. Out of breath, they overshot him, then turned around and slowly trotted to where he stood.

"Christopher Columbus . . . the queen demands that you come back!"

"Why?" Columbus asked firmly.

"The queen will grant all of your requests and demands for the voyage. We brought this horse for you to ride."

Columbus looked dumbfounded. Was it a trick to humiliate him again? Should he trust her? But then, he thought he really had nothing to lose by returning.

"I'll follow you to the queen," Columbus said, and left his mule in the care of a peasant in the field.

The kilometers back to Granada flew by in much less time than his trip out as he rode the sleek third horse, keeping up with the feverish pace of his escorts.

Again he stood before Isabella, whose benevolent smile reassured him that it was true. His heart thumped loudly in his chest as he tried hard to retain his composure and not jump for joy.

"We've agreed to your terms, Cristóbal Colón," Queen Isabella said. "You'll keep one tenth of all the gold, revenue, and treasures that are returned to Spain. You'll now be called Don Columbus and 'Great Admiral of all the Oceans,' and governor of the lands discovered for the crown of Spain. You'll pay for one-eight of the voyage and for all expenses, as you've already promised. Now go, Admiral Cristóbal Colón!"

Columbus remained standing, apparently speechless. Fray Perez, standing near him, threw him a sharp glance, shaking him out of his trance.

"My most gracious and benevolent queen." Columbus bowed. Standing upright, he faced the queen and continued. "Words cannot express my deepest gratitude and joy. My seventeen years of waiting have now been well worth it. I can't thank you enough from the bottom of my heart."

"Go, my admiral, with the blessings of our mother church and on behalf of my husband, King Ferdinand, and the people of Spain. Go in peace and much success." Isabella made a sign for him to withdraw.

Columbus felt as if he were walking on air as he left the hall of ambassadors in the Alhambra. Outside the palace, he walked slowly among the gardens flanking the entrance and smelled the sweet scent of ripe citrus fruit, still in the air of this chilly January morning. He thought that life could be as sweet as the succulent orange fruit, and it could reward those who labored. Much awaited him when he returned from his voyage. He smiled.

28

The March of History

THE PEACEFUL DAYS AND NIGHTS passed rapidly for Miguel, Josè, and Isabella. They'd become integrated into the Beneluz family, folded into their daily household duties and the prayers before and after the meals. Miguel watched Isabella observing silently the strange yet in-some-ways-familiar rituals of bathing and of washing hands before eating. The patriarch, Isaac Beneluz, patiently helped all three of them to become familiar with family members and household rituals.

Of the four Beneluz children, the eldest and most pious was Avram. He was about the same age as Miguel, almost eighteen, a ripe age for marriage. The second son, León, was Avram's opposite. He was seventeen and showed promise with his hands in the skill of woodcarving. He made drinking and food utensils and had undertaken furniture building for the household, making both his father and mother pleased with him. The youngest two children, Guerson and Mica, were twelve and ten, respectively. They both helped their mother with the daily chores of gathering water from the outside well and feeding and attending to their animals in the attached rear barn—when they weren't filling the house with their rambunctious youthfulness.

Miguel learned that Isaac Beneluz made his fortune in commerce: shipping wool and goods by mule train north to Aragon and south to the Granada border. He owned two ships to ferry the wool west; grain and luxury items such as silks, brocades, precious jewels, and expensive woods went to the ports in Seville, and as far as Portugal. Miguel's father, Nahum, had been a young lad when Isaac took him along on lengthy sea voyages to the lands of spices in Asia. Isaac taught his brother, Nahum, the skills and knowledge of commerce, and how to use a fee to appease the lords and nobles whose lands he had to cross. Nahum learned the trade fast and became a full partner to the Beneluz estate. Isaac said that Nahum proposed branching out into the northern Castilian valley, the surrounding areas of Seville in Alcalá de Guadaira, and north to Carmona.

Isaac's business provided his family with comfort without his having to worry about his future and the futures of his four sons. He feared that the farther his commerce took him, the more dangerous the journeys would be. He told Miguel the consolidation of Spain's lands from the Moors made journeys life-threatening, with robbing bandits on the roads, higher fees demanded by nobles, and tax surcharges levied from the royal houses. He refused to allow Nahum expansion of the trade. Strife built between the two brothers until one day Isaac discovered Nahum had left for Seville. Isaac sent missives and letters to small-town governors and to Seville with mail carriers to search for his brother, but Nahum couldn't be found.

Two years later, Isaac received news from Nahum that he had married, had a small son, and fared well in his own commerce. Isaac Beneluz also learned that Nahum had converted and changed his name from Beneluz to Costa. It was the only news he received until he learned from Téresa of Nahum's death. For a long time he mourned the death of his brother, blaming himself for not expanding his territory as Nahum had suggested. Now he had to do right by his brother and protect his children along with his own family.

"May I help you with your work, Uncle?"

Isaac turned around to find Miguel standing on the doorstep of his study.

"Dear Nephew, you remind me now of your dear father—*zichrono le bracha*, his memory be blessed." Isaac pulled up a small bench and gestured for Miguel to sit down next to him. After shuffling the papers on his desk, he turned to Miguel.

"I have many metals in the fire," he said. "My ships provide much work and payroll for my sailors and my managers, and the most important aspect of my business is my land-travel commerce. Without my voyaging travelers, I have no commerce."

"How do you know, Uncle, if the buying and selling is conducted with honesty?" Miguel asked.

"That's a clever question, Nephew. I have an overseer who reports to me any misdeeds, and who supervises all my workers. The managers report to him, and he reports to me."

"What if your overseer steals from you?"

"That is always a possibility, but I have to trust him. Without trust there is no commerce, and without commerce there is no living."

Miguel lowered his head in thought. His uncle was a trusting man. Would the authorities trust his judgment? His mother had trusted them and where had it gotten her? He creased his forehead under the painful memory of her arrest. Where could she be right now?

"Now, now, Nephew. Don't give your thoughts too much time. Help me here with this paperwork." He laid before him a pile of documents with columns. "Add these numbers for me. Sometimes, I find them tedious and procrastinate to finish the task."

Miguel took the quill from his uncle's hand.

Isaac left Miguel to his work and headed for the kitchen, where his wife was kneading dough for the Sabbath. Wearing a white apron, Isabella helped her with flour that spread wide swaths on her arms and forehead, and smudged her beautiful features. His two youngest children were busy stirring a hot cauldron on the fire: no doubt, his wife's favorite chicken soup for the Friday meal. Isaac let out a sigh of contentment, savoring the peace and satisfaction of well-earned rewards in his advancing age. The city of Cordoba was a haven, protecting him and his family. Now, in turn, his home protected his nephews and the young girl under his roof. No one would come looking for her in this corner of paradise, he assured himself.

Inspector Guerida sat gloomily at his makeshift desk in a tent in Santa Fé. He was befuddled by the turn of events taking place in Granada, where his search had met with a dead end. He sent his Moro spies into the midst of the exiled moors in Andarax, the region where Boabdil would find peace in a much smaller kingdom. Guerida quizzed various Moors about Isabella, but to no avail. The young woman had disappeared from the Alhambra. Guerida was stumped about Isabella and had no leads in the disappearance of the Costa brothers. He feared his career as chief inspector was at an end. Perhaps now it was time to return to Seville and begin the search anew.

"Pedro!" Guerida called his orderly. Pedro appeared instantly in Guerida's tent. Guerida issued new orders. "We're leaving for Seville. Make haste!"

Pedro left to carry out his duties, and a beggar looking like a Moor made his way into Guerida's tent. He looked disheveled with dirty black matted hair descending to his waist. His beard fared no better, with debris stuck in it, and his bushy eyebrows concealed dark impenetrable eyes laced with red veins.

"What's the meaning of this?" Guerida roared. "Who let you into my tent?"

The beggar reached a hand to Guerida. "Please, hear me out!"

"Out with you! Out!"

The beggar swallowed, then stuttered, "I'm . . . I . . . have information . . . for you."

Guerida came near him, and then recoiled at the repulsive odor coming from the beggar's unwashed clothes. "What kind of information?"

"I know where the young woman you're searching for is," he said, this time in a steady voice.

"What do you know exactly?"

"You've been looking in the wrong places," he announced.

"What do you mean? Out with it! Or I'll throw you in chains into a dungeon!"

"Please, Inspector, let me explain."

"Unleash your tongue, beggar!" Guerida yelled.

"I have information for a price."

Guerida grabbed him by his clothes and tried to drag him to the door.

The beggar fought back with vigor. He planted his two feet squarely on the ground and resisted being dragged. "All I need is a warm meal, clean clothes, and a few maravedís!"

Guerida stopped, looked into his eyes, and said sternly, "It had better be reliable information."

"Inspector, with all due respect. The young lady left Granada a while ago before the surrender."

"How long ago was it?"

"Perhaps ten weeks," the beggar said.

"And how do you come by this information?"

"I was a guard in the palace at the time of her disappearance. She and the two Christian boys were seen going into the *Jennat al Arif* gardens, the enchanted gardens of the architect *al Arif*, praise is to Allah!"

Guerida exploded with impatience and the rapid information coming at him. He grabbed the beggar by the throat and squeezed his hand around his neck. "If you're telling me lies, I will personally see to your execution!"

The beggar tried to free himself from Guerida's grip. He coughed as Guerida's hand loosened up. "Please . . . please, Your Excellency . . ." He coughed again. "I haven't eaten in a long time. My memory is weak. Can I please have something to eat and drink?"

Guerida saw that the beggar would not cooperate until he had his way. He called his orderly again. "Delay our trip to Seville, and see that this beggar gets something to eat."

The orderly complied by reappearing with bread, cheese, olives, and a jug of water. The beggar fell upon the provisions and ate them voraciously. When done, he wiped himself on his sleeve and waited for Guerida to address him.

"Now talk, you miserable wretch—my patience is at an end!"

"About that time," the beggar began, "I was posted in the gardens of the al Arif, the paradise gardens above the Alcazar fortress." He stopped for a moment to recollect his memory. "That's when I noticed the young woman, looking fat—"

"What do you mean?" asked Guerida.

"She was attired in many clothes piled one on top of another to look like the fat maiden Maha in the harem. I couldn't be fooled. I gathered that she was fleeing."

"Then why didn't you go after her?" Guerida fumed.

"Because, Excellency, I was interrupted by the two boys following her. They were running fast. So I followed them through the descending gardens, but they became hidden by the trees and underbrush below the hill."

"Then what happened?" Guerida asked anxiously.

"That's when I lost their tracks," the beggar said.

Guerida exploded, this time with a paroxysm of fury. "Why didn't you alert the palace, or the king himself?"

The beggar remained silent to Guerida's anger. He then said, "I couldn't. You see, if I had told anyone about it, I would have been beheaded on the spot for failing in my duty."

Guerida couldn't refute the logical explanation the beggar had just given him. All three fugitives had slipped between his fingers again. All he had to do now was retrace the steps of the escape. The beginning of their flight would be a starting point.

March sea air wafted gently over little waves that lapped onto the hull of a four-masted carrack ship prepared for a grand voyage and ready to sail. Farther down the shipyards, two other caravel ships that had been commissioned for the voyage were being outfitted. Men and builders hovered over hulls, the rigging, and masts.

Captain Martin Alonzo Pinzón, a friend of Columbus, took over all the operations for sailing, provisions, manpower, and most vital: the trading baubles and trinkets to appease the inhabitants of Cipangu they would encounter. Captain Pinzón knew his fortune would be made at the completion of this voyage. He and his wife and children would reap incredible monetary rewards, and he would be given a prestigious position in the town of Palos. Not that his family hadn't already held important positions within Palos; his ancestors had occupied the town for centuries and contributed to the wealth of its inhabitants with the Pinzóns' skilled mariner's hands. He and his two brothers began learning those skills when they were children, as apprentices to their father's merchant marine business. Now that he had taken over the family business, which provided amply for the Pinzóns' livelihood, they all prospered. In addition to repairing hulls, damaged masts, or plank floors on the caravels and carracks coming into the dry docks for repair, Pinzón supervised the docks by having full control over customs and the import and export of goods.

This had been an unusual year, with provisions being unloaded on the docks, then finding their way south to Granada. Supplies for the troops fighting the Moors until the conquest of Granada had daily brought fully loaded ships with arms, food, and horses to Seville. All supplies had been shipped to Cadiz and all the way up to Malaga and by mule to Santa Fé. It had all been for a good cause: the conquest and expulsion of the Moors from the jewel in the Spanish crown, the legendary land of Granada.

A great commotion suddenly hit Pinzón's ears, and he scurried from the docks to find out where it had come from. A crane holding a precious cargo of food and water had crashed into the hold. Pinzón ran up the ship's plank to where the sound had originated to find out that the platform holding bales of hay, jugs of wine, and crates of dry goods had spilled deep into the hold over the stored provisions.

"What moron did that?" Pinzón asked with anger in his voice. He scurried to the gaping hull and squinted his black eyes to see into the darkness. The only thing he saw were the silhouetted figures of laborers toiling to bring in the cargo.

"All's well, Master!" the reassuring voice of his foreman shouted back at him from deep within the bowels of the hull.

Still squinting, Pinzón replied, "*Bueno*, Manrrique. Continue the work!" He walked back down the plank to resume his operations on the dock. A number of men waited in line for him near a table. Pinzón sat and shouted, "First man!"

"Name?" Pinzón asked the first man in line.

"João Treves."

"What experience do you have with sailing?" Pinzón asked.

"Ten years total. First in Lisbon, then Seville, and all the way up to Malaga along the coast."

"And who were your masters?"

"Masters Fábio Domingos and Benedito Caetano. The dates were 1470 all the way to 1480."

"And what happened between 1480 and 1490?" Pinzón asked suddenly.

João said, "I was employed in the wool industry, Don Pinzón."

Pinzón fixed eyes on him then said, "You can call me Master Pinzón from now on. You still report to Juan Manrrique, my foreman."

"Thank you, Master Pinzón," João said. He turned and smiled at the men behind him.

"Next!" came Pinzón's booming voice.

One by one, men were hired, then joined the others waiting for further orders. They were then shown their quarters down in the hold behind the cargo. The following hours were filled with loading the heavy bales onto a wooden platform that was lowered into the hold, and the bowels of the ship.

Not far from a carrack ship in the port of Palos, work progressed on two smaller caravels being outfitted for the sea voyage. João asked the workmen at this construction site where they were bound, but they wouldn't tell him. One youngster helping his father said, "We were only told that a voyage would take place in August."

"Juan!" the older man supervising him called out in an angry voice. "You're paid to work, not to play!"

"Sorry, Father," said the youth.

João turned away, his curiosity piqued. He noticed that more men had been hired by Master Pinzón to work on the two caravels standing next to his ship. He wondered if there was a link between these three ships. They were named *Niña*, *Pinta*, and *Santa Maria*—the latter was a proper religious icon befitting a voyage blessed with great expectations. If his intuition credited him with good fortune, these ships must be leaving on a great voyage—the type of voyage he advocated to his friends to join in search of a haven for Jews and Conversos hoping to escape their threatened existence.

This could be their escape to a new world free from persecution and unfair living conditions at the hand of the Inquisition. His heart leapt. He'd also heard rumors that Queen Isabella had contracted a foreign mariner with a dark history to lead this voyage. His excitement grew. He anticipated his predictions might finally come true. He communicated his thoughts and excitement to his companions, planting seeds of hope in their hearts.

"*Dime*, João," said Hernán Çavallos. "Where did you hear these rumors?"

"Could it be true?" mused Alfonso Sabatin. He removed his cap and wiped sweat from his forehead.

"Take it easy, my friends," João replied in a calm voice. "We don't want to show too much interest. As far as we're concerned, we are skilled and hard laborers making a living. We don't want to attract any attention to our mission and goal."

Hernán nodded while smiling.

"We'll be careful, João," Alfonso said, half-smiling.

"Yes. And don't look too pleased, either," João said. "We can't look too complacent. We're employed on a ship that will bring hardship and danger to our lives. So, no smiling!"

The men returned to their long hours of work in sweltering temperatures in the stuffy hold, enduring meager rations and admonitions from the foreman, who was none too pleased with their pace. At last, the hold was filled to its ceiling. The hatch closed on the deck, and they were left in darkness. The paraffin lamps were lit, and the men washed from pails filled with water. Supper was black bread, olives, and dried meat with cheap red wine. When the lamps were dimmed, the men fell into an exhausted sleep, giving thanks for their tired muscles and elevated spirits.

Don Obrigon sat forlorn and hopeless in his dark study. All communication from Guerida had ceased since he came back from Santa Fé before the surrender of Granada. The last news Obrigon had heard about Isabella was that Guerida had searched the Alpuxarras, where King Boabdil was to remain with his household, family, and numerous harem, but to no avail. This was bitter news to Don Obrigon. It seemed only yesterday that Isabella came into their lives. Her beautiful smile and squealing baby laughter lit up the household. His dear wife, Estrella, may she rest in peace, delighted in the antics of their beautiful daughter. Every Christmas, after the evening supper, they opened up their presents when Isabella dictated to everyone that she wasn't about to wait all night. The household had revolved around their daughter, whether it was her lessons, her dressing, or being on time for meals. Everyone around her cajoled and forgave her any mild tantrums or the tapping of her right foot when she insisted on getting her way. Don Obrigon and his wife gave in to Isabella's fancies and demands. And Isabella was affectionate to all: parents, servants, animals, and strangers who stepped into their home. Where had this happy time gone? Don Obrigon was now a widower bereft of his beloved daughter.

"Why is this room dark and airless?" dada Hannah exclaimed as she barged into the room. "You'll get ill breathing this stale air!" She ran to the windows and pulled the heavy damask draperies apart and opened the windows. The sunlight penetrated the room instantly, specks of dust dancing in its rays.

Don Obrigon shielded his eyes with both hands at the piercing light coming into the room. "Can't I get some peace?" he lamented.

"We all want some peace in this house. Doña Estrella, may she rest in peace, made me swear to look after you. Since you can't or don't want to, I'll have to do it for you." She stood over him with her hands on her hips and a stern look on her face.

Don Obrigon looked up and suddenly burst into laughter. "You sound . . . like . . . my mother!" He held back a tear or two of relief that came to him abruptly.

"I'm only your employee, not your mother," dada Hannah replied.

"And what a faithful employee you've been to the family!" Don Obrigon said. "You've been a trusted member of my house all these years, Isabella's governess, and a second mother to her." At the mention of Isabella's name, Don Obrigon fell back into silence.

Dada Hannah quieted down at the mention of Isabella. "They're looking hard for her. Mark my word, she'll return to us within a short time. I feel it and can almost hear her voice." Dada Hannah nodded and clasped her hands together prayerfully.

Don Obrigon wanted to believe dada Hannah's words of hope. He wanted to believe that Isabella would enter their home any time now.

"Let me know right away if you hear anything?" Don Obrigon said.

Dada Hannah nodded at him, then left Don Obrigon still seated in his study.

It was true that Isabella had to be found, having the entire police force looking for her, he reassured himself. He wanted to believe in dada Hannah's prophetic words; she had shown strong intuition in the past. He recalled a number of years ago that a young child went missing in the neighborhood, and dada Hannah sensed that the child had ventured away from town on his own. The authorities found him wandering and unharmed near the Guadalquivir River two days later. There was another instance when dada Hannah solved a mystery for the Obrigon household, when food kept disappearing from the pantry. She predicted they would find that an animal had found a way into the food reserves, not that staff was stealing. He thought she should look into her crystal ball to see where Isabella dwelled at this moment. He sighed, but a commotion interrupted his reverie.

"Don Obrigon, Don Obrigon!" Pilar barged into the study. "Inspector Guerida is here with news!" She stepped aside to let Guerida in.

Guerida trudged into the room with his heavy boots, a whip in his hand. He sat in front of Don Obrigon in a grandiose fashion.

"I don't want to give you any false hopes, but we found a fresh lead, a good one this time!"

Don Obrigon raised hopeful eyes.

"A few weeks ago, a shepherd watching over his flock saw three children crossing the vega leading north to Cordoba."

"Three children?" Don Obrigon raised eyebrows.

"Yes!" Guerida said in triumph. "She was with the two sons of a woman called Téresa, who happened to be under the Inquisition's custody."

A veil passed over Don Obrigon's eyes. "Why the Inquisition?"

"Because that woman was one of two people seen with Isabella at the inn. Apparently she's the kidnapper. The other one, a man in his forties, has disappeared."

"I still don't understand why the woman is in the Inquisition's hands and not held by the local police."

Guerida frowned but didn't answer Don Obrigon's question. "All I can tell you is that we're getting close," Guerida said.

Don Obrigon held back the multitude of questions bursting through his head. "Thank you, Inspector. I'm very grateful to you," he said.

"We'll keep you informed with any developments."

"¡Muchas gracias!" Don Obrigon shook both Guerida's hands vigorously before the inspector left.

Dada Hannah waited in the doorway with a smile on her face. Don Obrigon returned her smile. He would count the hours until Isabella was safely home with them.

29

The Alhambra Decree

THE EARLY MORNINGS AT THE Beneluz home were filled with peace for Isabella. The sun played games on the closed shutters as it spilled through the slats then moved to the right of her window. She remembered sun rays penetrating her room in Seville not long ago and waking her in a fine linen bed with embroidered pillowcases and sheets made for her by dada Hannah, who doted on her. It wasn't the same love as her mother's love; her mother acceded to Isabella's every request because the child pouted for hours if she didn't get her way.

"Let her have it," her mother would say.

This gave Isabella the notion that all was allowed in her case. That's why she couldn't accept or resolve her precarious situation this past year. This state of affairs was bound to end, the culprits would be arrested, and she'd be reunited with her parents in Seville. *Why is it taking so long for help to arrive?* She was sure the Beneluz family would be shocked by rumors that someone was looking for her. Not that Isaac Beneluz and his wife Rivka had mistreated her in any way. On the contrary, they made her stay most pleasant and agreeable. Her bed wasn't attired in fine linens, but it was comfortable and clean. Rivka Beneluz gave her modest clothing that was compatible with the general population's attire.

Her only reluctance about the new clothing was the red badge sewn on the outer sleeve of her garment proclaiming her to be Jewish. Rivka gently explained that wearing the red star, as each one of them did, made her a member of the Jewish community. For her own protection, she no longer wore the veil and Moorish pantaloons. Isabella thought ironically, *Am I not a Jew myself?* She was free to reveal her face, and she attracted many appreciative glances from all who saw her. As she'd strolled down the street the other day, she caught several merchants casting long glances at her.

When the Beneluz family arrived at Cordoba's great synagogue on Friday evening, the mothers who were searching for eligible young women of marriageable age for their sons descended on Rivka Beneluz with questions and smiles. Rivka turned them away with the final word that Isabella was spoken for in her hometown. Isabella's origins were hidden from prying ears so as not to arouse suspicions.

Isabella was curious about the religious service conducted by Isaac Beneluz officiating as a priestly rabbi for the Sabbath evening service in the synagogue. She found it strange that she had to sit with the women, who were adorned in rich silks and broad gold lace, on the second floor of the hall and separated from the men by a latticed window. She noticed that no statues were displayed throughout the hall, and there were no displays of religious icons except for the Star of David carved on a closet behind a blue silk curtain. The ark was opened and closed several times throughout the service. When the ark was opened, Beneluz retrieved a cylinder holding the scrolls of prayers written on parchment. The congregants prayed at times with low voices, while at other times they stomped their feet loudly when King David's enemies, such as Edomites or Philistines, were mentioned. Some of the congregants were called to come up to the ark when it was opened. They first bowed, then the scrolls were kissed and replaced inside the ark. Rivka had not instructed Isabella on the prayers or on the bowing that she as the matriarch of the family did with the other congregants. At other times the assembly prayed silently while standing up, in the Hebrew tongue that she didn't understand.

Isabella looked down at the Beneluz sons praying while helping Miguel and Josè with the prayers. Her gaze fell on Miguel's lustrous black hair as he bent down during the prayers. He stood taller than all the other young men in his row. Isabella admired Miguel for the affection he showed for his brother, his strength and resilience in the face of adversity, and his gentleness when he spoke to her. For some reason that she couldn't explain, she felt warmth in her heart and her pulse quickened whenever Miguel looked at her. She admonished herself and tried to replace the feeling with thoughts of Juan. Where was Juan now—in Seville or fighting the Moors in Granada? Her head and shoulders sagged. She was heavy with disappointment about the lost anticipation, the missed wedding, the missed happiness, and the shocking revelation of her origins. But the seeming impossibility of being reunited with her family was what oppressed her the most. As these thoughts ran wild in her head, she caught Miguel looking up at her through the partition lattices with a worried look on his face. His eyes seemed to ask what was making her so unhappy. She lowered her eyes in confusion and tried to calm her thoughts.

Rivka suddenly called her name. "Isabella? Isabella?"

"Yes, Rivka?"

"We're leaving, Isabella. The service is completed."

Isabella followed Rivka in silence as they descended the marble stairs to the first floor of the synagogue with the rest of the women. Isaac Beneluz and his sons were waiting for them, and everyone kissed each other with the *"Shabat Shalom"* greetings. Miguel approached her and planted two kisses on Isabella's cheeks. She blushed instantly, and brushed her cheeks lightly against his, but didn't kiss him back. Miguel, nevertheless, smiled at her with the same tender gaze in his blue eyes. She quickly went to rejoin Rivka and the rest of the family walking to the exit.

"What about me?" A soft voice stopped Isabella in her tracks. She looked back to find Josè with a lost look in his eyes.

"What about . . ." She stopped and quickly bent down to hug and kiss Josè. "Let's join the others." She grabbed his hand and led him toward the entrance.

The Beneluz family, flanked by their visitors, strolled through the twilight to their home. Other congregants had emerged from the service on their way home talking and laughing, their children sauntering and playfully chasing each other. As they reached the town plaza they saw, in the dim light of lit torches, some of the congregants clustered in groups, talking and gesturing. Isabella saw that Isaac Beneluz reacted with surprise to the gathering. By now she was accustomed to seeing most families enter their homes to eat their Friday night meals right after the Sabbath service. Beneluz separated himself from his family and advanced to the center of the plaza, where a great commotion was taking place. Isabella saw that men were mumbling to each other, their wives were weeping silently, and other people in the vicinity stood with stony expressions on their faces. She and the rest of the family came near to the main fountain and the statue of Saint George, where jet streams fell back gracefully into the shell bowl. Below the large bowl on the center base was affixed a large banner written in bold red letters. By the light of torches on either side of the banner, they read:

The Alhambra Decree

ON THIS BLESSED DAY OF April 29, 1492, by the grace of God, and by the authority of Queen Isabella and King Ferdinand of the line of Trastámara and the House of Barcelona, King and Queen of Castile, Aragon, and Sicily and all dominions under the crown, a decree is hereby proclaimed that there are in our dominion bad Christians who Judaized by committing apostasy against The Church and our Catholic faith. The Inquisition was established in 1480 to remedy the apostasy between Jews and Christians. We were informed by the Inquisition that these Jews still draw New and faithful Christians and instruct them in their evil temptation in observing their laws, circumcising their children, teaching them their Passover observance and to eat of their unleavened bread in observing their Law of Moses, and making them believe that there is no other law. It is clear that if the diabolical temptation that is causing great damage to our Catholic faith and has resulted from the perversion of these Jews is not removed, we would succumb in this war against our Catholic faith; thus, we are forced to expel said Jews from this land.

TO SEVER ALL COMMUNICATIONS BETWEEN said Jews and Christians, all Jews—men, women, and children—will leave, by July thirty-first, this Andalusia land forever, and never set foot again on this Catholic soil. These Jews and Jewesses will be granted permission to sell or dispose of their properties and homes till the end of July, and exchange their furniture and households without harm to them. They may leave by land or sea without impunity to their safety with conditions that they may not take gold and silver. We then order all officials of cities and villages to see that these Jews not be harmed, and to facilitate their leaving from this land. Anyone infringing upon these rules will be punished severely.

IF ANYONE SO DESIRES TO convert to our true faith, the faith of our ancestors, of our Lord Jesus Christ, along with their children, they may do so within two weeks' times without impunity, and be exempted from leaving. They may continue to dwell in this land and keep their possessions, their estates, their professions and trades.

WE THEREFORE PROCLAIM THAT THIS edict be displayed in all the plazas in all the cities and villages, and announced by the town crier so that no one may claim ignorance of this decree. Anyone doing the contrary in aiding the Jews will be punished severely and deprived of their offices and have their homes and goods confiscated by the crown.

THIS SIGNED TESTIMONY THAT WAS ordered and provided to the court is given in the city of Granada, the thirty-first of March 1492, the year of our Lord Jesus Christ.

Signed *I the King Ferdinand I the Queen Isabella*
Present *Juan de Coloma, Secretary of the King and Queen*
Registered *by Cabrera, Almacan Chancellor*

"¡Oy, El Dio!" cried Rivka. She pulled her younger sons nearer to her by pressing their heads tightly to her chest and began to sob. Isaac Beneluz stood with his head down, his right hand stroking his beard over and over.

Isabella felt a shiver go through her body. *Why is this happening?* Why was this family, the family who sheltered and welcomed her in their home, being forbidden to remain in their home, in their land? It was an inexplicable feeling, squeezing and trying to permeate her brain.

Miguel stood by without a word. Josè came near him and grabbed his hand.

"Don't worry, Miguel, I won't be afraid." He smiled at Miguel.

Miguel grabbed both José's hands and held them close to his heart.

Isabella looked at both of them and felt a sudden pity for Josè. *So young and so vulnerable*, she thought. Having to experience hardships, the loss of his home, parents, and now his land. Perhaps his youth was protecting him against this blow. Not understanding the enormity of this decree may be a blessing for Josè.

Suddenly, Isaac Beneluz recovered his speech. "We'll go home and confer as a family about what to do. Make haste, Sons. Miguel and José—follow me." He turned to Isabella, who stood at a distance, and said, "You too, Isabella—you're part of this family."

Isabella didn't reply, and followed them as they headed back down the narrow lane to their home. Other families shuffled along in shock searching for their homes for security and to soothe and comfort their wounded spirits.

What can I say to them? Isabella felt personally responsible, as if she had initiated the decree. It was the Christian church and her Christian brethren who decreed that all Jews should leave this land. She belonged to the Christian community, and the Christian faith that contributed to that decree—didn't she? Was she a Jewess after all? Doubts crept back into her thoughts. Her head was muddled, her thoughts confused. If only she could go back home to find her parents, confront them, and find the truth! She felt torn between opposing thoughts and opposing faiths. Silently, she followed the Beneluz family home. As she walked, she sensed Miguel's eyes upon her. She kept her eyes fixed on the cobblestones beneath her feet.

"Come in, come in, my children," called Rivka. "Isabella, please come with me to the kitchen."

Isabella followed her to the warm kitchen, where a steady fire burned in the hearth. Isaac always stoked the fire before the Sabbath set in, placing enough wood to burn for twenty-four hours until sundown the next day. Rivka immediately began working feverishly, placing food on platters. She handed them to Isabella with a nod of her head into the direction of the courtyard. Isabella carried the platters to the family in the open court.

When Rivka joined them from the kitchen, Isaac Beneluz recited the bread prayer *"Ha Motsi"* in Hebrew*: "Baruch Ata Adonai Ha Motsi lehem min haaretz."* Beneluz's lips then moved in a silent prayer.

Grabbing the Sabbath bread near him from a platter, he tore it in small pieces, dipped the pieces in salt, then passed them around the table. They ate the meal in silence. No one ate much or talked or raised any questions. Everyone waited for the head of the family to speak first. At last, Isaac raised his eyes from his plate and addressed them.

"My dear wife, sons, and guests in our humble home, today . . ."—he hesitated—"Today on this Friday, as we welcome the Sabbath bride," he continued, "we are witness to a great injustice. An injustice caused to the Hebrew people that will resonate and reverberate into the entire world. Today the Pharaohs of olden time have arisen again to punish us. We're now forced to abandon the land we love dearly. This is a land where we have dwelled for more than a thousand years. Again, we mourn *Tisha B'Av*, the ninth of Av, when our second temple, our holy of holies, was destroyed in Jerusalem in the month of August in the year 70 CE (5450). We were here before the Visigoths, when our ancestors populated this land, and before the Berbers and the Moors made war on them. And we were here in Cordoba when Tariq ibn Ziyad fought and defeated the Visigothic King Roderick. Now those same Christian people who have conquered the land from the Moors have made war on us by expelling us from our homes, our lands, and tearing us apart from our communities and our friends. Just as the days of old, justice will be done. God will rain his justice upon them as in the Exodus of our ancestors. Amen." All repeated after him, "Amen."

Beneluz then said, "We have living among us three dear guests: our dear nephews and our dear Isabella, who joined our family and whom we look upon as a daughter. I want to drink to their health!" He raised his wine glass and everyone followed. Putting down his glass, Beneluz began to speak gravely. Everyone in the courtyard trembled and anticipated the words he was about to say.

"After the Sabbath is over, we'll begin to prepare ourselves to leave our home and join a caravan heading for Seville."

Isabella's heart jumped. "When are we leaving?" she asked, her voice trembling.

Beneluz eyes rested on her for a moment. "We have three months to get ready or as soon as our affairs are in order," he said.

Isabella felt remorseful for negating their hospitality and the warmth they had shown her. "It's important for me to see my parents."

"Of course it is. Any child would want that," Beneluz replied.

Isabella caught Miguel's eyes on her as he got up to help with the dishes that contained food only partly eaten. She ran to help him.

Rivka, who had sat quietly throughout the meal and the short conversation, remained sitting with a pained expression. She didn't stop Isabella or Miguel.

When they found each other alone in the kitchen, Miguel said, "You know that I'll help you to go back to your parents."

Isabella nodded. "I wouldn't be here if it weren't for your mother, who took me away." Seeing the pained look her words caused to form on Miguel's face, she quickly added, "But I met the wonderful Beneluz family, and . . ." She stopped as a slight redness covered her face.

Miguel came close and embraced her, holding her for a long moment. Isabella didn't pull back and remained breathing against his chest. Slowly, Miguel lowered his face to hers, touched her lips with his, and both fell into a magical time where reality disappeared. Miguel pulled his head away first, then hugged Isabella again. She felt happy and at peace.

"You are more dear to me than anyone else," Miguel said tenderly.

Isabella smiled at him. "We ought to join the others. The Sabbath is still on."

A palpable gloom hung over the three men in the antechamber to Queen Isabella's council chamber. Don Abraham Senior sat with Don Isaac Abravanel and Senior's son-in-law, Rabbi Meir Melamed. He tried to avoid their gazes as if both men could destroy him with one look. As the private treasurer to the queen, Senior had begged for an audience to rescind the expulsion order, or at least postpone it. When Isaac Abravanel came to him with the request, he flatly refused at first.

"The queen's counselors will take this request as favoritism on her part, and will raise a great protest," he told Abravanel. "But you're also her financial advisor, and her most precious man, one to whom she can't refuse to give a favor." Abravanel pleaded with him to make the request. After several more pleas, in which Abravanel told him he was a stubborn man, he agreed to request an audience with the queen. All three of them sat nervously.

The chamberlain to the queen approached them and said, "The queen will see you now."

All three rose from the wooden bench and followed the chamberlain. Inside the royal chamber, Isabella sat on her throne affixing her signature on documents that were held for her by an aide. When finished, she motioned to the aide to retire.

"Please approach the steps, Don Senior, Don Abravanel, and Don Melamed," Queen Isabella said with a smile on her face. All three came close to where she sat, and bowed.

"What brings you to my chamber, my subjects?"

Don Senior saw that Don Abravanel was piqued at being called her subject. This designation would not last much longer for him. This was a pointed remark on the part of the queen and a slightly sarcastic one.

"We're here," began Senior, "to beg you to reconsider your decree for the expulsion." Senior pulled a kerchief from his long robe pocket and wiped several beads of sweat off his forehead. "There is no possibility that all the Jews in your realm could leave this land, where they have dwelt for over a thousand years, in such a short notice. They have fields, cattle—"

Queen Isabella interrupted him with a motion of her hand. "My dear Senior, you know that it was on the highest authority that this decree had been promulgated. It's God's will that guided our hands and hearts to expel the Jews." Queen Isabella's face showed neither benevolence nor harshness. Her bonnet covered part of her forehead, showing less of her face.

She looked unmoved to Senior's eyes, carrying divine providence and wishes from the Spaniards' pulpit. A stick on his back would have been more appropriate. *So much for Spanish justice*, he thought bitterly. At this moment her face resembled the images of saints carved in leaded glass on the windows he had seen in their churches. She presented a cold image, not one that was alive, or one that breathed life from God's will.

Senior remained silent to the queen's final remark. Both his arms hung slack along his body in an attitude of defeat. He felt himself to be a weakling at this moment, not the rabbi leader of the Jewish community. He also felt weary in his old body, and weary from having to appease the Jews and his monarchs at the same time. His son-in-law, Melamed, a secretary to the king, also stood mute, accepting defeat by his silence. They were at the mercy of their queen and king, and were pawns in their hands.

"My dear queen, may I speak to Your Royal Highness?" Abravanel spoke with deference to the queen.

"Speak," Queen Isabella said without a stir on her face.

"Most venerable Queen," he began, "the Jewish communities have dwelt for many centuries in this blessed land. They have acquired properties and wealth, lived in peace under your reign and your father's, John the II of Castile—may his memory be blessed for always—but they also contributed great wealth to your realm through their acumen in trade, knowledge, and benefaction upon the poor and the downtrodden. We have also worshipped in our synagogues without interference for many, many years." Abravanel stopped for a moment.

The queen remained silent yet attentive.

Don Abravanel continued. "We've also provided many of our sons to fight the enemies of España. The Jews of this land don't deserve this edict. It would be an unjust sentence upon your most devoted and faithful subjects. Please, benevolent Queen, have mercy upon our families, upon our children and the elderly, who would be most affected by this edict. Many would not survive the uprooting, nor would they survive the voyages to other lands. Please reconsider this act. Have mercy on us! I am willing to offer the Crown six hundred thousand pieces of gold right away to rescind this edict!" Abravanel's voice had risen with his plea as a cry of despair.

This time the queen's face softened in response to this heartfelt and moving request from Abravanel.

"My dear Abravanel. It's a most generous offer, especially since our coffers suffered from the war against the Moors. You've been a most faithful servant and advisor in the past to my husband, the king, and for the last two years as my treasurer. It's upon this recommendation that I will look into this request and confer with him and my advisors as to what path we will follow. I will inform you of my final decision shortly. Now, go in peace."

The audience was now closed. All three men bowed to Queen Isabella and left her chamber. Outside the chamber, they all spoke at once. Senior raised his hand. "Be calm, my friends. The queen was most understanding. We should now wait and be patient."

Abravanel lowered his head and silently took leave of Senior and Melamed.

In the rising mist in the Palos dockyards, a flurry of activity took place. Mallets and hammers sounded all over the shipyards. Woodworkers carried large planks and fitted them into the hulls of two caravel ships, and long saws manned by two men each ground through tree trunks that had been transported from as far away as Granada and the Sierra Nevada mountains.

Not far from this hive of workers and foundry men, a larger ship was ready and being provisioned with water and food for a long voyage. This proud four-masted carrack swayed as the waves lapped its rounded stern. A colorful round flag bearing the Spanish kingdoms of Castile and León with yellow castles and red lions flew at the top of the main mast. Large red crosses were painted on the square sails to show that faith would protect the ship on its voyage. Emblazoned on its bow was the name *Santa Maria.*

On the docks below, the builders on the other two ships being refitted were hard at work, sweating despite the weather being mild for a June day. One of the caravel shipbuilders lay down his hammer, pulled a red scarf from his pocket, and wiped his brow. His naked torso was wet with sweat, gleaming in the morning sunlight.

"You'd think we're in mid-July," he said.

His coworker laughed at him. “Come on, Alfonso. We’re heated by the work and not the sun.”

Alfonso laughed back and turned to his coworker. “You know, João, I can’t imagine what the next months will bring after the ships are ready.”

“That’s what I’d like to find out, too. I do know that an envoy was here last month talking to our foreman, Juan Manrrique. I’m glad we were hired to work on these other two ships. The large carrack stands empty of sailors for now. Once the two smaller ships are finished, I know we’ll sail.”

Alfonso stood silent for a moment, letting the hammer hang idle at his side. He checked out of the corner of his eye to see that Juan Manrrique wasn’t watching, and turned to João. “I wonder if we’ll find this blessed land where our brethren will follow.”

“You must have faith,” João said. “Meanwhile, you’d better put your hammer to use.”

“What’s this?” The angry foreman, Juan Manrrique, fell upon Alfonso. “This is the last time I see you idle. Next time you’re out!”

“I’m truly sorry, by the Madonna”—Alfonso crossed himself—“I just stopped to wipe my brow.”

The foreman didn’t reply and stood with both his hands poised on his hips. “Get back to work!”

Alfonso rushed to hammer nails into the plank in front of him.

That was close, João thought while communicating that thought to Alfonso with his eyes.

Alfonso acknowledged his look and continued working. The two ships now had masts standing erect. The mainmast on the *Pinta* was presently being fitted with square sails, and the foremast with the triangular-lateen sail. The mizzenmast stood empty, waiting for its sails. The *Niña* was already rigged with three-masted lateen sails. Several other workers, perched on a wooden plank that was attached from the ship’s starboard, spread large swatches of reddish-brown paint to the outside of the vessel.

The work went on for many hours, stretching into late afternoon with one break for lunch. By six o’clock in the evening, the sun had dimmed considerably, then began to descend on the horizon. The entire sky took on a yellow hue, painting the scattered clouds with vivid orange colors.

At the sound of a bell, all workers put down their hammers and mallets, the twine ropes, and brushes still dripping with paint. Wet rags and mops used for scrubbing the planks floors of the deck were put away to dry. Filing one by one, the shipworkers passed the foreman at a table. Each man received his twenty maravedís for the week and left his thumbprint smeared with ink on the foreman's large sheet on the table.

"You, Alfonso," said Manrrique with a threatening finger pointed at him. "You watch out that this isn't your last pay!" He slapped down twenty maravedís in front of him.

Alfonso took the coins, then bowed before Manrrique with seriousness and true humility. "Your Excellency, thank you for my humble pay. I'll be hard at work tomorrow, I promise you."

Manrrique waived him away with his hand, turning his attention to João waiting for his pay. "Don't get too chummy with this coworker," he warned him. "Your work could be affected by his laziness. I like you, your work, and your pace. Keep this up and I might slip a good word to the admiral."

João bowed his head in appreciation. "It's my pleasure to work for such a worthy enterprise, Master. When will the admiral arrive?"

Manrrique raised his head, scrutinizing him for a moment. "I have no knowledge of his arrival, but it will be known soon."

"Thank you," said João, and he walked down the plank to reunite with Alfonso and Hernán on the docks.

"Let's celebrate tonight, my friends. I have good news to report."

Senior stood in Abravanel's cool hall, where a fire burned in a marble fireplace. The nights in Seville were still cool despite the heat during the day. He leaned over to warm his hands and wrapped his shawl tightly around his chest and skinny neck. He was eighty years old and felt he had used most of his active years on behalf of España. He'd served Ferdinand as an advisor, a tax farmer, and a tax collector. He'd funded and supplied the war against the Moors, paid ransom for four hundred and fifty Jews after the fall of Malaga, and patronized scholars. He'd done it all. He'd saved many Jews from expulsion from Valmaseda by mediating with the king to let them stay in their homes.

He felt España owed him a debt. Hadn't he effected the reconciliation between Isabella and her brother, Henry the IV, that led to her acceding to the throne? Would she be now the queen of all territories in Castile if he hadn't? He'd succeeded in bringing forth the marriage of Isabella to Ferdinand and facilitated España's victory over Granada today. Yes, he'd done all of that—and more.

His father had been treasurer and advisor to John the II of Aragon, King Ferdinand's father. Senior sighed. His daughter was married and he had no sons; he felt his line was at an end. His son-in-law. Melamed, was to take over his duties as head rabbi of the Jewish communities. He was a good son-in-law, as he obeyed his duties with devotion.

"My dear Senior," exclaimed Abravanel as he entered the room, "my apologies for making you wait." He waited for Senior to speak first.

Senior sat on a blue satin dais, his knee creaking as he lowered himself. He brought his hands together as if he were going to pray, but instead shook his clasped hands several times. "You know how hard I've worked as the court rabbi for the Jewish community throughout the years in Aragon and now in Castile?

Abravanel nodded.

"You know," continued Senior, "that I want nothing better than to help all of my brothers and sisters in time of need. I've tried in every way to counsel the queen and king to listen to reason. I've foretold the countless way that España would suffer if they lose the best-skilled people. The best artisans, financiers, weavers, metalworkers, physicians, and royal treasury minters are members of the Jewish community. España will lose collectors of crops and owners of vineyards, soldiers and navigators and makers of scientific instruments, shoemakers, all the silk mercers and spice dealers, silversmiths and gilders, the foundry workers, carpenters . . ." Senior stopped, out of breath.

"Tell me the truth, Senior? Was the queen's heart closed?"

Senior's head went limp on his chest. He was exhausted and lacked spirit. "Have pity on me, my friend."

"The ones to be pitied are the countless families with children to be uprooted and thrown into the path of hardships and dangers on a voyage they did not want. We must get the communities ready," Abravanel said with mournful eyes.

"The queen, though, gave three more days, till August the third, for all Jews to leave," Senior said in an afterthought.

"That is most magnanimous of her," Abravanel said sarcastically. "She's no longer my queen, nor do I consider her a human being. She must have a maravedí instead of a heart."

Senior tried to stop Abravanel with both his hands waving through the air. "You mustn't say such things. You could go to jail for treason! Against your monarch!"

"She's no longer my monarch! She's my executioner. Do you know how many will perish undertaking this voyage? Maybe hundreds—no, thousands will die. Think of all the elderly, the young children, and the sick. You can call that a royal treatment. I'll send a missive to Her Highness to tell her what I think of her!"

Senior said with horror, "You mustn't, you mustn't!"

"You must excuse me now, Don Senior. I have much to get ready." Abravanel showed his guest to the door. Senior vacillated as he got off his seat. He headed for the door with difficulty, then turned back to Abravanel.

"Believe me, I did all I could."

As soon as Senior left, Abravanel rushed to his desk and prepared the long letter to Queen Isabella. When he was satisfied with the contents, he blotted the excess ink and prepared to write to his three sons. Judah, Joseph, Samuel, and their families must join him immediately for Lisbon. He also left letters of credit for everyone to whom he owed money, then sent for his old servant, Ernestino.

"Ernestino, prepare my clothes, food for the road, and transportation. Tell Conchita to do the same for my wife. We're leaving within the hour for Portugal."

Ernestino's face went blank. "What about your guests for tonight's banquet?" he asked.

Abravanel grimaced, then hit his forehead in a gesture of exasperation. "I will write a letter of apology to my guests. I also want you to be in charge of delivering this letter to the queen."

Seeing Ernestino's bewildered expression, he hastened to explain, "But only in two days' time. Make sure it is delivered into her hands!"

Ernestino nodded. "Won't you take me with you?" His wrinkled face bore witness to his long service for the Abravanel family. His expression revealed his complete trust and his sadness at parting with his benefactor.

"My dear Ernestino," said Abravanel, "you've been a trusted and obedient servant in my house for many years. There's nothing I'd want more than to take you with me. To do so would endanger your life as a Christian, and the life of your daughter and her children. It's for their sake and yours that you should remain here. You'll need money to survive. Here's enough for you to live in this house. And you may bring your family to live here, until . . ." Abravanel's voice broke as he handed him a money-filled purse. "Until the house is repossessed by the authorities."

Ernestino bowed to kiss Abravanel's hands with tears in his eyes, then left him to prepare for their long voyage.

Abravanel then went to a painting on the wall and swiveled it away to reveal a strongbox. He opened it with a key that hung on a chain around his neck, and withdrew all the cash, jewels, and notes that made up all his immediate wealth. His estate and lands he would entrust to his loyal foreman, Francisco de Torres, to see to the tenants' needs and collect the rents. He signed a document to that effect and left it on his desk in full view.

His agitated wife, Gracia, swept into the room. *"¡Por la vida del Dio!,* what's happening?"

"We're leaving tonight for Lisbon. Do as I tell you. Gather your things. We'll meet with the children at the city gates."

Doña Gracia looked at him questioningly.

"It's for our lives that we must leave," Abravanel impressed upon her.

She nodded and left him to make her preparation for the long journey.

At the hour of midnight, Abravanel and his family met at the gates and formed a small caravan.

In the Alhambra, the Friday morning audience didn't go as planned for Queen Isabella. She arrived late and was interrupted by her daughter Juana's distress call. Then her younger daughter, Catalina, requested to be heard, too. The affairs of Catalina's heart were most pressing. Prince Arthur of England's advisors had arrived the previous day, pressing for Catalina's answer as to her future betrothal to Prince Arthur.

"My dear daughter," she told Catalina. "Your prince will wait for your answer. Your betrothal is most important to the treaty between England and España."

"But—"

"You will do as I've told you!" interrupted Isabella. She turned her back and went to attend court.

She found her loyal subjects gathered at the court to have their voices heard and their demands for justice met. Her reluctance to attend her court of justice was partly due to the boredom she felt at presiding over peccadilloes and the lack of civility and good manners on the part of some of her subjects. Queen Isabella felt pressed for time when she granted the first audience of the morning.

"My queen," began her advisor, "your first subject requests audience to redress an injustice."

Queen Isabella nodded. "Begin," she said.

"Citizen Arturo Gomez requests that his neighbor, Fadrique Martinez, pay for damages that occurred on the blessed day of the sixteenth of March, 1492, when Martinez's cows entered Gomez's fields and damaged his crops."

"What's the damage in *reales*?" asked Queen Isabella.

"To replace the damaged field, the future value of the crop, and the damaged fence would take more than one hundred maravedís or three hundred reales."

Queen Isabella thought for a moment, then asked, "How did the cows damage the fence?"

The advisor turned to Fadrique Martinez, who stood shyly, twisting his hat with his hands. "Speak to the queen!" he ordered him.

"With respect, my queen, the cows didn't damage the fence. It was already damaged before they entered the field."

Queen Isabella turned to Arturo Gomez. "Why was your fence in disrepair?"

Arturo turned red to the tip of his black hair. "Because . . . I hadn't the time to fix it, my queen." He bowed deeply to Queen Isabella.

Queen Isabella looked at him fixedly for a moment. She turned to her advisor and said, "Martinez will reimburse Gomez by paying him two hundred reales only. The other one hundred reales he will have to spend from his own moneys to repair his fence."

Both men looked uncomfortable but, nevertheless, accepted the queen's judgment.

"Who's next?" Queen Isabella asked.

The advisor read from the list on the parchment in his hands.

"We have Ernestino, the humble servant from the house of Don Abravanel, my queen."

The queen felt slighted. "Don Abravanel didn't have the decency to call himself?" she asked.

The advisor turned to Ernestino for an answer, but he stayed mute.

"You may speak," Queen Isabella said to him gently.

"My benevolent queen," began Ernestino, "my master left two days ago, instructing me to deliver this letter as of today."

"Why didn't you come sooner?" the queen asked.

"Those were my instructions. I had to travel for many days to Granada. My travel was impeded because the roads were filled with soldiers and mercenaries returning to their homes in the north."

Queen Isabella nodded to her counselor to hand her the letter. She opened the seal and began to read its contents. No sooner had she laid eyes on the letter that she stopped reading. She handed the letter to her counselor. "Read the content!" she ordered him.

"My dear and illustrious Queen Isabella," the councilor read. *"It's with great despair and protestation that I write to you and to King Ferdinand. It's a disgrace that the great nation of España has to bask in the glory of their conquest of the Moors by expelling its most devoted subjects—the Jewish communities that have lived here for millennia. You're expelling the finest flowers of Castile—your artisans, silversmiths, blacksmiths, physicians, merchants, and goldsmiths. All your taxpayers, who supported*

and filled your coffers for the war machine, are being expelled. We can't understand how we're a threat to you and to the realm. Haven't you, already, confined us to restricted quarters, forced us to wear the red badge, taxed us excessively, and terrorized us with the Inquisition? This crime you speak of, the crime of being a threat to Christianity, isn't committed by Jews but by you and in the name of your faith. It's a great error that you're committing in the name of justice. And what justice? We're the true victims of the zealots that carry their own violent beliefs in the name of your religion. You've been misguided by those zealots and churchmen, the same ones who want to burn these great libraries of knowledge built by the Moors, and burn thousands of books in bonfires throughout the countryside to destroy the power of knowledge.

"There's still time to correct this terrible injustice before your country goes down in shame for centuries to come. The great name of Spain will be tainted when it could be great. We, instead, will live with dignity and courage to stand for our beliefs. If this edict of expulsion stands, it will live forever in infamy.

"Signed this blessed day of April 1492,

Don Abravanel,

Treasurer to Castile, Queen Isabella, and King Ferdinand."

Queen Isabella looked shocked. She silently got up from her golden throne and walked to Ernestino, who was standing and shaking. He immediately prostrated himself before the queen.

"My most illustrious queen. I'm humble before you. I had no knowledge as to this letter's content. I swear on the Virgin Mary! No knowledge at all!" He wiped tears of fear in his eyes.

"I believe you, my good man," Isabella said as she offered her hand for Ernestino to kiss her ring. "You must cooperate with the justice now and help them to locate Don Abravanel."

Ernestino nodded his head in submission, then seeing that he was being dismissed, left the hall in a hurry.

Isabella then turned to her councilor. "Fetch for me Don Senior, immediately! Dismiss all the other attendants to come back next Friday for an audience."

Within the hour, Don Senior walked unsteadily into Isabella's presence.

"Did you know of Don Abravanel's letter?" she asked sternly while handing him the letter to read.

Don Senior took the letter and read its content. His face drained of all color. "I knew that he would write you a letter, but I didn't know its content, I swear!"

"I believe you, Don Senior. You've remained my most trusted advisor, financier, and tax collector in the entire realm. Without you, my marriage to King Ferdinand may not have taken place. You've played many important roles by financing my armies during the war with the Moors. It goes without saying that you were an important man for your people as court rabbi. We owe you and your family a great debt, and the king, as well as I, could not do without you. I look upon you not only as my financier and right hand but as an old uncle and member of my family." She stopped for a moment.

Don Senior remained silent.

"You know," continued Queen Isabella, "That I can rain down my wrath on the entire Jewish community! That I can bring prison and death on them all?" She looked to Don Senior for a reply. He stood in front of her with his head down. His weary body showed a slight tremor—from old age or undisguised fear, she couldn't tell. Her voice took a softer tone, one of true and familiar friendship.

"One of our dearest wishes is for you to convert. As a Catholic man of importance, your family and descendents would be assured wealth and health. The King, Cardinal Mendoza, and Papal Nuncio have all approved and are ready to sponsor your baptism."

This time Don Senior began to tremble in earnest.

Queen Isabella didn't know if it was fear or the great honor she'd bestowed on him that made him silent. She knew he couldn't refuse her, nor would he stop trying to help his brethrens.

"What say you?" Queen Isabella asked gently.

"My dear queen," Don Senior began, "there's nothing more that my heart desires than to have peace in your realm, peace in my house, and peace among all my brothers—Jews and Christians alike. Whatever decision I make is bound to offend someone on one side or the other. I need time to consider your request. Time to communicate with my God as to which way I should lead."

Queen Isabella stood silent for a moment. She then spoke to Don Senior with a gravity he'd never heard her use. "My dear Don Senior," she began in a measured tone of voice, "I also have to think of my people's well-being and faith. I don't want to lose you, nor do I want your people to suffer from your decision. I promise you that if you do not convert, my wrath will fall upon your people, and they'll be persecuted before they leave my shores." Her voice was calm and measured. She knew he had no choice but to relent, at least for the sake of his people.

Don Senior bowed his head. "I will do as you bid me, my queen."

She smiled at him. With a nod of her head, she motioned to Don Senior that her audience with him was concluded.

30

Trek of Tears

THE SUN HAD BARELY RISEN over the horizon when the noise level in the street grew higher than the Christian inhabitants in Cordoba had ever heard. They ran to their doors and roofs to see the source of the commotion. A shock awaited them. The streets were filled with their Jewish neighbors and their households leaving the Juderia. Donkeys and mules strained to pull loaded carts, children were crying, and exhausted parents' tired expressions said it all: We want to cry until we feel nothing.

Nina, a Jewish neighbor of the Beneluz's household, rushed into their courtyard.

"Rabbi Beneluz, I don't know what to do, or where to go!" she exclaimed while wringing her hands.

Isaac Beneluz took her aside and said, "You must be strong! You hear me?" He shook her gently by the shoulders. "We all have to be strong."

Nina nodded her head and slowly returned home, while his wife, Rivka, watched her with sad eyes.

She said to him, "I'll start by contacting some of our Christian neighbors. They may want to buy some of our furnishings. I'll also prepare our children and our guests for the trip." She mentioned "trip" casually, as if they were going to the next town to visit friends.

Isaac forced a smile. They had taken many trips throughout their married lives. Before their children were born, Rivka traveled with him to faraway destinations while they traded their goods. After their small family grew to four children, Rivka stayed home to raise them, but helped Isaac with the details of the business when he was traveling. She dealt with traders, shipped orders by caravan, and kept both home and business running smoothly. Rivka had been his companion, his partner in life and adversity. They were about to be tested on another level, and they didn't know the outcome. He pushed aside the frightening sense of the unknown they were facing.

As these thoughts ran through his head, Isaac went to his study to pack his books, and was much surprised to find his nephew waiting for him there.

"Uncle," Miguel said to him with a serious look on his face, "I must ask you questions."

"Of course," Isaac said. He pushed aside piles of prayer books on the bench by the table and said, "Sit here."

"When we reach Seville, I need your help to find my mother."

Isaac, startled by Miguel's comment, fell silent. He said, "Miguel, this is a dangerous and foolish enterprise."

"But, Uncle—"

Isaac put up his hand to stop him. "You mustn't do anything to jeopardize yourself! Think about your brother. Who'll protect him if you're caught?"

Miguel lowered his face. After a long silence, he said, "You well know that it'll be dangerous for all of you if Isabella, Josè, and I travel along?" said Miguel.

"All I know," replied his uncle, "is that we're one family, and that includes you, Josè, and Isabella."

"But it was my mother who kidnapped Isabella, so Josè and I must be wanted by the Inquisition and Torquemada."

At the name of Torquemada, Isaac felt a shiver. He was a man feared by all. "We'll travel together, or we'll stay here to be charged with disobeying orders."

Miguel didn't reply. Then he said, "Thank you, Uncle. I do feel . . . no, I do know that both Josè and I are members of the Beneluz clan, and for that we're grateful."

Isaac smiled and nodded at his nephew.

"However," Miguel continued, "having Isabella with us might be highly dangerous. How can we make sure she isn't recognized?"

Isaac suddenly burst into laughter, and Miguel looked at him as if he'd gone mad. When he stopped, he said to Miguel, "It's touching that you're concerned about her safety."

Miguel turned red at his uncle's remark. He tried to defend himself. "I just wanted to make sure . . . you wouldn't be in danger because—"

Isaac cut him off again by saying, "No, no." He made an arresting motion with his hand. "It's prudent that you're concerned for Isabella. It's healthy and wise. Rivka will instruct her in the daily prayers, the duties of a woman, and the obedience of a daughter so she can blend with the rest of us," Isaac said.

Miguel looked reassured. "I'll go and help my aunt."

On his way down to the courtyard, Miguel asked himself what his uncle meant by "healthy." Was Isaac aware of his feelings for Isabella? As he thought about Isabella, he felt his heart jump slightly. Her name, her appearance, and the subtle scent that enveloped her when she was near him made his whole being faint with joy and happiness. He felt the same way about her speech, the way she formed the words with her lovely lips, her flashing green eyes when she was excited, and her pouting when she disagreed with him. He was desperately in love with her. Did she feel the same for him? She hadn't pulled back when he kissed her, and she rested her head on his chest. That was a sign that she loved him in return, wasn't it? Lost in this happy conclusion, he jumped at the sight of her waiting at the foot of the stairs.

"Did you need me?" he asked her, blushing.

"No, but your aunt wants you."

The disappointment on his face made her burst into laughter. When she stopped, she said quickly, "I do need your help with these loaded baskets."

She turned around and pointed to large overflowing baskets to be mounted on the waiting mules outside the house.

Miguel ran to the baskets and began to attach them to the obedient mules munching on grass. He threw furtive glances at Isabella, but she left him for the kitchen, where Rivka was painfully sorting her wares.

The small village and retreat of Guadalupe had never seen such a distinguished assemblage as the one gathered at the queen's request. On the fifteenth of June, 1492, the small streets were filled to capacity when Queen Isabella and King Ferdinand's carriage passed. They both wore regal attire with ermine robes, carried scepters in hands, and wore crowns on their heads as they headed for the royal monastery of the church of Santa Maria de Guadalupe. Both monarchs' faces showed their jubilation as they prepared for the conversion of Don Abraham Senior. Already assembled in the monastery of Santa Maria de Guadalupe were the court's guests and dignitaries, also dressed for the occasion. His wife, Doña Violante, sitting next to him, looked austere under the silk bonnet that covered half her face down to her eyebrows. The rest of the Senior family consisted of his daughter Reina; Reina's husband, Rabbi Meir Melamed; and his two grandsons. Their faces, too, were somber.

At the sound of the *Te Deum*, Queen Isabella and King Ferdinand walked into the church following the procession of Christ's cross, led by the cardinal of Spain, ambassador of the Holy See, officiating as the *papal nuncio.* The monarchs sat on their ornate gold-and-red velvet chairs. Roderigo Maldonado officiated for the royal council, and Senior's closest friend and Converso, Luis de Santángel, was there to witness. Queen Isabella made a motion to the priest to begin Mass.

After the Litany of the Saints and the Blessing of the Baptismal Waters, the priest looked to Queen Isabella to begin the Rite of Baptism. At that moment Don Senior, court rabbi, stood and walked with a slow gait to the altar under the church's apse, where the priest in his white cassock and violet stole stood smiling. Don Senior genuflected at the feet of the priest. The papal nuncio stood at his side.

"Dearly beloved Virgin," said the priest, "honored King and Queen, and noble guests. We are here to instruct and welcome in our midst an honored son of Spain who has proudly served his king and queen with devoted faith." The priest stopped for a moment as he looked in the direction of Queen Isabella. A nod of her head and a smile told him to continue.

"We are gathered here to baptize Don Senior and his family into the family of Christ. *Ergo te baptizo in nominee Patris, et Filii, et Spiritus Sancti.* I baptize thee in the name of the Father and of the Son and of the Holy Ghost." As he said those words, the priest slowly poured holy water on Don Senior's forehead each time he invoked the divine name.

The priest whispered a few words to his acolyte, who gave him a piece of paper. He opened it and read: "You will be known from now on by the name of Don Fernando Núñez Coronel of Castile—Fernando after our King Ferdinand, Núñez for the house of Mendoza, and Coronel for your rank. That will also be your family's name." The priest made a motion for the bishop to confirm the new congregant into The Church of Christ.

"I sign thee with the sign of the cross, and I confirm thee with the chrism of salvation. In the name of the Father and of the Son and of the Holy Ghost." The bishop turned to the congregation and asked, "Who sponsors this confirmand?"

Queen Isabella rose from her seat next to King Ferdinand and said, "As Don Coronel's godparents, we—Cardinal Mendoza, the papal nuncio; and King Ferdinand and I, Queen Isabella of Castile—sponsor him and his family to be confirmed into the family of Christ."

The assembly bowed to Queen Isabella as she took her seat next to her husband. The monarchs held hands and smiled at each other.

The bishop stretched his hand over Don Coronel's head and recited, "May the Holy Spirit come down upon you, and the power of the Most High keep you from all sin."

"Amen," Don Coronel said solemnly with the congregation.

The prayers followed and all congregants sang, "From thy holy temple in Jerusalem, confirm, O Lord, this confirmand. Alleluia!"

When the golden chalice holding the wine was brought to Don Coronel's lips, a teardrop fell and dissipated into the red liquid.

Columns of dust rose in the early morning over the plain of Granada leading to Castile. Occasional openings in the dust cloud revealed long caravans of carts and carriages loaded with furnishings and chests, with children perched on top. The noisy rumbling of wheels over rocks and depressions in the ground added to the din. The sleep-deprived mothers of crying children looked haggard. Fathers and old patriarchs from each family rode horses in front of the carts, helping to lead the reluctant mules.

The more fortunate of this motley assemblage of human exiles were the Jewish nobles and rich merchants of Toledo, Cordoba, and surrounding towns and villages who rode at the front of the column in their carriages, protected from the beating sun and dust that coated everything and everyone.

In one of those carriages rode Isaac Beneluz with his wife, Rivka; their sons, and guests. León was perched outside and leading the horses. Each bench held four of them respectively. Isabella sat tightly between Josè and Miguel on one bench with Mica Beneluz, the youngest son. Tied to the back of the carriage were four mules carrying their personal belongings.

"We've traveled for days since we left Écija. Can't we at least stop for the noon meal?" said Rivka. She wiped her face, which was wet with the sweat and humidity from the hot July sun.

Isaac Beneluz looked at Rivka with tired eyes. "Let's continue until sunset. Then we'll be eighty-five kilometers from Seville."

Rivka held Isaac's gaze and said, "Stopping or not, we'll eat now in the carriage. The children look hungry." She opened a large satchel at her feet, pulling out bread, cheese, and fruit. She distributed food and water for all of them and handed the same to León through the carriage window.

Isabella's bread and cheese tasted delicious. She had never been so hungry before, not in her parent's home, when a prisoner of the pasha in Granada, or at the Beneluz home. Abundance had been the norm. Thinking of her family caused her to long for them and home, and most of all for Juan. *Please God, keep him in health, she prayed.*

The memory of Juan's features was now becoming indistinct, except that she did remember his tall stature and willowy appearance. His eyes, smile, and voice had become somewhat of a blur. She felt a slight tug at her heart, but it dissipated when she found Miguel's eyes upon her. Her cheeks suddenly felt warm, and a deeper tug pulled at her heart. She lowered her eyes to the floor of the carriage, hoping none of the Beneluz family members had noticed her confusion. She then looked to Isaac; his face reflected contentment as he read his prayer book. Rivka was knitting, and the rest of the children were playing on a check-a-board square from which the pieces fell each time the carriage bumped on the road. She looked up and caught a strange look on the face of the eldest Beneluz son, Avram, looking at Miguel with anger in his eyes. Then he turned his face toward her with sad eyes. *Why should he be angry at Miguel?* she wondered. Could it be? No! It wasn't possible. She hoped that Avram wasn't in love with her. That would complicate everything for her new loyalty to the Beneluz family. She quickly dismissed the thought, and turned to Josè, who was sitting next to the window.

"Dear Josè, may I change places with you for a few moments?"

"Of course, big sister," said Josè with a mischievous smile on his face.

"Thank you, little brother." Isabella replied in kind, hugging him.

They changed places, and Isabella could now look outside the carriage for distraction. She did note, however, that Miguel looked disappointed.

Isabella parted the gently flapping curtains and observed the vast mass of thousands of people, carts, and animals before her eyes. An uninterrupted moving caravan descended the hills from the horizon behind them to the hills beyond the plain in front of them.

It was late afternoon, and the pace of the caravan had slowed considerably. Carts and carriages pulled off the road, their occupants lighting small fires with which to begin cooking their food. Children sat quietly, observing their parents prepare food for them. From her vantage point, Isabella found those children lethargic and on the thin side. Their clothing looked unkempt from the rigors and dust of the road. She then noticed an elderly man walking around with a goblet in his hands and asking for some water from the travelers. The answer was mostly no from many who turned away from him, until one man gave him water and some bread with it. Isabella felt relieved. She wondered why some travelers were running out of water and food. She found it troubling.

She heard a commotion and saw a cloud raised by horses advancing toward them. When the horses came nearer, she saw a group of soldiers with swords heading for Granada. As they passed their carriage, Miguel grabbed the curtains and pulled them closed. Isabella understood immediately. Her heart jumped with fear and joy at the same time. She was getting closer to being reunited with her dear parents, but as the kilometers decreased, the danger of being found out increased. She couldn't betray Miguel or the Beneluz family. She had to rely on the promise Miguel made to her, to bring her back to her parents. She nodded her reassurance to Miguel.

Isaac and Rivka Beneluz hadn't noticed the fear that permeated the carriage just now. They went on with their reading and knitting. Isabella couldn't help feeling that she now shared secrets with Miguel—their feelings for each other and fear for their safety. She sighed quietly.

As the day went on, more carts and carriages pulled over to the side of the road—to remain there permanently, it seemed. The journey was taking a toll on the longest travelers, the ones who had left weeks ago from the most northern regions and cities—León and Aragon, and Salamanca and Toledo. Most travelers were now running out of provisions and water, and some of them, thirsty and hungry, began to visit the nearby churches. The priests and townspeople were there to greet them. Isabella saw in a flash several Jewish travelers kneel down and take the food given to them, then make the sign of the cross. They were being baptized!

The inhabitants along the road shouted to them, "Stop and be baptized! Don't go on with your march to death! Think of your children!"

This new element became routine in each town. The Beneluz family still had plenty of provisions, so they turned their eyes away and closed their ears to the shouts for conversion. They were now in their sixth week of arduous travel, and each of them was exhausted, dusty, and longing for an end to the road. The kilometers kept rolling by, but many more cities and towns lay ahead. Isabella longed for night to arrive and to collapse on the makeshift bed on the ground.

At the first ray of sunshine, the Beneluz family knew this would be the hottest July day for them. The night before hadn't cooled as expected, and the ground felt warm and humid to the touch.

"Hurry up!" Isaac Beneluz shouted to all of them. "There's still some moisture in the air coming from the fields. If we leave now, we'll reach Marchena before nightfall," he urged them.

They all pitched in, lifting their bundles, gathering the mules, and checking their provision baskets. Their neighbor Nina, from Cordoba, who was traveling in her cart some meters behind their carriage, approached them in her black widow garb, holding her young daughter. Nina's eyes were lackluster and somber.

"Please, please, Rabbi Beneluz. I need a doctor for my daughter," she begged.

Isaac Beneluz approached the child and held her wrist between his thumb and forefinger. "Her pulse is weak and she's feverish," he said. "We can fetch one at the next town or search among our brethren."

Nina's eyes lit up with hope. "Please find him fast. She's been like that for the last three days." She sobbed.

"For shame!" Rivka admonished her. "Why didn't you come to us? We were only ten carriages and carts ahead of you. I saw you at the well in the last town. Why didn't you tell us that your little Sarah was ill?"

Nina lowered her eyes and sobbed silently.

Isaac searched the column of carriages for any sign of a physician. The sight that greeted him wrenched his stomach and tightened his chest. All around him were old men and women and small children lying on the side of the road, moaning and sobbing. Charitable men and women attended to them, but had to walk away after covering the heads of the dead with blankets. A stench filled the air. The dying fixated their eyes on the sky above them, looking for salvation in another world. *"Shema Israel, Adonai Eloheinou, Adonai Ehad."* The eyes were sealed with the prayer. For a shocking moment Isaac forgot his mission. He shook himself and searched the crowds still marching to their destination—the Port of Seville.

"Do you know a physician? I'm looking for a physician?" He pushed through the crowds, the dead and the living, the carriages, the loaded carts, with the dust everywhere.

"I'm a physician!" shouted a voice.

Isaac looked where the voice originated and found a small man holding a physician's wooden case. "Where's the patient?" the man asked.

"Follow me."

They ploughed back through the multitudes to the spot where Nina held her child. The physician took the child's pulse again, checked her eyes, and forced her mouth open to look at her tongue.

"This child is very sick," he pronounced. "Same as all the others I've treated for the last week."

Nina broke into a loud wailing while everyone around her was aghast. Isaac felt a shame deep inside of him. Why weren't they told? Why was this happening? How could they have traveled in their peaceful trek while others had fallen sick and were dying? He felt enormous guilt. He had been the rabbi of his city in Cordoba and the leader of his people. Where had his attention been? Perhaps in the luxury of his carriage and the abundance of his provisions and in the midst of his loving family he had forgotten his brothers and sisters in their hour of need.

Rivka stood next to him wringing her hands, silent tears sliding down her cheeks. The rest of the children stood around them with grave and fearful faces.

Isaac felt the agony of his fellow travelers. Why, he asked himself, why was this happening to these good people? Why were they being expelled from their homes and the land they loved to face death and the rigors of a grueling trip forced upon them? Where was justice for them?

"I'll give this child water mixed with lemon juice. Bring clean water," said the physician.

Rivka ran to the water jugs inside the carriage and brought it to the physician. He tried to squeeze drops of lemon juice from a bottle he carried into the girl's mouth. She gagged and coughed weakly.

"Do you have onions with you?" he asked. Rivka nodded. "Add crushed onions to the water and keep her warm with lots of water to drink," he told Nina, who broke into tears. "Make sure you boil the water over fire pits!" Then he left to attend to others.

"You can stay with us until little Sarah is better," said Rivka. "Avram, and you, León, go to Nina's mule and attach hers to ours.

"But," asked Avram, "how are we to travel?"

"You will both ride Nina's mule for now," Isaac said with a stern face.

Avram looked unhappy with his father.

Guerida sat at his Seville garrison looking completely dejected. All his searches had been fruitless. Every lead led to a dead end; it seemed Isabella had disappeared into thin air. All those months—practically over a year—nothing had turned up. Where could she be? It was the same for the Costa children. They, too, had vanished. They could be hidden anywhere. Where, though? These were two children who had been baptized; the oldest, Miguel, attended school, and the young one, Josè, was apprentice to the mason's school in Seville. Neither one had showed up in their respective learning places. It was the same with their house—it was watched night and day but stood empty. Guerida was completely baffled. Now he had to answer to the Inquisition Office. He trembled at the thought. They were pressuring him to come up with a lead and fast. He did know, however, that their mother had been deceased for a number of months. Her children were bound to inquire as to her whereabouts. That information had to be kept from Téresa's children, keeping her death a secret. It was the only way to lure them back.

"Inspector! Inspector!" His aide barged in, red in the face, the fat around his stomach shaking with excitement and his face beaming with joy. "We found a true lead this time," he said.

Guerida sprang from his seat. "Where?" He kept his voice calm. He'd been disappointed so many times before that now he wanted to be sure. "Tell me everything you know."

"We've been tracking down those three since España took over." The aide crossed his forehead and chest. "The trail became cold just after the infidel Moors left for the Alpuxarras—"

Guerida interrupted him with impatience. "Get to the point."

"*Sí, mi Alguacil*. We questioned many people in many towns, and we put up notices with the descriptions of the three suspects and—"

Guerida became impatient again. "But how did you get to them!"

"We got a lead from a Marrano in Cordoba. A woman reported seeing the three youths leaving from Jewish Friday-night services."

"Are you sure of your source?"

"Absolutely. The woman is a good New Christian. She wouldn't lie to us. She described the girl as a seventeen-year-old young woman with black hair and beautiful green eyes. The two boys were one very young and the other about eighteen or nineteen years of age."

"But where could they have gone from Cordoba?" Guerida asked.

"That's the mystery. All three joined with the Jews leaving Cordoba, about three weeks ago." The aide lowered his head. "That's where we lost their trace. There are hundreds of thousands of refugees marching from many cities and towns in Andalusia, and from Aragon heading to ports they can get to. The Cordoba caravan is headed for Seville. But they could've gone on to the ports in Aragon, Cartagena, or Barcelona."

"You've done good work," Guerida told the aide. "You're to dispatch twenty men to various ports, to look out for them. Report any news to me immediately!"

"*Sí, Alguacil.*" The aide saluted and left the room.

Guerida felt some relief to his morose mood. All he had to do now was supervise every port of departure in southern Spain.

Under a partially hidden silver moon, clouds had gathered by evening's end, and the chances for showers were beginning to materialize. Rain in the month of July was unusual, but this season had been one of unpredictable surprises. The spring was late in coming, and summer began in earnest in the middle of July. Temperatures had soared, and the humidity was unbearable.

Beneluz was sweating profusely and couldn't sleep. It was very late at night. He looked beyond the area where his family lay on blankets on the ground, beyond the makeshift night camp where the rest of the masses lay, to the massive silver mountains of Sierra Nevada above the plain. He saw some snow still clinging to the peak of Mulhacén. Beneluz felt he may as well be on the moon—that was how far away the solution of his dilemma seemed. What future waited for them at the end of their trek? He didn't know. He knew for certain that ships moored at the harbor in Seville would receive them with open arms. The ship's captains were sure to empty the pockets of the miserable wretches coming to them. Since Jews were barred from taking silver or gold with them, the ships and mercenaries would be the inheritors of great Jewish wealth. Beneluz had taken with him enough gold, sewn by Rivka into the linings of his caftan cloak, to cover their trip and allow them to cross the straits of Gibraltar. From there it was a quick passage to Tangier; then perhaps Fez would be the final leg of their trip.

He heard Nina's little girl moaning quietly. He went to the child and found her uncovered. Her breath rattled. Beneluz tried to cover her, but she was sweating heavily. Her clothes were wet and her forehead hot. He shook Nina slightly by the shoulder to wake her up.

"What! What is it?" she asked with a fearful voice.

"You daughter needs you. She's burning hot."

Nina shifted her body next to Sarah and felt for her forehead. "My God, what can I do? Her fever is worse!"

"Give her more of that water with lemon," Beneluz suggested, but he suspected it might be useless. He sensed the child was dying.

Beneluz woke Rivka from a deep sleep. When Beneluz whispered in her ear, she jumped from her blanket to go to Nina.

Now we wait, thought Beneluz grimly.

In the dark hour before dawn, little Sarah, who had been a playful and happy child, died in Nina's arms. At the sound of her wailing, other people began to awaken to the dreaded news. A low rumbling moved through the throng, then furor began to erupt.

"Another senseless death! Oh God, why are we being persecuted?" Cries rose in many groups while mothers hugged their children as if to protect them from the arms of death. Up till now, many old folks had succumbed to the rigors of the march, the heat, and lack of water and food. Now it was the children who suffered. Their small bodies could not take the hunger and hardship. Disease stalked them.

"May God protect us," Rivka moaned to Beneluz. "May he see them safe!"

The morning hours revealed a gloomy camp. Preparations were hastily made to bury little Sarah on the side of a hill. Her name was scratched on a small rock with a flint stone, making a headstone. Beneluz officiated as rabbi while Nina cried inconsolably. By noon, Beneluz, Rivka, and the children were ready to take to the road. Nina was asked to join them, but she refused. As the carriage pulled away, Beneluz watched Nina disappear into the background, a small figure dressed in black.

31

Exodus

A LONG CARAVAN OF WAGONS, carriages, and carts led by mules, with haggard men, women, and children on foot made its way down ravines, then emerged into Castile's fertile green plain. Orchards and rows of wheat, barley, and oats grew side by side in the flourishing fields. All around them was growth and green plants, the image of new life in contrast to the refugees, who were broken in body and spirit. Families had decreased in size due to the loss of many of their members. The remainder of a once-prosperous middle class of traders, artisans, and peasants now comprised only ghosts of a past that fed upon dreams of a once-flourishing society.

Amid the throng of emaciated people, the dusty carriage of Beneluz and his family creaked along, some of its wheels wobbling and on the verge of detaching from the main carriage body. Of the four pack mules, only one was left, carrying a light load of personal belongings; the other three had died of thirst and labor. Without these beasts, the Beneluz family was forced to distribute the excess personal belongings to more unfortunate families, and the rest was discarded. The two front mules were still pulling the carriage, but very slowly and reluctantly.

Several times along the way, soldiers stopped them to check the occupants of the carriage. Isabella was dressed as a young peasant woman with matted hair obscuring parts of her face, which was now smeared with soot and dust. Miguel, Josè, and the others were disheveled and grimy from the road. Now they looked more like gypsies in their own country. The little water they had left was held in one jug, and their food was now meager. Rivka took pains to divide the provisions evenly. She gave all the children their parts, leaving a few crumbs for Isaac and herself.

Isaac Beneluz, who saw the panic and worry on her face, said to her, "We're getting near Seville. Once there, we'll feast on the best foods your eyes ever beheld. We'll wash and sleep in comfortable beds. You'll see."

Rivka lifted hopeful but tired eyes at him, then nodded quietly.

It was almost noon, and few kilometers remained as they approached the town of Alcalá de Guadaira, and the last stop before Seville. Travelers in the opposite direction slowed their carriages to observe the thousands of people marching toward the city. Their eyes gazed in amazement and shock at the sight of these bedraggled and emaciated voyagers. As they approached, the townspeople came out of their whitewashed homes to look upon the spectacle of ghostly figures still trudging on the road.

An older woman shouted at the top of her lungs, "For the love of Christ, convert for your souls! For your dying children!" She brought them bread to show her empathy. The bread disappeared as hundreds of hands lunged for it.

"You Jews can't be too smart!" a man yelled, standing with his hands on his hips. "Look at you! The true faith is the Christian faith. Convert or perish!"

One of the Jewish women in tattered clothes, her face smeared with dust that had caked over, spit at his feet. "We know which is the true faith. It's our Mosaic Law! You wouldn't understand!" She passed the man with her head high.

Rivka and Isaac Beneluz, who had watched the scene from their carriage, shook their heads in disbelief.

"We don't have to prove our Jewishness to the peasants who were once heathens themselves," said Beneluz, addressing his children and without looking in Isabella's direction. "When their peasant ancestors were worshipping the sun and the moon under their Visigothic rulers, our forefathers had one God and no other gods. How can they doubt our religion, the one that spawned theirs?"

Isabella saw in disbelief the chasm between the two opposing views. She now felt torn between the two. Who was she? Or what was she? A Christian or a Jewess? She looked surreptitiously at Miguel on the opposite bench in the carriage. He had remained silent during the outburst between the two camps. Could he, too, be feeling conflicting emotions? At that moment, Miguel's eyes rested on her in a loving gaze. She smiled back at him and caught Beneluz's eyes watching them. Both Miguel and Isabella blushed at the same time, and turned their heads in opposite directions.

Beneluz broke up in an uproarious laughter. Rivka looked at him strangely with worry in her eyes.

"My dear Isaac, what's making you laugh so? Perhaps you can tell us. We could use something other than the misery around us."

Beneluz coughed as he tried to stop laughing. It only produced a renewed laughter. He caught his breath, wiped his teary eyes, and said, "It warms my heart to see that love can be born despite everything that wants to destroy it."

"What do you mean?" Rivka asked. Her face reflected a mischievous smile. Rivka seemed to know that what passed between Miguel and Isabella was more than concern or affection for each other.

Beneluz remained silent for a moment. Then he said, "I think it is high time that you declared your love, Miguel."

Isabella sat silent but fidgeted with her hands.

Miguel turned crimson red. "What do you mean, Uncle?"

Beneluz bent down and reached for Isabella's hand, then for Miguel's. He put their hands in each other's keeping. "You are blessed, my children. Blessed for your love for each other and blessed for the propagation of our people to continue in our faith. *Mazal tov!*"

Miguel broke into a tender smile as he looked at Isabella, who lowered her eyes with a shy smile.

Rivka got up from her seat and went to hug them both. "Good luck, my children, and congratulations to you both!" She then clapped her hands and broke into a song.

"¡La espozada es muy hermosa! ¡El espozado es muy alegri!" She kissed them on both cheeks.

José, whose face beamed during the surprising news, hugged Isabella, then his brother. "I'm so happy. I'll be your witness at your wedding."

Miguel laughed, then seeing José's contrite face, quickly said, "Children can't be witnesses, but you can be my ring bearer."

Contented with the task, Josè beamed.

"Now I can be your real sister," Isabella said to Josè, then hugged him tightly.

The only one not smiling was Avram, whose face looked somber. Beneluz noticed the change on his eldest son's face and looked intently at him. "What do you say, Avram, heh?"

Avram hesitated at first, then he shook Miguel's hand and hugged Isabella. She answered in kind.

While the congratulatory hugging and kissing went on, Beneluz's second son, León, who led the mules, stopped the carriage and came down from his perch. He appeared at the window and peered in. "What's all the commotion?" he asked.

"It's a happy occasion!" Beneluz shouted. "Miguel and Isabella are engaged!"

"This is indeed a happy occasion," said León. "Can we toast, Father?"

"Of course!" Beneluz replied. "Rivka, you know what to do?"

Rivka smiled, then told her other two sons to get off the bench. She then opened it and produced a bottle of sweet wine. "We will drink to you two," she said.

The glasses were filled, and the young couple drank first, then everyone else drank. Outside the carriage, the mules brayed loudly. Avram barely wetted his lips and left most of the wine untouched. Beneluz, seeing that his eldest was having a hard time accepting the happy event, turned to him,

"Avram, it's your turn to lead the mules up front."

Avram nodded, and without a word climbed up to the outside perch, and the carriage moved again sluggishly.

The rest of the Beneluz family sat back inside the carriage, temporarily relieved from the dreariness of the voyage. Lulled by the swaying of the vehicle, they fell asleep one by one. The only ones awake were Isabella and Miguel, who marveled in their happiness by holding hands and smiling at each other. Beneluz read his Torah and mumbled the words to himself.

The day was now winding down, and by evening they arrived in Seville. It was still light, and Beneluz began his search for an inn. An hour later, finding that most inns were filled to capacity by the influx of road travelers who paid exorbitant prices for a room, he came back to the carriage on the outskirts of town.

"I'm afraid there are no more rooms," he said dejectedly.

"Offer them more money," said Rivka resolutely.

"You don't understand, my dear wife," he said to her without a hint of reproach. "All rooms have been taken. I've visited every inn for the last two hours. We have no choice but to sleep in the carriage one more night."

Rivka shook her head, unhappy. "Could we at least get a warm meal at one of the inns?"

"I've already taken care of that. It isn't very far. Come with me, everyone." He turned to Avram and said to him, "You'll have to stay with the carriage and the mules. We'll bring food for you back with us."

Avram didn't answer his father. He nodded respectfully.

The rest of the family, including Miguel, Isabella, and Josè, walked to the nearest tavern. It was crowded to capacity inside. The owner cleaned a large table for them, and the food came quickly: hot bowls of rice, fried fish, onions, beer, and *buñuelos* for dessert. Afterward, Beneluz ordered the same for Avram, who waited with the carriage and mules. When he came to pay, the owner of the tavern declined to take money. Confounded, Beneluz opened his mouth with surprise and was about to say that it was a mistake, when soldiers with swords burst through the door. They fell upon the table where the Beneluz family was seated. Rivka pulled two of her younger sons to her breast, and Beneluz stood, pale and shaky. Miguel paled too, grabbing his brother and Isabella by the shoulders.

"What's the meaning of this?" Beneluz asked in a trembling voice.

The soldiers didn't answer, but turned their heads toward the tavern's door. The entrance of a police inspector made the diners who had stopped their meals speak in low voices.

"I'm Guerida, chief inspector of Seville and all of Andalusia."

Beneluz sat on the bench with shaky knees. "What's your business with my family and guests? We're leaving Seville within a few days as scheduled. We've done no wrong!"

"That will be determined by the courts. You have here fugitives from the law, and we're here to capture them."

Beneluz's face blanched again. He sat as still as a statue without looking at anyone seated at the table. "Who are those fugitives?"

Inspector Guerida came around the table to where Miguel sat still with his arms around his brother and Isabella. Guerida looked at Miguel and said, "We're here to arrest you, Miguel Costa, and your brother for kidnapping Isabella Obrigon!"

Miguel startled. His arms went limp but he still held onto Isabella and his brother.

"We've done no wrong!" Josè shouted.

Miguel shook his head to Josè to silence him.

Isabella, who had sat with a stunned face, sprang from her seat and turned to Guerida. "You're mistaken. I wasn't kidnapped! I went to these people here on my own free will. I was their guest, and they didn't know who I was!"

Guerida smiled ironically. "I know you're protecting them. But if I were you, I'd want to spit in their eyes. Because of them, your mother is dead! Dead, you hear!"

Isabella jerked back in shock and collapsed hard on the bench. Rivka let go of her sons and turned to hug Isabella, who sat next to her sobbing.

"Provecita niña, Oy, mi provecita niña." Rivka murmured as she hugged Isabella tightly.

"How could you be so cruel!" Beneluz shouted at Guerida.

Guerida didn't answer and turned to Miguel and Josè. "And your mother is also dead!"

Josè immediately threw up the food he'd just eaten, and Miguel swayed, dazed. Then he straightened.

"You're lying! You're lying!" Miguel shouted at Guerida.

Guerida's face became somber. "Seize them!" he ordered.

The guards grabbed Miguel's and José's arms and tried to tie them behind their backs without succeeding. Josè's small body shook as if the Devil had possessed him, and he began to yell and kick the guards. Miguel fought them, too, by rocking himself back and forth, thus preventing the ropes from being tied. Rivka had let go of Isabella and joined in the fray by shouting at the guards, "*¡Ellos son sólo niños*!" Isabella extended her arms to stop them too, but more guards came into the hall, and helped tie them. They lifted both boys on their shoulders and carried them outside the tavern.

Isabella sat stunned and wordless. Guerida approached her and spoke gently for the first time. "Please follow us, señorita."

Isabella raised her tear-stained face. She felt numb and dazed by the series of events. She stopped crying for a moment at the realization of these shocking events. Her most desired wish was about to be fulfilled—to see her father and . . . She stopped suddenly at the thought that her mother was now dead. She renewed her crying now in a low and wailing sound. Rivka came again to hold her in her grief.

"*¿Por favor, señorita?*" Guerida spoke again. "Your father's been waiting for you for one year."

Isabella got up reluctantly, started to walk a few steps, then turned around to hug Rivka. Rivka received her with open arms. "Don't you worry—we'll track Miguel and his brother and report to you."

Isabella lifted teary eyes. She turned around and hugged Isaac Beneluz and the three Beneluz children.

As he hugged her good-bye, Beneluz said, "I promise you we'll help them."

Isabella shook her head somberly and stumbled after Guerida.

The sounds of horses' hooves against the pavement died down as they slowly trotted away.

Beneluz sat frozen on the bench, his eyes staring at the tavern door. Rivka looked at him aghast and white-faced.

"Isaac?"she said in a mournful voice. Beneluz didn't answer, still in a trance. "Isaac?" Rivka called out to him in a louder voice.

Beneluz shook and looked at her. “What is it, my dear?” His voice broke.

“We’re still safe? Aren’t we?”

Beneluz looked at her, then his face turned confounded. “But why? We should’ve been arrested too—we were with them!”

Rivka looked confused. “What are you saying?”

“Don’t you see?” he said. “We were accomplices, and yet they didn’t arrest us.”

“I don’t understand.”

Beneluz stayed quiet for a moment. He then raised lifeless eyes to her. “I knew.”

Rivka said, “How could you know?”

“Miguel told me everything. Their mother, Téresa, was involved in kidnapping Isabella.”

“But why didn’t you tell me?” Reproach was in Rivka’s eyes.

“Because I swore to Miguel to keep this secret from the rest of the family.” To Rivka’s shaking of her head, he hastened to explain. “It was to protect everyone. It was to prevent any of our children from speaking or confiding in anyone. Don’t you see—secrets never remain secrets!”

Beneluz felt exasperated for a moment with his wife’s naïve attitude. It was a trait of her good nature. Rivka saw no wrong in people. She’d been protected and inured from grief and disaster, and his position as rabbi and leader of the community had given her and his children this added protection, even though the authorities suspected everyone in the Jewish quarters in Cordoba.

“And yet, we weren’t arrested?” She came back again to his original question.

Beneluz couldn’t answer her. He, too, was befuddled. “We ought to leave and get to the docks as soon as possible,” he said, getting up.

“How could you think of that now?” she cried at him. “What about Miguel and Josè? Are we to abandon them?”

“Of course not!” he shouted back at her. We’ll come back and enquire as to their fate. Besides, they’ll be released soon. As soon as the authorities realize their mistake.”

"But they're your brother's children!" she came back at him with reproach.

Beneluz stood silent for a moment, then wiped his brow as if sweat was there. "I don't know what made me say that," he said suddenly. "I was thinking about the deadline to leave Spain. You're right. How can I abandon my nephews and blood kin? We'll wait here until we hear word about their fate."

Rivka smiled at him with affection. "I always knew you to make the right decisions concerning the welfare of this family."

Beneluz didn't answer her. "Let's go," he said.

They all walked back to the carriage where Avram waited for them. Silently, they got into the carriage. León lead the mules this time on the outside post.

After a long silence, Avram spoke. "Where's the hot meal you promised me?"

Beneluz raised his eyes at him and mumbled a few words of apology.

"I don't understand, Father. You never break a promise."

"I said, I'm sorry," said Beneluz. "We completely forgot."

"How could you forget?" Avram asked with impatience.

Beneluz then related to him all the events that transpired. "So you see, when we left, I completely forgot all about the food."

Avram remained silent, accepting his father's explanation.

"Here, I still have more bread and cheese for you," Rivka said as she told her sons to get off the banquette and searched in the bin below. She gave Avram the leftover food and then went back to a muted silence.

Within less than an hour, they veered away from the moonlit road leading to the port and left the throng of fellow travelers. Instead, they entered the heart of Seville to await word on the fate of Miguel and Josè.

32

End of an Era

ISABELLA RODE IN A MODEST carriage that belonged to Inspector Guerida. He sat opposite her in regal uniform with gold epaulettes over his shoulders. His face looked satisfied, but he had tired lines around his eyes. She saw him fiddling with his nails as the carriage neared her ancestral home.

Isabella looked at Guerida with anger. Because of his zeal, Miguel and Josè were now in jail or worse. She shuddered at the thought. She'd heard whispers in the past from her servants that the Inquisition searched out with vengeance all those who transgressed the Catholic faith with Judaizing. She also heard horror tales of dungeons and burnings. She shivered and rubbed her arms.

"My apologies, señorita. You must be cold." Guerida slipped out of his highly decorated jacket to wrap it around Isabella's shoulders. She accepted the jacket without thanking him and remained silent.

"I know," said Guerida, "that you've been through an ordeal. Now you can rejoice in your father's home and be protected from criminal elements."

Isabella felt blood rushing to her head. She contained herself from blasting at Guerida. Right now she had to play the role of a rescued young señorita.

"I was thinking about my mother," she said simply.

"My poor girl. We'll see that those culpable are brought to justice. I promise you!"

Isabella felt sorry she had stirred Guerida's confused state of mind as to where culpability lay. She felt that same sort of confusion as to which faith she owed allegiance. Now that she would be reunited with her father, she would seek answers to this disturbing question.

Deep in thought, she'd been unaware that the carriage had come to its final destination. They'd traveled from the outskirts of Seville to her family home in its upper heights. The whitewashed wall around the house looked inviting in the moonlight drenching the narrow streets and alleys. All looked the same to her: the citron-scented trees overhanging the surrounding walls, the boxed flowers hanging from the upper floor windows, and the quiet enveloping the entire grounds.

Guerida turned to her and said, "Please stay put. I must prepare your father for your arrival. He's a tired man now."

It was strange to have to wait at the door of her own house, but Isabella understood the request and nodded. She watched from within the carriage as Guerida walked to the front gate and pulled the bell. At the sound of chimes, a servant appeared.

Isabella heard him ask the servant to see Don Obrigon.

An interminable wait began for Isabella. She could hardly contain her impatience and descended from the carriage. Approaching the front door, she opened it and quietly slipped inside. She heard voices coming from the kitchen, and the hallway was empty. Her slippers shuffled silently on the red tile until she came near her father's study. She heard Guerida talking soothingly.

"Now, Don Obrigon, prepare yourself for the good news I bring you."

Isabella heard her father's trembling voice. "You found a lead?"

"You must not get excited. For your daughter's sake."

"Please give me the news."

Guerida recalled the events at the tavern, the arrests, and the fact that he would see his daughter shortly.

Isabella heard a rustle of skirts behind her and turned to face dada Hannah standing in shock with her mouth opened wide and without a sound. Isabella put her hand over her mouth to silence her, then fell into her warm and expansive arms.

Dada Hannah sobbed deeply and quietly. Isabella kissed her forehead and turned toward her father's study. She couldn't wait any longer. She stepped into the room and stood on the threshold. She saw her father bolt from his chair, then swivel around. She ran to him before he fell and embraced him as he collapsed on his knees.

"Mi povre padrecito." She bent down to him and kissed him over and over.

"¡Mi querida hija, mi amor!" Obrigon yelled at the top of his lungs. *"Gracias, gracias, Madonna Sancta. Gracias para la vida de mi hija."* Obrigon prayed with his eyes closed, thanking the Virgin Mary for his daughter's recovery.

Isabella tried, but couldn't pray. She'd never before had trouble reciting the Hail Mary and asking for intercession for her father's and mother's well-being and protection. In the past she'd also enjoyed handling the rosary to recite prayers while caressing the stones' smoothness and reciting the fifteen promises. Now she could hardly bring herself to pray. Her mother was dead, Miguel and Josè were probably in a dungeon, and her father's hair had turned white over the period of one year. She had nothing to be thankful for and least of all for herself. She was now of two different religions, belonging to two different cultures and two different creeds. Was it the Trinity or the Jewish star that would claim her?

Just then the memory of her mother surfaced. She broke into in tears. Her father tried to calm her. "What is it, my querida?"

"*Mi madre*. I'll never see her again." She cried harder with bitter tears. Was she not responsible for her death? If she hadn't been impulsive and used to getting her way immediately, her mother would be here right now to hug and hold her.

Her father tried to console her. "Your madre said one thing to me. She said, 'Find Isabella. Find her,' she said to me."

Isabella raised her eyes to him.

"At least I found you. And now your mother in heaven is happy," Obrigon said.

Isabella was bursting with questions. She looked up, becoming aware that Guerida was still standing in the room. She whispered into her father's ear, "Father, I want to be alone with you."

Obrigon understood his daughter's wish for privacy. He nodded to Isabella, then turned to Guerida. "My good chief inspector. My daughter and I are now tired and need to be by ourselves."

"If there's anything you need, please let me know?" Guerida said.

Obrigon nodded then said, "Muchas gracias, Inspector. Thank you for bringing my daughter back."

Guerida smiled and turned to leave, but stopped and turned back to face Obrigon. "His Excellency, the grand inquisitor, Torquemada, may need your help, and your daughter's help, to investigate the culprits further."

Obrigon shivered at the name of Torquemada. He nodded to Guerida.

As soon as Guerida left, Isabella ran to her father and asked him to sit down. Obrigon, looking somewhat puzzled, acquiesced to his daughter.

"Father, do you know why I was kidnapped?"

Obrigon didn't reply. He looked at her with a blank face. After a moment he said, "To ransom you?"

"You know, Father, that isn't true, don't you?"

Obrigon moved uncomfortably on his chair. "I don't know what you're talking about."

"You do remember . . ." she said. She moved her chair closer to him. Putting her arms around him, she snuggled into his chest. ". . . how I used to sit on your lap and snuggle up to you when I was little?"

Obrigon nodded and smiled tenderly at her.

"You were my hero then and you're my hero now. There's nothing that can change the way I see you and love you as my father."

"What change are you talking about?" he asked suddenly. His face reflected a tinge of worry.

"I know about my origins and the fact that I was adopted," she said with a firm voice.

Obrigon now turned white. "It's not true!"

"Please tell me. Father; I must know! Or I'll pry it from you in any way I can!"

Obrigon took a kerchief from his vest pocket and wiped a cold sweat from his brow. He remained silent for a long time. Isabella saw that it would be difficult for him to speak the truth. She hugged him again, then kissed him on the forehead.

"You're the father I grew up with, and you'll remain my father till the day I die."

Obrigon lowered his head in agony. He raised his head and looked her straight in the eyes.

"You, too, will be my daughter till the day I die. I will have no other daughter but you. What you ask of me is very difficult. I swore an oath to never speak of it."

"But you must, Father, you must!" Isabella insisted. "I must tell you something I would not have told anyone." She swallowed, then spoke fast. "I'm in love, Father, in love with a wonderful young man." She beamed as she said those words. Then her face took on a dark shade, and she shuddered, and tears began to show in her eyes. She bent down, wringing her hands.

Obrigon fell silent. "Is it about Juan?" he asked her with pain on his face.

She looked up at him confused. "Juan? No. It's not Juan."

Obrigon fell silent. "What is it, *mi alma*? Why should you cry when you're in love?"

"The boy I love is Miguel Costa. He's been arrested, and I don't know where he is." She cried again.

This time Obrigon looked confounded. "Miguel, Miguel?" he repeated.

"I will have to write to Juan and return the engagement ring," said Isabella. "I'll explain everything to him, but now that I'm in love with another, I have to tell him the truth."

Her father was strangely quiet, almost reflective.

"What is it, Father?"

Obrigon said quickly, "Tell me about Miguel. I want to know everything."

Isabella related to her father all that had transpired during her absence. "So you see why you have to tell me the truth about my birth. You must!"

Her father seemed aghast. After a long silence he said, "Yes, we adopted you."

Isabella kissed her father on both cheeks, then hugged him. "Tell me everything?"

He told her about her uncle, who had brought her to their home, his request to keep this information a secret from her, and for her to marry within the Jewish faith.

"But how could he have thought that I'd be raised Catholic then marry within the Jewish faith?"

"Because he wanted to protect you from reprisals. Eventually at eighteen years of age, we would have to tell you the truth."

"And did my mother know of this?"

"Yes, she did."

"Yet, she loved me as her own child," Isabella said pensively.

"She did more than that. She went overboard to grant your every wish."

A smile appeared on her wet face. She wiped it and said, "We must save Miguel and his brother. You must help me, Father. You must!" She grabbed his arms and shook them.

"I will talk to Guerida and others who can help." He then said, "We have powerful friends now." He put his finger to his mouth, then whispered, "The king and queen."

A sign of hope appeared on Isabella's face. "Thank you, Father," she said.

Miguel woke up to a gray and cold morning. The stones under the straw bed felt frigid to the touch, and he couldn't wait for the sun to rise. At least they could stand by the barred window to bask in warm rays of the sun. He looked at his sleeping brother and felt relieved that José still found nourishment in his deep torpor. "Who sleeps, eats," his mother used to say to him when he was a small child. Whenever their father was gone on one of this road travels, José couldn't fall asleep. He would constantly ask for food, then water to drink, then a story. Their mother would acquiesce to his first request, then, when her patience wore thin, she would rock him to sleep. *My poor mother,* thought Miguel with deep sadness. Her lot in life had been hard. First losing their father as a husband and companion, then becoming the breadwinner for him and his brother, then a fate that she did not deserve. *Why had she become involved in kidnapping Isabella?* He had warned her the night of the arrest, and she had confided in him the reason she had whisked away the Obrigons' daughter. He told her it was dangerous to become linked with the Moorish enemy. He thought with irony that if his mother hadn't been involved in this kidnapping, he would never have known Isabella, never experienced this sweet love and burning need for her. But now he had lost them both.

The unlocking of the cell door brought him out of his thoughts. A priest with black robes entered their prison cell. He walked silently with a sunken and ashen face, and his body was caved in as if he had been perpetually starved.

"Miguel Costa?" the priest asked.

Miguel lifted his head from his ground position and looked into the eyes of the priest without a word.

"Are you Miguel Costa?"

"Yes," Miguel answered after a long silence.

"I am the grand inquisitor, Tomás de Torquemada."

Miguel shivered. He had first became familiar with this dreaded name during his mother's arrest. With contempt he turned his head away from Torquemada.

"I know how sorrowful you are about the death of your mother," Torquemada said.

Miguel didn't answer, but dug his nails into his arms.

"Your mother was a courageous woman. She only thought of her sons and their safety. She had a bad heart, and she died a martyr."

Miguel turned his head with pain to Torquemada.

"My poor boy," Torquemada said in a mellifluous voice. "You've suffered greatly. You and your brother can be exonerated from the kidnapping if you tell me why you were with Isabella."

Miguel kept his mouth shut. Another word from Torquemada and he would charge.

"I won't press you right now," said Torquemada. "But if you change your mind, I can have you both released immediately."

Miguel lowered his head over his chest, and his fists were clenched tightly under his armpits. He wouldn't give him any information. It would incriminate his mother in death. Yes, the Inquisition had been known to exhume dead persons and throw them on the pyre to clean their souls. Horror filled him at the thought.

When he lifted his head, Torquemada had left as quietly as he had entered the cell.

Thank God José was asleep, he thought. He would've been scared out of his wits.

In the early hour of four o'clock in the morning, Rivka woke up to find Isaac pacing back and forth in the small bedroom in the inn. With luck on their side, they had found the last room in that inn. It was clean, with a bed for him and Rivka. Their sons slept soundly on mattresses on the floor. Rivka watched him pace. Isaac looked haggard from lack of sleep and hadn't eaten in the last two days. She knew that he was under great pressure to resolve his nephews' release while meeting the deadline for their departure.

"You're worrying yourself to death. Come and rest now." She hushed, afraid to wake the boys.

Isaac turned to Rivka's voice. "How can I rest? Are my nephews resting now? They're probably scared and hungry."

Rivka lowered her head in despair. If Isaac continued in that vein, he would become sick. "You must rest and eat something. We're leaving in a week. Are we to carry you on a stretcher? The ship may refuse us passage. They'll think you're ill! You know what'll happen if we stay behind. Forced conversion!"

Isaac stopped pacing suddenly. Rivka may have talked some sense into him—who would seek advice from a converted rabbi? He turned to Rivka and laughed.

"Are you going mad too?" Rivka asked, startled.

"Why didn't I think about it? How stupid I've been."

"What do you mean?"

"I forgot about my friend Don Abraham Senior. I know he will help us. He is 'Rab de la Corte,' and has the queen's confidence, and he is also financial advisor to King Ferdinand."

Rivka raised hopeful eyes. "But doesn't he reside in Segovia? How are you to go there and be back in time for our voyage?"

Beneluz passed a hand over his brows. "Yes, I'm aware of this impossibility. Perhaps I can see his friend Abravanel. I know he's in Seville."

"Then you must go right away to him. Take Avram with you."

"That is what I'll do. You're a treasure, my dear wife. Get Avram ready."

Rivka went to Avram's mattress and shook him gently.

"What is it?" Avram said, startled.

"Shush. Don't wake up your brothers. You're going with your father."

"Where to?"

"He will tell you everything," said Rivka. She helped him find his clothes that were strewn all over the mattress on the floor.

Avram looked up to see his father getting dressed. He approached him and stood silently behind him.

Isaac felt his presence and turned around. "As my eldest, you are to come with me on an important mission."

"What mission is that?" Avram asked.

"To save your cousins from certain death."

"My cousins, always my cousins. What about us? As Jews, and second-class citizens, we must keep to ourselves."

Isaac was taken aback by his son's outburst. "It pains me very much to see your lack of compassion."

"I have great compassion for you and mother and my brothers."

"You must have compassion for every human being, every living thing. That's what *Atorá* teaches us."

Avram didn't reply. He lowered his head.

Rivka felt pity for her older son. His father always drove him harder than his brothers, giving him the hardest tasks and leaving no space for indulgence. She knew that Isaac didn't acknowledge Avram or praise him like he did his other sons, but she couldn't interfere with her husband's discipline. She turned to a smoldering fire burning in a small fireplace and poured hot liquid into a goblet from the hanging pot.

"Here, Avram. Take this warm milk with you," she said softly.

Avram took the metal goblet from her hands and kissed his mother's forehead.

"I'm ready, let us go now," said Isaac.

Obrigon waited in Guerida's small office for over an hour. He was about to give up when an aide came in. "He will see you now."

Obrigon had been known to be a patient man, always finding a cause, then acting upon it without losing his head. But if this unimportant inspector thought he was powerful, he would tell him otherwise!

"Please come in, Don Obrigon."

Obrigon sat down without acknowledging Guerida.

"How can I help you?" Guerida asked.

"I'll come to the point. I want the two youngsters you have in custody."

Guerida was shocked. "Why would you want them? They're criminals!"

"I know that," Obrigon answered patiently. He quickly said, "They've deprived me of my daughter for a year now. I want to see them squirm like fish without water."

"Oh, come on, Don Obrigon. We don't have to be so cruel. They're children, after all."

Obrigon was incensed that Guerida would've discovered compassion suddenly. "I only want to scare them, that's all."

"These two are now out of my jurisdiction. Torquemada has them, and he'll make them squirm, I assure you."

"I've no doubt about that. But couldn't you give me this satisfaction? No one will know. You'll deliver them to me in the morning, and by night they'll be back in prison custody."

Guerida shook his head with a smile on his face. "I can't do that. As an officer of the law, I'd be betraying my oath of duty to the public. You know I can't do that."

Obrigon stood up and searched in his overcoat's large pockets. He pulled out a coin pouch and placed it in front of Guerida.

Guerida's face went from shock to surprise. "I'm ashamed, Don Obrigon, that you should think me easily bribed!"

"Just look inside. They're *doblas* . . . gold coins!"

Guerida shook his head. "I'm afraid I can't take them. My post is at stake."

Obrigon sighed, took back the coin bag, and pocketed it. He turned and walked out in silence. He couldn't face Isabella, who was waiting for him.

After a short ride, Beneluz and Avram arrived in the affluent part of Seville. The carriage stopped at Don Abravanel's large estate with the imposing house sitting in the midst of a fragrant citrus garden. Beneluz pulled the handle on the bell.

"I want to see Don Abravanel; it's urgent!" he told the servant who opened the door, but the servant remained frozen. "Don't you understand me?" Isaac yelled at the man.

"I'm afraid Don Abravanel isn't here." the servant then said.

"What do you mean?" Isaac yelled again. "Where is he?"

"My name is Ernestino, and Don Abravanel left me in charge of this house. He left Spain for Portugal, never to return again, I'm afraid."

Isaac stood stunned on the threshold. "Why has he left?" he asked.

"I don't know. His whole family left with him."

Isaac dropped his head in defeat.

"Father?" Avram said in a hushed voice. "We must go back."

Isaac looked at his son with empty eyes. "Go where?" Then as if possessed by some devil, Isaac pushed Ernestino aside and ran into the house. "Abravanel?" Isaac called out. "Abravanel, where are you?"

Avram ran after him, thinking his father had been touched by a demon that made him leave his senses.

Ernestino ran after them. "Please, please don't scare my daughter and grandchildren living in the house!"

At that moment, the bell to the house rang, and Ernestino stopped his search to run back to the front gate. There he saw Don Abraham Senior standing in silk and velvet attire.

"Ernestino, I have to speak to your master quickly!"

"There's another gentleman asking the same. He's in the house. Please come in."

Don Senior followed Ernestino into the house and came face-to-face with Isaac Beneluz. He recognized him right away from a rabbi conference in Toledo years ago.

"What are you doing here, Beneluz?"

"I should ask the same of you, my friend," Beneluz said, having come to his senses.

"I'm looking for Don Abravanel."

"I'm also looking for Don Abravanel," Beneluz replied.

"If I may speak?" Ernestino interrupted. "Don Abravanel has fled for Portugal with his family. He's entrusted me his house until the authorities come to seize it."

There was no surprise on Don Senior's face. He seemed to take it all in stride. He pulled Beneluz aside and hastened to explain.

"I'm afraid Don Abravanel has displeased the queen, and he's fled Spain."

Beneluz remained speechless by the news.

Don Senior turned to Ernestino. "I understand. Thank you for looking out for his possessions in the meantime."

Beneluz grabbed Don Senior's arm and, trembling, said, "You must help us, Don Senior. For the love of God and the love of your Jewish faith, you must help me!"

Senior stood surprised by the request. "I'm no longer known as Don Senior. I've converted, and I'm called now Don Coronel."

Beneluz was astonished. "But you were a Jew all your life! You served the queen and the king as a Jewish court rabbi! How can you change your faith now when your people need you most?"

Don Coronel said sadly. "I'm now eighty years old, and I don't have too many years left. The queen . . . it was she who pressured me. She warned me of retaliation on the entire Jewish community if I didn't convert."

"She's already retaliated. She's kicked us all from our lands, our homes, and our communities. What more could she do to us?" Beneluz said angrily.

"I don't really know what more she has in mind, but believe me, it could be a worse fate than we know. Now what was it you needed help with?"

Beneluz told him of his nephews and their arrest. "We must help them as soon as possible."

"Come with me," Don Coronel said firmly. Beneluz rode in Don Coronel's carriage, and Avram led theirs behind.

Within the hour they arrived in front of military police headquarters. They left Avram to look after the carriages and went looking for Guerida's quarters. In one of the small offices they found Guerida sitting at his desk. His surprise at seeing Beneluz again made him open his mouth wide, but when he saw Don Coronel he refrained from saying anything.

"You've arrested two of my relatives, two boys by the name of Costa. I want them released right away!" Don Coronel ordered him.

Guerida took his time answering. "I'll do no such thing. Beside, they're being held in Seville's prison."

"Do you know who I am?" Don Coronel's voice thundered. "Do you know that I can have you arrested, thrown in a cell where everyone will forget who you were?"

Guerida looked at Don Coronel with curiosity. "And who might you be?" he asked in a mocking tone of voice.

"I am the foremost tax farmer to the realm and the counselor to Queen Isabella and King Ferdinand! That's who I am. And if you don't believe me"—he came close to Guerida—"here's the seal of chief tax collector." Don Coronel extended his right hand and showed him his ring with the seal.

Guerida's face changed color. "I believe you, Don Coronel. But how can I help you? They're in Torquemada's hands now."

Just then, Avram entered the room looking for his father and Don Coronel. When Guerida saw him, he got off his chair and came to greet Avram.

"My dear boy, what are you doing here?" Guerida asked.

Avram looked at Guerida confounded, then at his father, and then tried to leave the room in a hurry. Isaac ran after him.

"What's the meaning of this, son? You know Inspector Guerida?"

Avram kept silent, but tried to free himself from Beneluz's viselike grip on his arm.

"Speak!" Beneluz voice was strong and terrible.

"You're hurting your boy," said Guerida. "That boy of yours is a hero. He led us to the tavern where the Costa boys were. You should be proud of your son."

Beneluz looked at Guerida with fury, then to Avram with anger and pain. "I had a son," he said with sadness.

Don Coronel interrupted. "We're losing time. You take us right now to the prison, or I'll have the queen herself sign your execution warrant!"

Guerida looked at Coronel and saw in his eyes the real arm of the law—one greater than his and Torquemada's combined. "Follow me, gentlemen."

They all rode in Coronel's carriage with Avram sitting next to Guerida. Isaac didn't look at his son nor react to his son's hand on his knee. He pushed Avram's hand away with anger. He knew that his son was begging for acknowledgment. He ignored him.

The sun rose on the horizon as they approached the prison gates, where they were shown in without stopping for identification. All the wardens apparently knew Guerida, and his presence validated their admission by the prison's manager, thought Beneluz. They entered Miguel and José's cell after the guard unlocked the door, and found them asleep. José slept on Miguel's lap, his face drawn even in slumber. Don Coronel shook Miguel by the shoulders and put a hand over his mouth to keep him from screaming.

"You're being released. Wake up your brother and follow us." José's eyes opened, and he tried to move, but he was too weak. Beneluz lifted him by his arms, and they exited the cold, dark corridors of the prison.

Outside, Coronel turned to Beneluz. "Where will you take these boys?"

"We're staying in an inn, where my wife and three of my boys are waiting for us."

A plaintive voice then rose from Beneluz arms. "Please, put me down," José asked in a weak voice.

"You're in no condition to walk," said Beneluz.

"I want Isabella. Where's Isabella?" José asked.

Don Coronel looked at Beneluz with a question in his eyes.

"He's talking of Don Obrigon's daughter, Isabella. She's right now in her home in Seville."

"Then this is where we will go," said Don Coronel.

They left a very pale Guerida behind them.

When they arrived at the Obrigons' home, Beneluz turned to Avram and told him harshly, "You'll stay outside until we have a talk."

Avram obeyed his father without a word.

The rest of them were all shown into the parlor right away, and Beneluz gently put José on a sofa.

With a great cry, Isabella ran into the room and into Miguel's arms. "You're saved! You're saved!" she cried with joy. "Father, come quickly, quickly."

Obrigon came into the room and laughed with relief at the sight awaiting him. "How can I thank you all?" he said with tears of relief.

When the tears of joy and laughter subsided and more hugs took place between Isabella and Miguel and José, then Beneluz, Don Obrigon said to all in the room, "Nothing can express my joy and gratitude to all of you. You must tell me how I can repay you."

"There's nothing to repay," said Beneluz. "It is all due to Don Coronel."

Don Obrigon looked at Don Coronel and asked with respect, "I thought you were Don Senior. Or am I being too presumptive to ask such personal question?"

"No, you're not. You knew me before by that name from our mutual friend Don Abravanel. It's the queen who has dubbed me Don Coronel. I'll keep this honor bestowed by Her Majesty."

Don Obrigon didn't reply. He turned to his joyous daughter. "We must all share in this joy. "He turned to Beneluz and said, "Please bring your wife and children to my home so we can celebrate."

"I thank you, Don Obrigon, but we must make haste for our departure on August the third."

At that moment, both Miguel and Isabella looked at each other. Miguel went to her and whispered to her ear, "Will you be my wife?"

Isabella's heart exploded with joy. She nodded.

Miguel turned to Don Obrigon and said, "Don Obrigon, may I please have a private word with you?"

Obrigon looked at Miguel, then at Isabella. She silently communicated to her father her great happiness. He turned to Miguel and said, "I must attend to my guests right now, and I'll speak with you afterward."

"It must be now," Miguel said with a firm voice.

Isabella's pleading eyes were on her father.

"Please, would you excuse me?" he said to both Beneluz and Don Coronel.

Don Obrigon and Miguel went through the corridor to another room in the house. This room belonged to his deceased wife, Estrella, and all her belongings were still there, untouched since her death. He guessed what Miguel would speak to him about, and he wanted his wife's spirit to be present.

"Speak," he told Miguel.

"Dear Don Obrigon, You know I love your daughter and she loves me in return?"

"Yes?" Obrigon said, half smiling.

"With your permission, I would like to marry your daughter."

Obrigon hesitated.

Miguel fidgeted in his chair.

"I know you love my daughter," he said to Miguel. "I believe your uncle that you were wrongly arrested. I just want to make sure that you'll make her happy."

"I swear on my honor that she will be as my eyes, and as my heart." Miguel said with emotion.

"In that case, I don't see any problem," said Don Obrigon, smiling.

Miguel breathed a sigh of relief. "Thank you."

"However," continued Don Obrigon, "what future will you have? Isabella comes from a different background than yours. She was raised a Catholic."

"But, I—"

"I know," interrupted Don Obrigon, "you've also been raised in the Catholic faith, although you were older than Isabella when it happened. She's never known any other faith. Can you understand what I'm saying to you?"

Miguel nodded. "I understand, and I'll do anything to make her happy."

"Then, my son, I give you and Isabella my blessings."

When Don Obrigon and Miguel reentered the room where the guests waited, they smiled at Isabella.

Isabella ran to her father and cuddled into his arms. "Father," she said with gratitude.

Don Obrigon took Isabella's hand and put it into Miguel's hand.

"I give you my blessings, my children, and hope that your union will be happy and blessed."

Everyone in the room shouted at the same time, "*Mazal* tov*!*" and *"¡Felisitar!"*

José got off the sofa with difficulty and went to hug his brother.

Then a dark cloud passed over Obrigon's eyes. Isabella went to him and hugged him. "What is it, Father? Is it Madre?"

Obrigon looked at her with sadness in his eyes. "I wish your mother could've been here to share in this joy."

Isabella became sad, and she hugged him again. "Yes, I miss her too."

At that moment, Obrigon held back that Juan had died. He couldn't bring himself to ruin her joy. *Someday, I'll tell her,* he thought.

Just then, the servants in the house came to the door to congratulate the young couple. At their head was dada Hannah, who received Isabella into her bosomy chest. "My dear child, my precious child," she said with tears in her eyes.

"We all want to congratulate you, Don Obrigon, Isabella, and the groom," said Emilio, the head servant.

"Thank you, thank you," replied a happy Don Obrigon.

Miguel turned to Isabella and spoke words in her ear. She nodded with a big smile on her lips. She then ran to her father.

"Father, we want to get married now."

Don Obrigon looked at her with surprise. He went to Beneluz and asked him, "My dear Beneluz, my daughter and Miguel have expressed their wish for you to marry them."

Beneluz thought for a moment, then agreed. "We must do that right away," he stressed.

"We will!" said Don Obrigon. "Quickly, dada Hannah, take Isabella and prepare her for her wedding!"

All the servants shouted and sang together, *"¡La novia, la novia, ella es muy hermosa!"* Isabella followed her nursemaid dada Hannah, but turned around to gaze at Miguel as she left the room.

Miguel was led by the menservants to another room in the house to prepare him.

Twenty minutes later, Isabella and Miguel appeared from opposite sides of the house, both dressed in white. Miguel wore Don Obrigon's old wedding suit, which hung loose on his body. Isabella wore a white satin wedding gown with a lace train.

"My dear child," said Don Obrigon, "you're dressed in your mother's wedding gown. Now we can both feel her presence with us." He wiped a furtive tear from his eyes. Isabella kissed him and went to stand near Miguel.

Beneluz asked two male servants to hold a white silk scarf attached to two poles over the head of the young couple. Beneluz turned to both of them and said, "We're here to unite Miguel Costa to Isabella Obrigon. According to the tradition of our forefathers, while I read the seven blessings for the bride and groom, Isabella will circle Miguel seven times. This will create a bond between the families, and it represents seven days it took God to create the earth. These blessings will also bring prosperity and health to this young couple." Beneluz then faced east, in the direction of Jerusalem, as he read the seven blessings.

As Beneluz read the seven long blessings, Isabella circled Miguel while holding her white train. When Beneluz read the last blessing, he asked for the cup of wine. First Isabella took a sip, then Miguel, while Beneluz said the wine blessings. *"Boreh Pri Ha Gefen."*

"Miguel, you may now break the glass, as our heart broke when the holy temple in Jerusalem was destroyed."

Miguel stepped on the empty glass to break it.

Beneluz then called on José—who was holding the rings on a small satin pillow—and two witnesses among the servants. He showed them two gold wedding bands that had belonged to Isabella's parents. "Do those rings have value?" Beneluz asked. The witnesses replied, "Yes, they do."

"Now, Miguel, repeat after me: 'Behold, thou are consecrated by this ring to me by the Law of Moses and Israel.'"

Miguel repeated word for word: "Behold, thou are consecrated by this ring to me by the Law of Moses and Israel." He then slipped the ring on Isabella's right index finger.

"Isabella, you do the same for Miguel," Beneluz said.

Isabella slipped the second gold band on Miguel's index finger of his right hand, and repeated the same words as before.

Beneluz said, "Go and rejoice, find exultation, delight in each other's comradeship, and peace. This couple's happiness and joy should be heard in all of Jerusalem! I now pronounce you man and wife. You may kiss the bride."

"¡Alegria! ¡Alegria!" Shouts came out of the servants' mouths as they applauded and ran to throw grains of wheat over the couple's head. "Be fruitful and multiply!" they shouted.

"Mazal tov!" Beneluz congratulated the young couple.

Don Obrigon went to kiss Isabella and hug Miguel. "I know that you'll make her happy," he said to a beaming Miguel.

Next it was José's turn. He took Isabella's hands and said, "Now you truly are my sister."

Isabella hugged him back with a tender smile. She then went to dada Hannah, who stood shyly aside, and kissed her. Dada Hannah hugged her tight with her big arms. "My dear child, I'm so happy for you." She cried with joy.

"I now part from all this joy," said Beneluz. "I must get back to my family and to my son, Avram, waiting outside for me." He turned to Miguel and his brother and said, "I know you'll be in good hands. I also give you my blessings for your joy and your safety. Thank you, Don Coronel, for saving my nephews—and to you, Don Obrigon, for their safety." He then hurried out of the room.

33

Bliss

THE SCENT OF ROSES AWAITED Miguel and Isabella in her room. The floor and the bed were strewn with rose petals of every hue. They stopped at the threshold to admire the enchanting sight. Dada Hannah had decorated the room, knowing how much Isabella loved roses. Now that the house was empty of all servants and Don Obrigon and José, she and Miguel were alone. Isabella entered her old room with Miguel's arm around her waist.

"This is the only world I've known since I was a child. Now I want to share it with you."

Miguel bent down and kissed each finger of her right hand. "And I thank you for letting me share it."

Isabella pealed with laughter and pulled away from Miguel. She flung herself around the room, dancing a pure flamenco *Zambra Mora*. Clicking her heels with her hands on her hips, she twirled about the room. Miguel watched her, smiling. After a few minutes, Isabella fell on her bed, out of breath, and extended her hand to Miguel. He approached the bed slowly and lay down near her, finding her trembling lips and kissing her. She returned his kiss with a love he could never have imagined. He slowly undressed her, exposing her upright breasts, graceful hips, and shapely legs. He undressed and joined her in a locked embrace. The delight they found in each other was reciprocated back and forth as they gave each other their young and deep love. Afterward they lay in each other arms, their breath mingling.

"My beautiful wife," Miguel said to her.

"What is it, my most loving husband?" she asked.

They both broke up in laughter at the strange sound of "husband" and "wife."

"Now that we are husband and wife, we have to plan for the future," said Miguel.

"I don't want to think about the future," Isabella said, pouting. "Right now, I only want to know my life with you."

"So do I, but as your husband, I have the duty to take care of you and provide for your well-being."

"You don't have to do that right now, do you?" she asked with a coy smile on her face.

He replied by kissing every curve of her still-wet and moist body. Within moments they embraced again with a passion surging for each other. When they stopped, Isabella fell asleep in Miguel's arms.

He watched her sleeping and considered how innocent she still was. Having grown up in this protected environment where every one of her whims and desires were met had left her vulnerable. He thought of himself, growing up with danger around him. His mother had tried her best to shelter him from the perils of growing up as a New Christian, but his peers never missed a chance to remind him that at one time he had been Jewish. The insults—being called "pig"—had flown around him no matter how hard he tried to block them out. To the old Christians, he was still a Jew and always would be. He now felt more than ever that his destiny was to return completely to his parents' ancient faith. But then, what of Isabella?

A moan from Isabella brought him to the present. She was so lovely, he thought as he stared at her. Just then, Isabella opened her languid eyes and found Miguel looking intently at her. She rose on her elbows and kissed him.

"Why are you thinking so hard?" she asked him.

He laughed. "Does it show?"

"Yes, it does. I don't want my husband to think too much right now," she said, smiling.

"I'm only thinking about you."

She stayed silent for a moment, then said, "You know, I've been thinking too."

"What've you got to think about? You let me do all the thinking for both of us."

"No, listen," she said with a seriousness he had not seen on her face before. "I've been thinking about this uncle of mine named João. I wonder where he is right now."

"And why must you know?" Miguel asked her, intrigued by her comment.

"Don't you see? He's the link to my past."

"I thought you only wanted to think of the present," he jested.

"My past will determine my present. I still want to know my birth mother. Not that I don't love and cherish my adoptive mother's memory, but I feel that I must know who she was. My adoptive father, as well, is the only father I love, but who was my real father?"

"The answer is shrouded in the mists of time. We can never know all the details of our past lives. Take my father, for example. I have some memories of him, but I will never know in depth some of his past life or what his childhood was really like. My Uncle Beneluz filled in some details about my father, but a good portion of his past will always remain unknown to me."

"That's why I want to find my uncle—so he can tell me about my past."

"But we don't know where he is!" Miguel said.

"I still want to know. Can you tell me what you knew about him?"

Miguel recollected in silence for a moment, he then said, "All I remember is that he came to our home when I was young and asked me what I wanted to do when I grew up."

"Yes?"

"Well, I told him then I wanted to travel like my father, but I wanted to become a seaman and travel the seas."

"And what did he say to that?"

"He encouraged me and told me of his past sailing experience."

"That means he was a sailor," Isabella said, sounding confident.

"But I don't know the details of his merchant travels. Oh yes, he told me that he used to sail from Portugal on his travels, and then stop to see his sister on the way to port."

Isabella sat up on the bed. "She must've been my mother!"

"I'm not sure about that," Miguel said hesitantly.

"I'm sure," Isabella said, with strength in her voice. "Mi querido, I must find out who was my real mother—it may lead me to my real father, too."

"You mustn't feed yourself with false hopes. You might be disappointed."

"If you love me, Miguel, you'll help me find them," she said, determined.

"I love you more than you can ever imagine a man loving a woman."

She laughed at the sound of the word *woman*. "I'm a grown and married woman."

"You sure are." Miguel lifted her fingers and proceeded to kiss them one by one all over again.

She gently pulled her hand away. "I must know, Miguel. I must!"

"Very well," he said, convinced that she would pursue the matter no matter what. "We can ask my uncle, if we can catch up with him."

34

The Expulsion

TORQUEMADA STOOD IN FRONT OF Guerida. His pale face was livid. Only his black eyes showed life; lightning seemed to pour from them. Guerida squirmed on his seat, not knowing whether the light streaming from Torquemada's eyes would scorch or strike him dead.

"You have undone all my work! You fool!" Torquemada became animated as he yelled. "How could you give your consent to Don Coronel. He's a Jew! A Jew will always be sly, undoing good deeds and the work of The Church!"

"But, Your Holy Excellency, He had the seal of the realm on his ring! How could I know it was a fake?"

"It wasn't a fake, you idiot! The queen herself gave him this power. He still is the chief tax farmer for España. But that doesn't give him power to release prisoners. That power belongs to me and The Church!"

Guerida sat with his head hanging over his lap. How did he sink so low? What black magic did Don Coronel use on him to convince him of his absolute power?

"How can I undo this terrible mistake?" Guerida begged Torquemada.

"First we must find them. Go to Don Obrigon's house and arrest them immediately! You hear?"

"Yes. I'll do that right away. I'll bring them back and redeem myself in your eyes."

"You'll pay with your life if you don't find them!" Torquemada threatened.

Guerida trembled down to his bones. He left Torquemada and hurried to his police headquarters, where he gathered a group of strong men armed with swords and knives.

The men mounted black horses; left the outskirts of Seville, where the headquarters were located, to stop merchants or foreigners without papers from entering the city; and headed for the heart of Seville. When they arrived and burst into Don Obrigon's house, no one was about. No servants, no host, and, worst of all, no youngsters.

Guerida was ashen with fear. He couldn't return empty-handed to Torquemada. It would be a sure death. But where could they be? Perhaps if he found Miguel's cursed uncle he might then find some answers. At the inn, where he had found them the previous day, the innkeeper knew nothing of their whereabouts, except that the whole family had left in a hurry.

"But where to? Where, you idiot man?" Guerida yelled.

"I don't really know," the innkeeper said with a trembling voice. "They seemed to be traveling toward the port."

Guerida laid his hand flat on the innkeeper's face and pushed him to the ground.

"Let's go!" Guerida ordered his men. They all mounted their horses and galloped in the direction of the largest maritime port in Castile.

At the port in Seville, hundreds of empty ships were moored at the docks with sailors and workers preparing for their occupants to board. Two hundred thousand people, carriages, carts, horses, and mules covered the port grounds as far as the horizon. The cries of lost children, and the screams of mothers and fathers looking for them, were deafening. Once a child let go of his parent's hand, he couldn't be found again.

Amid the masses of people at the end of the docks sat the Beneluz family. They'd waited on the docks for two days, and Rivka and the children were exhausted and short of patience.

"When can we board the ship?" asked León.

"Father, I'm tired and sleepy. Let's go back to the inn, please?" begged Guerson, his third son.

"Patience, Guerson. They're bound to announce the voyage soon."

His youngest son, Mica, was lethargic, and Avram stood aside, moody and silent. Beneluz hadn't opened the subject with him nor demanded answers for his conduct since they left Seville. In time, these questions would be put to Avram. Isaac hadn't told Rivka yet of the sellout of Miguel and Josè by their eldest son. He neither understood nor accepted his son's betrayal. He had always taught him right from wrong—why this behavior? He was in a quandary to explain it.

A great hubbub of activity began to arise on the docks. Sailors were running about, knotted ladders and white oak planks were being lowered, and captains were taking their position at the tops of landings. A sudden cry rose from the crowds. "We're leaving! We're leaving!" As one people, the crowd stood up and gathered their families and belongings. The captains on the ships began the painstaking task of checking papers and baggage. A great sign at the foot of the plank was posted for every passenger to see:

"No gold, silver, or object of value is to be carried onto the ship. If found, they will be confiscated by order of the court."

"Move along, move along, people!" the orderlies yelled at the embarking passengers and shouted over a horn.

The Beneluzes were near the landing platform, when they heard a cry behind them. "Uncle, Uncle, over here!"

Beneluz turned around to spot his nephew, Miguel, and Isabella running toward him. In his surprise he dropped the large bundle from his arms.

"Miguel! Miguel!" he shouted at them.

Rivka followed his gaze and looked at the newly wedded couple with a smile.

Miguel fell into Isaac Beneluz's arms. Isaac hugged his nephew, then Isabella. Rivka took Isabella in her arms and said, "I heard of the beautiful wedding. My dear niece, may I call you my niece now?"

Isabella laughed as she hugged Rivka. "Yes, Aunt Rivka, I'm your niece now."

"I'm sad that I couldn't attend your wedding, my children," she said as she now hugged Miguel. "But why are you here?" she asked. "You should be on your honeymoon!"

Isabella spoke first. "I wanted to know about my uncle."

"Your uncle?" asked Rivka, befuddled.

"I mean my other uncle, João Treves. My mother's brother."

Beneluz looked at Isabella and Miguel, puzzled. "What's this story of an uncle?" he asked.

Miguel interjected, "When my mother had gatherings at our house, there was a man called João Treves. My mother told me in confidence that Isabella's uncle, João Treves, had her kidnapped so that she would not marry outside the Mosaic faith. He's the only one that can help her find her parents' identity."

"But, my dear children," Beneluz started out, "it's all history now. Yes, Miguel, your mother wrote and told me João was Isabella's uncle."

"Why didn't you tell me?" Miguel asked, a surprised look in his eyes.

"I didn't tell you because it wouldn't have helped. He'd been in prison, and associating with him would've jeopardized all our families. Your mother risked her life and put both you and your brother in danger. May she rest in peace," he concluded.

Miguel's face turned sad. "Yes, she did risk her life."

"But where can we find him?" Isabella asked Beneluz. "Please Uncle, please, I must know!"

Beneluz sighed with heaviness in his heart. "I can't tell you because I don't know the answer."

"You must remember something. Please, Uncle," Isabella said. "Anything from your correspondence with Miguel's mother?"

At that moment, passengers pushed them aside, trying to get on board.

"Let's move aside for a moment," said Beneluz. They all moved away with difficulty, with the throng of people around them pushing and shoving.

Beneluz stood reflecting for a moment and said, "He'd always been a sailor. You must look in Palos, where he might've embarked on a merchant ship."

"Thank you, Uncle Beneluz. Thank you!" Isabella jumped and kissed him.

Miguel shook hands with him and turned to Isabella. "Let us . . ." He stopped in midsentence. From all sides, he saw soldiers with swords searching the crowds. Not far from them stood Guerida urging them on. He blanched and met Isabella's eyes.

Beneluz, who'd observed the scene, suddenly pushed Isabella and Miguel forward toward the plank ascending the ship. Rivka looked at him bewildered.

With panic on his face, Miguel pulled Isabella's arm and dragged her to the plank.

"Hurry! Hurry!" he urged her.

Isabella understood the danger awaiting them. She ran up the plank pulled by Miguel, then the entire Beneluz family followed. When they reached the top, the captain asked Miguel and Isabella to pay for their passage. At that moment, Miguel looked back to see Guerida's men approaching their ship. Beneluz came forward and slipped gold coins into the captain's pocket and locked eyes with him. The captain nodded and waved them on. They ran down the deck and descended into the hold where other families huddled. They found an empty spot on the plank floor large enough to accommodate the whole family at the opposite wall of the hull, away from the ladder. Beneluz took all of their bundles and piled them up in front of Miguel and Isabella, hiding them from prying eyes and from anyone that might search the hull. They waited.

Before long, soldiers descended the ladder into the hold and began to search its occupants. When they reached the Beneluz family huddled in front of their bundles, they asked for papers. A soldier held Don Obrigon on one side, and Guerida stood on his other side.

"Look at him!" he yelled at Don Obrigon and pointing to Isaac, "Isn't this the man you sent to the prison with Don Coronel? You wanted the boys released! Didn't you!"

Don Obrigon remained silent.

"Speak, man! Speak! Or I will have your tongue cut off!"

A muffled cry came from the throng. Guerida searched the floor near him, then turned around to locate where the sound had come from. But he saw nothing. A woman sitting near them suddenly raised her hand and hit her young son. "Stop your crying!" she yelled at him. The young boy she hit yelled and screamed loudly, then began to cry.

"I must teach him manners," the mother said sheepishly to Guerida, whose eyes were fixed on her.

Guerida took another look at all the refugees sitting on the hull's floor and said to his men, "We're wasting time. Let's search the next ship."

Before Don Obrigon turned to follow Guerida, he locked eyes with Beneluz, then nodded silently.

Beneluz saw the grateful look in Obrigon's eyes and acknowledged the don's gaze with a nod of his head. *This father is parting forever from his beloved daughter,* he thought.

After Guerida, his men, and Don Obrigon climbed the ladder and disappeared from view, Beneluz sighed with relief.

"Stay there a little longer," he whispered in Miguel and Isabella's direction. When a few minutes passed, they emerged from behind the bundles and hugged Beneluz, then Rivka.

"We must still be on our guard for Guerida's return before we sail," warned Beneluz. He turned to the woman who hit her child and saw her cuddling the boy and shushing him to sleep.

"How can we ever thank you?" asked Beneluz.

"You don't have to thank me. I was just avenging my husband, who died at their hands. Good riddance to all those evil men!" She spat on the floor.

"Thank you, just the same. You saved my niece and nephew."

The woman smiled and went back to rocking the boy.

Beneluz said to Rivka, "We must take care of the woman and her child. See that they have enough food to eat. We can split our provisions with her."

Rivka nodded in agreement.

Just then, they felt the floor move beneath them. They were in motion and sailing on the high sea. The ship swayed gently and took an easterly direction toward the Gulf of Cadiz, Morocco, and Tangier.

Isabella cried silently, tears running down her cheeks. Miguel tried to comfort her.

"We'll be back. Back to your father and back to your home. You'll see," Miguel said to her in an encouraging voice.

"Certainly I will miss my father, my home, and especially my nursemaid, dada Hannah. I'm also crying that I'll never find out. Never find the truth to my birth."

Miguel stayed silent and unable to comfort her. "You're weeping for your father, and I'm weeping inside for my young brother. I don't know if I'll ever see him again."

Isabella immediately stopped her crying. She said with regret in her voice, "I'm so sorry, Miguel. In my sorrow I forgot about Josè. But don't fear. I know my father will protect him and keep him well. If anyone can be strong, it's my father."

Miguel pressed her hand with gratefulness.

Beneluz addressed them. "Let's go on deck. I'm sure now we're beyond the reach of Guerida and his evil intentions. Follow me."

He led them up the roped ladder to the upper deck. The bright light blinded them as they emerged from the semidarkness of the hold below deck. They were surprised to see the ship at a far distance from shore. Beneluz called Rivka and the boys to come up and enjoy the fresh air. They made their way onto the deck crowded with men, women, and children. Old and feeble grandfathers and grandmothers, who had been traveling for weeks and months from the northern parts of Spain, sat on coiled ropes. The decks were filled to capacity.

Beneluz grabbed Rivka and his two young sons, then called to Avram and León to approach them. He then let go of his youngest and put his arm around his eldest.

"Look! Look! This may be the last time that we see España. This was the land of our ancestors from the dawn of time in Iberia, before the Spaniards, before the Moors, and before the Visigoths. We came here in the time of the Romans. For more than a thousand years we slaved and raised our crops and beasts of labor and had children that begat more children. We built with our sweat and our blood. Now look for the last time as we leave these beloved shores."

He heard weeping as Rivka and Isabella sobbed.

"We'll build again on other shores, and our young will grow and have their own children. We won't disappear nor will we become extinct," continued Beneluz. "God in heaven will protect us."

Suddenly Avram broke into sobs on Beneluz's shoulder. Beneluz hugged his eldest son and said to him in a low voice, "Cry, cry, my son. There's redemption in tears."

Isabella wiped her tears and felt Miguel's arms around her. She pushed her windblown black hair away from her oval face. She felt suffering mixed with happiness. A resolute determination settled in her heart and mind. She vowed to return someday to find her father, who had raised her with love and care, and visit the grave of her dear mother. For now she would live peacefully with her beloved Miguel. But some day she would seek the answers to her origins. Some day . . .

Epilog

August 3, 1492

THE WAVES LAPPED GENTLY AT the swaying hulls of the *Pinta*, the *Niña*, and the *Santa Maria*. The ships' sails billowed with the full-blown wind coming into the harbor from the open sea. Sailors checked final details such as coiled ropes, food and wine, and water jugs. The admiral and captain's quarters were fully provisioned with various instruments and maps.

A fanfare lined up on the docks to receive all travelers for the voyage. Musicians began playing on their drums, flutes, and tambourines. The populace of Palos in Huelva all came in force to cheer the voyagers on their perilous voyage. Banners bearing the cross and the crest of Spain flew high above the heads of bystanders, their poles held with difficulty by altar boys. A priest led the parade, swinging a thurible with incense.

Several carriages stopped in front of the moored ships, creating a dust cloud. Admiral Christopher Columbus, a tall man in his forties with blue eyes, reddish hair, high cheekbones, and a ruddy complexion, alighted from one with Juan de La Cosa master and owner of the vessel; the pilot, Sancho Ruiz; followed by Diego de Arana, his master-at-arms. They took their places and marched with Columbus at the front of the procession to the master ship, the *Santa Maria*. A priest to bless the voyage and sailors to man the ship followed them up the ramp of the *Santa Maria.* The rest of the procession, composed of Martin Alonso Pinzón and his brothers, sailors, artisans, physician, and the king's reporter, climbed aboard the *Niña* and the *Pinta.*

A silence fell on the docks and the crowds when the priest crossed himself. "We pray today that these ships go in peace to their destination with the protection of our Savior," the priest said. The spectators and the men on the ships crossed themselves in silence.

Columbus stood on the *Santa Maria's* deck facing the crowds on the docks that cheered him with shouts of *"¡Que Dios los acompañe! ¡Vaya con Dios!"* He waved back at them with pride and satisfaction. This voyage was his life's dream. It was the fulfillment for all the years that he'd spent waiting. Victory was on his tongue and in his lungs as he tasted and breathed the salty air, and his heart beat fast with the excitement of the voyage.

"For our beloved Virgin, noble and proud citizens of Palos." Columbus addressed the crowds below the ship. "We're leaving on a voyage of mission and adventure. The mission is to conquer the route to the east for our kingdom and for the illustrious Queen Isabella and King Ferdinand of España!"

The crowds on the docks cheered again with shouts, some crossing themselves and some looking on with skeptical smiles.

He continued. "We'll bring back fortune and pride for España, and win millions of new souls for our Catholic church!"

The crowds cheered again and the band played. Bystanders waved flags, some with tears in their eyes.

When the anchors were lifted, the waves gently billowed the sails and pushed the three ships to sea. As the docks began to recede behind their ship and the port became a miniature town far in the distance, tears filled the eyes of the captain, and the master-at-arms.

Christopher Columbus turned around and faced his crew. "We go with God's help. May he have mercy on our voyage and souls!"

The crew cheered, and Christopher Columbus dismissed them. He then caught sight of one sailor lingering on the deck and looking strangely at him. His eyes fixedly burned as two emerald jewels. In those eyes he saw contempt. The sailor's gaze startled Columbus. These were similar eyes to those that had haunted him for many years. These eyes brought pleasure and pain at the same time. He raised his hand and wiped his brow as if to erase the thought. He must've been imagining a ghostly memory buried deep inside him. He discarded the thought and returned to the task at hand. He turned to the sea in front of him, the ship's prow parting the white foam waves, and the wind whipping the rigging.

Now begins my voyage to fame and fortune. A voyage dedicated to God and country.

The End

Flower from Castile Trilogy

Cast of Characters

First Family

Isabel Gonçalves Zarco — mother of Christopher Salvador Colón (Columbus)

João Gonçalves Zarco, great Portuguese navigator — father of Isabel Gonçalves Zarco

Cristóbal Colón, explorer — also called Christopher Columbus

Infante Ferdinand of Portugal — first duke of Beja and second duke of Viseu, son of King Dom Duarte

Sarita Treves — Cristóbal Colón's first love affair (no marriage)

Felipa Perestrello e Moniz — Christopher Colón/Columbus's only wife

Diego Colón — Christopher Colón's firstborn, with his wife, Felipa Perestrello e Moniz

Beatriz Enriquez de Arana — Colón's second love affair, (no marriage) after first wife died

Fernando Colón — Colón's second son, with Beatriz Enriquez de Arana

Spanish Nobles

The Obrigons, Noble Spanish Family of Seville

Isabella Obrigon — sixteen years old

Doña Estrella Obrigon — Isabella's mother

Don Arturo Obrigon — Isabella's father

The Obrigons' household and friends:

Obrigon Household:

Dada Hannah — Isabella's nanny

Carmelita — Obrigon's maid

Pilar — Obrigon's maid

Emilio Gomez — servant

Obrigon Friends:

Duke de la Mancha — Isabella Obrigon's godfather
Don Alvarez — physician to Doña Estrella Obrigon
Mayor José de Gerondi — friend of Don Arturo Obrigon

Escobar Family and Friends:

Juan Escobar de Santilla — Isabella's fiancé
Doña Maria Escobar — Juan's mother
Don Pedro Escobar — Juan's father
Corporal Antonio Peres — Juan's army friend

Queen Isabella and King Ferdinand's Palace in Seville

Queen Isabella I of Spain in Castile and León
King Ferdinand, King of Spain, Aragon, and Sicily
Tomás de Torquemada — Grand Inquisitor
Fray Juan Pérez — friar of Convent de la Rábida
Fray Antonio de Marchena — friar of Convent de la Rábida
Doña Beatriz de Bobadilla — Queen Isabella's retinue

Don Abraham Senior — financial advisor to Ferdinand and Isabella and rabbi to the court in Spain. Baptized Don Fernando Núñez Coronel of Castile
Doña Violante Senior — wife of Don Senior
Doña Reina Senior — daughter of Don Senior and wife of Don Melamed
Don Meir Melamed — Don Senior son-in-law
Don Isaac Abravanel — Jewish Columbus supporter and financier to King Ferdinand
Doña Gracia Abravanel — Jewish wife of Don Abravanel
Luis De Santángel — Columbus's friend and Converso
Alonso de Quintanilla — Christian Columbus supporter

Carmela — palace servant, friend of Maria Donarojo
Fadrique Martinez — court petitioner
Arturo Gomez — court petitioner

Meeting of Jewish and Conversos' Dissenters at Téresa Costa's House

João Treves — Converso, Sarita's brother
Maria Donarojo — Converso
Téresa Costa — Converso, Miguel and Josè's mother
Alfonso Sabatin — Converso
Pedro Grasin — Jewish
Salamon Moresco — Jewish
Ana Sarauel — Jewish
Esther Castelan — Jewish
Benvenide Matigoro — Converso
Hernán Çavallos — Converso

The Families

João Treves and Sarita Treves — brother and sister
Téresa Costa — mother of Miguel and Josè
Nahum Costa — Téresa's deceased husband
Miguel Costa — Téresa's son
Josè Costa— Téresa's son,
Master Torres — José's sculpting master
Blanko — the mule
Isaac Beneluz — Nahum's brother living in Cordoba
Rivka Beneluz — wife of Isaac Beneluz
Isaac and Rivka Children — Avram, León, Guerson, and Mica Beneluz
Nina Leon — Beneluz's neighbor
Little Sarah — Nina's three-year-old daughter
Francisco and Adela de Medina — Moriscoes, and friends of Ana Sarauel
Conchita — old woman

Granada

King Boabdil el Chico, King Muhammad XII — last ruler of Granada and of the Nasrid Dynasty
Morayma — Boabdil's wife

Noor — Concubine
Amina — Concubine
Sarah — Isabella's friend in the harem
King Muley Abul Hassan — Boabdil's deceased father
Ayxa la Horra, (Ayesha) — Boabdil's mother, first wife of Muley Abul Hassan
Zoraya — Boabdil's stepmother, second wife of Muley Abul Hassan
Pasha El Zagal — Boabdil's uncle, and king in Granada 1485 to 1486
Yusef Aben Comixa — Boabdil's general
Abul Cazim Abdel Melic — Granada's old governor,
Muza Ben Abel Gazan — Boabdil's general and valiant fighter
Moussa El Zayari — Boabdil's treasurer and finance minister
Ahmad Kalil — Moor scout
Mansur Abbas — Moor scout

Spanish Nobles and Soldiers

Constable Guerida — chief inspector in Seville and Andalusia serving under The Church and Tomás de Torquemada, grand inquisitor
General Don Alonso de Aguilar — elder brother to Gonzalo Fernández de Córdova and able general
Captain Gonzalo Fernández de Córdova — younger brother to Alonso de Aguilar. Distinguished for his military skills and ten years fierce fighting in the Reconquest
Rodrigo Ponce de Leon, Marques of Cadiz — noble and powerful owner of estates and soldiers
Don Enrique Pérez de Guzmán, second duke of Medina Sidonia — noble owner of estates and armies
Rodrigo Ponce de León, marques and duke of Cadiz — noble owner of titles and estates
Don Diego de Cordova, count of Cabra — noble owner of titles, estates, and armies
Don Iñigo López de Mendoza, count of Tendilla — noble

Don Juan Téllez-Girón, second count of Ureña — noble
Fadrique Enriquez — second grand admiral of Castile
Don de Torres — adjutant to King Ferdinand
Don Diego de Enriquez — fighter under Gonzalo de Córdova
General Hernando Perez del Pulgar — noble

The Port of Palos

Captain Martin Alonzo Pinzón — mariner and shipbuilder
Captain Gomes Manrrique — pilot of the Pinta
Juan Manrrique — foreman
Sancho Ruiz — pilot of the Santa Maria
Benedito Fernando — Santa Maria shipworker
Benito — Pinzón's foreman
Gomes — coworker of João Treves
Master Fábio Domingos — João Treves's past employer
Benedito Caetano — João Treves's past employer

www.ingramcontent.com/pod-product-compliance
Lightning Source LLC
LaVergne TN
LVHW020525100826
845148LV00010B/1345

9780970273512